Praise for Ronlyn Domingue and the Keeper of Tales Trilogy

THE CHRONICLE OF SECRET RIVEN

"Lush descriptions and a mythic tone. . . . In Secret's world, anything can happen."

—*Publishers Weekly*

"Mysterious manuscripts, arcane languages, and sinister silences animate the wonderfully inventive realm of Secret Riven, a character so powerful that we are both startled and enchanted as we tumble headlong into her world."

—Maria Tatar, author of *Enchanted Hunters:*
The Power of Stories in Childhood

"An extraordinary mix of a fresh voice and an Old World sensibility. . . . This is a book that reminds us of the power of silence, of paying attention, of intuition, and of protecting the most vulnerable among us."

—Susan Henderson, author of *Up From the Blue*

"An epic fairy tale for a new age; Ronlyn Domingue has created a mythos all her own. *The Chronicle of Secret Riven* deftly braids the story of love, loss, magic, myth, and ancestry together into a hauntingly beautiful tale."

—Signe Pike, author of *Faery Tale*

THE MAPMAKER'S WAR

"Legend, allegory, fantasy—Domingue's novel entwines genres to cast a spell upon its reader. . . . Curious, thought-provoking."

—*Kirkus Reviews*

"A fun read for fantasy lovers."

—*Publishers Weekly*

"Beautifully capturing the tone and voice of a classically told tale, Ronlyn Domingue crafts a deeply intelligent, richly enhanced tale of magic, power, greed, and the infinite resilience of the human heart."

—*New York Journal of Books*

"Domingue deftly explores themes of motherhood, gender equality, and the powerful ties that bind us to our roots, while at the same time mesmerizing the reader with the story of a mythical land struggling to protect itself from the greed and jealousy of the slowly encroaching outside world."

—*Booklist*

"It'll entrance you."

—*The Advocate*

"Ronlyn Domingue's jewel of a book has a big canvas, memorable characters, and intimate storytelling. You will be swept away by this otherworldly tale that charts the all-too-human territory between heartbreak and hope."

—Deborah Harkness, *New York Times* bestselling author of *The Book of Life*

"An extraordinary tale of a woman's courage in an ancient Utopian world. Domingue has taken on the herculean task of inventing a new legend, and the result is a remarkable novel at once absorbing and heart wrenching, but above all mesmerizing!"

—M. J. Rose, internationally bestselling author of *The Witch of Painted Sorrows*

"What a stunning, original book this is—restrained and sensual, cerebral and lush, always blazingly intelligent, expansive, yet filled with the most precisely and lovingly observed details."

—Carolyn Turgeon, author of *Mermaid*

"This novel is a celebration of brave women and men, of expansive vision, and ultimately, of a humanity not easily denied."

—River Jordan, nationally bestselling author of
Praying for Strangers

"Evokes not mere fantasy, but the real magic I found as a child, reading by flashlight under a blanket. As then, the story took me by the hand to exotic lands and noble people and held me under its spell."

—Ava Leavell Haymon, award-winning author of
Why the House Is Made of Gingerbread

Acclaim for Ronlyn Domingue's unforgettable debut
THE MERCY OF THIN AIR

"This is that rarest of first novels—a truly original voice, and a truly original story."

—Jodi Picoult, #1 *New York Times* bestselling
author of *Leaving Time*

"Entrancing and ethereal."

—*Seattle Post-Intelligencer*

"Through the alchemy of Domingue's rich, lovely prose, we are transported back and forth through time."

—*The Boston Globe*

"Filled with vivid descriptions of scents, sounds, and marvelous human sensations that people take for granted and that spirits can only wistfully recall, this is a novel that gets under one's skin."

—*Library Journal* (starred review)

"Blending the practical matters of marriage with the sentimental, Domingue has fashioned an emotionally satisfying story of love and longing."

—Meg Wolitzer in *The Washington Post*

THE CHRONICLE OF SECRET RIVEN

Keeper of Tales Trilogy:
Book Two

RONLYN DOMINGUE

WASHINGTON SQUARE PRESS
NEW YORK   LONDON   TORONTO   SYDNEY   NEW DELHI

Washington Square Press
A Division of Simon & Schuster, Inc.
1230 Avenue of the Americas
New York, NY 10020

First Washington Square Press trade paperback edition April 2015

Washington Square Press and colophon are trademarks of Simon & Schuster, Inc.

For information about special discounts for bulk purchases, please contact Simon & Schuster Special Sales at 1-866-506-1949 or business@simonandschuster.com.

The Simon & Schuster Speakers Bureau can bring authors to your live event. For more information or to book an event, contact the Simon & Schuster Speakers Bureau at 1-866-248-3049 or visit our website at www.simonspeakers.com.

Manufactured in the United States of America

10   9   8   7   6   5   4   3   2   1

The Library of Congress has cataloged the hardcover edition as follows:

Domingue, Ronlyn.
  The Chronicle of Secret Riven : Keeper of Tales Trilogy : book two : an acccount of what preceded The Plague of Silences / Ronlyn Domingue.—First Atria Books hardcover edition.
pages cm.— (The Keeper of Tales Trilogy; book two)
  Sequel to: The Mapmaker's War, 2013.
  Summary: "An uncanny child born to brilliant parents, befriended by a prince, mentored by a wise woman, pursued by a powerful man, Secret Riven has no idea what destiny will demand of her or the courage she must have to confront it in the breathtakingly epic, genre-spanning sequel to The Mapmaker's War"—Provided by publisher.
    1. Gifted children—Fiction. 2. Women cartographers—Fiction. I. Title.
  PS3604.O457C47 2014
813'.6—dc23   2013045442

ISBN 978-1-4516-8891-7
ISBN 978-1-4516-8892-4 (pbk)
ISBN 978-1-4516-8893-1 (ebook)

THE

CHRONICLE

OF

SECRET RIVEN

—

AN ACCOUNT OF WHAT PRECEDED

THE PLAGUE OF SILENCES

THE CHRONICLE OF SECRET RIVEN

— I —

The Babe Born Evensong Riven

MOMENTS AFTER HER BIRTH, THREE BIRDS SWEPT INTO THE room through an open window. The pigeon, the dove, and the sparrow circled the newborn three times, widdershins, lit upon the wooden sill, and settled their feathers. They turned to one another in conference, or so it seemed to the baby's father, who saw their heads bob and heard them coo and chirp. He had respect for the uncanny and, believing the birds' council to be that indeed, watched them come to their enigmatic conclusion.

The meeting adjourned. The sparrow fluttered toward the infant, snatched a wispy hair from her head, and guided the dove and the pigeon into the autumn twilight.

Her father would one day tell her this, and about how he walked to the window to decide what to name her. He hadn't expected the dark tiny creature she turned out to be. She was third born but an only child. Two brothers, born blue, had preceded her. Her father looked to the sky at the crescent moon and the bright star rising at its side. She was named Evensong, for the time of her birth, but she would be called Eve, then become Secret soon enough.

She was an odd little thing with black hair, tawny skin, and eyes the colors of night and day. Except for the occasional cry or laugh, she would be mute until her seventh year, skilled with only one mother tongue until her fourteenth. From Secret's first breaths, the girl was hushed with a silencing hiss, a sound of menace, not comfort, by her own mother.

The child became a watchful being.

Secret remembered the room where she spent the days of her first three years. The door to the room was always closed, and she was penned off by a guard of wooden slats with a soft pallet and toys on the floor. She occupied herself with colorful blocks, leather balls filled with sawdust, and dolls stuffed with wool. Secret took pleasure in the crawling things in her space. She wiped her hand through webs to watch the spiders build again. Beetles danced on their backs if knocked off their feet. Ants marched in lines to carry off crumbs she left for them. She was glad to have the insects to amuse her because they helped her feel less lonely.

Out of reach, in a corner of the same room where the windows faced east and south, sat her mother. There, Zavet bent over manuscripts and books, often muttering and burbling, caught in a rushing stream of words.

Madness? No.

Zavet was gifted with the languages of the entire known and ancient worlds. She did not, and could not, explain the mystery of her many tongues. Whatever language she heard or read, she grasped instantly, as if she remembered rather than learned it. She spoke all of them like a native without the accent of her own. The words burbled out of her as if from a deep, hidden spring. She dammed them with her work as a translator, but the flood could only be slowed to a trickle.

Now and again, this strangeness happened in front of other people. With Secret comfortable in a little wagon, Zavet went to market or for afternoon walks, and sometimes Zavet would mutter aloud softly. Some people seemed to try to ignore her, but Secret observed the suspicious glances from others. She saw them lean close, eyes narrow, fingers pointing. She rarely heard what they said, but she could sense their scrutiny. This is how she knew her mother was not quite right, and perhaps neither was she. Zavet and Secret did not look like their neighbors and, between her mother's muttering and her silence, did not sound like them either. Still, the other women were polite toward Zavet, and she was polite but cool toward them, and they allowed their children to play within view as they filled their baskets and remarked about the weather.

As for Secret's father, Bren was often gone while it was light but home when it was dark. Now and then, Bren went away for long periods of time but always came back. When he returned, he brought presents. Secret remembered a set of thick cards marked with colors, shapes, images, and symbols. Glad for the attention, she sat on his lap as he named them. She learned quickly and delighted him with the deft accuracy of her pointing finger when he asked her to identify the images for the words he spoke.

Her mother was always surrounded by books, but her father was the one who filled her with stories. Zavet taught her respect for the texts, which Secret was allowed to look at but not touch. What Bren gave her she was allowed to handle, with care. She turned the pages and, with his voice, he guided her into other worlds, slowly reading with his finger under the symbols that became words, and the words became images. Many of the books had illustrations, but they couldn't compare to what emerged in her mind as she listened.

Although she was very young, Secret discovered she, too, could divine the symbols again and conjure what they told. What marvelous tales of wonder, adventure, and possibility! Her father found her concentration unusual and tested to see whether she understood what she read on her own. He gave her books he had never read to her. He asked her questions to answer yes or no, which she did with nods and shakes of her dark head. My mute little prodigy, he called her.

Secret knew her mother possessed this magic as well, but Zavet was parsimonious with its use in regard to her daughter. Some of the books her father brought he couldn't read and promised that her mother would. She rarely did. With those, Secret sat in silence—such a good, obedient child was she—and studied the mysterious marks on the pages. She wondered what they meant, what tales they told.

One ordinary day, Zavet gave her coloring sticks and used paper with which to draw. The little girl sat on the floor and marked the page with all manner of symbols like ones she had seen. As she wrote the unintelligible words, Secret's heart pounded. Her tiny hand gripped the coloring stick as her head flooded with images. There, within her, was a story she could not yet tell. One she must reveal herself. All at once, she felt its burden, its danger, and its re-demption.

Secret cried out with wonder and dread, unable to understand what had opened in her but fully able to feel its power.

From the sunny corner, her mother hissed long and harsh. The noise startled the girl, and she spilled a half-empty cup of water with a jolt of her hand. Her mother hissed again, louder. The girl felt a tight knot at her navel loosen into a heavy force, which spread through her belly and chest. She held her breath, kept her glare to the ground, and pushed the hot feeling deep into her body, coiling it back to where it lived. Secret struck the page with thick black marks, but quietly, quietly.

"This spill is but an accident, yes, little scourge," Zavet said under her breath as she wiped the floor clean.

A Visit to Her Grandmother

WHEN SECRET WAS THREE YEARS OLD, SHE HEARD TWO words she knew but didn't understand when paired together.

Zavet said they were going on a journey to see the child's *grand mother*, an old woman who lived far away in a place Zavet hadn't seen in many years. She had never mentioned the woman or the village where she was born.

Secret's father, a historian trained in geography, tried to explain the distance to her. She sat on a stool as he faced a map on the wall. "You are here, in this kingdom, in the town of its very seat, in a ward near its center," he said, pointing to one dot among many. Bren drew his finger up and far to the right, then tapped the chart once. "You're going there, to another kingdom, to a village in the woods. An adventure, my pet!"

Secret knew what that was because almost every story her father read to her was an adventure. She could hardly sleep knowing she would soon have one of her own.

On a cool, sunny morning, a large carriage pulled by six brown horses arrived at Secret's small house. Her father carried three trunks to the road where two stout-armed men strapped them on the roof. Bren patted Secret's hair and kissed her on the forehead. Then he and her mother wrapped their arms around each other, whispering and smiling, and quickly kissed full on the lips. Zavet walked up the steps into the carriage, then reached for Secret. The girl saw her mother had tears in her eyes. Several other travelers were already waiting inside. Clean yellow curtains with green sashes framed the windows.

In this carriage, Zavet and Secret traveled for many miles. Day after day, Secret rocked to and fro, sometimes on a seat by herself, sometimes on her mother's lap if the carriage was full. She was used to sitting alone, and she felt uncomfortable on Zavet's thighs, a hard place where she rarely ever sat. Secret was glad when they stopped for meals and for nights in sparse, tiny inns.

Never before had Secret been among so many different kinds of people. They were young and old and in between. Some were dressed in clothing that was worn and patched, others in clean and flawless garb. She watched them with attention, observing their movement and manners, what seemed proper and what did not. She listened to their private conversations and ones they had with her mother, who hardly muttered at all, her mouth busy speaking to the fellow passengers, nervously it seemed.

Secret didn't escape observation either. People stared at her mismatched eyes the colors of night and day but smiled at her. She looked down at her books or out the window for hours on end, but never said a word. In these circumstances, Secret realized, her silence was welcomed. An inquisitive person or two asked her mother why she didn't speak. Zavet said no physician who had examined her could explain it, and this was true. But most who bothered to remark at all said, "Oh, what a well-behaved little girl." Her mother replied with a thank-you, in a tone that made Secret think she was truly pleased.

Then the roads became narrow, and the buildings and houses were farther and farther apart. Secret and Zavet were the last passengers in the carriage, which left them at a large stone cottage near the edge of an endless thicket of trees, rows of green triangles. When her mother went into the cottage, a small creature with triangular ears and a thin tail circled Secret's legs.

Cat, Secret thought. The soft beast made a puttering sound as she stroked its fur. She smiled, her palms warm. Although cats and dogs often approached her when she was out to market or on walks with her mother, Zavet never let her touch them and scared them away with a stomping foot and threatening hiss. The little girl secretly felt they went to her on purpose but was powerless to attend to them.

Secret heard her mother's sharp call. Zavet warned her to get away before it bit her, but the innkeeper, an old woman, said the cat loved nothing more than children's cuddles. Secret pressed her face to the cat's, then Zavet pulled her away.

The little girl heard hoofbeats and watched a black horse approach. It and the carriage it drew stopped at the cottage gate. A man in a dark-blue coat and breeches stepped down. He spoke words she didn't understand, but the adults clearly did. He and a helper from the cottage strapped their trunks on a wide, solid shelf on the back of the carriage. It was the same color as the man's clothing with wood trim and light-blue leaves painted around the windows and doors. The old woman gave Zavet a basket filled with food.

Inside the carriage, Secret leaned on the windowsill. Soft shade and a cool breeze surrounded them. As far as she could see, there were trees and plants coming into leaf. Spring had followed them along the journey and finally met their stride.

They stopped along the way to rest. Secret stepped off the dirt road and trampled what looked like hay. She looked up into the green tree and sat upon the dry whiskery leaves it had shed, the smell sweet and thick as syrup. Never had she seen anything like this before. Birds and shadows scuffling in the trees and shrubs, the spiraling ferns, the dense moss. Soon enough, Secret would be able to name everything she saw, but in that moment, she did not yet have a word to describe how she felt. The awareness was familiar, as if she might have experienced it before, but not so intensely, not in a way that filled her with laughter and tears of joy. She sensed herself a part of everything around her—what was green, alive, Beauty, all that belongs together and was meant to be.

A cord of sunlight parted leaves and attached to the glow of a pale yellow cone on the soil. Secret knelt next to it, entranced. The coachman saw her and crouched at her side.

"That is a mushroom," he said with an unfamiliar lilt to his words. "It's beautiful to see but poisonous to eat. Not all mushrooms are that way, and you must learn the difference. It has emerged too soon in the year. How strange."

Secret stroked the cool, smooth cap and smiled. The man mirrored her joy.

"Oh, Eve, don't touch that dirty fungus," Zavet said. As soon as she spoke these words, she turned her back and walked to the carriage.

Secret's smile ebbed away as her finger fell to her side.

"Come, child," the coachman said. He reached out his gloved hand and pressed her delicate fingers in his blue silk palm the color of the sky. "Your grandmother is waiting for you."

Secret had learned who this *grand mother* was. The visit was to see her mother's mother, who had never laid eyes on her only daughter's daughter. Secret had heard Zavet speak about this with strangers on the journey.

They were traveling to the village where Zavet was born, hundreds of miles northeast of the kingdom her husband and child claimed as their native land. Insular and isolated, the village was founded long ago within a forest dominated by spruce trees and bitter winters. There, people were born and left only in death. They spoke the language of the region with an obscure dialect, rarely heard outside its geographic borders. The village did not feel like home to her, Zavet said to one passenger, because she had been away for long periods of time since she was seven years old. Secret listened closely. Her mother didn't explain the reason for these periods of separation, but Zavet did say that the times away showed her how much existed beyond the village, a place that felt abandoned rather than independent.

Secret could tell by the way Zavet bit her lip there were more words to say that she would not speak.

At last, after weeks of travel, the carriage stopped in a quiet village in front of a wooden cottage. Secret stood behind her mother.

She heard a metal door knocker, *clack clack clack*. The door opened with squeaks and groans.

"Zavet," a woman's voice said.

"Ahma" was the reply, then several words Secret didn't understand. For a moment, Secret thought her mother had lost herself in muttering. Then the child realized the old woman knew what was being said. The two women spoke the same unusual tongue. Hesitant and stiff, they leaned their heads close together and kissed the air near each other's cheeks.

Zavet stepped aside and placed her hand on Secret's shoulder. More incomprehensible words, then a name, hers, Eve.

Her grandmother was not as old as she imagined a grandmother to be. That is, her face was lined but not shriveled. She had downy cheeks and jade eyes, with skin tinted green, as if somewhat rotten. The woman was strangely tall and sturdy, her shoulders wide, her hands mannish, a body suited for physical labor. Her hair was white with a thick black streak at her temple, the mass of its darkness braided and coiled on top of her head, held by metal pins. Her straight skirt hovered low but revealed narrow ankles and feet.

Ahmama stared at Secret with such force that the little girl crept backward. The old woman appeared to search the child, then Zavet, her eyes fixed on theirs in turn. Then, as if she had received an answer she wanted, Ahmama sighed and smiled.

"Kiss your ahmama, Eve," Zavet said.

Secret pressed her lips to her grandmother's fluff and then went inside the house.

The rooms connected one to the next with no hallways or doors. There was a place to sit with a heavy couch and padded stools, a place to eat at a trestle table and benches, a place to cook at a hearth surrounded by huge metal pots, and a place to sleep on high beds surrounded by heavy, rough curtains. Secret was to share a bed with her mother. She wished for a bed of her own again.

In Ahmama's room, Secret saw a cupboard that had doors at the bottom and shelves on the top. Colorful bowls, mugs, and vessels crowded the space. At the very top was an oval object painted brightly with the image of a woman. Secret had seen such a thing before, one like this but more worn, stored in the room where her mother worked, never touched, though sometimes glimpsed.

"See," Ahmama said. She took the object and gave it to Secret. Again, word sounds the girl could not comprehend.

"Nesting doll," Zavet said to her mother.

"Nest-ing doll," Ahmama said with effort.

Her grandmother settled to the floor. Her broad-fingered hands twisted off the decorated woman's head and chest. In the doll's hollow wooden body was another body, and within that, another and another. Secret counted thirteen dolls while her ahmama spoke as if telling a good story.

"She is talking to you about an old tradition," Zavet said. "In our family, the firstborn girl receives her mother's nesting doll when she is seven years old. The mother gets a new doll for herself to remember the old one. You are three now, closer to four. You must wait your turn," Zavet said to her daughter.

Secret tried to fit the dolls back in place, in order. She was gentle in her actions.

"Care full child," Ahmama said.

From the corner of her eye, Secret saw her mother smirk.

"Hmm, bothered to learn a few foreign words, did she?" Zavet said in a cheerful tone that masked her meaning.

Secret stacked and twisted as best she could. Her grandmother watched with her hands on her knees. Zavet had disappeared. After Secret put the dolls back together, with Ahmama's help, she looked at the woman's face.

"You no smile. Zavet no smile child," Ahmama said with surprise.

But this would change for Secret, for a time, during the visit to her grandmother's house. Ahmama followed Secret's lead, which sent them outdoors every possible moment. She learned the names of things drawn in books, but in the woods and near the village, she saw these same things alive, with her own eyes.

Ox sheep goat owl hawk bird—so many birds—deer rabbit fox hedgehog squirrel.

Vine fern moss bark branch twig tree shrub flower seed nut fruit.

Ahmama gave the proper names in her tongue then, and years would pass before Secret would learn them in her own. Although they spoke different languages, Secret understood her grandmother judged the named things. That which had bright colors and sweet smells received loving caresses. Ahmama spit on the ground for what was nasty, soured her face for the ugly, and dusted her hands for the dirty.

Secret's heart resisted these declarations because she felt great pleasure in all she saw, heard, touched, and smelled, even when it was strange to her senses. She accepted them as they were. Secret thought the caterpillar could no more change its stinging spines than the owl could lose its hoot or the chamomile flower transform from white to red. They were what they were, and it didn't seem fair anyone might wish them to be otherwise.

With such a conviction in mind, that summer in the woods was a wonder for her. She felt cheerful among the sprawls of evergreen spruce, light under the leafy birch, and strong near the occasional oak. She knew her mother had lived there as a girl and did not return when she became a woman. How could she leave this place? Birds sang all day. Where Secret lived with her parents, all was wood, brick, and stone with dogs on leashes, cats in windows, and birds mere blurs in flight. That world seemed barren, even sick, to her now. The little girl hadn't known she'd been starving until she received her fill of what had been denied.

In the final days of their visit, distant relatives arrived in the village to see Zavet and her daughter one last time. They resembled one another with dark hair, swarthy skin, subtle slanted eyes, strong jaws, and muscular bodies. Secret's hair and skin looked like theirs, too, and a calm sensation within her made her feel as if she belonged among them. She didn't feel that at her own home and wished she could stay in the village.

Old cousins, ahpapas to their grandchildren, lifted her to stand on their knees and stared into her eyes. She pushed her chin down, quite aware of the strangeness they observed. The cousin-papas laughed and called her a name meant with kindness. Duckling. Secret had seen a brood of them at a pond. There were far worse things the old men could have said, she thought. Now and then, she'd seen women at market stare at her and her mother and draw close to whisper. Cold fish. Batty. Freak. Evil Eyes. Witch.

Ahmama and the women prepared a picnic feast for everyone. With baskets and jugs in hand, young and old walked along a narrow path through the woods into a wide clearing with room to run. They ate, then ate more. Some of the men had drums and stringed instruments, which they played while the adults and children sang and danced. The women twirled and gestured to one another and the willing men.

Zavet didn't join the revelry. This didn't surprise Secret, because her mother never once danced or sang in her presence. What Secret noticed was her mother drift among everyone with physical grace, her head held high, her hands turned up at her sides toward the sun. That day, Zavet's usual awkward, cautious movement disappeared.

Nearby, Secret hid so she could safely watch and avoid the cousin-papas who snatched little children and held their hands to sway and step. Although a part of her desperately wanted to join in, the little girl who always watched and listened did just that. She stared at her feet as the music pulsed through her, urging her toes to tap in time.

Then Secret heard the hum. A beckoning. A welcome. She approached the sound with all of her being. She left the picnic and walked into the woods with the hum as her guide.

The sound came from a dead tree with a terrible wound, its scar so thick Secret gasped. She felt afraid of the tree and its dark hollow, but the hum called her. As she stepped forward, a slight noisy breeze drifted overhead. She looked up. A beeline, she knew, because her grandmother had pointed out one to her several weeks before. Ahmama had told her the insects were easily angered and would painfully sting, but Secret saw no harm in the flying creatures gathering gold from flowers and carrying it away in pouches on their legs.

Secret crept closer as bees went in and out of the hollow. The dizzy sparks of their wings and the hum that had changed ever so slightly entranced her. She peered into the heart of the gap. Then she walked inside and sat down in the center. The space was as large as a tiny hut. She could imagine a bed, a chest, a fireplace, but it was only a thought as the hum became louder.

A bee landed on her cheek. Still and silent, Secret realized it was telling her a story. She closed her eyes to focus on what streamed into her—sights she saw but couldn't see, sounds she heard but couldn't hear, and feelings she couldn't know to feel. Her body felt caught between waking and sleeping, almost paralyzed, as if pulled between two worlds. The little girl shuddered as if she were frightened, but she was not afraid. What came to her was like a memory, a dream, a moving illustration. There were no words, but she formed them in her mind to describe the impossible knowledge that revealed itself.

One, two, three shadows of angry men. Then a sad man, alone, called out in a gentle voice. A terrified child, a girl, ran through the woods. A shadow man grabbed her. Coiled rope, dead hare, ancient tree. Too much at once—too fast—a blur of image and sound. Screams severed by silence, blackness. The grieving man had a bloody wound the length of the front of his body. Then a silver wolf was howling, then digging, digging to find the man.

Around them were bees, so many bees. The wound and the wolf, covered with honey.

Someone called her name. Secret opened her eyes. Tremors coursed up and down through her small limbs. She blinked. The world beyond the hollow was a blur, then came into sharp focus. She meant to leave the tree, but the bee wished to tell more of its tale and its sisters persisted in their hum. She wanted to stay in the hollow with the faintest scent of flowers.

"Eve, my little fungus. Where have you gone?"

The little girl opened her mouth to try to speak. As always, since she was an infant, the knot at her navel remained tied to her tongue.

"Eve!" her mother called. "Eve! Where are you? Come here this instant!"

Secret looked past the tree's dark threshold. Bees continued to stream in a line, a sparkling ribbon of life, joining the others within. She felt them crawl on her skin and hair, their breeze above her going up into the dark, deeper in the dead tree's wound. The hum suddenly changed.

There was her mother, darting toward her. She'd been found. Zavet reached to grab her, but Secret retreated farther back into the hollow. The bees' hum rose again, an angry noise. Zavet reached for her a second time, and the bees swarmed out into the light. Zavet screamed and thrashed, dancing wildly.

Secret stood to look and, as her head topped her full height, she felt three sharp stings above her eyes, one after the other. She cried out in surprise, not in pain, not yet. By then, others had heard Zavet's screech. A cousin called Zavet's name as Secret emerged from the darkness, a poisoned node rising hard on her forehead.

She saw her mother's face grow red, misshapen. As familial hands moved across her skin and limbs, Secret watched her grandmother's nails pinch throbbing spheres from Zavet's face.

She heard her name uttered in a question. A young man and woman knelt at her sides. With their tongues, they spoke her language.

"Three holes. No barbs, Duckling."

"Stung by queen."

Zavet said nothing, nothing at all. She turned her head ever so slightly toward her daughter before the swelling closed one eye shut. On Zavet's skirt and on the ground were dead and dying bees. In time, Secret would learn that bees give their lives for the hive and their queen, the cores of their bodies released with the stings. That afternoon, she knew those bees had died to protect her but not the reason why.

Before bedtime, Secret stood at the full-length mirror, with candles lit on a nearby table. There on her forehead, between eyes the colors of night and day, were three dots.

● ●

●

One point, two points, three points. A triangle, Secret thought.

From a pocket on her dress, she took out a bee's corpse. She observed its black oval eyes and thin broken legs. She put her ear near the body, but there was no hum. Was this the bee that told her of the wound and the wolf? How could it tell her such a thing? Its mouth had no lips, not that she could see.

For a moment, she doubted what had occurred. Possibly, she had trailed the beeline, fallen asleep within the hollow, dreamed of the tale, and awakened to see her mother grasp at her.

Secret looked in the mirror and saw the bed in a shadowy reflection. She remembered instances when she was somewhere else, being chased or left alone in blackness, and suddenly, she was not, her mother leaning over her, dutiful in her effort to stop the nightmare. There were other times Secret was in beautiful places she had certainly never seen in her short life, a jeweled palace, a blooming garden, a rocky seaside. How lovely and peaceful those other places were, sometimes light, sometimes dark. Those times, upon morning, she'd felt disappointed she had to leave the comfort of the dream.

Perhaps the bee had told her nothing at all, but Secret believed in her heart that the creature had. She felt, did not merely think, this truth. She was confused by what had happened and some of what was revealed, but that didn't mean her experience wasn't real. Grief for the bees filled her throat as a lightness opened in her chest, gratitude for the strange gift of the story and their sacrifice.

The little girl sensed a presence near her. She turned to see Zavet in the doorway. Her mother's face was monstrous, a feverish glow above a gray dress. Secret closed her hand around the dead bee. As Zavet approached, Secret's flesh tightened and cooled, shriveling like a fallen leaf. Her mother was in one of her dark moods. Zavet knelt by the child and waved her hand above the node on the girl's forehead.

"Does it hurt?" Zavet asked.

Secret shook her head and held her fingers near Zavet's swollen lip. Egg-sized lumps covered her face. One eye was still closed, the other's violet iris lost in a red wetness. The injuries looked terribly painful. With a look of sympathy and a gentle hand, Secret tried to stroke her mother's cheeks. Zavet leaned away from the gesture. Secret's lashes thickened with tears from her mother's rebuff.

"This is what happens when a bad girl doesn't listen to her mother," she said. "Good thing you were found. Your father would be distressed if I lost you."

Zavet took a comb from the table and began to run it through Secret's long black hair. The strands fell forward over her eyes, which she had furiously wiped. In that instant, Secret realized she could see out but her mother could not see in. The sensation took her back to the moments in the hollow tree—a place of protection. A place where she could hide.

The Town, the Kingdom's Seat, Before the Plague

DESCENDANTS AND SURVIVORS, TRAVEL NOW TO A TIME BE-
fore the Plague of Silences.

A good imagination will serve just as well as a map, although
there is one to reference in the appendix, if one wishes.*

Begin the journey with the morning sun at a visitor's back.
Approach the seat of the kingdom. In the center is the town, built
long ago over the ruins of a village and in the midst of a once-great
forest. There are vestiges of the forest still. To the north is a tract of
private hunting land. A wide clearing separates it from the virgin
fragment of its former self to the west. To the east, there is a corridor of trees along the road of entry.

Continue due west. Stray for a while to walk in the shade of
those nearby trees. Beyond the margins of leaf, tree, and root are
a meadow and a pasture. On the left, the wind swirls the tall grass
and partners leggy wildflowers in a dance. Past this meadow are
arable lands near the river, in use for ages before and after The
Mapmaker's War. On the right is the pasture, which was not one

---

* See Appendix I on page 361.

until the land was cleared for its timber and animals were brought to graze on what grew.

Sure-footed again on the cobblestones, advance toward the east entrance into town. When the signs appear, there is not far to go. The signs are flat, painted with tremendous skill, and mounted on great standing stones. They hawk in silence all manner of product and thought, temptation and warning, ye olde and the new and improved. What is this marvelous town?

Consult, or imagine, the map. Orient north, although the direction is arbitrary, as it once had been to first face east. There, where the sun moves in secret, is The Castle. A map suggests the land is flat, but the body will see and feel the earth rise to a hill under its foundation. Stand facing its facade, which rises beyond its circling wall. See that it is a regal castle that meets all expectations and mirrors imagination. Note the sturdy bridge crafted by tough-handed carpenters, the forbidding portcullis forged by bull-armed smiths, and the thick stone walls erected by skilled masons. Uniformed guards walk the walls, peer out from the towers, alert to threat. Bright flags herald that its days are not over.

Below and beyond The Castle, north to south, east to west, is the town. Crisscrosses and coils of cobblestone streets separate and bind the wards. The wards from one end to the next do not resemble one another. The buildings reveal evolving designs and tastes, shifts of innovation and fortune. This is where most of the people live and work, die and dream. The rest do so in the fine manors to the northwest and on the small farms southeast, near the river.

The town gives way to a long plaza. Stand at its geographic center and look left and right. The gold-toned tiles reach vanishing points. There are no benches, planters, or trees. Ahead is a tall building, the tallest one in town, twelve stories high. The architecture hints at a time well before its time, as well as ahead. Observe the visual weight, the symmetry, the columns. On either side of the building are smaller ones. They are older than the tallest one, shells of themselves. Within, the interiors have been removed, the walls and floor rearranged.

Behind The Tallest Building and its companions is Old Wheel. Such is the name of this ward in town and no one knows why. Despite its age, Old Wheel has not been wholly abandoned. The squares are busy with entertainment for all ages—plays and music, and on occasion, puppets and magicians. Here, there are streets at right angles and terminal points at wide squares.

In one square, there is a portable stage. A trunk yawns open upon it. Costumes sprawl lifeless. A mask lies nearby. It has the forked tongue, flared nostrils, and red scales of a dragon.

Across the square, neglect is evident. Jagged cracks compromise the walls of several buildings. See that the mortar is weak and the bricks can no longer rely on its strength. Where bricks have fallen away, other wasting layers lie behind. Wooden beams support cavities of crumbling mud. The decay cannot be stopped now.

If one had an older map, it would reveal this place had been connected to the river. The port and its docks, as well as its artery to town, are farther east and south, downstream. The river is unchanged, although its boundary once separated one domain from another. Now the water cuts through only one kingdom, the lands joined by force.

Much has been seen today, and the evening draws late. The maw of darkness swallows the sun.

Return to the plaza. Watch the lamplighter touch a flame into a lamppost's brass shade and see the tongue leap within. Warm glows are cast down on the shadowed cobblestone streets ahead. Find lodging. Find an amusement. Rest, because tomorrow will be a busy day.

A Change of Fortune

ON THE RETURN HOME FROM HER GRANDMOTHER'S HOUSE, Secret remained under the spell of the woods. She sat on or near her mother's lap and peered at the meadows and woods as the carriage whisked past them. Green gave way to red, yellow, orange, and brown. She thought of all the beautiful things she had seen, touched, smelled, and heard. Each time there was a rest from the journey, Secret sought whatever trees, plants, or animals she could touch, or at least observe. She knew none of this existed where she lived with her parents. When she realized she might never encounter such beauty again, she cried without a sound. Her palms ached with the pain of absence. Her mother hissed, not caring who heard, and told her there was nothing to cry about.

When at last the carriage approached Secret's house, the night was cool. The lamps were lit on the streets of the ward, and moths fluttered against the glow. She saw her father waiting at their doorstep. She smiled at the sight of him, clutching the cloth bag Ahmama had given her to hold leaves, petals, bark, and stones. Bren lifted her for a brief embrace, kissed her where the stings were no longer visible, and set her on the sidewalk. Her parents reached for each other's hands and pulled together for a kiss. Zavet caressed Bren's cheek as he spoke to her quietly. They stood this way until the coachman unloaded the last trunk and cleared his throat.

The next morning, Bren set aside the longsheet he was reading and, while Secret ate her breakfast, admired the treasures she had brought. He asked her questions to which she nodded yes and no.

She noticed her father wore new clothing. He looked like the fancy men she'd seen in Old Wheel, a ward in town where men walked around with their hair brushed back and shiny—if they had any at all—and their matching coats and trousers were without wrinkles. Bren had never dressed so finely. Clipped at his side on his belt was a small contraption she'd seen other people wear, men and women both. He cleared the table and asked if she would like to join him for an outing. Secret was confused because her father was clearly dressed for a day of work.

On occasion, Bren had taken her out for an afternoon. They would attend a performance, usually one of the ancient tales because he knew she liked them best, then to a teahouse for a treat of her choice. But that morning, she clapped at the novelty and rushed to ready herself with a cloak and mittens.

They walked three blocks to a stable where a liveryman checked the straps on a brand-new two-horse cart. If she'd spoken, she would have asked what happened to the smaller one he'd had since long before she was born. Bren lifted her to the seat that wasn't worn or patched.

"Hold on. We'll go for a ride first to see the sights," he said as he urged the horses to move.

Behind the horses, her father sat high, in good spirits, as he directed her attention to this and that point of interest. Secret had been to different wards in town before, but only to go to a certain shop or amusement.

From the center of town, where they lived in a modest ward, her father drove them slowly through a particular northwest ward of clean, large, well-kept row houses with polished entries and rear courtyards.

"Very soon, we will move here, closer to where we are meant to be," Bren said. Secret thought his voice seemed choked and his eyes damp.

Bren crossed a wide street and told Secret to look up to her left. "Can you see The Castle on the hill? That road leads past its surrounding wall and right up to the gatehouse. One day, I will be granted entrance, mark my words."

Secret glimpsed its imposing gray exterior and saw flags waving at the tops of its towers. She turned to search for them again as they wound through the northeast wards, full of row houses, more narrow and some quite shabby compared with the others.

Her father drove them through the central east and west. Some streets were lined with brick walk-ups several stories high, and other streets had many small houses that all looked different. As they went along, Secret realized they passed through the ward where she had lived since she was born.

"Oh, to finally escape this hodgepodge!" her father said as he looped north again, the sun at Secret's back.

The sun warmed Secret's little face as her father traveled southeast. There, single-story hovels were built right next to each other, and the streets were not tidy. Old barrels and crates and scraps of wood were piled on the sidewalks. Paint was missing or peeling from windows and doors. She realized people were staring at them as they passed. Children with torn and dirty clothing shouted, sometimes chased behind them.

"Could you have imagined that I, your father, rose from such soot and ashes? Look well at what you'll never have to suffer," Bren said. Suddenly, he flicked his hand as if shooing a fly. A boy close to Secret's age with greasy hair and wide brown eyes trotted near the cart. "Go away! I have no coins for you! Run along!"

The boy's dejected expression made Secret feel heavy. She looked at her father who scowled, his jaw tense.

"No, you will never know what I endured . . . Let me tell you of another past," he said as he prompted the horse to step up its gait.

Part of what he told her that morning she would piece together with other fragments over time.

Bren Riven claimed he was from an old family, people of a waned wealth. He knew, for he'd seen some documents, that the land they'd held became smaller and smaller until there was nothing left, for complicated and mundane reasons. There was little record to note why such prestige fell. Something as simple as the displeasure of a king, a debt to be paid, a loss to endure. Do not such circumstances happen all the time?

Those ancestors, now dead men, did little, of course, other than tell other men what to do. No real work came of them, some would say, but Bren believed such an assessment was not just. Management and governance are their own vocations at times. Still, they were men who did not use their own hands, soiled them not, knew no hobbies other than eating, drinking, and being merry. Generations later, their descendants had no time for hobbies or the means to be lavish.

There were some among them, it was rumored, who were scholars. It was said a number of them left to pursue studies in mathematics, some in the natural sciences. One may have been a poet.

Each generation or so, there was at least one who claimed a link to the right hand of the king. A place of counsel. He possessed a tenacity that suggested something great had been taken away. This man told his sons, one supposes his daughters, of a former prominence. Bad luck or a fickle king or two had stripped a fortune from him and his heirs.

Bren had yet to confirm but felt confident that their lineage dated back before The Mapmaker's War. This was a subject he knew well, to the verge of obsession. His personal library contained translations of old chronicles, analyses of the events, and histories related to those days and times.

As Secret would learn in school, but first from her father, the war started because of a disobedient mapmaker's apprentice, who was not mentioned by his proper name in any of the chronicles. The apprentice defied the king's order not to cross the river that separated their land from another. In that land was a wealthy, well-weaponed people whose ire was provoked by this action. As a result, a war began. The apprentice was executed by sword. The fighting waged on for three years, spreading to distant lands east and north, less so west and south. Triumphant, the kingdom doubled its holding. Good King Wyl moved the seat of power across the river to where the first battle took place, a village that grew into the very town where Secret was born and lived.

Since then, there had been other wars at the fault of men, as well as droughts, famines, floods, and plagues at the fault of Nature. Yet for those with living memories, in recent years, prosperity thrived and peace reigned, or so it seemed.

Bren had made trips to pore through tax records and annals to trace a link back to those ancient days. This was difficult because the war had occurred a thousand years earlier. He encountered sparse documents, many details lost to fire, water, inconsistency, and carelessness. Bren had yet to close the gap between himself and his oldest known ancestor—who was born several generations after the war—and advisers who had counseled the king to go to war. Bren was sure one of those advisers was his forefather, whose misfortune slowly swept the family into obscurity and poverty.

"Good fortune was once a matter of noble mercy," Bren said to his silent little daughter on the seat of the two-horse cart, "until times changed and men could make proper names for themselves. I am such a man, and I intend to take back what was lost."

The story over for now, Secret turned her attention to what was around her. She had not seen so much of the town before.

As they entered the southwest wards, Secret enjoyed the heat on the top of her black head. There, walk-ups and houses were mixed together, as if they came from different times and places.

Although some of the wards seemed to be cared for better than others, Secret noticed that they were still linked by sameness.

In most of the wards, entire blocks were fenced to create lots for carts and horses. She saw buildings with strips of grass next to them and children playing out in the open. Some of the places that looked like houses were instead shops and eateries, with displays in their windows and signs hanging near their doors—with pictures and words that Secret could easily read, even though she was only four. Every few blocks seemed to have a group of carts, shaded by umbrellas, the same as where her mother went to market.

Cobblestone streets with sidewalks and deep hidden drains fronted each threshold. Every few turns of the cart wheel, a spindly tree grew through a square cubit of dirt or an iron lamppost with a bronze shade stood to cast night light. Hitching posts lined the shop fronts. Pump spigots anchored most corners.

Newsboxes, small as puppet stages, held the center of many intersections, and the speakers inside shouted out the day's events. On top of the newsboxes, clocks made no mistake of the time, all of them perfectly synchronized. Here and there, young men stood waving stacks of longsheets, purchased by those who did not have them delivered to their doorsteps.

The streets curved, angled, and continued. Secret felt lost and was glad her father was there and knew the way.

Near an intersection, all movement halted. Secret looked around. There was a plain one-seat wooden cart behind them, and she watched the aging nag grimace against her bit. On Secret's side, going in the same direction, she saw an immaculate six-seat wagon, drawn by two enormous field horses, with gold trim, leather cushions, and rain roof. The little girl reached her hand toward the horse closest to her. The beast exhaled on her fingertips then nibbled them with its lips. Secret grinned with delight.

The newsbox chatter suddenly became louder.

"*Why talk only to yourself when you can Tell-a-Bell what you have to do?*" the voice said. "*Get through your day with more clarity and success with the latest self-communication aid. Keep those lists of chores and left-to-dos all in one place—at the tip of your tongue. Make your bell toll today and never forget a thing. Visit your nearest Time Matters shop for your very own.*"

Her father kept one hand on the reins and touched the caged bell at his belt with the other, as if to ensure it was still there. Until that morning, Bren hadn't worn the contraption. She knew people who had muttered them to themselves like her mother but didn't receive the same strange looks. Maybe Mother should wear a bell instead of Father, she thought. She wondered if Bren had much more to remind himself of than he had had before.

Finally, the carts moved again. Secret realized her father was going in the direction of Old Wheel, the ward at the southernmost end of town. She didn't know why it was named that. She had never seen any unusual wheels there, certainly not old ones, or a shop that sold them. Secret thought places, like people, sometimes had names that made little sense. Nevertheless, she did know—because her father told her—that Old Wheel was the oldest part of town, where narrow streets intersected into open squares. That was the ward where archaic plays and performances were held, under tents or in small amphitheaters with stone seats tiered like a fancy cake.

She hopped lightly in her seat, excited that her father was taking her to a favorite location. After Bren crossed the gold-tiled plaza, he didn't turn on to a familiar little lane. Instead, he approached The Tallest Building, which cast a sharp shadow across the flat ground in front of it.

A wide overhang protected visitors from rain and sun. Her father turned the reins over to a uniformed liveryman and told him to tie the horses to a post. The errand would be brief.

Secret had never visited that building before although she'd often seen it from a distance. The entrance had large narrow windows separated by smooth black marble columns. Within the two wooden doors were glass panels with the letters F and M, each in a block style of emerald green bordered by gold.

Inside, black and emerald marble tiles covered the floor. Smooth gray stone walls rose as high as ten men standing on each other's shoulders. On the wall to the left were doors to a pulley lift, and across the lobby on the right was an open stairwell. In the middle of the back wall, there were two doors behind a tremendous desk. Warm and oily from the touch of hundreds of idle hands, its front panel was carved with sword-carrying men on horses. No one was at the desk, but above it, between the two doors, was a grand display of names.

Against a high black marble slab were large gold letters—pure gold, her father informed her—which read FEWMANY INCORPORATED. Underneath the letters was a recess of emerald-green marble filled with gray stones that were stacked on and next to one another with sharp precision. The stones were carved with names, but none that appeared to be of people. Secret turned her eyes toward the words. Amalgamated Metals, Appleseed Industries, Bellingear Wheelwrights Ltd., and many more.

Bren reached over the desk and rang a bell. He glanced at the doors and tapped his foot.

"I've taken a new job and will begin work here next week. What do you think of that, Eve?" he asked.

She nodded as if to approve, but she didn't know of what. Her father's occupation was a mystery then, one she'd eventually comprehend as a constellation of skills and desire.

As a historian and geographer, Bren was interested in the way people lay claim and keep it. He wondered how a thing such as land could be so arbitrarily taken and marked. Invisible marks, as if they are real and binding. He concerned himself with shifts of power that led to changes in what the mighty thought—hoped— was immutable. In times past, these moments were necessarily bloody, but often they were quiet, met with little resistance because few resist men with weapons or decrees.

But on that day as Secret stood in the grand lobby of Fewmany Incorporated, she assumed her father was involved with a business of buying and selling, which in a way he was. Several shops in town bore the name Fewmany in some way, where goods were bought and sold. That Fewmany might be a person didn't occur to her, since the word was always connected to a place. She stood in an enormous, imposing place indeed.

As her father waited for someone to come to the desk, he

shook hands with three men and had a brief conversation with another who honked when he laughed. Secret watched as men in fine coats and polished shoes moved in and out through the lobby doors, talking, checking timepieces, pondering their own thoughts.

Bren's hand hovered over the bell to ring it again. A man in a red coat emerged from one of the doors behind the carved desk.

"Welcome to Fewmany Incorporated, inspired by innovation, anchored in tradition," the man said.

"I was informed a parcel would be left for me."

"Your name, sir?"

"Bren Riven."

The man gave him an envelope sealed with wax. He opened it immediately. A small wooden frame was attached to a plain leather cord. Inside the frame was a printed card with his name, a title, and a miniature sketch of his face.

"Look at my badge. It's proof I belong here," he said. "When you sit with your toys and books four mornings from today, I will be on my way here—to my new office on the top floor."

As they walked through the lobby, Secret observed that her father seemed excited about, even proud of, the badge. She didn't understand why a card was needed, but she did understand being in a place where one belonged. She half-closed her eyes to remember the woods, her body in The Tallest Building, her thoughts miles away.

"This common man's son has taken his place on the wheel of fortune. I expect to rub royal elbows in due time," he said. Her father opened one of the huge doors and let her pass through.

Out of the stark building, she thought she heard a voice calling for attention with a needy tone. Several steps away, there was a tree dotted with yellow leaves in a large pot. A tenacious root had pushed its way down into a crack between the cobblestones.

Secret paused. She felt drawn to help and knew somehow what to do. She wandered away from her father as he waited for their cart to return. After she tucked her mittens into her pocket, she scooped soil with her hands from the pot's edge, careful not to make matters worse. She heaped the dirt over the unprotected root. A pail of water near a hitching post was half-filled with water. Carefully, she lifted the pail and tipped it over into the pot. She thought she heard a sigh.

The girl hugged the tree, as she had done with many trees in the woods far away. She kissed its bark, pleased with the rough texture on her soft lips.

Her father grabbed her arm. "Didn't you hear me call you? Look at you—these filthy hands and a damp cloak. What were you doing—playing with the tree?"

With a solemn face, Secret shook her head. She pointed at the sickly leaves and covered root.

"You were tending it?"

She nodded.

Bren stared at her, his own expression searching. "What a strange child you are." He pulled a handkerchief from his pocket and wiped her palms. "Come on then. There's a good girl. Let's get your treat now, my pet."

The Row House and Its Creatures and Plants

NOT LONG AFTER BREN STARTED TO WORK IN THE TALLEST Building, Secret and her parents prepared to move to a new house.

Where they were moving was a compromise. Her parents, who rarely had harsh words between them, argued frequently about the decision for weeks.

Bren wanted a brand-new house with its own small stable and an open lawn, built among the manors just outside the town's north wards. Zavet, set in her ways, didn't want to move at all. He insisted they needed to live in a house befitting his new position, and she thought it hardly mattered where they lived as long as he was successful in his work. He said she didn't understand the necessity, and she said the pauper's son would do well to realize he wasn't his father. He said the change might do her some good, and she said change usually brings trouble.

So, in the end, Secret's parents agreed to purchase a home in a prestigious ward, respectable enough because some of the town's best families, past and present, resided there as well. Zavet was pleased she wouldn't have to walk far or learn to use a horse and cart in order to go to market or to shops.

Zavet delayed her translation projects to prepare for the move. Secret tried to be as good and helpful as possible. She assisted her mother by carrying items to pack in wooden boxes, which were stacked in clusters near the walls and furniture. Zavet stumbled and bumped into them. She seemed confused and bothered that things were out of place.

Then their belongings were taken from the house. Secret and her parents slept on pallets for three nights. Her mother worked as best she could during the day but found no comfort on the floor. She preferred things as they always were.

On a morning near the end of winter, her father sat them on the two-horse cart and took them away. Secret and Zavet arrived on an unfamiliar street in front of a fine three-story brick row house with window boxes overflowing with ivy and freshly painted shutters with black iron hinges. A wide alley separated their row house from one neighbor and a shared wall kept them close to another. Secret could hear the unmistakable chatter of newsboxes nearby.

"This is our new home, Eve," Bren said.

Secret allowed Bren to take her hand and lead her through the rooms and up the stairways. There was far more space than they needed. Upon entry on the first floor was a large parlor with an enormous fireplace. The staircase was straight ahead. To the right was a narrow hall with a modern water closet and a storage room that held a mop, a broom, and buckets. To the left was a long room with a heavy back door. On one side was a kitchen with an older wood-burning stove and water basin, and on the other side, her mother's workspace with her tables and shelves. Secret studied the heavy back door with a great bobbin and latch and wondered where it led.

Bren and Secret went up to the second floor. Secret's room was above the parlor. On her left, she saw a little fireplace. Straight ahead were three large west-facing windows. Her bed had been placed under one in the far right corner, and next to it was a table with a lamp. At the foot of her bed was the small, faded blue chest with the painted animals—her mother's as a child—that served as a bench, for it was never opened even though it had hinges and a keyhole. Against the wall opposite the fireplace was her old wardrobe, which still held her little clothes. She walked a few paces to her right to admire the new cupboard that held her books. Next to it was the large chest that held her toys, and she peeked inside to make sure they were all there. After she was done, Bren showed her the storage room above the water closet, where he had placed his maps and records and some of Zavet's belongings. Above her mother's workspace and the kitchen was another room, clean and sparsely furnished, as if ready for a guest. Secret hoped her ahmama might come to stay with them for a while.

The third floor had a low, sloped ceiling because it had once been an attic. The bedroom above hers was for her parents. Across from it was yet another storage area. The remaining space was Bren's. It was already packed with his desk, map table, and books, books, books. Secret looked at a small panel in the hall's ceiling. Her father smiled as he whispered that the garret was crammed with mice and monsters. Better to leave it closed.

As he led her down the stairs, he asked if she liked the house. Secret nodded. She did very much, especially the new water closet, her room with space to play, and the old floor with scuffs and gouges.

"Your mother wants to wait until we're settled, but sooner rather than later, we simply must fix the cracked plaster, paint the walls, hang new drapes, and buy new furniture." He stopped on the last step and tilted her chin to him. "Our fortune has taken a turn, and we must keep up proper appearances."

Some things were the same and some were different in the new row house.

Their old cleaning woman, Elinor, had come once a week. Now she came three days, but she still wasn't allowed into Zavet's workspace. A new laundry woman, Hildith, delivered their clothes and linens pressed and folded, wrapped in a lovely fabric instead of bound with string.

Still too young for school—Secret was only four—she stayed home with her mother but she was no longer forced to play in a corner. She was allowed to amuse herself wherever she wished as long as she didn't make a sound.

Her father worked most days and came home later than he once did at night.

Her mother once had small stacks of books and manuscripts waiting for her attention. Before they moved to the row house, Zavet had many translations to do. Each courier, or patron, who had arrived at her door with a shrouded treasure and departed with two took her word for the translation. Who knew, in fact, what was accurate? What part of her work was conjecture, speculation? Within the words was intent—hidden or otherwise. Not all things are so clear, Secret thought to herself many years later, long after this part of her story was done.

Now, at the new house, Zavet translated documents stored in leather portfolios and had only one aged text or tome at a time. Secret didn't know, because her mother didn't say, whether Zavet missed the variety.

Although she had only one manuscript or book on her tables and all of those official-looking documents, Zavet used the same tools—five old pens with different nibs, several bottles of ink, rocker blotters, and her grids.

Her mother wrote on paper she specially ordered. Each page was covered with a grid. The lines were sometimes brown, some-times blue, and they were perfectly straight, up and down, side to side. They met to make perfect squares. On all four edges, where the lines ended there were dots alternating in black and red. A tiny red X appeared at the top left corner and the middle of the page. The paper was delivered in a wooden crate so heavy that a parcel man had to carry it inside and leave it next to Zavet's chair. Secret was allowed to use only the pages her mother discarded.

Zavet had other grids, too, glass ones etched with lines that were colored in with paint and surrounded with wooden frames. The frames had dots burned into the wood where the lines ended. These Zavet placed upon the pages she read and translated. Secret wondered whether the people who sent valuable books to her mother knew, or minded, that a thin glass pane was all that protected the words from her ink-stained hands.

What was new for Secret was the memory of fresh breezes and sunshine, what she felt those few weeks with her ahmama. Secret looked out of the house's windows at the moving clouds and the occasional dart of a bird. She felt lonelier than she ever had before, once again surrounded by roads and buildings, removed from the creatures and plants she had loved in the woods.

She found herself staring at the heavy back door and its great bobbin and latch. The mechanism seemed ancient to her, not at all like the doorknobs and locks in the rest of the house. The sight of it gave her a feeling of anticipation. It was too high for Secret to reach, but she knew if she could, she would be able to go outside. A trail of ants that made their way back and forth from the kitchen under Zavet's tables to the door's crack showed her so. Secret wished she could be a fly, an ant, or a beetle, and crawl around inside and out as much as she liked.

With daydreams she comforted herself, imagining that outside the back door there was a beautiful forest that awaited her company.

But Secret's only company was her mother.

Every morning, after feeding Secret breakfast with her father, Zavet supervised her bath, combed her long hair, and helped her into her dress. Soon after, on most days, they went to market. Upon their return, Zavet told Secret to quietly play while she worked. Her mother prepared a simple lunch, which they ate together, then both went back to their activities.

The afternoons, however, were a tenuous time of day. Zavet took a walk with Secret in tow in a wagon and, before they returned home, she let the little girl run along the sidewalk. Sometimes, Zavet took a long break with tea and bread that lasted through Secret's nap. Other times, Secret lay awake to hear her mother shuffle about the house. She could hear busy sounds—books placed on shelves, a cabinet opened and closed—but also the mutters. If her father was home at those times, he would call to his wife and say, "You're talking to yourself, dear." His words made Zavet pause, then stop. However, he was often not there when the mutters became angry, when Zavet seemed to hardly notice what came out of her mouth. If a noise Secret made distracted her, Zavet startled and glared at her daughter, releasing a hushing hiss that robbed the girl's body of light.

Weeks after they had moved into the new house, Zavet had a fit worse than any Secret could remember. The girl awakened from her nap and walked into the hall. She heard cabinet doors and drawers open and close, open and close. Words slammed with each shutting. The child couldn't understand the language, but she understood her mother was very angry by the tone of her voice and because of the straining knot at her navel that cramped her belly and tugged harder at her tongue. Secret crept to the ground floor, more frightened than she'd ever been. She crouched under a parlor table in the darkest corner. She hoped her father would come home soon or that Zavet would exhaust herself, as she sometimes did, to drowse lightly, head dropped on folded arms, at her table.

Secret felt tears on her cheeks, but she didn't make a sound. Her breath was tight and noiseless. She thought she heard the word Ahma, yet Secret could never be certain what syllables came from her mother's mouth. So she sat with stillness not suited for a child. She pressed herself closer to the wall, farther under the table. She glanced to her side and saw a fly there, the dim cast of twilight giving glint to its eyes and wings. I see it, and it sees me, she thought. Its company wasn't enough to soothe her.

Suddenly, Secret heard her name. She heard it called several times, but she didn't want to leave the hiding place.

"Eve!" her mother shouted. "Eve! Show yourself!" She gasped a deep breath when Zavet passed the parlor doorway. In an instant, her mother entered the room, hands outstretched and flailing. Zavet paused, suddenly calm. Then, as if the woman had eyes in the back of her head, she twirled, dropped to the floor, and grabbed Secret's ankle. Zavet dragged the child into the open.

"Your tongue may be dumb, but your ears are not," her mother said as she stood. "Don't try to hide from me, girl. I will find you."

As Secret curled her legs to her chest, Zavet tossed her arms around her head as she had when the bees came. Secret heard a fast, familiar *zuzz*. An insect circled Zavet with persistence. Secret glanced at the wall where the fly had been. It wasn't there. A soft, short giggle tickled Secret's throat as she watched the fly spiral around Zavet's ears. Its acrobatics annoyed her out of the room and away from the bewildered child.

After that, Secret became even more wary of her mother.

Then spring arrived, and with it, sweet breezes, but the heavy wooden door with the great bobbin and latch was never opened. Secret saw light in the crack that changed with day and night. She watched the ant trail flow through the space. They went to a place she could not, and she wished to with desperation. Secret began to bang on the door and reach for the bobbin several times a day while her mother worked.

"There's nothing out there," Zavet said. "Play with your toys and books. *SSSSsssss*."

Secret persisted, even at night, when her father would find her.

"If you stop that noise, I'll give you a cookie," Bren said. This worked for a time, but then cookies lost their appeal. She had spoonfuls of honey and hard syrup sweets. Her father's distraction didn't change her mind.

Then one day as her mother spoke to a courier at the front door, Secret pushed a stool against the back door and climbed on top. She pulled the great bobbin, the latch lifted up, and the door creaked to a narrow crack. Secret leapt from the stool. Her tiny fingers curled at the door's edge. The hinges groaned awake. She slipped into the gap.

Once, the courtyard had been beautiful. The ground was dry and bare, but long, raised planters and large ceramic pots, all cracked and crumbled, bore proof of greener times. Dead shrubs and weeds poked through dust. All around was a high stone wall with dismal moss clinging to one face. Yet in all this grayness, there was green.

Near the corner, close to the house, a single unfurled leaf topped the uppermost branch of an ailing fig tree. Secret stepped over the threshold to approach it, then felt her footing come loose. She kicked her legs in midair.

"If you wanted to go outside, why didn't you say so?" her father said with a chuckle.

Secret thrashed hard, and her father lost his grip. She fell on her feet, planted them on the spot. Bren cocked his head and tousled her hair. She kept her face still but frowned inside. Secret followed him as he walked around the house on the alley side, where the stone wall continued then ended at a barred iron gate with a rusty lock. Bren shook the handle and knocked his fingertips between the tight bars.

"There's no way for you to escape," he said.

He picked her up and took her inside. When he set her down again, she stamped her foot and pointed at the door with an outstretched arm.

Bren blinked at her, then smiled. "You want to be outside, don't you?"

Secret nodded. A cry of relief welled up in her throat.

"I'll let your mother know," Bren said.

The next day, Zavet opened the back door for Secret. She ran into the courtyard and skipped in the dust. She considered what to do first. Then she knew.

She approached the fig tree that grew in spite of itself, twisted toward what light it could get. Most of its limbs were broken away. What branches it had were spotted with crumpled pale-green leaves. Only the leaf at the top hinted that any strong life was left. There was no way it could survive here any longer without help.

There had been many times Secret felt sad for a broken flower, a limping dog, or a crushed insect. Like people, they suffered from neglect and illness and death. She'd seen it for herself in the woods and in her town. To love creatures and plants as she did caused her pain, too, knowing the pain they felt. She endured heartache for the fig tree, seeing it so alone and abandoned.

When Secret discovered the tree, it had been dying a slow, thirsty death because there was no one who gave it a drink when the rains stayed away. Its death was a dark one, too, as the sunlight moved far away and no matter how it stretched and spread its wide leaves, it could not get enough.

Secret loved the sad fig tree and climbed into its reach. The branches that did not break bent, and bent well. She sat in the curve of one, which swayed and rocked with grace. She knew that trees should be covered with leaves, and this one was not. She determined it was ailing. When she was ill, she was given cool drinks and warm soups, and so Secret shared her meals with the tree. Still, it got no better.

If she could have spoken, she might have asked her parents why the old tree was sick. Even she knew, as young as she was, they would have said it was old, and old things die.

But Secret didn't speak, not yet. Still, she wasn't wordless or thoughtless, so she sat upon her favorite branch to think. She touched a knot that once leafed. She watched the branches fall heavy, as if giving way to rest. There was no one nearby, but she was sure she heard a groan.

I feel sore with your tenderness, the fig tree said without saying.

Secret gasped. So it happened again, this talking without sound from that which could not speak. She remembered the bee in the tree, that told of the wound and the wolf. In the hollow, she hadn't tried to respond. But there, alone in her courtyard, Secret felt herself ask a question: *Why are you sick?*

The fig tree replied with images, and, as before with the bee, Secret could perceive the story she was told and transformed that into words. The girl learned her house had once been small and the grounds spacious. As the many years passed, the little house was torn down to build a larger one, with others built side by side. The walls rose, taking away the sun.

How can I help you? Secret asked.

Rub my limbs you can reach. Look with kindness on what you cannot. Pour water when the ground dries. Listen to my tales, she said.

Secret cared for Fig Tree. She filled a wooden pail with as much water as she could carry and gave the tree long drinks. Each day, Secret stroked the branches, careful not to break the leaves, and as she did, more life came into the barren courtyard. The tree had new strength to reach toward the sun. She was misshapen, but the limbs that grew produced leaves and then, by summer, fruit which Secret ate with sweet pleasure. In the tree's shade, the girl watched as insects trailed up and down the maze of dead ends and gentle bridges. A sparrow built a nest in the eaves of the house, and the fledglings took their first flights from her heights. Now and then, a bird perched within the branches and pecked a rosy kiss into the fruit.

Even the loneliest of children find a way to tolerate breathing, and Secret discovered that when she was very still and open, she could hear the stories of creatures and plants.

What began as chance occasions became as frequent and easy as blinking her eyes. Those times she listened, or so it seemed, although the words were not quite words and the feelings were not quite feelings. In those moments, Secret knew something new. And the things they told her—of places far away! Once, a little odd flower began to grow in a mossy spot. It shared a fanciful tale of another land and how beautiful it was and how breezes carried the scent of salt. Even though the flower hadn't lived there—so recently had it been a seed—this was all true, for it had the memory. Secret cared for the flower as long as it was able to grow and bloom. It was weak, away from where it truly belonged. Secret loved it anyway and because of this.

She went outside often to visit Fig Tree and those small things that were drawn to her. Secret liked to sit in the sun and feel her dark hair fire like clay. On temperate days, she took her books and studied them surrounded by air and light. Sometimes, she would read to her friends, as her father did to her, and declared before each one, as he did, what it was. Fact or fiction. History or story. Tale, legend, or myth. Bren had explained the differences, and so she explained them to her friends.

Fact is what happens in real life; fiction is what is make-believe. History is fact, and story is fiction. Myth is the make-believe history of the beginning and ending of everything. Legend is the strange child born of history and make-believe. Tale is a phantom with a body of fact and a heart of fiction, she said without saying.

Secret thought of the wonder tales her father had read to her of animals that could talk, lead people to safety, and bestow magical objects. Would her father believe her if she could tell him what she knew? The distinctions he taught her were not as rigid as he might think.

When she wasn't playing or telling stories, Secret did her best to tend a flower garden. She had conveyed her wish to have one by pointing at illustrations of gardens. Her mother had a load of manure delivered to the yard and had the man turn the soil. Secret helped with her own small tools that her father bought her. Then Zavet acquired seeds and showed Secret how to plant and water them. Her mother seemed pleased to see the girl occupied, even content. Sometimes, Zavet stood at the back door's threshold and watched Secret without comment. Secret waved and, often enough, Zavet gave a perfunctory wave back.

Life and color filled the courtyard. The reward for her efforts was the visiting bees that told her of meadows not far away. Sometimes, she kicked her balls around the courtyard, and Fig Tree sent them back her way when she could reach it. At the tree's roots, Secret played with her toys and drowsed with a thin blanket.

However, when the days were stormy or cold, and night fell, Secret had to leave the tree's comfort and go inside. If the days were too cloudy, Zavet didn't work. There were lamps and beeswax candles in the house, but she found the light insufficient to concentrate. Instead, she stood in the kitchen over long-cooking stews, or took lengthy sonorous naps, or knit a slow-stitched scarf. Sometimes her mother was in a dark mood, and Secret had the sense to squirrel away in her room and not leave until she was called for dinner.

But there were times when the indoor days were not so bad. Secret had a name for them, in her head—the good mother days. On these days, Secret didn't feel like a chore to be done or an obligation to tend. Secret felt what she thought other children felt, the ones whose mothers walked with them hand in hand and looked at them wistfully as they played. She didn't feel the need to hide in her room, aware of the smallest sounds and imperceptible changes in the air.

Now and then, when the clouds thickened, Zavet lit candles and allowed Secret to look at the works she was translating and books from her own small collection. In this way, Zavet could point out the differences in materials, craftsmanship, and age. Zavet showed her contracts that were new, with straight, tidy writing or printed with type. Some were old with curling scripts and edges that were scalloped, indicative of a time when agreements were written in duplicate and cut away from each other, the bottom edge of one mirroring the top edge of its mate. Secret liked to look at the wax seals and gold stamps pasted in the corners.

Secret studied books and manuscripts that were beautifully bound or loose without covers, their pages sometimes out of order. Some had missing pieces or intentional replacements, sometimes blatant ones. A few were little more than scraps and tatters. Zavet said cramped, small writing suggested a paper scarcity or a fastidious mind. Elaborate colors and decoration hinted at scholarly leisure, a moneyed patron. There were telling indicators of famed scriptoria and individual scribes.

If she was lucky, Secret was allowed to touch, exploring the difference between parchment, which was skin, and paper, which was plant pulp. She smoothed her hand across the bound texts, sometimes in wood, sometimes in leather. When she was given permission to handle a book by herself, which was rare, she loved the giving sound when it opened, the whisper of her fingers against the pages, and the smells released, different each time but always familiar.

Other days, Zavet read to Secret from books the child couldn't read herself because she didn't know the languages. Zavet's stained fingertips pressed the words on the page as if she could feel the ink. Secret felt a ghostly envy that her mother could understand any word, and thus any story, that came under her gaze.

Sometimes, Zavet took her nesting dolls from the shelves and allowed Secret to play with them. The girl thought of her ahmama then, how patiently her grandmother had helped her piece the dolls back together, how much Secret had loved and missed the woods. Secret remembered her mother's statement that the dolls would be given to her when she was seven. That seemed so long to wait.

What Secret liked best was when her mother sat with her and played memory games. Zavet smiled as her daughter matched picture to picture with precocious ease.

"Your mind remembers well," Zavet said. "Good girl."

– VI –

The Squirrel and the Woods

SINCE SECRET HAD BEEN ALLOWED TO PLAY IN THE COURT-
yard all day, she was content to amuse herself with toys and books
and stories shared among her plant and animal friends. Her father,
however, had words with her mother, that the girl would benefit
from outings in town several times each week. By then, she was
five years old, nearly six, and soon she would enter school. The
activity and interaction among others would prepare her for the
inevitable, Bren said.

Both of her parents knew she liked story times and puppet
shows and clapped loudest for the old tales. Her father thought
that was peculiar and charming, especially because few children
attended those performances, partial as many were to the bright
costumes and fast talking—amusements which kept the children
fixed and staring through a hypnotic use of sound and color and
movement.

So her parents arranged for a caregiver, a woman Secret already
knew, whom she called Auntie. The older woman had kept Secret
on the occasional nights her parents went out for an evening alone.
Usually, Secret was on her way to bed once Auntie arrived and
so didn't know the woman well, but the girl thought her pleasant enough. Once Auntie began to take her for outings, Secret
made certain to smile and brighten her eyes each time the woman
walked through the front door. The girl meant to show her appre-
ciation. This was not only for the chance to attend a performance
but also because Auntie treated Secret with kindness, taking her
hand as they walked, something her mother never did unless there

was clear and present danger, and then it was a jerk or a grab rather than a gesture. Auntie was patient as well, though with Secret patience was rarely a struggle.

One afternoon, Auntie took her into Old Wheel to see a performance. Auntie found a spot for her two-seater cart, clever for getting about town, and tied up the pony. As she had begun to do, Secret thanked the pony for his work and received a nuzzle in reply. Then Secret and Auntie walked to the square, which had a large tent to cover the storyteller and audience. They sat toward the back because they were late. The day's story was an ancient dragon tale. Secret knew it would be when she noticed the storyteller's old-fashioned attire and caught a peek at the dragon costume, the purple fabric faded to mauve. Several children groaned and protested. These had less spectacle and fire than the newer ones. Yet Secret was pleased and waited for it all to begin.

The storyteller strummed his miniature harp to announce the program's start. Then, as she always did, Auntie folded her arms, bent her head, and went right to sleep.

Secret was attentive to the story and not easily distracted. However, movement near the closest tent pole caught her eye. She looked away from the stage and searched for the dog or cat that had likely sniffed nearby. But it was no dog or cat. On all fours, with bushy tail and tufted ears, was a red squirrel. In its mouth was a yellow mushroom, stem and cap. It leaned back on its hind legs to eat what it had found. Secret twisted her head in all directions. No one else seemed to notice.

When it finished, the squirrel looked into Secret's eyes. The little girl saw an image of a squirrel leaping forward and glancing back.

She understood what it said although it didn't speak a word.

Follow me.

Secret looked at Auntie, who slept as if entranced, and looked at the children and adults around her, who watched the stage or fiddled with the belongings they'd taken along. Someone's Tell-a-Bell rang out, and the person began to repeat a list of chores a bit too loudly. Secret wondered whether she was the only one to see the squirrel, or the only one who was aware.

The caregiver whiffled deeper into sleep. Secret told herself she would only go so far, just so far. The squirrel jumped ahead. Secret left her chair and followed its halting steps. It stopped at the entrance of a narrow alley. Secret turned to look toward the tent. Auntie remained asleep.

The girl followed the red squirrel into the dim space. The day was warm, but cold air rose from a grate. Suddenly, she felt the soles of her feet press into the ground. The joints of her hips and shoulders ached. A fluttering tingle moved from her toes to her head. She closed her eyes and beheld the image of a low, circular stone wall. Where is the well? she thought, then shuddered. She knew she stood next to a drainage grate, not a well.

Below, in the darkness, a rat squealed. *The water has long been gone,* it revealed to her.

The squirrel slipped through the narrow bars. Secret couldn't fit, so she pulled from this angle and that until the grate lifted up on a hidden hinge. A metal ladder led down to a tunnel. Her feet splashed in a puddle. Dripping noises surrounded her.

I am Cyril, he said.

I am called Eve, she replied.

Dim light entered from grates along the way. She brushed her hand on the rocky wall at every step. Then there was nothing but darkness and a trickle.

Secret followed the sound of this splashing and kept close to the wall, more curious than afraid.

Come along. Have no fear of the dark. A few more steps to go, Cyril said.

Then, indeed mere steps forward, a hazy glow appeared from above. A spiral stair of stone led up to a hole at the base of a half-hollow tree. She climbed, touching the tree's exposed roots, and watched Cyril bound through the open space into the woods.

Yes, the woods!

This place was different from the woods near her grandmother's house but somehow the same as well. As far as she could see, there were trees and shrubs, ferns and vines. She wondered how far she had wandered from home.

Secret climbed from the hole and stood in front of the hollow. She laughed aloud and watched Cyril leap and tumble with silliness, urging her to come along. With dancing steps, she followed him. Her fingers brushed over leaves and branches, and her eyes met those that peeked out from hiding.

Cyril skittered along a narrow trail, past a leaning birch, and then stopped.

Secret looked ahead to see an enormous, noble tree that stretched from root and branch wider and higher than any she had ever seen. Its trunk coiled out of the ground, a helix between earth and sky. Secret rushed to the tree. She felt moss cushion her feet.

Unlike the petrified tree in the woods near Ahmama's village, this one was alive. It had no hollow, no wound. She touched it with affection. She could not have dreamed a more perfect being. A low, warm drone reverberated through her middle. She listened as an image formed above her closed eyes. She could not comprehend the voice. It was too old, too deep, but she discerned what came to her, heavy limbs rising gently to the clouds. She translated a word.

Is Reach your name? she asked.

The wondrous tree hummed under her hands. Secret took that as her answer. She understood by feeling that he wanted her company, and this made her smile. She pulled herself up on a low branch and climbed into the cradle where the largest limbs intersected.

She sighed. Her blood seemed to slow, its rhythm different from the throb she felt in her chest so often in town and at home. She listened to the calls of the animals, their particular communication among one another. The yip of a fox, the bell of a deer, the screech of a hawk. When she climbed down from Reach, she strolled in circles around him, wider and wider, but still in view. The little girl admired everything she could see and smell and hear and touch.

Then she began to run with arms flung wide. She caressed leaves and branches, leapt over logs, felt the fresh breeze on her face and hair, and laughed in unison with a crow's caw. Winded, she dropped to the ground, lay on her back, and splayed her coursing limbs. She gasped for breath and, after one deep inhale, she burst into tears. The cries ripped through a widening hole beneath her chest. She wept until she felt clean.

Cyril dabbed his paws on her cheeks. She sat up and thought perhaps the tears had come because she missed being among such quiet and beauty. She felt she belonged to herself, although she wasn't certain what that meant.

Insects began to whir in looping spirals of sound. Their even-song, she thought, and smiled at the connection to her given name. But their song meant night was about to fall and, with it, her heart, because she would have to leave this peaceful place.

The squirrel led her back to Reach to say good-bye, then to the portal at the base of the tree.

You are always welcome here, he said. *Trust your way in the dark.*

He didn't bound ahead of her. She was meant to return alone. She did, more fearful of the trouble she suddenly realized she'd get into for running off than of the trickling echo of the tunnel that led her back to town.

She surfaced in the alley. When she reached the square's edge, the audience had finished their applause and was beginning to rise from their seats. She ran to Auntie, who yawned, blinked, and stretched. Secret couldn't believe everyone was still there. She had to have gone quite far away, well outside of town, and she felt she'd been away for several hours. For a moment, she wondered if she, too, had fallen asleep and dreamed of a journey into the woods. If it was, it was one of the best dreams she ever had.

"Oh, it's twilight. Such a long story today. A lovely one to be sure," Auntie said as she nudged Secret gently ahead.

Secret nodded and felt a plucking sensation at the back of her head.

"How did you manage to get leaves tangled in your hair—and a twig?!"

Secret looked up with innocent eyes and shrugged.

"There isn't even a tree nearby. How do you children get into such peculiar messes?" Auntie asked.

When they returned to Secret's house, Auntie gave her mother the usual report on the child's behavior—a model of obedience, no trouble at all—then accepted her wages in copper coins and said her farewells. Secret waved as the door closed.

"So, Eve, did you enjoy your outing today?" Zavet asked.

Secret thought her mother seemed to be in a pleasant mood, but she didn't respond right away. The back of her neck prickled and the sensation spread to her arms. Secret drew herself still and closed inside although nothing outward hinted that she should. Secret's mind flickered with an image of Reach and Cyril then focused steadily on the faded dragon costume she'd seen.

The girl nodded with enthusiasm. Zavet smiled as if satisfied, and because Secret thought it safe to do so in that moment, she smiled, too.

The next day, under Fig Tree, Secret lay on her belly and drew pictures of the woods and told her friends what she had seen. The birds confirmed the woods she had seen were real, for they had flown above the treetops and nested in their branches. She looked into their round black eyes and, as she did, the birds revealed a view from the sky, The Castle to the north, The Tallest Building to the south, and the town in between. To the east and south of the town were sparse trees, to the north a large treed area surrounded by open land, and to the west the green edge of the woods.

Then a crow lit upon the courtyard's stone wall. His presence was unusual. Secret couldn't recall seeing such a bird in her small yard before. Their gazes met, then Secret closed her eyes. Within her, she saw a young tree, then Reach, then the young tree again. She understood they were one and the same. Next she saw, from the sky, a village with a nearby meadow and fields nestled among miles of dense trees, then an image of her town as the little birds had shown her, and once more a circling view of the village.

What is here now wasn't always so, the crow said. Secret felt a tingle through her body. It was unnerving to get a glimpse into a long-ago past.

That night, her father returned home after a long time away on a trip. He seemed glad to be the one to put her to bed. Secret was pleased, too, because he told her tales by candlelight, sometimes gave her a kiss good-night, and always left the door open. Her mother did not tell stories, put her to bed in the dark, and closed the door with a terse *thup.*

Bren sat next to his daughter. On the floor nearby was the little basket she kept close to the back door to store her drawings. He asked her to choose one, so she did.

"If you could tell me a story, I wonder what you would say," he said. "But, because you cannot, what can I tell you?"

Bren tucked the covers at her neck, stared long at the drawing, and conjured a tale of magical and frightening things that happened in a dark wood to a little girl just like her.

VII

Hurried Days in Town

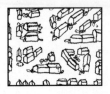

ON AN ORDINARY MORNING, THE DOORS CRACK OPEN AND the streets flood with motion. People hurry to the stables with satchels, children, and responsibility pulling at their shoulders. The horses can't be hitched fast enough by the liverymen. Once they are, the beasts wait their turns behind the others as the people twitch the reins. Some adjust the small cages belted at their hips, which hold bells instead of birds.

Hoof and wheel clatter on the cobblestone lanes. The drivers look straight ahead as the carts lurch forward. A loud, lone voice speaks with an instructive rhythm. Closer, the carts approach a newsbox in the middle of the intersection. A person stands at a small podium within and reads from a stack of paper. There was a murder in another ward, the voice announces. People shake their heads, spit slurs under their breath, and stare into the distance. Suddenly, the carts move faster and as that voice fades, another continues the story in another newsbox at another intersection. Everyone and no one is told that those with information leading to the killer's apprehension are encouraged to contact the authorities. A long cart half-filled with children is given way into the traffic.

Most of the schools are rectangular buildings in need of repair, surrounded by bands of short grass. These buildings are maintained

by the town. There is one school supported by tuition and philan-
thropy, which keeps up appearances. Children step down from the
carts, heavy with their own loads, and wait for the bells to call them
indoors for the day. The smallest children go elsewhere to sit, play,
nap, and snack. They will graduate to sitting, listening, and learning
soon enough.

The carts roll along. The beasts befoul the ground and leave the
dung behind. A street cleaner walks into the fray with a shovel and
scoops a mess near a drain. The pace slows more, and people scowl.
Movement is tighter because the hitching-post spaces begin to fill.
People walk in and out of teahouses and shops. Now and again,
people with bells at their hips speak aloud to no one in particular.
They hurry on to where they're going and disappear into doorways
behind which their work awaits.

Stop. Stand near the man who digs through his pockets and the
woman who rolls her thumb and finger at the stem that juts from
the bell's cage. The stillness disrupts the flurry. Adjustments must be
made in the flow. People furrow their brows. Stay there. A newsbox
voice continues. The rhythm is different, faster and forceful. The
town's joust team won a recent match. A lone cheer erupts nearby.
The team's favorite member was injured. A grumble rises.

The streets calm but are not quiet. People rush about their
business. Some adults with small children scurry along. The street
cleaners connect lengthy hoses to the corner pumps and wash the
morning's manure into the drains. At the newsboxes, voices double
for a moment as the news-speakers who started the day turn the
stories over to the next shift.

At the schools and day nurseries, children who sit for hours
inside burst out to the available grounds. They join in active games,
cluster in talkative groups, and venture off alone to sit quietly. Small
bodies move over climbing bars, swings, and seesaws. Balls and jump
ropes reach the sky. There are squabbles and fights. Some children
appear shunned and humiliated. The adults intervene, or don't.

Beyond the town's streets, where the earth breathes, human

hands and their tools tend crops. Beasts bear their burdens as help-mates and fresh meat. The work is not easy, but sun and air reach all in abundance. The people here are busy but also waiting. They know the anticipation to plant, to harvest, to be born, to slaughter. They know uncertainty, but theirs is of the natural mind, not the civilized.

VIII

Secret and Her Mother Go Shopping

SECRET FOLLOWED CLOSE BEHIND HER QUICKLY MOVING mother as they walked from the ward where they lived and through several others. Horses and carts hurried by. People whisked past, in silence, or with caged Tell-a-Bells ringing at their waists, or chatting with a companion. The newsboxes announced the events of the day from near and far. Shop doors opened and closed, opened and closed, opened and closed. In a way she hadn't before, Secret noticed the rush, so different from the way she felt in the woods.

At some point, the ward they were in looked familiar. She remembered going with her parents to an occasional performance at a hall only a block or two away. She also realized they were near Old Wheel, which meant the alley, the grate, and the tunnel weren't too far away. Secret had escaped to the woods several times since her first visit, thanks to drowsy Auntie and the squirrel.

In time, Secret and her mother entered an old shop with a new sign. The narrow building had tall front windows, and row after row of clothing hung on bars mounted along one wall. On the other side, shelves held shoes, hats, and folded garments. She and Zavet were there because Bren wanted his daughter to have something special to start her first year of school, a wardrobe befitting a child of a fine family.

A haughty-faced shop woman greeted them tersely and turned back to two women dressed as if they had a fancy engagement to attend. One of them glanced at Secret's mother as Zavet brushed her fingertips along the skirt of a small green dress. Secret walked to the tall windows and peeked at the items on display. She knew not to touch, and she didn't.

One of the women approached the counter to settle her bill. The other woman who had looked at Zavet earlier stood before a mirror, tucked loose brown strands of hair under her hat, and adjusted her belt, rattling the gold cage of her Tell-a-Bell. She cut her eyes in the mirror, staring behind her.

Zavet suddenly turned to face her direction, which made the brown-haired woman startle. She whipped around then and said with convincing surprise, "Why, Mrs. Riven, isn't it?"

"How good to see you, Mrs. Agister," Zavet said cordially. "I hope you and your husband enjoyed the ensemble as much as my husband and I did."

"Fine music soothes the heart," Mrs. Agister said, then introduced her friend Mrs. Knolworth, who had finished her shopping. "I was so sorry to miss you at the orphan asylum luncheon. The queen spoke quite beautifully and inspired a number of new volunteers. We are always in need of more kind souls."

"Of course I support your cause, but as I related to you at the time of your gracious invitation, I am otherwise committed."

Mrs. Agister's lips curled into an appraising smile. "Yes. Yes. What is it that you . . . do . . . again?"

"Translation. I work as a translator."

Secret could not see her mother's face. Still, she knew from the way Mrs. Agister drew backward that Zavet was not quite looking her in the eye but gave the impression she was staring intensely. Secret knew that look very well.

"And how did you . . . acquire . . . those skills?" Mrs. Agister asked.

"I graduated from an eminent high academy in the discipline of linguistics."

"You attended a high academy, and you have an occupation. How . . . unprecedented. Mrs. Knolworth, her husband works for Fewmany Incorporated, *on the top floor*."

"Does he?" Mrs. Knolworth said. Her eyes swept down from Zavet's head to her toes.

Zavet brushed her hands at her hips, smoothing the line of her skirt, and squared her shoulders.

"A charming man, he is, so gregarious, and with certainty, so . . . accommodating, as he does quite well for himself and his family."

"I am understandably proud of Mr. Riven," Zavet said.

"You have a child, yes?" Mrs. Agister said.

"We do. Eve, please come here and greet our acquaintances."

Secret took a long breath and approached the women. As she had been taught, she looked at the two women, held the sides of her dress, and dipped her knees in a demure curtsy. The women smiled with approval.

"How do you do, Miss Riven?" Mrs. Agister asked.

Secret nodded once, deeply.

"A taciturn child. What a rarity these days!" Mrs. Knolworth said.

"Oh, no, she doesn't speak—" Mrs. Agister said, catching herself in the revelation. "But she is delightfully polite."

Secret could sense her mother trembling although not a part of her moved. Secret tilted her chin down. Her silence usually didn't cause her shame; that is, until she felt the judgment of those who didn't comprehend that she couldn't help how she was.

"How interesting you understand so many words and your daughter says none," Mrs. Knolworth said.

"Nevertheless, she is an intelligent girl," Zavet said.

"Like her mother, to be sure. And she resembles you as well. Your accent is perfectly indicative of the central region, yet no fine family I can recall bears your . . . striking . . . features," Mrs. Agister said.

"I'm afraid the name wouldn't be familiar to you, Mrs. Agister. Please forgive my brusqueness now. I simply must get Eve prepared for school and complete our errands before Mr. Riven arrives home for dinner," Zavet said.

That instant, Mrs. Agister's Tell-a-Bell rang with a frenzy, the mechanism which activated the bell whirring behind the metallic *tinktinktinktinktink*.

"Time for my toll. A pleasure, Mrs. Riven, Miss Riven," Mrs. Agister said. As she and Mrs. Knolworth scurried from the shop, Mrs. Agister loudly declared the chores she had for the first-floor maid.

"Let's be quick about this. It's not the only item on our private toll today," Zavet said.

Secret understood what had happened was trying for her mother, and she resolved to be cooperative. Young as she was, she realized Mrs. Agister had been prying, bordering on rude. However, Secret hadn't realized it was strange, even unacceptable, for her mother to have studied at a high academy or to have her own work. Her father didn't appear to mind. As to the latter, he never discouraged her or suggested she should stop. Intelligence and personal interests mattered to him.

After a brief conversation with the shop woman, whose haughty face had softened with a friendly, warm smile, Zavet thrust dress after dress under Secret's chin, her violet eyes somewhat unfocused. As Zavet decided which ones Secret would try on, the shop woman unhooked a deep-purple cloak from a high bar and dangled it near Secret's mother.

"Will she need winter wear?" the shop woman asked. "A durable, fine wool. A bargain for its quality."

Secret reached for the hem, and the shop woman lowered it to her. The girl fingered the bronze-colored buttons as the woman told her mother they had been reproduced from a button mold found in the ruins of a lost village. That detail made it ever more appealing to Secret. The cloak fell off its hanger. The shop woman shook it fiercely then opened it for her. Secret was delighted to find the cloak had sleeves. Her fingers peeked past the vine-embroidered cuffs.

She flipped the hood over her dark head with a dramatic flourish and smiled.

The shop woman and her mother gave a small laugh.

"Too big now," Zavet said. Her gaze fluttered across her daughter's face. "But she will grow. It does suit her nicely."

No one else entered the shop as Secret tried on dress after dress and five pairs of shoes. Even though Secret thought her mother meant to rush, she didn't. She carefully felt the fabric and seams of the dresses. She allowed Secret her choice of seven among twelve.

Everyone was in a cheerful mood when the shop woman tallied the bill and noted the address where Secret's new school clothes should be delivered.

Secret followed her mother out of the shop onto the busy sidewalk. As they crossed the street, Secret heard the stumbling clap of hooves and startled whinnies. She turned to see a small red blur rush between the horses' legs. Her heart's beat became fluid and quick.

Zavet called her name and led her into a perfume shop. Through the windows sunlight reflected off the nearest bottles, which were perfectly arranged on a table with elegant, curved legs and carved claw feet. A miasma of cloying, delicate, and intoxicating scents swirled around Secret's head. While her mother spoke with the shop woman, the girl crouched to look under the display tables.

Her mother eased toward the back of the shop and began to float her hands above the beautiful vials. A sharp *chit* pierced Secret's ears. She whipped her eyes toward the noise. There was Cyril, black eyes bright, red fur shiny.

Within herself, Secret saw the grate, the hole in the hollow, and Reach.

No, she said to Cyril.

The squirrel glanced at her mother, and Secret looked, too. Zavet's thick lashes fluttered as she held an open bottle under her nose. Her hips swayed almost imperceptibly. The woman seemed lost in whatever pleasure was unleashed. Secret welcomed a flood of warmth for her.

Secret's feet pattered in a nervous dance. She wanted to join him, but she would be punished if she left. Auntie was always asleep when she went away, but her mother was there, wide-awake. Cyril jumped on a display shelf and rattled the delicate vials.

"Eve. Be careful! Don't touch!" she said, her back turned.

Go away. I'll get in trouble, Secret said.

She won't miss you, Cyril said.

The words struck her in the chest. She gasped. All the good feelings she'd had tore away like a flimsy veil. Unexpected tears came to her eyes. Her shoulders collapsed inward, and she bumped against a table.

She heard a bottle fall over. In an instant, she turned to see it precariously roll to the edge. Her hands thrust forward. There was no shatter of glass. Her palms were empty. It did not fall. Carefully, Secret set it right.

Still, her mother whipped around and hissed into her ear. "You will be the ruin of me, won't you, girl? You will not make a mess here. Go to the window and stand there until I'm done."

She did as she was told. The warmth she'd felt for her mother and for their otherwise pleasant afternoon vanished. A bitter chill took its place.

Another customer entered the shop. Secret knew then Cyril had gone. She stared at the parquet floor until she heard her mother's voice. Secret watched her open her purse, pay in gold, and slip the wrapped bottle into a pocket.

As Secret crossed the shop's threshold to the street, her body felt heavy and dull. She had done no harm but felt as if she had. Then she saw a feather on the ground. She picked up the beautiful blue lightness at its white, hollow stem. She wondered where the blue bird had been, where it was going, and wished she had seen it herself.

Her mother stood in front of her. "Put that dirty thing down and come along," she said.

Secret released the feather. It drifted with grace until it spiraled around the legs of a man and was trampled under another's feet.

The following evening after dinner, her father asked to see the clothes that had been delivered. She took him upstairs to her room, removed the new frocks from her wardrobe, and placed them neatly on her bed. Bren held a lamp steady as he peered at the little dresses.

"These are very fine, my pet. Very fine," he said.

Secret removed her new cloak from a hook inside the wardrobe's door. She slipped it on and glanced up at her father. He looked at her with a waiting expression. Secret twirled fast until she bloomed like a topsy-turvy tulip. Bren clapped and smiled until the corners of his eyes crinkled. She smiled, too. The cloak was magic, she decided.

IX

Lessons in the First Year of School

ONE MONTH AFTER THE SHOPPING TRIP, BREN TOOK SECRET to school on her first day. He was knotted, buttoned, and shined, and she was clean, combed, and pressed. Although she was apprehensive, despite what her father told her to expect, she discovered she was excited once she entered the building. There would be things to learn and others to play with and no muttering mother.

At the threshold of her classroom, he knelt on one knee and tickled her chin. Bren focused on her eyes. "Now, a bit of advice on your first day. Don't let your silence get in your way. Smile. Remember to share. Make friends—lots of them. And, whatever you do, don't cry. The others will jump you like a pack of wolves."

He patted her head before the teacher took her hand and led her to a tiny stool at a round table where a boy and girl had taken their places.

"This is Eve," the young woman said, then told Secret the names of her classmates. Each had a puzzle with large pieces. The teacher offered her a choice among three. She picked one with interlocking birds.

When she looked around the room, she saw children she recognized from going to market with her mother. Some of them she'd played with on the sidewalks. She knew they must live near her, although they had never been invited to play at her house or she at theirs. She was hopeful, here, that she would make friends.

She had been with groups of children before, but never so many for so long. She was familiar with being alone and entertaining herself. The noise and bustle made her nervous sometimes.

Aside from that, she liked that the days had a rhythm—lessons, snacks, and playtime.

She was proud of herself that she could already read. When the teacher had the students match letters and words with pictures, Secret didn't talk, but she walked up to the front of the room and pointed from 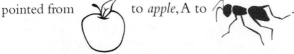 to *apple*, A to .

The teacher soon allowed her to read by herself as she played these games with the class.

For the first few weeks, all was well. Secret was a model student and a good girl. She never complained. She shared toys, took turns, and listened well. She was always cooperative, neat, and clean. Oh, she was perfect, except for the silence.

Secret tried to fit in, even though her silence kept her from a certain intimacy. When there were games to play with others, she knew what to do. She could play tag, jump rope, and hide-and-seek following all the rules. She quickly learned the boys didn't want any girls to climb the wooden towers, kick balls, or shoot marbles with them. With the girls, she could play clapping games, but not sing along, as well as play with dolls, only not make them speak.

The latter, she discovered, was very important.

She sat with the same group of girls and shared a basket of dolls. Secret listened to their conversations with serious curiosity. Secret received glimpses into other children's lives through the dolls. The girls gave them names, often Baby, Mother, Father, Brother, and Sister. The mothers talked to the daughters and the fathers sometimes talked to the sons. They were make-believe, but they were quite real in their kindness and affection but also in their cruelty and sternness. There were brothers and sisters, too, who were the best of friends or brutal enemies. Secret found this especially interesting because, as she always had seemed to know, her brothers had been born blue, which meant they never truly were.

While the other girls toddled the dolls and put words in their mouths, Secret did the same, but without sound. She used them to imagine what it might be like to have another father or mother, or a sibling. How would she be different? Would she speak like the other children her age? Would her eyes be the colors of night and day? Would she be charming or spirited or petulant? Would she still love animals and plants?

Of course, the dolls became whoever the girls wanted them to be. They giggled over mocking a teacher or a prissy girl in another class. And Secret was shocked when the group she often played with turned on her.

"*I'm Eve,*" one said, parading a dark-haired doll across the grass. "*I'm a teacher's pet and a goody-goody.*"

Secret's eyes grew round. She didn't think of herself that way.

"*I can read better than anyone but I can't talk,*" the girl added.

"Why not?" another girl asked, introducing a blind poppet with a shorn wig.

"If she can't talk, *you* can't talk for her," a third girl said.

"Of course I can," the first girl said. "*Why can't I talk?*" She spoke in a high voice. "*Because my mother is a witch from another land and she put a curse on me so I wouldn't tell all the bad things she does.*"

"That's only pretend, isn't it?" the second girl said. "Eve, is your mother a witch?"

Secret shook her head so hard her neck popped.

"*Oh yes she is!*" the first girl with the Eve doll said. "*She says spells over the food at the market and makes people sick. Blech! Blech! Blech!*" She acted as if she were vomiting.

Secret grabbed the dolls from their hands and threw them as far as she could.

"That's not nice!" the third girl said.

"Eve, she was only teasing," the second girl said.

Secret ran toward the only tree in the schoolyard. She flung herself at its roots and pressed the ground with her fists. The oak tree showered her with yellow and brown leaves. With wet lashes, she glanced up into the dappled light coming through the limbs.

She told the tree what happened because she could tell no one else. She played over what the girl said in her mind. Secret was at school, away from her mother, but apparently, in the way of rumor, her mother wasn't away from her.

Afraid to be teased again, Secret began to spend her playtime under the tree. The solitude had its pleasantness. She read books or arranged leaves and twigs in patterns. She had the company of birds in the branches and insects on the ground. With her hair spread over her collarbones and shoulder blades, she sat still and held the tiny creatures. They twined her fingers, tickled her neck, and sometimes told of their hidden worlds.

She chose to hide behind the oak's trunk because she had never seen girls touch creeping things. She noticed boys playing with small creatures, sometimes with care, but often to the girls' horror. She didn't want to draw attention to herself this way.

But not long after, she sensed terrible distress, as if something screamed. She ran toward the pain, which was a feeling more than a sound. There was a boy crushing ants under his thumb and laughing as he did it. Furious and without pausing for a thought, she pushed him away and stood between him and the trail. He squawked at her. Secret shook her head no and looked straight at him as if that could pin him down.

"Stop looking at me, evil eyes," he said.

His friend went to his side. "Yeah, stop looking at him. You don't look like anyone else around here with that hair and skin and those eyes that don't match. Where do you come from, anyway? Bet that's why you can't talk."

Secret scowled with anger as her face burned with his insult. She looked down. Ants had begun to swarm at her feet, coming from all directions. The sight jolted her, and, for an instant, she forgot about the boys.

"Ugly bug!" one of them shouted.

That was enough to provoke his friend to taunt her and for other children to join in the laughter.

Secret stepped far to the side, sparing the ants her crushing feet, and walked away.

After that incident, a girl with wavy auburn hair began to watch Secret as she crossed the yard and sat behind the tree. Her name was Audrey. One day, Audrey whipped around the trunk. Two large beetles skittered in circles on Secret's open palms as a wren perched on one of her fingers. The wren flew away, Secret looked up, and several schoolmates, along with the girl, stared at her.

"Look at the bugs on her! She's letting them do that! Disgusting!" Audrey said.

Secret watched as the children gasped and giggled. Not one young face expressed curiosity or understanding.

A dull glow, like a distant bolt of lightning, pulsed through her dark head. Although Secret couldn't explain how she knew, she realized then that what she experienced with creatures and plants was special. No one felt the connection she did. Even as they made fun of her, which she hated, she felt awe and gratitude for what she could do. She was welcome among the creatures and plants.

Still, she didn't like being teased and vowed that she would be careful from then on. She would not attract attention again. Secret didn't play with the insects and animals, but this wasn't enough to avoid scrutiny. Audrey decided Secret's silence was perturbing as well.

She would sneak behind Secret's stool or stand in her way and taunt, "Say something, say something, say something!" Audrey's coldness deepened by winter and spread to some of the others who cajoled Secret as well. The girl tossed her auburn head, haughty with judgment.

On the first cold day when Zavet sent her dressed in the fine purple cloak, Secret sat on a root with the sun at her back, content in the warmth. She sensed a twittering, but not of birds, and turned to see a gaggle of girls and the one who teased her lean in to whisper to another.

"Look at those eyes! She's so ugly! And she never, never says anything. She's so stupid. And I heard her mother is mad. She must be, too."

Secret felt her skin draw to her bones, her heart to her spine. She felt herself shrink. She wondered what she'd done to provoke such meanness, which suddenly reminded her of what her mother meted out through silence or hisses. A part of her wanted to lash out against them, teeth and claws bared. She wanted to hurt them, too. She imagined many hateful things to say and places to slap and pinch. She took a deep breath, filled the hollows of her lungs, and exhaled long and slow through pursed lips. She noticed that the anger slipped for the briefest moment. In its place was the other part of her, the one that was purely tender in a world that was so often cruel. When she looked to the ground ahead, she saw a pigeon. The bird released a soothing coo.

I don't want to be mean like them, she said to herself. Secret lifted the hood over her head and gripped the buttoned edge and let the wool's gentle weight hold her down. She remained immobile, staring ahead, until the girls went away. Secret noticed her shadow on the ground. I cast that shadow. That's me—I'm there, too, in that place, she thought. Her body felt protected under her hair, under the hood. She was hidden in plain sight.

She insisted that she wear the cloak every day, no matter the weather. She liked the way it made her feel.

Once spring came and her mother determined the cloak was too heavy, Secret was told she could no longer take it to school. In a fierce, uncharacteristic frenzy, Secret refused to leave the house. She cried, which did no good. She flung herself to the ground, which served no purpose. She hid in every possible cranny, which only delayed the inevitable. Zavet found her, gripped her daughter's small arms, and hissed in her face.

"What has gotten into you?" she asked.

If Secret had been able to speak, she didn't know what she would have said. Shame had twisted her in knots.

Her mother let her stay home in her room that day, but that

night, her father made her sit at the dinner table as he scolded her in a way he never had before.

"Crying, writhing on the ground, refusing to go to school! I'll have none of this behavior. You know better than to act that way," Bren said as he loomed over her.

From the shadows of her workspace, her mother stood with her arms folded.

"And another matter which must be attended to. . . . Your marks are very good, but that is not enough. You must make a better effort to get along with the other children. Your mother and I are aware of how you scurry off behind a tree and keep to yourself."

Secret's mouth dropped open. She kept her eyes down.

"Yes, we were told of some children who teased you. These things work themselves out. The best thing to do is ignore them and keep your chin up. Find friends who aren't petty."

Secret held her breath. She knew if she breathed she'd cry.

"Of course, you know, this would all be so much easier if you would only speak," Bren said. "Until that happens, if that happens, you must do better. I will require a report from your teacher, and if I learn you aren't making more of an effort to belong, you will have no outings with Auntie this summer."

She faced him then, her mouth a tight, hard line.

"That commanded your attention. Good. Now, go to your room and think about how you can do better, Eve."

She went to school the next day, sitting in class with her hair spread around her, all the while wary of who might be watching her. Her purple cloak had given her a thicker layer between worlds, hers and the rest.

But at playtime, she forced herself to join a game of jump rope. She forced herself to be brave. She had to. The thought of never seeing Cyril, Reach, or the woods again was a worse pain than the rejection she believed she would endure.

X

Zavet Receives a Letter

THROUGH THE LAST MONTHS OF HER FIRST YEAR OF school, Secret managed to play with, or at least blend herself among, the other children enough so that her father was pleased with her teacher's reports. When summer began, Auntie returned to take her out three times a week. At least one of those days each week, they went to Old Wheel, which meant Cyril sought out Secret and led her to the woods.

The days when Secret was alone with her mother were the same as they had been before she was in school. Zavet worked at her tables; Secret kept herself occupied in the courtyard, happy to have Fig Tree's steadfast companionship. The greatest difference that summer was Fig Tree's fruit was more abundant than it had been the two previous years. Fig Tree had asked for extra water to plump the growth, a sweet gift for the kind child who bothered to love her.

One evening that same summer, Secret was with her father at the table eating her dinner when there was a knock at the front door. Her mother answered, then returned with a flat, rectangular parcel. Surprise, perhaps even affection, showed on Zavet's face when she returned.

Secret watched her mother's back as Zavet lit a beeswax candle and unwrapped the parcel in her workspace. She laid a manuscript to the side. Secret heard the soft rush of her mother's fingers across a piece of paper.

"So he is capable of humility after all," Zavet said with a hint of laughter.

"Who?" Bren asked.

Zavet turned and waved the letter in her hand. "My ancient adept."

Transfixed, Secret took the smallest nibbles of her meal that she could as she listened to her mother tell her father a story of her past.

When Zavet was a student at the renowned high academy, she had a professor who took her under his wing. Because of him, she met several dignitaries and diplomats, great men who sought to achieve accord through the power of words. Zavet considered an active use of her translation skills in such circles, until he invited her and several schoolmates to a special display at the library.

A tablet had been found in one of a complex of chambers, buried by intention or disaster, no one knew. It was made of stone, and the carved marks on its surface were worn in places. The marks had yet to be deciphered by anyone. Allowed to touch it with ungloved hands, the students skimmed their fingers across the tablet with awe, even reverence. Except for Zavet.

That evening, she returned to the library alone. Because of her reputation as the most promising linguist that academy had ever known, the curator allowed her to see the tablet again unattended.

Zavet realized she not only knew what language it was—a form of it still spoken in a remote cluster of villages near a southern sea—but also what was written. The tablet was merely a history, an accounting of time and place. She wrote the translation in her adept's native language, although she could have chosen among the many they both understood. When she gave it to him, he was incredulous. How could she so quickly decipher a script no one had ever seen? He said scholars must study the tablet and, until then, what she claimed couldn't be corroborated. Zavet risked adding that she was certain there were still some living speakers of the tongue and told him where they were, although she herself had never visited there. She could tell he didn't believe her although he didn't say so.

Secret noticed a hurt tone in her mother's voice. The professor's response seemed to have wounded her. The girl wondered how her mother could be so confident about what she knew, when no one else seemed to know.

She felt a lurch in her belly that pulled at her tongue. She understood Zavet's certainty very well. Secret knew the language of creatures and plants. Why and how that was so was a mystery to her, as unexplained as her mother's faculty with human languages. The connection Secret made between their abilities disturbed more than pleased her.

"And what did you receive tonight?" Bren asked after Zavet paused long enough to indicate her tale was done.

"An apology in his quivering hand. More than twenty years later, I've been proved right. Other scholars came to the same conclusion. They had additional tablets, too, more discovered in the same area. No mention of the people, however. The script might have been lost to them. Language and symbols have a way of becoming obsolete."

"Is that a manuscript he sent as well?" Bren asked.

Zavet patted the unbound pages. "Yes. Unusual though. He sent a transcribed copy even though he knows I prefer to work with the original. The text must be considered highly valuable."

"But you will decline and return it," Bren said.

Secret glanced at her father. His voice was quiet but commanding.

"Of course, Bren. I haven't forgotten the terms of the agreement with the patron," Zavet said.

"Good."

"Although I am quite tempted."

"Regardless."

Zavet walked over to him and swept one hand against the back of his head as she picked up his dinner plate. He brushed her fingers with his as she stepped away.

Whatever matter arose between them had been settled quickly.

"Finished your dinner?" Zavet asked Secret.

She nodded and took her plate to the water basin in the kitchen. Before she went upstairs, she patted her father's arm.

"Your mother's story wasn't enough, then. Go up and I'll be there soon," her father said.

Secret changed into her nightgown and sat on her bed. The windows in her room were open. A breeze lifted the curtains in billows. Over the rooftops, a stripe of sky faded to ever-darker grays. It was nearly dark when her father arrived and lit the lamp next to her bed.

"Your mother inspired a nostalgic mood," he said. "Tonight, I will tell you how we met, but first I will tell you of her and me before there was us."

Bren said that in a distant town in a nearby kingdom there was a high academy of great prestige that drew together many brilliant minds.

One of them was a young woman from a forest-circled village far away. Her family survived by the sweat of their brows and strength of their bodies. As a girl, she had no consistent, formal schooling but she was determined and brave. She demanded to be tested for admittance at the academy, and when she proved worthy, secured a scholarship to aid her study.

Zavet graduated from the academy in that quaint town and applied herself to an occupation no one could do better. After receiving fine letters of recommendation from her teachers and references for work, she soon acquired a reputation among collectors of old and ancient texts. Zavet completed translations in half the time of most others, yet charged the same fee. She guaranteed completeness and accuracy and welcomed any patron to verify her work with another authority. Few did in the beginning, none after her talents proved flawless.

Zavet lived in a turret atop a crumbling castle. The castle itself had been out of use for many years, a standing memory of a vanquished kingdom consumed by a greater one in times past. The chambers were home to students, apprentices, and eccentrics, who shared common cooking and washing spaces within the building.

These odd folk appreciated the queer woman who sat all day surrounded by dead voices. Zavet was known for taking moonlit walks through deserted streets. She was the first at morning markets, hands brushing over cabbages and potatoes and onions, eggs only hours from the hens, trout strung with the memory of weightlessness in their watery eyes. She spoke to few people, yet none found her especially displeasing. Mysterious and reclusive, yes, even somewhat dreamy or romantic. A young woman uniquely possessed of herself. She was coveted for gatherings of gifted intellectuals, which she never claimed or thought herself to be.

Bren Riven was born in one of his kingdom's oldest towns and lived in one of the poorest wards. He had been an athletic boy, competent with bats and balls, skilled as an archer although he didn't hunt. From boyhood to young manhood, he ran among jolly fellows with silly nicknames. Bren was one of the brightest among his group; fortunate to attend the schools he did because of his intelligence and full scholarships. He enjoyed the friendship of those who overlooked his humble origins. His good nature earned him a place in their company. This made the poor boy bold enough to ask friends for favors and recommendations that set him well on his worldly way.

He graduated with honors from a high academy in history and geography. Although suited for an academic life, he eventually chanced upon a position as a researcher for an ambitious but struggling land speculator. It was soon clear he was meant for more than scouring through old records.

Bren's natural affability made him the obvious envoy to convince property owners to sell what they had. He endeared himself because of his sense of history. Do you know what was here before? he'd ask. This was the site of an ancient battle, a partial holding from a great nobleman, where an important agreement was signed, where your great-great-grandmother was born, where a butcher shop stood for three generations. Sometimes, he'd bring a document. See here, he said, things change. Nothing stays the same.

He listened to the owners' resistance, but he knew their troubles. Oh, I know this has been in your family for years, but the taxes have become a burden, haven't they? Indeed, you cherish your home but the payments have become more than you can manage, not your fault, of course, times are tough. There is a lien. There will be a lien.

The scholarly man was good at this. As a historian, Bren had great patience for dust and detail, a keen eye for inevitability. He didn't mind the hours of research spent in windowless rooms, unlike Secret's mother, who grew feral in the absence of light. Although relentless, Bren was not heartless. He made promises to give buildings and areas a special name, an homage to the past, bound by contract. Negotiated prices were often quite fair.

He had been working for the speculator for ten years when he was assigned a complicated matter of a deed, disputed by a woman who claimed to be an heir. Bren was tasked to verify her lineage, document his findings, and obtain legal notaries whenever possible. He relished these generational dramas because they required him to travel and talk and research.

As was sometimes the case, when family members held on to letters, papers, or diaries no one could read—languages changed, what had been native became ancestral—Bren had possession of a ledger that a cousin of the woman allowed him to borrow so it could be translated. Bren would have to pay the fee for the work. He knew the town had a prestigious high academy for languages and linguistics, so he inquired for a reference for a translator. He received the name of their most gifted graduate.

With the address in hand, Bren walked to a quaint, decrepit neighborhood and was surprised to find himself at an old castle. Each chamber was marked with a number, but the one he sought had a letter. He knocked on a random door and asked for directions. A faceless finger pointed up, and a voice from behind the cracked door told him to take the stairs.

Up the spiral Bren climbed, with dim light from the arrow loops guiding his way. He reached no landing or visible door. The stairs stopped at a wood plank roof. Through the grayness, he spied two hinges and the telltale glow of a keyhole. He knocked above his head.

"What is your business?" a woman asked.

"I've a recommendation from the academy to see you. I need a translator," he replied.

The keyhole blackened, then the ceiling opened up. He climbed the last step and entered her room. It was a tidy space with the view of a distant mountain range and the whole town below.

The turret received light from all sides. A fireplace vented through the edge of the roof. Someone had affixed sturdy, shallow shelves between all of the windows on the curved walls, floor to ceiling. These were covered with books, odd objects of interest, and her nesting dolls. Shutters hinged above the windows, which were lowered and raised by ropes and pulleys and locked with iron pegs. Under each window was a table, and under each of those was a locked chest. There was only one chair, used for work. In the middle of the room was a long divan that served as seat and bed, a table that held her meals and teas, and another chest that served as seat and storage. As he would learn, Zavet lived sparsely but the richness was in her work.

When he finally looked at the translator, Bren noticed her hands first, splotched with ink, then her hair, dark as a shadow, then her eyes, violet as a rare woodland flower.

"You're the first woman I've ever met who has locked herself in a tower," he said before he gave his name.

"That implies you've met others held against their will," she said. "Does it?"

"To say *I've never before met a woman who was locked in a tower* offers a far different connotation," she said.

Bren apologized for his imprecision, which had caused no offense, and introduced himself. She inspected the document, stated her fee, and told him to return in three days. And he did. He climbed the dark stairs again on the fourth day to ask her to join him for an early dinner at an inn near the banks of a beautiful lake. To his surprise, she accepted.

They shared several meals together and nighttime walks through the town and around the lake. They exchanged addresses and correspondence. He was some years older than she, though not significantly or even noticeably so then. She claimed not to mind, as there was comfort in the difference. To him, her ability with languages was absolute genius, the gift of a rare intelligence. To her, his natural charm—as she called it—gave him movement through the world in ways that transcended words.

Bren had no official business when he returned to the town four months later. He had taken an extended break from his work. No other location tempted him. So it was that he and Zavet saw each other several hours every day. He bought a diamond ring from the oldest jeweler in the world and proposed to Zavet without knowing whether she could cook, clean, or sew.

When they arrived where Bren had his home, the town where he was born, which was formerly the kingdom's seat, his parents called him foolish for overlooking such details. Although Zavet proved competent enough, she soon had little to do because they could afford the luxury of hired help. Between the two of them, Bren employed as he was before, Zavet as a translator, they earned enough to hire a woman to clean once a week and another to do laundry. Zavet insisted she do the cooking herself.

Zavet's parents said nothing because they were not informed until long after the vows were spoken and her place in her husband's house comfortably made. Her contribution to the household was modest. She had brought few belongings of her own—several prized texts, her clothing, and a little faded blue chest painted with animals.

A few years later, after his parents died, Bren and Zavet packed their possessions and moved across the river to the seat of the kingdom to find their fortune. In time, they had a daughter who was born with black hair, eyes the colors of night and day, and a gentle spirit.

"And that, my dear girl, is where I shall conclude the tale, because we do not yet know the ending," Bren said.

The hallway outside Secret's room was dim but warm with light. A shadow moved at the doorway. It glided toward the darkness then took shape at her father's side. Zavet placed her hand on his shoulder.

"You would have made a fine bard in another time," Zavet said.

"You heard, then?"

"Every word."

"And what do you wish to add?"

Zavet reached for the lamp and extinguished the flame. The chair where Bren had been sitting creaked when he stood. Secret lay on her pillow. Her father slipped the bedsheet under her chin and kissed the crown of her head.

"I kept a small room in a high place where I translated forgotten books. It was in that town I met your father, who first reminded me of someone I'd known, then of no one I'd ever encountered," Zavet said. The threshold to Secret's room held two shadows then, joined in the middle. "He was the only one who'd have me as I was."

The door began to close. "Good-night," Zavet said.

It did not shut. A long rectangle of light remained. "Good-night, my daughter," Bren said.

Secret closed her eyes. Something about the story reminded her of others her father had told and ones she read to herself. She fell asleep with thoughts of courage, love, and rescue.

XI

The Grand Ball at The Castle

DURING THE SUMMER BEFORE SECRET'S SECOND YEAR OF school, her father was in a state of elation. The family had received an invitation to the annual grand ball at The Castle. Secret overheard Bren tell her mother that Fewmany, the man for whom he worked, had kept his promise and arranged this auspicious boon. Bren told Zavet to buy formal gowns for herself and their daughter—and only the finest would do.

On the night of the event, Secret was left to splash in a cool bath as her parents dressed. Her long black hair, washed earlier in the day, was pinned at the top of her head and held fast with a kerchief. She tried to imagine what the ball would be like, what people would wear, and what feast there would be to eat. She was excited, and nervous, to attend. This evening wouldn't be like the ones when her parents took her to a play or a musical performance. At those times, after greeting people and making small talk in the hall's lobby, they simply sat and listened and watched. At a ball, there would be many people walking about, and dancing, perhaps much dancing. What was she going to do?

Anxious to get ready, she dried off and wrapped herself in a light robe. She traced her finger in a crevice of cracked plaster in the first-floor hall and leapt over the step that always creaked on the stairs. She thought of her parents' recent squabble about the house—her father insistent on a renovation, her mother adamant that she could not work in the midst of chaos and fumes. To Secret, the row house had character. To make it as perfect as Bren wanted might sacrifice its charm.

She crept to the third floor. Secret peered into her parents' bedroom. Zavet faced Bren, her back to the open door. She was wearing her gown but it was not yet buttoned. Zavet straightened her husband's collar and ran the flats of her fingers along the length of his lapels. With the sides of her thumbs, Zavet smoothed the thinning hair at his temples, more gray than brown as it once had been.

Bren told his wife to stay where she was. He disappeared from Secret's view then returned with something in his hands. He draped it around Zavet's neck. She glanced down as he clasped it, and she gasped as her fingers traced the string of jewels. Slowly, he closed the gown's back, a row of round jet buttons, the length knobby as her spine. Bren kissed her neck.

Zavet turned then. Her hair had been set at a parlor, the thick, wavy strands lifted away from her shoulders, artfully arranged on her head, and held fast by hidden pins and a silver circlet. When she fluttered her lashes and glanced up at her husband's face, Secret let out a gasp of her own.

The flattering violet gown intensified the color of Zavet's own violet eyes. Never had Secret seen her mother so richly dressed and never, until that moment, had she considered Zavet beautiful.

"Little spy, go to your room. Time to prepare," Zavet said.

Secret hurried down and found her gown and slippers on the bed. She dressed herself, and Zavet soon entered to tend to the details. Zavet tied the sash at Secret's waist and polished her black leather slippers with a soft cloth. She brushed Secret's hair long and straight. The dark tresses surrounded her from her crown to far below her shoulders. The child wished for her hair to be left like this, because she wouldn't be allowed to wear a cloak that evening, she'd been told. But her mother traced a center part and placed a shiny silver comb on each side, like a curtain framing her face. Secret peered at Zavet's distracted eyes then studied her mouth. Zavet had painted her lips with a berry brightness. She had taken care to fill the two deep grooves on her bottom lip, where her teeth met the flesh out of habit not design.

Moments later, the three of them stood inside the front door to await the carriage. Secret decided they looked very lovely, more so than they ever had before. She imagined that people would remark on their comeliness and consider them happy.

This thought made her smile, until her father smiled back at her and said, "Eve, your mouth is crooked."

A knock startled her. Their carriage had arrived. Four brown horses with plaited manes waited as Secret, her mother, and her father climbed inside. The coachman wore a long coat and breeches, and his gloves were a tawny leather. Secret thought of the kind coachman with the blue silk gloves and the yellow mushroom that was poisonous to eat.

At the edge of a north-end ward, the road began to slope upward. Secret peered from the carriage window and saw distant torches blazing the approach to The Castle.

She remembered stories her father had told her about the days of The Mapmaker's War. Their town was built on the same ground where the first battle took place. Legend had it that the clan who once claimed the land had paved the roads with gold, which was gathered and melted down by the triumphant king. When Bren repeated these tales, the roads spiraled and spoked in her mind's eye, bright and beautiful, again and again. History told—and of this there was no question because the chronicles recorded it—that the kingdom's seat moved to the site. The land was not hilly, but the new castle was built upon one. After the war, hundreds of trees were chopped down, their roots exposed and burned, and the earth dug up to make a mound. A proper fortification, as a castle was, required a high, unobstructed view.

That instant, she thought of the crow that had come to her courtyard, soon after her first visit to the woods near her town. He had revealed the image of a village surrounded by a great forest. The hair on her arms prickled.

The feeling dissipated quickly when the carriage stopped at the heavy wooden gate set in the high stone wall surrounding The

Castle. A man in a handsome uniform confirmed their invitation, and the horses carried them onward.

Shiny lanterns hung on hooked metal poles along the paved road. A man in a different kind of uniform directed her father to pull their carriage onto the grass, where many others were already left, the horses tethered and given water. Up the hill ahead, at the end of a bridge, the gatehouse was decorated with ribbons and flowers. Secret and her parents walked under the raised portcullis and through the dark corridor. On the other side, fresh straw and herbs cushioned the courtyard. Yet another man told them to follow the colorful woven mats that made a path to a long, dense red carpet leading into the Great Hall.

Oh, what splendor Secret saw inside—elaborate tapestries, handsome furnishings, guards and servants in their finest uniforms, candles and oil lamps tricking night into day, garlands of blossoms and greenery, glints from polished jugs and goblets, and guests, so many guests dressed as beautifully as in a dream.

Secret and her parents walked behind a short line of people, cordoned off by a gold velvet rope. Then, as the couple ahead stepped away, a man's voice announced her family. Secret could hardly believe she stood in front of the King and the Queen. She curtsied to them and their two maiden daughters named Pretty and Charming. Their jewels and crowns glimmered. After the greeting, Secret wondered where the youngest of the royal family might be. She knew there was one, the third born and only boy.

A couple approached her parents, and the adults rearranged themselves, the women together opposite the men. While they talked, Secret stood within view of her parents as she watched a juggler and a mime. In the shadows, children chased one another with long sticks that had colorful tassel ends. She wanted to go closer and see what game they were playing.

Secret returned to her father's side. She tugged his coattail, but he didn't look down. She heard him ask the man if he'd seen Few-many.

By then, Secret knew Fewmany was both a place and a person. She had overheard her mother and father speak of *him*, not it or they. She knew he was important and powerful. She would learn eventually that Bren had swiped deals from under Fewmany Incorporated's fingers time and again when he worked for the land speculator. When the magnate's enterprise couldn't triumph over its competition directly, it resorted to oblique methods, wooing Bren away. With the flattery came the promise of a generous salary and bonuses. Bren accepted.

Bren was given the peculiar title of Geo-Archeo Historian. Entirely accurate in its enigma, official yet almost quaint and non-threatening, the title didn't convey his ultimate task. No, Secret wouldn't know that for years. Instead, what she was told was that he worked backward through time to make sense of disputed lands and unclear titles. If he could reach back far enough, even with hearsay, a loophole might emerge. Custom and law, he knew, had their own gaps.

But at the time, what Secret knew was that Fewmany sent her father on trips to lands near and far, had his desk on the same floor as Bren, and came from the same region as her father. What a strange coincidence that Bren grew up in the decrepit old town across the river, Fewmany not far outside its humble borders, Bren the son of a chimney sweep and Fewmany the son of a shepherd.

The girl watched her father and his companion glance through the hall. They both smiled when their eyes met with a man who recognized them.

When she saw him, she felt herself contract in her skin. The animal alarm made her body hot, her breath shallow, and her legs tense. What repelled her, she could not see plainly.

Fewmany was not so tall but seemed much taller still, with smooth-combed hair, lightly oiled, and gleaming eyes and teeth. The lines across his brow and at the corners of his eyes hinted at his age, temperament, or worldliness, perhaps all three. The silk wrap at his neck seemed about to burst. He wore a fine suit of exquisite weave and drape that somehow appeared stuffed underneath. A timepiece at his hip swung in rhythm with his gait. On his right index finger there was a splendid ring. His boots were so new they bore no dust or creases. When he bowed to her mother, Secret noticed a tiny caged bell at the end of a thin wire poised at the opening of his ear. She stared at the bell and the mechanism tucked behind the fold. The device resembled, in miniature, the Tell-a-Bells many adults all throughout town wore on their belts.

After a brief greeting, Bren's companion took his leave, and Bren introduced his daughter. Secret curtsied with exacting formality. She drew her hands behind her back and didn't look into his eyes. She stared at his coat pocket. The stitches were stretched away at the bottom. What resembled bread crust poked from the hole. The pocket appeared full, a handkerchief tucked neatly above the contents.

"A pleasure to meet you, Eve," Fewmany said.

Knowing she must be polite, she looked up at him and nodded. She took a half step back as she felt a subtle pull at the core of her body. He studied her eyes a moment too long. She knew he had noticed the mismatched strangeness there, a flaw she couldn't hide. Quickly, she pushed her chin down.

"Shy one, I see," he said.

She shook her head.

"Cat got your tongue? Goat in your throat? Louse in your mouth?"

Her parents laughed. She shook her head again.

"She doesn't speak yet," her father said.

"Mmm-hmm," Fewmany hummed.

Then, as if there were a flash of fire, she noticed a boy behind the imposing man. The constriction within her suddenly released and reversed. She felt a stream of light ease into her blood, as gentle as it was forceful.

"So, if I tried to eat you up, you wouldn't even scream?" Fewmany asked.

She saw the intimidating glint in his eye from the corner of hers.

"She can speak," the blond boy with the gold cup said. "She keeps a secret. If she says any words now, the secret might escape too soon."

The girl's eyes stared into the boy's. They held each other's gaze and smiled as if they shared a hidden, precious knowledge. He moved closer until she could clearly see his features. His eyes are the color of myth, she thought.

The adults looked at the boy until Fewmany bowed and said, "Ah, Prince Nikolas, my liege."

With an aloof nod and a slight bow, the prince acknowledged the man's greeting. "Good evening, sir," he said. Nikolas turned to introduce himself to The Castle's unfamiliar guests and learned their names, then asked the girl's parents if she might join him and the other young visitors. Of course, they agreed.

"That Fewmany raises my hackles," he said as he placed his cup on a servant's empty tray. "Come with me."

He led her to a waiting group of children. She skimmed their faces, afraid she'd see someone from her school, but no one looked familiar. They hardly glanced at her.

"Her name is Eve," Nikolas said, "and she is quiet, like her name. She will be good at hide-and-seek."

He smiled at her as an older girl began to count. Secret looked left and right to decide which way to go. Nikolas hadn't moved but watched over his shoulder.

"Follow me," he said. "You won't give us away."

Secret stalled. She thought he'd been kind to invite her to play, but she didn't expect a gesture of friendship like this.

Nikolas swept his arm to beckon her.

She followed him along a dim corridor that stretched along the Great Hall. From the glow of oil lamps, she could see chamber doors, all closed. Muffled, youthful laughter came from behind one. Heavy footsteps clamored in the distance behind them. Nikolas started to run, and she went after him, through a door he opened, and into the dark. He shut the door as quietly as he could.

The windows across from her had drapes, but they were not drawn. The faint glow of the moon and stars gave off some light in which to see. What looked like an enormous shield hung on the wall to her right. Curtains covered almost the entire wall on the left. In the center of the room was the longest, widest table she had ever seen.

In the corridor, a man's voice called out. Children giggled and screeched.

"Here," Nikolas said. He reached behind a curtain and lifted a hidden latch.

She found herself inside a narrow space with a long bench bolted to the floor. She touched the panels of the door, which were textured as if woven. She could see the filtered light on the other side.

"Only the bravest will sneak past the guards. Sometimes they play along. Tonight they are, so far," he whispered.

Cautiously, with kitten toes, Secret walked the length of the tiny room. She wondered where they were, no doubt someplace important if they weren't meant to be there and for it to have such an enormous table. She imagined the king there, with his men. When she turned to walk back, Nikolas was sitting on the bench. All she could see was his outline.

Suddenly, in a way she never had before, she wanted to be able to speak. She wished she could ask Nikolas question after question about The Castle, what hung on its walls, what kept everyone so busy there. She wanted to know if he had special duties and if he had to go to school like other children and if he could have anything he asked for because he was a prince.

"Is this the first ball you've attended? Knock on something quietly, once for yes, twice for no," he whispered.

She knocked once.

"Does your father have a new appointment?"

She didn't understand the question and shrugged dramatically, hoping he could see in the dim light.

"You don't know if he has an appointment, or you don't know what I mean?"

She held up two fingers close to him, unsure if he'd understand. He did.

"Is he new on the Council, or has he been given a title?"

Secret was still confused, but if something as important as that had happened to her father, she certainly would have known. As an answer, she knocked twice.

Before Nikolas could ask another question, there was a click, then a light in the room. The bench in the hidden space creaked, and Nikolas put his face to a woven panel that formed the wall. As he began to creep sideways, the thin door flung open and a lantern rocked under a ghostly hand. Secret pressed her fingers to her closed mouth.

"Next year, one of us will lock the door, and then what will you do, our fine prince?" said a man. He raised the lantern to his face and stared at Nikolas with good-humored sternness. The man was young, his face roughly pimpled, with a severe cleft chin. He glanced past Nikolas and saw Secret.

"You wouldn't ruin the fun, would you, Hugh?" Nikolas said.

The guard narrowed his eyes. "You and your accomplice must leave the premises—NOW!"

The shout made them startle. When Hugh the guard stamped his foot in mock threat, they ran from the chamber, down the corridor, giggling all the way.

Back in the hall, two boys close to their age gestured wildly to him. Nikolas looked at her. She knew boys preferred to play with other boys. The adventure she'd had with Nikolas had been a treat. She shook her head and waved her hand for him to go. He paused long enough to smile, then joined the boys. While she stood alone, Secret could still feel the light and spaciousness within herself. Many years later, they would speak of this night they both remembered well. She would tell him what she observed as he first looked at her. He would tell her he meant the uncanny words he said, knowing beyond knowledge he was right.

Secret studied the face of every child she could see. None of them was of a schoolmate. With a hopeful heart, she joined games and learned dances. She ate fruit and cakes more delicious than any she'd ever had and drank punch from a pretty silver cup. She sat on cushioned benches to rest and tapped her toes with mirth. She smiled to herself as she decided this had been the best evening of her little life, because the best mornings had been spent in the woods long ago with her grandmother and the best afternoons with Fig Tree and creatures in her own courtyard.

Across the hall, among the adults dancing, she spotted her parents in each other's arms. Her mother moved as if she were suspended in water, her father not as nimble but capable enough. Other couples surrounded them, but they didn't seem to notice.

Far from the dancers were several men of various ages, gold glinting from their timepiece chains and lapel pins. One of them was Fewmany with a goblet in his hand. She squinted her eyes and bit her lip, unsure why she had had such a violent feeling about him.

Then, nearby, within range of hearing if she concentrated, Secret saw Nikolas standing among the King and a group of men. The adults looked toward him then grinned at each other.

Nikolas furrowed his brow and asked with earnest bearing, "Why couldn't we invite the dragon to our kingdom and show him we wish to be friends?"

The King patted his son on the head as the men clutched their bellies and slapped their knees. Secret watched the boy's face and posture shrink and felt her cheeks burn on his behalf. Then, for a moment, the boy watched them with a calm expression and walked away with a scowl. Before he could disappear in the crowd, his mother noticed him walk past her, called him back, and placed her hand on his cheek. He frowned and appeared to answer her with few words. When she kissed the crown of his head, he seemed to lean into the gesture.

When it was time to leave the ball, Secret searched for Nikolas and, when she found him, waved good-bye. He returned the gesture and said, "I bid you a *good eve.*"

Well past midnight, in a linen gown in her soft bed, Secret unwrapped a favor from the ball. Twisted inside blue paper was an almond and honey confection embossed with a bee. She nibbled the candy. Her parents wished her good-night.

She thought of Nikolas, how kind and welcoming he was, how outspoken and good-humored. She wished she could see him again one day. She thought of what it might be like to have two older sisters, as he did, or two older brothers, like him perhaps. The two brothers who had been born were forever blue because they never had a chance to breathe, her father once tried to explain.

Her eyes the colors of night and day rested behind heavy lids. There in the dark, she remembered Fewmany, his swinging timepiece and tiny bell, the pocket of his coat, the gleam in his eye like the glint of a blade. Then Nikolas behind him, golden, speaking what she knew to be true deep within, yes she did, although she didn't know how.

As she fell asleep, she whispered to herself, "My name is Secret."

That night, Secret had a vivid dream.

Water lapped against a shore. The air was chilly. Her back felt

heavy, as if she carried a weight. Five men emerged from the woods. They raised their arms in greeting, no weapons in their hands. They were all dressed the same, in beautiful blue coats, flaxen leggings, and leather shoes. Their hair was swept back, cut short at the base of their skulls. One of the young men approached her. He spoke, but she couldn't understand what he was saying. She knew beyond knowing that they could lead her to a special, peaceful place, one where she belonged. She wanted to touch them and feel the texture of the blue coats they wore. She wanted to go with them and follow where they led and never look back.

Secret awoke with a shock in her body, her heart pounding as if she'd fallen from a great height. She sensed she had dreamed of them before but never with such clarity or urgency. In the rising light, the girl found her coloring sticks and paper. She drew a picture of the blue men and hid it in a box under her little bed.

– XII –

Secret Is Her Name

ONLY DAYS BEFORE SHE WAS TO BEGIN HER SECOND YEAR OF school, a few weeks before Secret turned seven, her father surprised her with an announcement. He was sending her to a new school— a day school for the children of prominent families in town and a boarding one for children whose prestigious families lived farther away.

"Thank goodness you're smart, but my important connections and acquired means were the keys. You'll meet many fine children and rub many elbows there," he said.

She couldn't tell Bren she wouldn't dare do such a thing and have them think her any more peculiar than the classmates at her previous school did.

"To acquire a place in this world, you must have intelligence but more so influence, in your power or on your behalf. I should know. When you come of age, my pet, you'll be assured your pick of the finest high academies and potential husbands as long as your marks are good and friends are great."

Her mother spared her a speech. She didn't take Secret to the shops where she could choose clothing for herself. Instead, Secret found new items arranged in her wardrobe—five white blouses, five brown overfrocks, five gold sashes, and five red, round caps. Secret had outgrown her favorite purple cloak. Even if she had not, she wouldn't have been allowed to wear it. Instead, she was to wear a handsomely made but drab and heavy herringbone cloak. A uniform, her mother called it.

Secret was pleased she wouldn't have to return to the other

school. She hoped circumstances would be better, that she wouldn't be teased as she had been.

On her first day, her father escorted her to her classroom, a brief walk made long as he greeted other children's mothers along the way. "Good morning, Mr. Riven, delighted to see you," they crooned with warmth.

When she entered her classroom, she paused to look around. Several faces were familiar. She had seen some of them in her ward and at performances she went to with Auntie or her parents. Then she realized she had met some at the grand ball at The Castle.

She looked for Nikolas and was disappointed when she didn't see him. The girl took her seat at a sturdy wooden desk with an inkwell and a groove that held a pen with a metal nib. Under its hinged flap was paper. At her other school, they had used waxed boards and bone sticks instead. Going up and down the rows, the teacher spoke the name of each child. Secret slipped a sheet of paper from under her desktop. She wrote her given name and crossed it with an X. Below it she printed the letters S-E-E-C-R-I-T. When the children were released to play out on the wide green yard, she laid the paper in front of the teacher. She pointed to the letters, then to herself.

"But Eve, you have such a pretty name," the woman said.

The girl tapped the word she wrote. The teacher smiled, reached for a pen, and wrote letters at the bottom of the sheet. S-E-C-R-E-T.

"Very well then, Secret," the teacher said. "This is the correct spelling."

Overcome with gratitude, she grasped the teacher's hand with both of her own. She ran outside and into a nearby hedgerow where she saw a spider and said without saying, *My name is Secret.*

Her excitement lifted her through the day's lessons, only to fall that evening. The teacher instructed her to give a note to her mother. Zavet lit a beeswax candle on her desk, laid the paper flat near the light, and skimmed the words with her fingers.

"Such silliness. That's not your name," Zavet said.

Neither is "my little fungus," Secret thought, but her mother called her that anyway. The girl willed her face and body into impassive stillness. Her mother sighed.

"As you wish, then," her mother said. "Children and their phases. This will pass."

But this did not.

In her pocket, Secret carried a small card that read, *My name is Secret.* She wasn't certain how often she would need it, only that she would.

Those first few days, she tried not to do what had set her apart before at her other school. There was nothing she could do about what made her obviously different from everyone else. Her silence had not disappeared, and her hair, skin, and eyes remained unlike the others'. When creatures communicated with her, she gave them quiet attention but didn't allow them to crawl or land on her. She sat under the trees but didn't touch them. She made an effort to join in games and take proper turns on the playground.

Although the teachers called her Secret, the children called her The New Girl. They were not cruel but neither were they welcoming. She was asked pointed yes-no questions, and she overheard some of their conversations.

She learned her family name wasn't appropriately old, the block of the ward where she lived was just good enough, and the consensus among the children's parents was that her father was well liked, family name aside, and that her mother was peculiar. Regarding her mother, those were the kinder assessments.

She resigned herself to the fact that making friends was going to be complicated.

But one day, as she sat below the too-tidy apple tree that bemoaned its phantom limbs, she thought she recognized a boy at the far end of the yard where the boys played each day. She crept closer and closer. She stayed hidden under her hood until she could see him clearly. Nikolas didn't seem to recognize her even when she waved, although he did wave in return. She realized she hadn't seen him before because she was in the other second-year class and any games she played were always with the girls. Bravely, she walked up to him and tossed the cover from her head. Nikolas grinned and said her name. He remembered her. Her feet seemed to lift from the ground. She showed him the card she carried.

"Hello, Secret," he said. "My name is still Nikolas."

He smiled in a way that quieted the whole world around her and filled a waiting place in her heart.

Quite soon after that day, Secret's school organized an outing to Old Wheel for a special program for the younger children. A traveling troupe from far away had come to town with jugglers, acrobats, and puppeteers. Everyone was excited, including Secret. When her group settled into their seats, she peered through the crowd for Nikolas. Their eyes met, and their hands waved. He was one row behind, on the end.

Horns and drums accompanied the rainbow twirl of acrobats. The children clapped and cheered. Secret craned her neck to see the stage.

She felt a light tap on her foot.

The red squirrel held up one paw as if in pause, then dashed under the seats.

Secret turned her head to search for Cyril. Had she imagined the glimpse?

When she looked behind her, there was a young man wearing a coat decorated with gold braid. He was Nikolas's guard, who lurked like a distant shadow wherever the boy went. The guard stood on the end of an aisle a few paces behind the prince. His eyes wandered over the crowd of children, then fixed on a pretty young woman at his right. The guard began to speak to her. When she smiled, his posture slackened and he smiled back.

Then Secret watched Nikolas startle and stand up. His red, round cap fell to the ground. He twitched as if he couldn't decide to sit, stand, or chase what his eyes tracked. Secret looked at him until he glanced her way. She gestured for him to follow her. Nikolas shook his head and pointed over his shoulder toward the guard.

Secret slipped from her chair. Cyril jumped into her arms. Nikolas widened his eyes, crept from his seat, and joined her. They turned to see that the guard hadn't noticed Nikolas was gone.

The boy was silent as Secret led him into the alley, to the grate, and through the tunnel.

He gasped when they emerged from the ground into the hollowing tree.

The red squirrel darted back and forth at Nikolas's feet, then dashed in Reach's direction. The boy ran after him. Secret stepped behind them without haste. She carried a butterfly on her fingertip until it flew away under the tree's canopy. She watched Cyril and Nikolas run in circles around the trunk. Secret breathed in a way she never could in school, at home, or in town. Her soles ached when Reach grumbled. She gave him a brief hug.

Nikolas had left his cloak on his chair, but he didn't appear cold. He seemed unsure of what to do.

"You've been here before," he said.

Yes, she nodded.

"With the squirrel?"

Again, she nodded. Secret knelt on the ground and scratched into it with a stick. She spelled S-I-R-I-L, then pointed at the squirrel. Nikolas fumbled with sounds until he formed a recognizable word.

"Cyril!" he said.

Nod, up and down.

"Do you ever speak?" he asked.

Shake, side to side.

"You can, can't you?"

She clutched her throat tightly and shook her head no.

"Do you mind if I do?"

Side to side.

"Are we far from home?"

She drew a circle on the ground and wrote the word *town* inside. To the left of the circle, she drew three simple trees. She touched her stick near the bottom of the circle and scratched a line from it into the trees, tapping the spot where the line ended.

Nikolas told her he had never been here before but had been to the woods in another kingdom. He had visited cousins who liked to hunt and insisted all the men and boys go along. He remembered the dogs, the crossbows, the shouting, and the boar's pooling blood.

This made her sad because she had encountered boars, their appearance more frightful than their demeanor. One had allowed her to touch him, his curved tusks, coarse bristled back, and thick shoulders. She could not imagine pursuing animals with the intent to kill them for amusement. They had thoughts, feelings, and memories just as she did, although they were different.

Secret beckoned Nikolas to follow her. They stepped beyond Reach and peered at what grew in the damp. Such things didn't grow on sidewalks and in courtyards. They chased the brilliant red, orange, and yellow leaves that fluttered from the sky. They sat for some time in a sunny patch without a sound made by human voices or invention. A sparrow flew into her hair and pulled at the strands until she laughed. The bird sat on her finger long enough to chirp a tune. Soon after, a doe peeked from the bosk and crept even closer as Secret quietly called to her. The girl rubbed the animal's flank.

He's a friend. Will you let him greet you? Secret asked.

The doe approached and leaned her face toward the boy. Nikolas gave Secret a wary glance, and the girl nodded. His fingers rubbed the deer's nose and the top of her head. Suddenly, she stomped her hoof and ran into the trees, her tail flicking. Nikolas blinked at Secret with interest.

"Do animals always go to you that way?"

No, she shook.

"Sometimes?"

Yes.

"Do you know why they go to you?"

No.

Nikolas sighed and eased back against his outstretched arms. A breeze tousled his blond hair. "I'm glad to have a rest today. I'm learning to shoot arrows and use a sword and staff, and my father makes me practice every day," Nikolas said.

She looked at him, waiting to see what he'd say next.

"Do you know why?" he asked.

Secret had her own ideas, but of course she said nothing.

"One day when I'm a man, I will have to fight enemies, protect the weak, and go on a quest to find a dragon."

Her eyes grew wide. She had heard ancient dragon tales in Old Wheel and several from her father. Now and then, she heard newsbox reports of the dragon menace, but she couldn't determine whether it was an actual beast or a person with a strange name. Regardless, the newsboxes made it seem real, dangerous, and unpredictable. Secret's expression prompted her new friend to explain.

"Yes. That's what I'm told. A long time ago, the people of our kingdom chose a quest for the prince. They sent him away to get proof of the dragon and to show it that they weren't afraid. So he went to a distant land and took a scale from the dragon's flesh and returned home a hero. Ever since, princes from kingdoms all over the world have faced this dragon to show their courage. And when I'm old enough, I'll go, too, as my fathers did before me."

When Nikolas looked straight at her, Secret shivered, as if a horde of ants had run across her skin.

"And my sisters told me after I return from my quest, I'll have to marry a princess and have a boy child with her. I'm not sure what's scarier—that or the dragon," he said. His expression was so earnest that Secret felt a twinge of sympathy, until she realized he also intended to make a joke of these serious matters. When she giggled, he smiled wide and revealed the gap between his missing front teeth.

Cyril kicked bark from a nearby branch, ran down a tree trunk, and skittered past their feet. The time had come for them to leave. As they approached the tunnel's entrance in the tree, the girl and boy paused when they saw an ancient stag step into the dappled light near them and lift its tremendous antlers. His body had visible scars. His appearance surprised her, but she had no fear. Secret met his eyes. She stared at him as if she had seen him before but couldn't remember where or when. Her heart quickened its beat. He and the children peered at one another in silence. Then, he gave a dignified bow before he slipped among the trees.

Through the hole in the hollow, along the tunnel, out into the alley the children went. They leapt into their seats to join the final applause. She sensed a stare at her back and turned to see Nikolas. He held a steady gaze on her. Above a mischievous smile and bright eyes, he raised splayed hands to his temples, like horns, and slowly bowed. Secret felt soft and light as a petal.

So it was that the two of them knew a way into the woods. If they found themselves near or in Old Wheel and Cyril appeared, they followed, whether they were together or alone. A trusted escort, the squirrel signified safety, the ability to come and go unnoticed. She thought he was magic, and Nikolas did as well. They couldn't explain how adults who were supposed to watch them became so distracted that they were able to get away without being caught. They didn't know why time lost its boundaries so that minutes seemed like hours. They were children who, like all children, believed in wonder, which granted them the gift of wishes come true.

As proof of their adventures, they gave each other little surprises—a stone, a feather, a beetle's husk. They shared them at school, but sometimes they left the gifts in the woods.

Secret was the one who found the snakeskin, a translucent ribbon she coiled at Reach's roots. Nikolas was the one who surrounded the skin with pebbles, twigs, and an ingot of gold molded into a hexagon that he'd found half-buried in the earth.

XIII

Hurried Evenings in Town

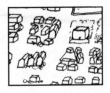

As THE DAY ENDS, CONTEND WITH THE NOISE, THE TRAFFIC, the newsboxes. People vanish behind their doors. Many come out again to slip into places that were active but less conspicuous during the day. The carts go out again, and people seek entertainment of all kinds. The night calls for distraction.

Walk around. Notice where the people cluster and flow. In Old Wheel, in several well-lit squares, tiered benches surround semi-circle stages. Almost every night, old plays are performed there, ancient by many standards and tastes. Cushions cover the ground of another square, where children sit to listen to stories as pimple-faced young people keep watch.

Stroll around west and east. Find a seat if you can to view *Revelation*. There is a wooden box and a brass horn that protrudes from a hole at the front of it. An anonymous person enters the box wearing a cloak and mask. He—or she—speaks without questions, admits his worst fears and shames, and leaves through the shadows. Those present shout, laugh, judge, and cry. The box is never vacant. The seats are always full.

Opulence can be seen in the center of town. Its stage is a manor built for show, not residence. A queue weaves from room to room.

Observe the splendor of wealth, the fine decorations, and the possessions. Look, desire, but don't touch.

Near a row of shops, slip through a doorway into a space with cushioned benches lined up on a slope. Wood shavings cover the stage. A whiskered man holds a saw in one hand and pats a wood plank cut at an angle. Behind him is a pegboard covered with tools. To his right, the mere frame of the wall. He is the master carpenter for a new favorite, *This Old Hut*.

Someone left a booklet on a seat. Check the paper for local listings. In seven rooms throughout town, there are simultaneous performances of *The Wenching Hour*, a bawdy comedy. Four others have recent episodes of *Rule of Justice*. In other venues, audiences watch all manner of drama, comedy, tragedy, and farce. There are also lectures on history, current events, science, and the natural world.

Most of the performances end in the evening and resume the following day. Yet there are places that entertain through the night, when sleep is elusive or loneliness cloys like another skin.

When the carts return to the places where the beasts will sleep, the street cleaners complete the last shift. Lamplight assists their work. Water blasts from the hoses and drowns out the newsboxes. There is no interruption in the word stream.

Notice, yes, notice no interruption at all, but the din becomes a murmur by midnight. Where fewer people live, the newsboxes close until dawn. An intersection here, an intersection there, the voices continue to tell of the world within and without.

Near a trickling drain, a man sits and smokes a pipe. He listens, or perhaps not, to the repeated report of speculation that the dragon menace laid waste to a distant village, so far away it hardly seems to matter.

XIV

A Gift from Zavet

ONE AFTERNOON BEFORE SECRET'S SEVENTH BIRTHDAY, while the girl chose a toy from her room to take outside, Zavet opened and closed cabinets and doors as she uttered speech unlike any Secret had heard before. This was not a familiar language stew or bout of muttering. The little girl crept into the hall to listen. The sounds were worse than her mother's hissing silence and more menacing than her usual twitters and gurgles. She chattered and sputtered and spoke so quickly she seemed to gag and choke on her words.

Secret trembled and remembered the last time she felt this way. Not long after she'd visited her grandmother, after they'd moved into the row house, Zavet had such an episode, and the little girl hid under the table. In neither instance did Secret know what had been unleashed inside her mother.

The girl did her best to find a place to hide. She slipped into the room where her father worked on the third floor and crawled under the table. A long sheet of paper was draped over the edge like a curtain. Secret swept her hair around her shoulders as if to shield her. She startled when she heard shouts. This hadn't happened before, her mother's voice raised until the sound hit the roof. Secret hardly breathed. Her lungs barely filled, thin as leaves.

Light came through a window and struck the paper curtain. Space illuminated between lines on the other side. Secret saw triangles, dozens of triangles, and when she widened her sight, she noticed points from which the triangles extended. Their lines intersected with more lines, creating other small triangles and parallelograms. She stared at them for a long time, drawn to them as if they had meaning to her, until her skin tingled and she began to feel dizzy. She held her breath to quiet the swirl. When she looked at the shapes again, there was order to what she saw. There she sat until night began to fall, and she worried how soon she would be hungry.

An earwig crept near Secret's knee. It paused to raise its pinching tail and drew the tines together. The girl listened for footsteps and heard, "Where is that little fungus of mine?" Secret shuddered and breathed thin as a hair.

"Where is my little fungus?" Zavet called again. "Hiding in the dark, waiting to release your spores?"

Secret didn't move. She hoped her mother would tire and let her emerge on her own. She didn't know what might happen with her mother in this state, worse than it had ever been. With the uncanny swiftness she sometimes possessed, Zavet knelt on the ground, grabbed Secret's ankle, and dragged her out with a yank. The little girl sat back on her hands, her legs splayed ahead, frozen. Zavet crouched on her hands and knees.

"Should I slap you as my mother did me to make you obey?" she asked.

Wide-eyed, Secret shook her head. Had she spoken yet, even then she wouldn't have known what to say.

Her mother cried out and flung her hand to the side as if bitten. Zavet stood and rubbed the side of her palm. She said dinner would be simple and soon, then told Secret to go outside until it was ready.

Secret waited until Zavet was gone then pounded down the stairs. She ran to the heavy back door and pulled the great bobbin with angry force. The latch clanked. Her mother hissed loudly. Secret almost doubled over as the knot below her belly seized and tore at the root of her tongue. She wanted to scream but of course she could not.

She stepped into the courtyard and noticed a solitary bee. It twirled near the flowers she tended and crawled into the hidden stores of gold. In spite of, or perhaps because of, what happened when she was three, Secret loved bees. She thought of the beautiful hum when they greeted their queen and the light that shone through their line. What had one told her of the wound and the wolf? She could remember, when she tried. The men and frightened child. Images and feelings she didn't understand then. The man with the bloody gash from his throat to his belly. The wolf that had to dig into the ground to find him. The bees that buzzed around them both.

At that moment, Secret watched the little bee leave in its loopy flight. She wished she could join the bee, flying far from her mother, who treated her with meanness for no reason she could see.

Secret went to Fig Tree. The tree bent her limbs around the child, giving her the cover of leaves. One leaf, healthy and green, fell to the ground. White droplets plopped near Secret's foot. Without words or sound, in a way of seeing beyond sight, Secret learned of the other children Fig Tree had held and given comfort. The tree remembered blood, sweat, and tears. She knew sad, terrible things, which she refused to tell. Secret wrapped her arm around her friend's thick trunk. She kissed her gray skin, cried for her witness, and thanked her for her impossible kindness.

Several days later, a parcel arrived and remained unopened on Zavet's table. Secret wasn't allowed to touch or open such things, and she did neither. She suspected it was a present. Her seventh birthday was near, as her father said each evening as the day approached. He seemed excited in a way that made Secret feel more expectant, too.

Then she remembered her visit to Ahmama and the nesting dolls. Zavet had told her the firstborn girl received her mother's dolls on her seventh birthday. Secret stared at the dolls high on her mother's shelves, the anticipation making her giddy.

On the morning of her birthday, Secret awoke to a dove, a pigeon, and a sparrow in a line on her windowsill.

She thought of all the times her father had told her of the day of her birth. She was never sure she could believe him, although she wanted to. He was, after all, a clever storyteller. The girl sat up and greeted them.

Our grandmothers told us of you, the pigeon said.

A child born with a great gentleness, the dove said.

And we have come to honor you today with a song, the sparrow said.

Secret clasped her hands at her heart. The three birds joined their voices as a peculiar trio, their coos and chirps woven together with unexpected beauty, plaintive and cheerful. When they were finished, Secret applauded and stroked each one on the wing.

She was still in a joyful mood that night when her parents gave her a celebration and gifts—sweet butter cake topped with seven candles, a puzzle, a toy owl with glass eyes and carved wooden talons, and a large, beautiful book filled with illustrations and old tales in a language she didn't know. With enthusiasm, her father said he had obtained the book from a little shop in the region where her mother was born. It was written in her native tongue, one she'd surely read to her. Secret had her doubts.

The parcel on her mother's table lay undisturbed. It had not contained a gift for Secret. She went to bed disappointed not for that reason but because the nesting dolls remained on their shelf, untouched. They were not hers.

Not long after, on a morning when Secret didn't have school, she sat at the dining table with her coloring sticks and old paper. The sky was dark from a coming storm. Her mother never worked on days like this, always preferring sunlight, although Secret didn't know quite why.

A cold wind blew through the windows. Zavet began to speak—to herself, to her daughter, Secret couldn't be certain. But the tongue in which she spoke was the one they shared.

"I had a brother once," Zavet said and then began to tell of a boy born to her father and not of her mother, years older than she. He was witty and charming, with a quick smile. Zavet found him mysterious and wondered how a boy so warm and bright could come from the father they shared. Nevertheless, his presence cheered her when she was with him. He lived with an uncle who taught him a woodworking trade, but Zavet's brother wished for adventure. She feared he would go far away and she would never see him again.

As it came to pass, she was the one sent away from him, against her will.

He had warned her time over time, Jabber—he called her Jabber—you must control the strange voices. People don't understand you and they think you're mad. You may be, but that is no excuse to send you away. Do you think you can speak with only one tongue? he asked. Do you think you can stop saying what you believe is in other people's thoughts? Promise me. Zavet tried and failed, not because she forgot her oath to her brother but because she couldn't fight the streams that flowed within.

Secret stared at her mother's back. She knew she must listen to every word. A story such as this her mother rarely told, and would never tell again.

Zavet's story continued. She said she couldn't remember her strangeness becoming worse as she grew older, but the adults around her, her mother in particular, grew less tolerant. They called her disobedient, bad, unclean. On her seventh birthday, her family gathered to mark the occasion. Zavet's ahma gave her the nesting dolls, which had stared down from a cupboard shelf as long as she could remember. Her brother, a young man then, with stubble at his jowls and hands scarred from the lathe, shunned the call to drink with his cousins and sat with her as she played with the dolls.

He didn't tell her, but she knew from him, in the way she simply knew things, that she would leave him. Her father avoided her, and her mother had given no hint. Her mother's mind was closed. Zavet had promised not to speak of others' thoughts, so she put her arms around his neck and kissed his cheek. He clutched her to his chest in a way she had never been held. She was very afraid.

Come morning, Zavet readied herself for the day and sat at her place for breakfast. Her brother had gone in the night. He left a fanciful carved creature upon her plate, a beast with a coiled tail and bird's wings.

Zavet's ahma gave her bitter tea to drink. The child was told she was going on a journey to stay with a distant relative. Zavet asked why.

Her mother replied, I need a rest from you.

So it was that Zavet went to the first foster home among many. She left behind the nesting dolls. She visited her parents' home between promises of correction and cure. She was away, always away, and that was where she was when her brother died.

"I last saw Szevstan the day my mother gave me these dolls," Zavet said as she placed them in her daughter's hands.

Secret's whole body jolted as if someone had crept behind and startled her. Her head was dizzy. She held the dolls to her chest, breathing with shallow pants. Her skin felt too tight, her chest too small. The arches of her feet curved, and she felt as if someone were pulling her arms from their sockets. For an instant, Secret thought another child was near her, but knew that couldn't be.

Zavet returned to her table, opened the waiting parcel, and removed a vase painted with geometric designs. Secret felt a jab in her stomach when she realized her mother hadn't followed the tradition she had learned about when she visited her ahmama. Zavet had not purchased new nesting dolls to replace the ones she handed down to Secret. She felt as if a promise had been broken.

"No such memories will ever plague you," Zavet said as she turned around again. "Your brothers Noose and Knot, dead before they were alive, spared you the grief of their loss, if you had loved them."

The mention of her stillborn brothers startled Secret, but her mother's raw pain held her attention.

Secret went to Zavet and took her hand. There were moments, no matter her mother's coldness and cruelty, in which Secret felt a rending compassion for her. The girl meant to thank her mother for the dolls she had waited to have and to comfort her in a sadness Secret never knew she carried. Until that moment, Secret had no knowledge of her uncle or that her mother had been in fosterage.

Zavet looked toward her child's face. "Lucky thing I kept you," she said.

Secret drew herself inward as she backed away. Her palms suddenly ached. A sharp stab spiked through her navel that spiraled up to her tongue, then dulled to a throb in her belly.

"Lucky thing," her mother said, "I kept you."

She took her nesting dolls into her room. Dingy light reached across the floor. Under the window, Secret sat down. She opened each doll until she reached the smallest one, the solid center. Top and bottom, she joined each doll to itself, their hollow cores unburdened by the others' weight. Secret separated the largest from the smallest. She pushed the smallest ones away. She danced the large dolls across the floor and the top of the little faded blue chest.

"When I get big, I will go far away," she said to herself. "When I get big, I will have my own house. When I get big, I will meet the blue men."

Secret remembered the nesting dolls at Ahmama's house so long before. As little girls, her grandmother, then her mother, had played with the ones that were now hers. How old they must be, the girl thought. Then Secret wondered how her ahmama, who had been so kind to her, could have made her mother go away as she did. Secret had glimpsed, but didn't understand, what made her mother so hard.

Secret glanced out of the window at the gray sky. She smelled the sharp edge of rain. The metallic tingle soothed her. She lay on the floor with the tiny thirteenth doll in her hand. Within herself, she fled to the woods, seeking comfort and shelter in the hollow tree where the bees sang for their queen.

XV

Old Woman's Cottage

THE WINTER WHEN SECRET WAS SEVEN, AUNTIE RARELY took her to story times in Old Wheel, susceptible as the woman was to the cold and damp. Nevertheless, on milder days, Auntie slept cocooned in her cape, muff, hat, and scarf while Secret ventured into the woods with Cyril. She loved the sparseness and clarity. How blue the sky was among the trees' brown grasp. How high the hawk flew, how sleepy the salamander, how loud the scuffle of hoof and paw. She drew her hood tight with mittened hands as she wandered under occasional evergreens and let it drop away where the sun brightened what was most often dim.

Then one day, the squirrel didn't leave her soon after they emerged from the tunnel and Secret went to Reach.

Come, he said.

Cyril led her to a path. It was within the area where she usually played, and she was surprised she hadn't noticed it before. Secret covered her long black hair with the shadow within her cloak's hood. Beneath a stand of pines, she shivered more from fear than cold. The path was narrow, a shallow impression on the woodland floor. Cyril leapt ahead, bounce by bounce. He skittered up a tree where the path curved sharply.

Follow, he said. *You will not be lost.*

Secret crept forward with anxious steps. The path connected to a wide glade. On the opposite end of the glade was a small tidy cottage. Its roof was thick thatch, its door was open, and its shutters were blue. In a nearby pen, sheep grazed in the sun. Secret dared not cross in full view, so she walked along the woods' edge. As she came closer, she saw raised patches of brown soil as wide and long as bedcovers, where greens and cabbages grew full. Under both front windows, there were plants waiting to come back into leaf. On the side of the house that Secret saw first, an unlocked, shallow wooden cabinet revealed jars, tools, jugs, and pails. Quietly, the girl stepped to the cottage's back. A low, thin-slatted fence enclosed a half-moon of ground and a miniature house with slit windows, one door, and a long plank leading to the entrance. Hens scratched in the dirt.

Secret's hand rested on the rear gate, which was metal and decorated with flying birds. She walked with evermore caution because she heard a woman's voice.

"Settle in, settle down, my little lamb, and I shall tell a tale," the woman said. She spoke in Secret's language but with a subtle accent as if she'd come from a faraway place. The girl twitched her shoulders with a sudden chill.

The girl reached the opposite side of the house. On a low stool sat an old woman, or so it seemed from the quicksilver color of her long braid. She wore a green dress with a blue collar. A small sheep with a black nose rested its chin on her outstretched arm.

Secret remained still as an owl and listened to a fanciful story about a dream of creation and a dragon that watched it come to be. A myth, Secret realized, one that told of a beginning. When the tale was done, the old woman stood tall. Secret escaped on tiptoe before she could be seen.

Several weeks later, after a gentle snow, Secret and Nikolas found themselves in Reach's shelter at the same time. She wondered if she should invite him to follow her to what she had discovered. She sat near him and watched as he built a tower of sticks.

With no hint at all, Nikolas told her, "I might have dreamed I met an old man in the woods, but it might have been real. He wore a red cap and a hoodless cloak that shimmered. Have you seen him?"

Secret shook her head and reached for a twig. She drew a dress on the ground.

"A woman?" Nikolas asked.

She nodded.

"Was this in a dream?"

She pressed her lips together, then shook her head.

"She didn't see you?" Nikolas asked.

A shake no.

"Were you afraid of her?"

Secret shrugged. She had thought of all the tales and lore she learned, so many that warned of old women living alone in the woods, and she knew she should be fearful. But deep in her heart, she felt more curiosity than dread.

"I wasn't afraid of the old man. He asked me to help tend saplings. We walked through the woods and stopped at little trees the man said he had planted. Then he let me water the trees with a bucket that never seemed to empty. That's why I thought it was a dream. That's not possible—a bucket that's always full. But the next morning, my hands were sore as if I carried too much weight with them."

Secret wanted to believe what Nikolas had done was real. She wondered if the old man lived in the cottage with the old woman. Then she hoped he didn't. She imagined there was much peace living alone in the woods with day, night, the animals, and the trees.

"If you see the old man, he's very kind. You have no reason to be afraid if he finds you, or you find him," Nikolas said.

Cyril appeared from behind a tree. He sat in front of Nikolas as the boy offered him walnuts one by one, which were hidden in a pocket.

"I haven't told anyone what's here," Nikolas said. "I don't want anyone to know. You don't either, do you?"

Secret shook her head.

Nikolas reached out to her with a fistful of nuts and let them fall into her open hands. She looked at him and smiled softly, a thank-you not only for the treat he shared but also for his friendship. She was content in his easy company.

He smiled in return. "I like that you're quiet. Then I can be quiet, too," he said.

She nodded.

Cyril stood between them eating the walnuts they offered. Rustling leaves, birdsong, and cracking shells were the only sounds. Secret thought of the noise that surrounded Nikolas—the constant press of children on the playground, the fuss when people saw him among them, and the commotion when the royal carriage arrived at school, Nikolas perfectly combed and pressed, a guard not far from his side. Although she so often felt lonely and strange, she didn't wish to have such bother and bluster. She simply wished for peace.

XVI

She Speaks

BLEAK COLD AND GRAY UNFOLDED INTO WARMTH AND green. Secret's beloved Fig Tree reached out with verdant tips. A random songbird, weary from flight, would rest in its branches and sing of its travels. The visits from the birds had become quite regular since Secret began to care for the tree. Some told her a part of them, deep within, remembered its sweet fruit from another time. She told them all about her visits to the woods and what she saw there, including the old woman who told a marvelous tale. Secret hoped Auntie would take her to Old Wheel more often so that she could slip away into the distant trees.

Fortunately, she received her wish.

Cyril appeared again and again. Secret crossed the tunnel's darkness and emerged in the woods. Reach received greeting, but he was not whom she wished to see. Her feet found the path to the old woman's cottage. There she listened to the woman. The quiet child had yet to glimpse the elder's full face, but that mattered little to her.

There, Secret heard tales of a time before time, of a dragon, a dwarf, a woman-wisp, and an orphan. She learned their names and deeds and felt their presence within her own skin. She listened to the myths, the impossible explanations of the beginning and nature of All That Is.

The old woman never took notice of her but on occasion, the animals did.

Who are you? they asked her.

My name is Secret, she told them, *and I wish to be one.*

They gave no cries of warning, as if they knew she posed no predatory harm, as if they knew to protect her.

Secret soon noticed that the animals brought their young nearby to listen to the old woman's musical voice and magical tales.

Then days after a lamb was born, Secret heard the old woman say—

"Do you remember, small one, before you opened your eyes, The Great Sleep, which came before All That Is?" she said.

Secret had heard that one before and longed to again. Of all the myths her father read to her, and she read to herself, this one was her favorite, somewhat the same but also unlike any other.

The girl hid herself as always. She and the creatures listened to what happened after The Great Sleep dreamed its wish to awaken. The dragon, the dwarf, and the woman-wisp came to know all the beings that lived among them. Then the dragon found the orphan Azul, who had been left to drown in a river. Azul loved the dragon, the dwarf, and the woman-wisp but had to find a new life among humankind. The humans often proved less than kind because Azul was a stranger in many ways. But in time, Azul made friends and allies, had children, and with them, formed peaceful villages filled with love all over the known world.

Before the end of spring, Secret heard a myth she must have missed. The last one of the cycle. The orphan died, and Azul's children gathered to honor the parent's passing. On the day of the funeral, there was a procession in Azul's honor of young men wearing the color of the ocean and sky. Young men in coats of a beautiful blue.

The little girl gasped in a bright rising note.

A spasm at her navel fluttered and rippled, twisted and turned. The knot released, the cord through her belly slackened, and its length spiraled up to tickle the back of her tongue. She pressed her hands to her mouth and crouched like a hedgehog under the cottage window where she hid among the ivy.

Secret heard footsteps ever closer, ever nearer, until the sound stopped. A blue claw pushed the vines aside and filled the hollow with light.

"Cyril, what have we growing here?" a familiar voice said, the slight accent melodious as ever.

Secret felt gentle pats on her head.

"Is it a dark moss never before seen?"

Blue fingers approached her eyes and swept a curtain of hair behind her small ear.

"Is it a mysterious beautiful mushroom unlike any other?"

A soft face round and bright as the moon appeared, aligned, in front of the silent girl's own.

"Oh, a special creature with eyes—yes, look—with eyes the colors of night and day! Behold, Cyril. Does it speak?"

Secret's forehead pulsed with heat and filled her body with light. Only with Nikolas had she felt such an immediate warmth, never so strong before or until this moment. The light streamed into her fingers and toes and before she knew it, a beam flowed from her throat and Secret said, "I dream of blue men."

"Do you?" the woman asked.

"Yes."

"What is your name, little dreaming mushroom?" she asked.

"My name is Secret."

"Oh, it is indeed," was the reply.

"What is your name?" Secret asked.

"Old Woman," she said.

"Has it always been Old Woman, even when you were a girl?"

Secret's new friend laughed. "Oh, no. I was called by another then. Long ago, when I was a little girl, then a wife and mother. Many, many years have passed since that time, and it served me no longer."

"You live alone then?" Secret took the offer of her friend's thin blue hands and stood on her feet.

"Of course not. I'm surrounded by trees and plants and animals of all kinds," the woman said.

"But no people?"

"Myself, and a rare visitor now and again."

Secret stared at her. The girl thought of her ahmama, so far away, then of herself, so often alone. "Don't you get lonely?"

"Yes, but not as often as you might think. I suppose you know as well as I do how many companions one can find in the woods."

Questions filled Secret's head, more than enough for months to come. The girl asked Old Woman why her hands were blue. She was led to the front of the cottage. There was a cauldron full and still with dark water. Secret learned the woman grew woad and sometimes dyed cloth as well.

Her new friend invited her into the cottage. There was only one room, ample enough. A sturdy old table was accompanied by a bench and two chairs. An enormous cupboard with doors stood against a wall. A large cauldron rested heavily in one corner of the fireplace and smaller pots surrounded it. The bed was low and appeared comfortable, and at its foot was a chest.

Old Woman sat her down, gave her a wedge of bread, and asked her to tell of the blue man dreams. Although she had never spoken before, Secret found she had no tension or clumsiness in her tongue. Secret told of men dressed in lovely blue coats, men who looked brave and strong and who made her feel safe. They stood guard at a place where the dreams wouldn't let her visit, although she wanted to very much. No matter, though, because it was pleasant to be with them. They spoke to her, and she to them, but she couldn't understand a word they said when she woke up. The girl said she had dreamed of them several times.

"Are the people all men?" Old Woman asked.

"I think so," Secret said. "That's how they seem."

"Have you told no one else of them?"

"No." Secret paused. "I've never said a word until today."

Old Woman nodded her head. She was silent for a long while then said, "Remember this, child. They are real. Let no one dismiss your dreams, which reveal the truth."

Cyril shook his thick red tail and moved his feet in a dance.

Secret glanced at him and rose from her seat. "I have to leave now," she said. She paused. Old Woman had used the squirrel's name earlier, but Secret hadn't said it. "Why do you call the squirrel Cyril?"

"When I first saw him and we became friends, I thought the name suited him. I've always called him Cyril."

"It is a good name," Secret said.

"As is yours."

"Thank you for the visit and the bread. I'll come again, if you don't mind." Secret began to walk toward the doorway. "Goodbye."

"Come here," Old Woman said, gesturing for Secret to go to her.

Secret approached with caution. Old Woman wrapped the child in her arms, patting Secret's head, which lay on her shoulder. At first, Secret wriggled as if she were trapped, as if she wanted to get away. She felt confined, not comforted. But then as Old Woman stroked her hair, Secret couldn't remember when she was last held, last touched, in this way. Suddenly, she desperately wished to sleep.

Old Woman kissed Secret's forehead, where the queen bee had stung her.

"You are always welcome here," she said. "Always."

As Secret ran through the woods and splashed in the tunnel, she who had never spoken sang a song with each step. She found her voice to be clear, and not too high, and even somewhat warm. A good voice, she thought. Then Secret wondered if it would disappear again once she reached Old Wheel and returned home. Perhaps that wouldn't be so terrible, if she could only speak in the woods.

She found Auntie where she'd left her, inside a stuffy music hall, and said nothing. She didn't try to speak. As they returned to Secret's house, Secret wondered if she wanted to speak at all. Her silence had kept her apart from the world. To speak would close a distance and reveal her. Her muteness, for all its difficulties at times, had given her the subtle power of protection.

Yet that evening, as her mother prepared a salad with fragrant oil and berry vinegar and Secret drew her favorite dream, the girl chose to speak.

"Mother, I dream of blue men," she said.

Zavet turned around.

"Did you talk?" her mother asked.

"Yes."

"Why now?"

"Why not? Aren't you pleased?"

"I was accustomed to my silent child. I'm surprised. How different things will now be," Zavet said.

Secret waited for her mother to ask what happened, not that Secret would tell her precisely and even Secret wasn't sure herself. She paused, expecting some show of emotion, but there was none. Zavet went about preparing dinner as if it were any other night. Secret went to her room, bewildered at her mother's response.

Later that night, as her father stood and ate the wilted leftover salad, her mother called her to the kitchen.

"Repeat what you revealed," Zavet said.

"Father, I dream of blue men."

Bren stared at his daughter. Tears crested at his lashes. He flung his plate and fork on the dining table and rushed to his daughter. He lifted her to his chest. Secret wrapped her arms around his neck, barely able to breathe because he held her so closely.

"For so long, I've dreamed of normal children. Now it has finally come true," Bren said. "Off to bed you go, but tonight, you shall read to me."

"Oh yes!" Secret said as he carried her toward the stairs.

"Oh yes—who?"

In the dim hallway, she peered into his face. His eyes widened with expectation. "Father," she said affectionately.

"Father . . ." he whispered. "Yes, my good girl."

She didn't have school the next day, and her parents had a day outing planned with one of Bren's colleagues and his wife. Auntie took her to Old Wheel for a puppet show. Cyril arrived to take her to the woods, and when she went to Reach, she found Nikolas there.

He waved, glad to see her.

She walked to him, trembling with anticipation. When she stood in front of him, she nibbled her lip.

"What is it?" he asked.

"Nikolas, I dream of blue men."

He smiled, open as his heart. "Oh, Secret, I'm so happy you dream, and now you speak. Tell me about the men!"

Secret took a deep breath. Then she paused. A swirling current rose inside her, and with it, a sense that she needed to begin with another dream, an earlier dream that wasn't hers. "I'd like to tell you the myths I learned from Old Woman first. She calls them the Myths of the Four,* about a dragon and dwarf and woman-wisp and orphan. The stories end with blue men, and that will lead to my own."

Nikolas sat on the ground with Cyril on his lap. He looked into her eyes the colors of night and day with his full attention, ready to listen.

---

* The full text of the Myths of the Four appears in Appendix II on pages 363–385.

XVII

Friendship with Old Woman and Nikolas

Secret had an enchanted time from the summer she was almost eight through her entire third year in school.

She couldn't help but to be changed by her use of speech. She was still quiet, by nature, but she was able to better express what she wanted.

Most of all, she wanted to go to the woods. That meant she needed to be in or near Old Wheel. So Secret asked to be enrolled in activities—handicrafts, science experiments, and other entertainments, all of which interested her. She was a willing pupil on the days she attended, but each time Cyril appeared in a doorway or at her feet, she slipped away with him, knowing it was safe to do so.

As those first summer weeks went by, Secret learned about one of her new friends.

Old Woman said she came from another land, though not as far as Secret might imagine. In this other land, Old Woman was born in a village where people lived simply and beautifully. There she had learned many of the skills, as well as the wondrous tales, she was teaching her young friend. The people grew, milked, butchered, baked, and milled all the food they needed. Sometimes, they traded with others from distant kingdoms, but usually, skilled craftspeople made clothing and shoes, pots and pans, tools and utensils, toys and games, furniture and linens, and dishes and cups. Some people in her village made lovely things to wear or put in one's home, and others could make music and tell tales. She claimed no one was ever hungry or without shelter, and everyone was given a chance to learn how they were gifted and what gave them joy.

Secret could hardly believe such a place existed, but she wanted to, so she chose not to doubt her friend.

Old Woman said she had lived happily in her native village, but when she became a young woman, she felt a call to explore. She knew there was more to the world than her own land and wanted to see the differences for herself. So she left her people and moved to the kingdom where Secret was born, to a small town near the far eastern border.

She found work in a textile mill dyeing wool, a skill she'd learned among her people aside from her knowledge of plants. Soon enough, she became proficient in the language, spoken and written, and learned the ways of the people there. She met and married a good, gentle man, and had two beloved children. Once her boy and girl were grown, after her husband died, she returned to her native village.

There, mourning the loss of her mate, Old Woman experienced a period of deep quiet. She spent many days and nights alone in the woods. She believed the stillness was a balm for her grief.

Several years later, she felt another call—to return to the kingdom where she'd lived most of her life. That time, however, she chose to live alone among the trees and plants and animals that gave her peace and comfort. She expected to remain where she was, in her cottage, until she was too frail to care for herself and needed the help of her own people again.

As the seasons changed one to the next, Secret and Old Woman walked through the woods together, which the girl enjoyed as much, and sometimes more, than sitting alone with stories. There was much to learn. Old Woman told her the names of what grew and explained how to use them—this plant's leaves cured stomachaches but had to be picked in summer, this plant's roots treated coughs but had to be gathered in winter.

She taught Secret through her senses. Secret rubbed this with her fingers, tasted that on the flat of her tongue. The textures, tastes, smells, and colors mattered. Everything mattered. A mistaken mushroom could bring death. The give of a pear's flesh noted its sweetness. The green tips of a certain tree assured the end of winter. Unlike Secret's grandmother, who found much in the woods to be nasty, dirty, and ugly, Old Woman declared all as it should be and was. Secret didn't know what made her ahmama think that way, but she was glad Old Woman saw things as she did, wonderful in many ways.

To collect what she learned, Secret decided to keep a log. Old Woman had written records of her own, gathered through many years, which Secret was welcome to study, but she encouraged her young friend to write her own observations.

"I'm old and this is rote. You're young and this is new," she said, making a special place for Secret to store her pen, ink, and blank book.

However, a log was not essential for Secret. All of this learning came naturally to her. There was a deeper wisdom in the practical knowledge. When Old Woman gave her a nibble of foxglove, before Old Woman could tell her what part of the body it affected, Secret felt a flutter in her heart. Sometimes, if she stood still and open, Secret sensed what plants could heal or do harm, or both, depending on how they were used. Her body tingled, cramped, or responded in some way to reveal the place inside where the plant's power would work. The girl was unsure whether to tell her friend this, so she didn't. Not then.

Secret also didn't tell Old Woman what happened when they went near a huge rounded rock that was not far from the cottage. It seemed to have been placed there deliberately, and impossibly so, because there were no other rocks comparable in size anywhere in

 the woods where Secret had been. Each time Secret was close to it, more so when she touched it, her little feet ached and she shook inside. She had a feeling the rock was a marker for this particular place and a guide that pointed to another.

But how could that be? she pondered as she pressed her hands against it and felt the core of her body spin like the needle on her father's compass. These thoughts she kept to herself, like a treasure.

When she and Old Woman weren't in the woods, Secret helped her with chores in and around the cottage.

At Secret's house, her mother prepared the family's meals, but Secret was rarely allowed to assist with washing, chopping, and cooking. Old Woman taught her to use a knife with care and how to make several simple dishes. These were all made of vegetables and legumes because her friend did not eat meat of any kind. When Secret asked why, Old Woman said her body felt better without it, but she also believed animals had a conscious nature with thoughts and feelings, different from plants, for which she had reverence. Although Secret knew this to be true, she didn't say so, not then.

Secret also did tasks that Elinor the cleaning woman, and on occasion her mother, tended to at her house, which mostly involved sweeping, dusting, and scouring.

And then there were the many tasks she had never seen done. With Old Woman, she helped to card wool and tried her hand at spinning. She harvested seeds, roots, and vegetables. Her fingers proved nimble with a needle and thread.

The mistakes she made as she learned—and there were many— were met with patient correction that did not sting. When Secret became noticeably frustrated, Old Woman soothed her with a quiet voice and gentle reminder to breathe. No adult Secret had ever known had such a manner. Most seemed to barely contain their frustration, including her teachers and parents.

"Where I am from, we have a saying. *Sticks and stones can break bones, but words and looks wound deeper.* Remember that, child, with yourself as well as others."

Secret thought the saying was very wise, and very true.

Now and then during the hours Secret spent with Old Woman, she thought of her ahmama. She remembered the unhurried attention she received, the delight her grandmother took in her actions and discoveries. She longed to see her grandmother again. Several times, during the first months after Secret spoke, the girl asked her mother why they didn't travel to see her grandmother. Too far, too expensive, too busy, had been Zavet's answers. Without being told, Secret knew she shouldn't ask why her ahmama didn't come to visit them. In all her years of silence, Secret had discovered that unseen boundaries were clearly not meant to be breached. There were some within herself she couldn't cross. For Secret, Old Woman filled a place her ahmama could not.

Sometimes, Secret wondered whether her friend would allow her to stay if she asked. With Old Woman, she wasn't afraid and didn't feel like a bother. The woman seemed to enjoy her company. Secret knew she would miss her father and he would miss her, but she wouldn't have to miss Nikolas because he could find her in the woods. Such notions she kept to herself. She knew they were bad, and she shouldn't think them, but she couldn't stop. They were with her whether she liked them or not.

So when Old Woman asked Secret about her family, Secret told the bare facts. Her mother could read, write, and speak all the languages of the world, make delicious stews, and didn't like to work when it was dark. Her father bought her books and treats, liked to look at maps, and worked in The Tallest Building at a very important job. When Old Woman asked about her friends, Secret didn't mention how she'd been teased at her first school and how difficult it was to make them at her current one. Instead, she told her about Nikolas, who was smart, funny, and brave and who liked to go to the woods as she did.

The latter was indisputable.

Nikolas managed to convince his father to let him practice with his sword and staff in the early mornings so that he could join his friends in the afternoon and at activities near Old Wheel. A guard accompanied him wherever he went and stood off at a polite distance. Even though the guard was sworn to protect Nikolas at the risk of his own life, the man's attention would sometimes drift.

If Cyril appeared in one of those moments, Nikolas knew he could make an escape and return before he was caught.

The first summer after Secret began to speak, their time together was brief. Nikolas explained that he went on a trip with his mother and sisters for several weeks every summer, and that this one would be no exception. Of course Secret was disappointed, but she was determined to have fun while they could. So, those warm days, they learned about each other.

Secret shared what she had with Old Woman about her mother and father. Nikolas talked of his two older sisters, who were as likely to coddle him as they were to ignore him, and of his parents, his father so often in meetings or traveling, his mother so often minding her children, servants, and charities.

They liked to observe and explore, so they spent much time at both. They stepped barefoot across slippery rocks in meandering streams and crept along the banks in search of newts, frogs, and turtles. When they found ripe berries, they gorged until their bellies ached. They walked in the sunny glades and under shady canopies. Secret taught him what she had learned thus far from Old Woman, the names and uses of plants around them. When Nikolas told her he liked learning the names because that made them special, not simply ordinary, Secret smiled. She, of course, felt the same way.

When autumn came and they returned to school, they waved in greeting each morning and sometimes played together when the children were let outside between lessons. Some of the children were more willing to include her in games and conversations. Despite being a girl from a family that wasn't old enough, Secret knew there were two reasons why circumstances were different. First, she could speak, which allowed her to interact in a way she hadn't before. Second, and perhaps most important, Nikolas was her friend, a fact he didn't hide or deny. That he accepted her was enough to prompt schoolmates to set aside their earlier judgments.

Together in the woods, they lay on the cooling ground to watch birds begin their journeys south and the rest gather in swirling groups that made them gasp with awe. They ate wild apples picked from ancient trees. They sat in the sun as Nikolas taught her to play his favorite strategy game with a set he kept hidden in a hollow tree. She proved a fast learner and good at the game. Secret entertained him with tales she had learned, more than she ever realized she'd committed to memory. As she had with Fig Tree and her little friends, Secret explained what made them different—history and story, myth and tale. Nikolas found this fascinating because the only tales he was told often came from old chronicles. Those stories were meant to educate him about his own history and legacy, rather than amuse him.

In the calm of winter, they walked to keep warm, searching the treetops and between trunks for birds and animals. Secret became pensive. The rush of spring slipped into the pulse of summer, which eased into the thrum of autumn. Winter was a waiting stillness. She thought of all she had witnessed through the seasons. Her quiet must have been profound then, because Nikolas asked what she was thinking. She told him. He joined her contemplative mood, and they shared thoughts on what they'd seen in the woods and at their homes. A mother hawk's diligent attention to her brood, that snatched a different mother's fledgling to feed her own young. Layers of dead leaves transformed into the foundation of new growth. A mouser stalking the royal stables, finding a nest of dead mice. How much birth and death there is, Nikolas said. Secret had to agree.

When spring returned, they found themselves mirthful and restless. They watched bees greet every new blossom. They ran through glades of wildflowers and grasses, pollen and seeds dotting their hair and clothes.

One day, he surprised her with the materials he'd collected to build two kites. They painted faces on the surfaces, his a dragon, hers a falcon, and watched them glare down from the cloudless sky. Secret laughed as she ran around the wide clearing, Nikolas opposite her, happy to be among the trees and breezes with her friend.

Month after month, season after season, Secret came to know Nikolas as much by the clandestine hours they had together as she did by observing him among others. She realized he didn't insist on being the leader or first pick in games. He didn't gloat if he won, and he didn't pout if he lost. When disputes erupted—someone went out of bounds, cut in, cheated—Nikolas was often the one to call for a pause to make sense of what happened. She never saw him be cruel to anyone on purpose or stand by and watch one child be hateful to another.

Near the end of her third year of school, one afternoon as Nikolas ran by in a blur, she thought of stories she'd read about boys of privilege who took what they wanted and were given all they asked for. She didn't know Nikolas to be spoiled or demanding. She wondered whether she would behave the same way given the same circumstances. If she'd been born that way, what would she claim and take, simply because she could? She felt a stir deep within her, something hollow and greedy, an emptiness waiting to be filled.

Nikolas suddenly knelt at her side, breathless. "I fell and found this. It's for you." In her hand, he put a blue-green cylindrical bead with a chip missing from one end. A friend grabbed him by the collar, and they ran off laughing.

She felt shame cover the dark place inside her at the same moment she smiled at the small wonder in her palm and the gift of his kind nature.

XVIII

She Reveals She Can Communicate with Creatures and Plants

BY SECRET'S FOURTH YEAR IN SCHOOL, WHEN SHE WAS NINE, she had become a girl more involved with the world around her. In school, she participated in a way she couldn't before, answering questions aloud and joining discussions. Her teachers encouraged her, glad to see her intelligence revealed in a way other than her tests and essays. She had made new friends, not many, but enough so that she almost always had someone to talk to at any time during her day. Nikolas told her he still appreciated her quiet ways, but he liked being able to talk with her, too.

Her parents noticed a great difference as well. Secret asked for what she wanted instead of pointing and engaged in conversations. Sometimes, Secret felt her mother wished she were still mute, but that was not the case with her father. Even though Bren had been angry when she said she no longer cared to eat meat—it had been a luxury in his own youth and only the poorest ate like cows and sheep—he took delight in her attempt to explain that she didn't want to eat what she thought could feel and think. Of course, her mother believed this was a phase, didn't argue, and fed her more beans, nuts, and cheese.

While Zavet did concern herself with Secret's marks in school, Bren was the one always curious about Secret's studies, what came easily to her, and what she found interesting. When he was home from traveling for his work, he still treated her to afternoon outings now and then. But since she became too old for story times, he took her to lectures he thought she, and he, would enjoy. Secret usually liked them, as well as the conversations she'd have with her father at a teahouse afterward.

To the friends she'd had the longest, Fig Tree and her courtyard companions, Secret appeared to have a new clarity in her eyes, a glow around her. What was special about her was always known to them, but they agreed most humans were not accustomed to such subtleties. Fig Tree herself posed a guess as to why Secret seemed brighter and others noticed.

A part of you bloomed when you began to speak in words. You were not meant to be so silent, Fig Tree said.

Secret felt the truth of this. She wondered what else she might not be meant to be, but nevertheless was.

More than her teachers or Nikolas or her father, Old Woman seemed the most gladdened by the difference in her young friend.

One day, Old Woman told her, "You're coming into your gifts."

"What do you mean?" Secret asked. She began to quiver, as if some part of her knew what was about to happen.

"What is essential about you is shining through to others. When you were silent, this was much easier to hide," Old Woman said.

"I don't tell everything. I hardly say anything at all, really."

"There's no need to. As my people say, gold's nature is to glow."

Secret brushed a lock of black hair from her face then stared at her hands. The feeling in her belly intensified, as if something wanted to escape. At times, she had thought about telling Old Woman certain secrets about herself but didn't. Right then, she felt the need to tell what she'd never told, what she treasured about herself but guarded with care.

"Are gifts like special powers?"

"You are kind and gentle. Being kind and gentle are both gifts and powers in your case."

"No—*special* powers."

Old Woman became very still and looked into the girl's eyes. "What example can you give me?"

Because she trusted Old Woman, she said, "I can hear and speak to creatures and plants."

The woman's eyes conveyed sincere curiosity. "In what ways?"

"Today, when I was fetching water at the stream, a bird flew to a branch nearby. As I do sometimes, I became quiet inside and invited her to speak to me."

"What did she say?" Old Woman asked.

Secret took a deep breath and paused. Then she told of the bird that shared the mystery of how she built her nest of mud.

"That is wonderful! What other stories have been shared with you?"

Secret blinked. "Bees tell each other where flowers are with dances that line up with the sun. And they are all female, except for the few that are male and live just long enough to mate with the queen. And they recognize faces. Remember when we first visited the hive in the beech tree and they bumped at our heads? They were seeing who we were. Those bees know us, and the ones who bumped us told the rest in the hive, and none of them will bat at us again."

"Fascinating. And what else?"

With hardly a breath between tales, Secret told of the bee in the petrified tree that told of a wound and a wolf and of her friend Fig Tree, who lived in her courtyard, and of the ants she saved from the mean boy's stomping foot. She spoke of the crow that showed her the land as it was long ago, a great forest that protected a village, a meadow, and a patch of fertile fields.

Old Woman nodded, her features soft. Cyril appeared suddenly, squeaking with alarm, and climbed up the woman's back. Although Secret asked in words that weren't words what had upset him, Cyril's reply was vague, the image of a lid shutting closed.

"There, there, little one," Old Woman said. She brushed his whiskers with her finger. "As for you, Secret, you were very brave to tell me this about yourself. You honor me with your trust. I want you to know I believe you."

"You do?" Secret asked.

"Yes, child. Everything, the trees and the bees, all things, speak in their own way. It is rightful to give them heed."

"I didn't think anyone else could do this," Secret said.

"Anyone can learn something if she pays attention. But you—you have a gift far greater. An extraordinary gift. When I was young, I had an affinity for plants and animals, but rare were the instances I experienced what comes with ease to you. Cyril is my loyal friend, but I cannot talk with him as you can. I know him through our familiarity and our feelings. You are very fortunate, child. Nature knows who you are and reveals the wonder of awareness, the mysterious bond of all things."

Secret was glad she told her friend and that Old Woman not only believed her but also thought the gift—the power—was a special one at that.

Encouraged by Old Woman's affirmation, Secret decided to tell Nikolas about what she could do. He had already seen for himself the interaction she had with animals, how the wild creatures had no fear of her, or she of them. She would attempt to explain why that was so.

The next time they were in the woods together, she told Nikolas all that Fig Tree had revealed about her life in the courtyard before Secret lived in the row house.

"That's a good story. Are you making up ones of your own now?" he asked.

"No," she said. "That's what she told me. I can hear and talk to creatures and plants."

The expression he wore revealed nothing. He asked her to share what she knew of Cyril, and Reach, and the robin that preened herself above their heads, so she did.

"When did you first know you could do this?" he asked.

"I went to visit my grandmother in another kingdom when I was very young. I heard bees humming and followed the sound. I went into a hollow tree where they were gathering. One told me a story of these men in the woods and a little girl and a man with a bloody wound on his body and the wolf who was with him."

Nikolas nodded, listening.

"That was the first time. It wasn't until we moved to the house where we live now, where I found Fig Tree, that I learned I could speak to them if I tried."

"Do they speak in words, like people?"

"Not as we think of it. Most of the time, I see pictures in my mind, but I know things about what I see. I know what they mean. I can translate the images into words."

"Similar to what your mother does, translating one language into another?"

Secret tensed and held her breath a moment. That observation, although accurate, bristled her. She didn't want to be compared to her mother, even if what they could do seemed similar. "Yes, in a way," she said finally.

"And when you speak to them, what do you do?"

"I think of images that have the meanings of what I want to say."

"Is it like having someone talk to you all the time without stopping?" he asked.

Secret shook her head. "Sometimes it happens without trying, but usually, I have to be still and concentrate. I have to be . . . open. I have to want to hear, and they have to want to talk."

"Very mysterious," he said with a grin.

His response put Secret at ease. Her closest friends had not made fun of her or shamed her, and this bolstered Secret's confidence.

At school, her friends liked when she told them tales she had learned from books, so Secret began to tell what she had heard from other sources. She assumed the stories from the creatures and plants themselves would fascinate them, too.

During playtime, she sat under the achy apple tree and recited stories. The two or three friends who listened at any one time increased to little groups of five or six, then to a small crowd. Secret was pleased so many others were curious and entertained. The children agreed she was an excellent storyteller. Secret was glad to finally be known for something other than her strange eyes or past silence or her parents' reputations.

Then one day, a boy asked where she learned the stories. With a clear, steady voice, Secret said, "From the animals, insects, plants, and trees."

He laughed at her and gathered schoolmates to hear her repeat what she said.

"I know these stories because animals and plants tell them to me," she said, her tone defiant but wounded.

The other children laughed in response.

"So when you go off to sit under the trees by yourself and stare at nothing, they're *speaking* to you?" a girl asked.

"In their way, yes," Secret said. Embarrassment twisted in her belly. Her skin flushed hot.

Nikolas appeared as the taunts and giggles grew louder.

"What a liar!"

"My mother said her mother is crazy, and she must be, too!"

"That's witch talk!"

"Everybody knows animals can't speak!"

"Plants don't even have mouths!"

Secret wanted to cover her ears and run but knew that would only make things worse.

Nikolas glanced at her as the laughter continued, then looked at the boy who had provoked the teasing. The boy told him what Secret had said.

She met Nikolas's eyes, the color of myth suddenly deeper. She realized she didn't know what he truly thought. He had listened to her explanation weeks before but didn't acknowledge whether he believed she told the truth. She suddenly feared his betrayal.

"That's enough," Nikolas said with an edge to his voice. "There's no reason to make fun of her. You can like the stories no matter where they came from."

He stood next to her, calm and quiet. He didn't argue with anyone or shout retorts. Soon, the children dispersed with whispers and giggles.

"Thank you," she said.

"You don't have to thank me, Secret."

She paused, then asked, "Do you believe me? That I can speak to them?"

"I have no proof to say yes or no. I can't do what you say you can do. But you aren't known as a liar, and I don't think you've ever lied to me," Nikolas said.

"I tell the truth," she said.

"Then I believe what you say," Nikolas said.

Secret was hurt by the way her schoolmates reacted, but she was grateful Nikolas and Old Woman had been kind. She had kept this ability to herself for so long. She wanted to share this part of who she was, especially among those closest to her.

She didn't expect what happened next.

One afternoon as her mother prepared dinner, Secret sat at the table with her schoolwork. Zavet was in good spirits, so much that she had hardly muttered in weeks. Secret had no idea what had made her mother seemingly so cheerful. The girl was glad for those good mother days, when Zavet's usual distant and somber mood seemed like a memory.

If there was a time to share a surprise with her mother, that moment was better than any. She called her mother's name and said she wished to tell her a story. Secret spoke of the apple tree at her school and how it complained of the limbs that had been cut and the worms that nibbled its fruit.

"You have a clever imagination," Zavet said. Her chewed bottom lip curved up in an uncommon endearing smile.

"I didn't imagine it," Secret said. "The tree told me so."

"Nonsense, Secret."

"But it's true."

Zavet set down a wooden spoon with a clatter. She pivoted her body away from the stove and toward Secret, her not-quite-looking but somehow staring gaze on her daughter.

"Listen to me," Zavet said.

Secret bent her head. Her hair draped around her face.

"Listen to me well, girl. A long time ago, I once thought I could hear things I couldn't possibly hear. People tried to set me straight when I was near your age, but I was stubborn and contrary. Oh, I knew what was real and true. Do you know what happened? I was sent away, put away, talked down, tied down, until I realized I was in error. I suffered from my mistakes in ways you cannot imagine."

Secret sensed her mother had turned back. She lifted only her eyes and saw she was correct.

"Nothing is wrong with imagination until it is confused with what is real. Sometimes you are only dealing with thoughts. If you ignore the irksome thoughts, they will go away. It's for your own good that you understand this. Anyone who tells you otherwise is trying to deceive you, or is simply a liar, or is very confused himself."

A feeling like loneliness, only colder, sapped Secret's blood of heat. "You don't believe me?"

"Of course I don't believe you," her mother said. "Who in her right mind would?"

"But—" Secret remembered what Zavet had said the day Secret received the nesting dolls, that her mother knew things she couldn't possibly know. Again, another reference, but this time Zavet declared she'd been wrong about what she perceived.

"Well?"

"But you said once before, you knew things you couldn't know. Your brother, he knew and you didn't and then . . ."

"I was confused, as you are now," Zavet said firmly.

Doubt flooded Secret from head to toe. Was she making up all of this because she wanted to believe it? But what about Cyril leading her safely to the woods? What about the crow's view of their town, which Secret could verify on a map?

"You haven't told anyone, have you?" her mother asked.

"No, Mother," she said. Secret understood that was the right answer, and she decided she wouldn't risk telling her father now.

"See that you don't. Now, go to the cupboard and give me the basket of mushrooms. There are extra for your stew, as you like."

Secret did as she was told. When she glanced at the caps, she noticed one unlike the rest that she couldn't identify. When she touched it, her body tingled, and a feeling of alarm rose in her stomach. No, that wasn't her imagination.

"Here. But that one doesn't look like the others. I don't want to eat it," Secret said, pointing.

Her mother took the mushroom in her hand and sniffed it. She frowned. "Hmm. The market vendor made a dangerous mistake."

"I'll throw it outside," Secret said, snatching it from her mother's hand.

When Secret went into the courtyard, she threw the mushroom under Fig Tree, mashed it with the heel of her shoe, and sat under the branches. The tree reached to brush Secret's face, but she dodged away. Her thoughts were gray and confused.

The difference between what was real and what was make-believe was typically clear, but her ability defied stark distinctions.

Nikolas believed her but he was only a child, and her schoolmates didn't, and they were children, too.

Old Woman believed her, but she lived alone with only creatures and plants to talk to.

Her mother did not believe her, but she claimed she could read and speak any language in the world, which seemed as impossible as what Secret could do, but people believed Zavet.

Secret spent many afternoons trying to sort through her confusion.

Why would Old Woman call what she could do a gift and her mother call it nonsense? What if Secret had convinced herself she could communicate with creatures and plants—tricked herself—because she had been lonely? If so, could she convince herself otherwise?

But what if the ability was genuine, a true gift? She would be able to ignore that away, wouldn't she? In the end, Secret didn't want to, not then, not yet, although that separation would come. She wanted to see the beauty the creatures and plants showed her even when it meant seeing anguish, too.

However, Secret realized she couldn't reveal herself in this way again. She hated being teased and feared what her mother might do . . . Secret decided she must hide and control the gift.

XIX

Her Father's Interest in The Mapmaker's War

IN SECRET'S FIFTH YEAR OF SCHOOL, WHEN SHE WAS TEN, HER history teacher announced a lecture to be held in town on a subject they were currently studying. Students who attended and wrote an essay about what they learned would receive bonus marks.

The lecture's title was "Paleography in the Chronicles in the Immediate Era of The Mapmaker's War."

Secret wasn't intrigued by the analysis of old writing or the war itself, especially not the latter. Her history teacher had lingered on that ancient war for too long. Endless accounts of battles that encompassed their kingdom and lands to the east and northeast. Minutiae about strategy and tactics. She was often nauseated or had a headache as the teacher droned on.

Several of the boys in her class, however, couldn't seem to get their fill, including Nikolas. Another side of him emerged as he argued about details with the teacher. Since he was a small boy, he had been taught the history of the kingdom he would one day rule. Even to Secret, who knew Nikolas well, his display of knowledge sometimes seemed tinged with arrogance.

She had no wish to attend the lecture—she didn't need the extra marks—but one evening, her father happened to see the handbill poking out from her schoolwork.

"How did I miss this announcement?" he asked. "Ah—with the traveling lately, so much escapes my notice. Do you know what the scholar will discuss, my learned pet?"

"We were told he's begun a new translation of the kingdom's earliest records—"

"That hasn't been done in decades! The old ones are somewhat tedious."

"This fellow noticed a difference in the writing itself. The shapes of the letters. There are questions about why and how that's the case," she said.

"I must know," her father said, "and of course you will join me to find out!"

Secret nodded. She knew she couldn't bear his disappointment if she refused. He did seem to miss her when he'd been away on a trip for some time.

"Perhaps I'll acquire a piece of the puzzle, mine and yours," Bren said. "We must find a means to return to our origins, my pet, to a moment before what was ours was taken away. I feel, though, it draws ever closer."

He patted her head as he stepped by to go to the stairs. She knew what he was referring to. As long as her father had told her myths, legends, and tales, he included the story of his quest for an apocryphal past. The lecture would feed his obsession that once, long ago, his family had been prominent and powerful, in service to the king.

On the day Secret went to the lecture with her enthusiastic father, that history, past and present, personal and collective, lingered in the periphery of her thoughts.

They arrived at the hall moments before the scholar walked to the podium. An easel stacked with placards stood close enough for him to reach. Bren rushed to the front row. He was dejected to find no vacant seats and settled them toward the middle of the room. She saw him flick the hidden lever that silenced his Tell-a-Bell. Secret pretended not to notice how he twitched in his chair, his anticipation so childlike that she felt embarrassed.

Secret removed a bound notebook from her satchel, opened it, and held her pencil at the ready. During the lengthy presentation—complete with large-scale drawings of what the scholar found—Bren sat as if under a spell. Secret hardly heard a word, bored by the excruciating details.

"Welcome, ladies and gentlemen . . . an honor . . . as the first illustration depicts . . ."

". . . the thickness of the parchment . . ."

". . . distinctive upward flourish . . ."

". . . syntactical idiosyncrasies . . . posit that this was *not* a correction in fact . . ."

Occasionally, Secret looked up from the tiny sketches she was drawing to study the audience. A schoolmate three rows away recognized Secret, and the girl rolled her eyes with exasperation. Secret pressed her lips together to stifle a giggle. Toward the front right corner of the room, she noticed the chestnut-haired boy who was in her history class but to whom she never spoke. Many of the girls in her year, and the ones above, thought he was handsome, and Secret had to agree.

She didn't realize she was staring until another boy next to him stared back. Nikolas. He raised his eyebrows and nudged his head toward the boy. Secret frowned at Nikolas then looked down before the warm flush in her chest flooded her face.

Eyes lowered, Secret turned a new page in her book and drew neat little circles in rows. Then she began to link them, careful of the symmetry, and colored in the blank spaces where they overlapped. She stared at them. Her focus shifted. The dark intersections, which held the spheres together, opened into voids. Deep within, she pitched forward, her body threatening to follow the spiral that had begun inside.

Her father's wild applause startled her. She was surprised to find herself in the chair, in that room. Secret joined in, hot and shaky as if a horrible fever had taken hold.

"That was excellent! Riveting! I want to speak to the scholar. Will you indulge your father with patience?" he asked.

"Why don't I meet you at the teahouse we both like, the one on the south corner a few doors away?" she said.

"Very well. This is a safe ward, but don't wander too far if I'm delayed," he said. Bren squared his coat and hurried to the front of the room.

As Secret packed the bound book in her satchel, Nikolas appeared next to her. His guard stood out of earshot.

"That wasn't nearly as interesting as I'd hoped," he said.

"Well, it wasn't about the war. This had nothing to do with the event itself," Secret said. She forced herself to still her trembling.

"I've seen the original chronicles. The pages and writing didn't seem different to me," he said.

"Now you'll have to look more closely," she said. In the corner of her eye, she glimpsed the chestnut-haired boy. He slipped through the thinning crowd, headed toward them. Her palms moistened, and her head throbbed. "I'm supposed to meet my father at a teahouse now. I'll see you soon." She glanced behind Nikolas and hoisted the satchel on her shoulder.

Nikolas turned his head quickly. His smirk was playful. "Good-bye then."

Instead of going straight to the teahouse, Secret decided to take a brief walk despite the dreary weather. She found that movement soothed her shakiness, but she was weakened as though she'd had a frightening shock. She followed along the gold-tiled plaza, to the east, looking toward the sharp edge of The Tallest Building's shadow at her side. Old Wheel was hidden behind it. She paused to see whether Cyril would appear, but he didn't.

She turned left into the ward. She could hardly hear a newsbox, which was just as well because she hadn't yet developed the ability to ignore them as others appeared to do. Secret could only tolerate so much of the endless, repeated litany of horrors, misfortunes, and trivia.

She heard the sound of scraping metal and tumbling debris.

When she turned a corner, a rope blocked her entrance. Men loaded high-sided carts with crumbled mortar and broken bricks. Muscular dray horses tousled their manes and tails. Their hooves kicked at bare earth. The cobblestone street and sidewalks were gone. Several buildings had been demolished. A large sign read: NEW DEVELOPMENTS COMING SOON (COURTESY OF FM INC).

Secret reached over the rope to caress one of the horses. A wound on his shoulder was inflamed, and the skin around it was crusted. Carefully, Secret hovered her hand above the sore place, wishing she could heal it. The horse pressed his nose against her forehead. He told her their loads were too heavy and they weren't given enough rest. Secret patted his neck and shoulder until she remembered she must meet her father.

Bren was outside the teahouse absorbed in a jovial conversation with a man he seemed to know well. Her father introduced her and handed her coins to purchase a treat. She held the gold and silver circles in her palm, separate, no bond between them.

"Father, I'm not feeling well," she said.

He looked at her with concern, ended his chat, and led them to the lot where he had secured the two-horse cart. The entire way home, she could hardly breathe. Her father let her off at the front of their house before he went to return the cart and stable the horses.

Secret unlocked the door with the hidden key near the steps, hoping her mother was away on a walk even on a darkening day like that. Zavet was not at her worktable when Secret wrenched the back door's great bobbin, slipped through the gap, and crawled under Fig Tree's branches.

A vibration rippled into her chest, beyond her ribs, deep into the well of her belly. Her heart beat faster. She breathed in rapid bursts. Dizzy, Secret clutched the tree's limbs as sharp pains ripped like lightning through the front of her body. She looked down expecting to see a ragged hole between her ribs.

The piercing intensity waned to an ache that pounded through her feet, hips, and shoulders.

She shook as she remembered she'd had this wounded sensation before.

The first time was in the alley next to the grate, when she seemed to know a well had stood there once. She experienced it next when her mother gave her the nesting dolls, then again every time she was near the big rock in the woods.

In those moments, the impressions and images that emerged made her curious and her body twinged as if to hold her attention. But this time, she was afraid and felt intense pain.

As she sat under Fig Tree and huddled her legs to her chest, she tried to figure out what the moments had in common, as if that might explain what caused them, but they seemed random. They happened without warning.

That notion frightened her even more. What if it happened again, but worse? Why did it happen at all? Secret was certain no one else experienced such things. She had never read about or heard anyone speak of it. The impressions and images seemed to come from nowhere but sometimes felt as if they were hidden, then found, within her. It wasn't quite the same as when she spoke to creatures and plants, although there was a similarity in the way the images formed clearly in her mind. But with the creatures and plants, she never endured physical pain or fear.

"I'm sick. Something is wrong with me," she whispered.

You have a mystery in your blood, Fig Tree said. *Breathe, little one. Breathe.*

She lashed out and struck one of the tree's branches with her fist. Her forehead pulsed where the queen bee had left her sting, which enraged her all the more. She had neither sought nor asked for what happened to her in the dead hollow tree—what had followed since, to this very moment.

"I'm not right, not right at all," she said as she pulled at her hair and shut her eyes.

You are wondrous, Secret, Fig Tree said.

Quiet! Secret said.

She folded her arms on her knees and dropped her head. Her pulse slowed although she was still shaking from the shock. Without a doubt, she knew she couldn't speak of this to anyone, not her father, especially not her mother, not even Old Woman. She was not ready to discuss it, to admit it to anyone else.

"This is all my imagination, this is all my imagination, this is all my imagination," she whispered, as if repeating the words could make them true.

XX

Foreboding in Town

NO SMELL OR TASTE, NO SOUND OR SIGHT, BUT FEEL WHAT IS here. Look over a shoulder. Glance at the closed door. Search the empty room. Nothing is different, yet nothing is the same. It seems ominous, but what could it be?

The newsboxes give no clear hint. Outside, away, brutality erupts in distant places. Such mayhem is considered unstructured, uncivilized, by those who don't participate. Elsewhere, violence conducts itself with planning. Such activity is justified by those who condone it. Yet, somehow, the familiar disorder seems closer, pressing, as if it's right outside the gates. But the town has no gates, no walls.

Let the day go on as usual. Wait among the carts and the reined beasts. Deliver the children to their safe destinations. Enter the buildings, the rooms, the niches where honest work earns honest pay. Sit. Feel it. What is that sensation which runs up spines, lodges in throats, and sinks stomachs?

Children of the same ages sit clustered together in various parts of town, as they do almost every day. They learn the exact same things at the exact same time. Such is the intent, which serves a purpose. In the day nurseries, the small ones sleep and play according to schedule. The training begins when they are young so that later, in another form, in another setting, the monotony will be expected and comforting.

Within The Tallest Building, there is talk of doing more with less to get more. Such is the logic of efficiency and progress. This is expected by the few. Within the smaller buildings, most of them owned by the owner of the tallest one, the talk becomes whispers. The ones who whisper understand the want for more. Because they do, they will do more for less. Such is the logic of security. This is expected of the many.

Foreboding enters into and emanates from The Tallest Building. Speculations arise. Opportunity knocks. Proposals develop. All is kept secret. Those within identify a danger to contain, or block. Perception is nine-tenths of the truth. Everyone knows the common enemy although no one has seen its whole face. The newsboxes do not speak its hidden name, yet everyone knows what it is. Even the children.

XXI

The Dreams of a Mysterious Symbol

THROUGHOUT THE REST OF HER FIFTH YEAR OF SCHOOL, SE-
cret kept herself busy with schoolwork, chores with Old Woman,
and games with Nikolas. She discovered she didn't think of the
peculiar things that happened to her as long as she kept her mind
and hands at some task. Whether this was a matter of distraction or
focus, she didn't care. For almost a year, she didn't endure another
one of those occurrences.

Then, not long after her eleventh birthday, during her sixth
year of school, Secret was in the courtyard reading a collection of
folklore her father had given her. She was having a peaceful day. All
seemed well until a sudden exhaustion drained her strength. As the
soles of her feet and joints of her arms and legs began to ache, she
knew what was about to overtake her.

There at Fig Tree's roots, in the dream that formed, she stumbled through a dark forest. A beast, stealthy and menacing, followed
her at a distance. She tripped and turned to look at the obstacle.

In the darkness, she could see a symbol carved in flat stone. She
paused despite the pursuer's persistent gait. She tried to lift the
stone but it was immobile, as if rooted in the
dirt. She memorized the square with the circle,
triangle, and flame within. She knew she had to
seek another symbol. If she did, it would lead
her to a place of safety. Then she ran and ran
until she was awake.

She sat up and stared at her throbbing palms.

Believe what is in you is true, Fig Tree said without saying.

For several weeks, the symbol returned again and again in her dreams, but the dreams weren't always the same. The symbol appeared in different places. It was etched in a cobblestone, or painted in front of a shop, or scribbled imprecisely on a slate board. Yet when she dreamed of it set in stone, on the ground, she awoke with a sense of longing. She wanted to know what it meant, to what person or place it was linked. Again and again, she drew what she had seen, sometimes coloring or decorating the various sections, as if that would help her understand.

One day when her father was not at work and Secret was not at school, Bren found her in the courtyard and asked if she wanted to go into town for a sweet. During the past year, he had been traveling more often and was away for longer periods. Bren hadn't treated her to an outing in months. Secret gladly agreed to join him. As she gathered her materials, her father bent down to pick up her half-finished drawing. Her reach was too short to grab it from him.

"What is this?" he asked. He studied it closely. "May I have it?"

"I haven't finished coloring it," Secret said.

"This is lovely enough. The figure looks familiar. Where did you see it?"

"It appeared in a dream," she said. She saw no reason to lie, although she wished he hadn't seen it. She didn't want to talk about it.

"Did it? Are you certain?" her father asked.

"Yes."

"What a precise design to dream." He studied her face, then patted the top of her dark head. "Come, let's have our jaunt."

Secret was glad he asked no more. However, from that day onward, Secret's father would occasionally ask about the symbol she claimed to have dreamed about.

"Did you see it while on an outing at school?"

"No, Father," she said.

"Did you spot it while marketing with your mother?"

"No, Father," she said.

"Did you notice it while with Auntie?"

"No, Father," she said.

Between inquiries, he surprised her with books of myth and lore so magnificent even her mother remarked on their beauty and expense. After a while a shadowy feeling rose inside Secret. He wanted something, she sensed. Then the gifts stopped, but the questions did not.

By the middle of winter, each time he asked, Bren became ever more angry, his voice dark and stern. Secret wasn't lying, but the truth mattered little to her father.

"You could not have dreamed this. Where did you see it?"

"In a dream," Secret said.

"You are a bad girl. That's a lie. You've been places you shouldn't be."

Secret willed herself to be still. Any movement of her face or body might give her away. She had indeed been places neither her father nor her mother knew, without their permission. That was a fact. However, she was honest that she recalled the symbol from a dream.

"No, Father. I tell the truth," she said.

"Admit what you've done, or you'll be punished. You have one night to consider your decision. If you don't tell me where you saw the symbol, I will—" Then he paused, his eyes narrowing, to think of the perfect penalty. "I will cut your hair, bit by bit, until you reveal the answer."

Secret's jaw fell slack. The shock of his words made her numb. "No, you can't. You won't. I'm telling you the truth," she said.

"One night!" Bren said. "Go to your room."

Secret chose not to lie, although she knew what she would lose.

On the first night, as her father trimmed away the edge of her black hair, her mother stood in the corner and said, "It's for your own good."

Each night, her father asked, "Where did you see the symbol?"

"In a dream," Secret said.

Again, *snip, snip, snip*. Her father swept the pieces into her mother's hands. Zavet walked into the parlor and threw them in the fire.

"Go to your room," he said.

On the third, sixth, and ninth nights, the girl tried to convince her mother she spoke the truth.

"It is wrong to lie to your father," Zavet replied.

"I'm not lying," Secret said.

"He believes you are."

"And what do you believe?" Secret asked.

Each of these three nights, Zavet closed her eyes, put her face in her hands, and sighed with a loud huff. The girl stared at her mother. She suspected Zavet thought she told the truth. Secret couldn't explain why she felt that way or why her mother so easily complied with her father's intentions. Zavet cooperated with her father in word and deed from the first cut. But she had done so with detachment, as if she were not fully present in her own actions.

As confused as she was by her mother, Secret couldn't fathom her father's sudden cruelty or what she had done to deserve it. There had been instances when he teased her or brushed her aside, which hurt her feelings, but he had never been as harsh as this.

Night after night, day after day, a hard knot in her stomach became larger, tighter, hotter. Sometimes it pounded under her skin and sometimes it threatened to push up her throat. But Secret knew better than to cry or scream because neither would do any good. They wouldn't listen to her. She felt guilty for her hateful thoughts about her parents, but she could not stop them, as it seemed they, too, could not stop themselves.

On the twelfth night, a full foot of Secret's hair was gone. How much more would her father take? Cut until it was short as a boy's? Shave her bald?

On the thirteenth night, there was a loud *rap-rap, rap-rap* on the door soon after dinner. From her room, Secret couldn't distinguish the voices. A courier might have arrived with a package but Secret couldn't recall a delivery being made so late before. She couldn't fathom there was company for her parents. They never had guests in the house, rather meeting couples instead at an eatery or hall. Secret was certain no one had come for her. She never asked to have a friend visit to play. She was afraid of the unpleasant impression her mother would make.

A few moments later, her father called her down to the kitchen. Her heart thickened with dread.

She paused at the base of the stairway. She heard her father talking. He sounded apologetic, even timid, as he spoke of plans to redecorate their modest home, an undertaking he and his wife had yet to find time to attend to.

Secret entered the room. Her eyes traveled from the floor to the dining table, where the scissors lay shiny on the edge of a bowl of pears. Next to that was a bound parcel of papers held down by an open book. Richly colored, the illustration on one page was a girl reaching her foot toward a shoe. The facing page was text, embellished with decorative initials. Its beauty distracted her for an instant. Then she stood straight and faced the three adults in front of her.

"Good evening, Secret," Fewmany said.

"Good evening, sir."

Secret had encountered him since their first introduction at the grand ball four years earlier. On rare occasions when she went with her father to his office, and once or twice at an evening performance, Secret saw him, minded her manners, and kept her distance. Fewmany always made it a point to greet her, attentive to etiquette as well, even with a child.

That night, as her father offered him a seat and they lowered onto cushioned benches with purpose, Secret thought that Fewmany looked the same as he had the first time she met him. The bright eyes, glinting teeth, and fine coat. The tiny bell at his ear.

She suspected he was quite older than her father, but she couldn't determine how much. The magnate had a timeless quality to him.

"Thank you for personally delivering the documents I forgot," Bren said, his hand gesturing toward the parcel nearby.

"'Twas no trouble. My carriage passes straight through this ward every morning and evening," Fewmany said.

Secret took a slow, constricted breath. She glanced at her mother, silent and apart from the seated men.

"While you're here, there is something I'd like you to see," Bren said. He pulled a sheet of paper from below the bound documents and slipped it toward Fewmany. Secret's drawing of the symbol was exposed for all to examine.

"My daughter drew this. Do you recognize it?" Bren asked.

As Fewmany leaned over the table to study it, Secret glanced at the scissors. Her eyesight blurred not with tears but with fury. She pressed her arms to her side to resist the fierce compulsion to drive the blades straight through Fewmany's heart, then her father's, then her mother's, twice.

"Why, it does seem I've seen it somewhere before," Fewmany said at last, pushing the drawing aside casually. His fingertips moved to the gilded edges of the book within his reach. With a mindless flick, his attention elsewhere, he turned to a new page. The illustration was of a fox chasing a hen. "Secret, think carefully about what I'm about to ask. Tell me, did you see that in town?"

"No," Secret replied. In the silent pause between words, her head tingled and her hair grew one inch.

"Did you see it in a book?" Fewmany asked.

"No," Secret replied. Again, her hair grew.

"Did you see it in a wooded place?"

"No," she said. Then again, another inch. She lowered her eyes to her chest.

With each truthful answer, Secret's hair crept longer, curling in loose black spirals past her shoulder blades, reaching down her back. A primal will, stronger than her conscious one, had seized her. It evidenced that what had been taken could be restored to her.

Then with the thirteenth question, instead of answering no, she chose to say, "I saw it in a dream."

She glanced at her mother. Zavet set her teeth in the grooves of her bottom lip. A drop of blood landed on Zavet's hand and she wiped it away.

Secret looked at each adult in turn. Their eyes were wide. To ensure there was no doubt about the mystery they'd witnessed, Secret's hair descended to her waist with a lithe serpent stretch. Her father blinked and rubbed his eyes as if he'd been asleep. Her mother cast her gaze to the floor as she folded her bloody bottom lip under her top one.

The magnate narrowed his lids with ambiguous scrutiny. His eyes reflected a sinister amusement. Secret forced herself to face him. As they looked at each other, she felt a rending tension in the pit of her stomach, a force pulling her forward and pushing away equally. She stood inert, confused by her feelings.

Then Fewmany smiled as if he were charmed. Secret understood that, for him, what happened was a game, one he intended to win. She knew neither the rules nor the prize, but that the symbol she'd drawn was valuable to him. Fewmany closed the book gently, spread his hands across the top of it, and pulled it toward his chest. His ring glimmered. She knew, somehow, the book had been meant as a reward for her cooperation, withheld now that she hadn't given an answer that satisfied him.

"May I be excused?" Secret asked, her gaze fixed downward.

"Yes," her mother said.

"Goodnight, sir," Secret said.

"Mmm-hmm. Indeed, indeed," Fewmany replied.

As Secret crossed the threshold to the stairs, a spider descended on a silk thread and landed on her shoulder. The spider said she marveled at Secret's ability to spin so many threads at once. Secret didn't know how her body managed to grow her hair so quickly, but the effect was sufficiently unsettling for the conspiratorial adults who had wanted something from her she couldn't give.

Secret sat on her bed. She felt the drape of her hair anchor her in place and its warmth give her comfort once again. The knot that had been in her belly for days constricted and buried itself, hidden like a motive. Secret looked at the nesting dolls on her shelf. She remembered the game she once played with them, which she called When I Get Big.

"When I get big," she said to the spider that crept along her arm, "I'll go far away and never come back."

Although Secret had managed to cover what her father did under a cloak's hood for almost two weeks, drawing stares from her classmates and teachers, she hadn't been able to hide it in her thoughts. Even with her hair grown back now, she felt herself touched in a way she didn't wish to be. Her father had never struck her, but there had been violence in his hands as he cut what was hers, a threat in his voice when he spoke to her. Secret felt suspicious of her father—and, too, of her mother. Zavet was no mere witness. The truth behind their actions would be revealed in due time, months before the Plague of Silences finally struck, but the damage to Secret could not be undone.

The dark child seemed darker to those who knew her best.

When Secret visited Old Woman not long after that terrible night, the girl spoke only when spoken to, and then only in brief replies.

"What troubles you so?" Old Woman asked.

Secret kept her head bent as she sat on the floor near the door and sorted seeds into a bowl. Her friend was rarely so direct, allowing Secret to talk of her thoughts when she wished to. For a moment, she wanted to tell everything but couldn't.

The woman brushed a finger against the girl's temple and held up her hand between them. A spider swayed below her fingertips on an invisible line.

"Spin elsewhere, small one," she said to the spider. "Secret, you are safe here. You're free to speak without judgment or punishment. Do you know that?"

"Yes," Secret said, but she didn't believe it. She knew nothing was without consequence, even the truth.

Old Woman turned away and walked to the table. Secret glanced at her friend's stooping back where the white braid trailed along her spine. The girl swallowed an unwanted sob, continued her work, then said, "I had a dream which frightened me. I dreamed I was being chased by something, or someone, and I tripped, and on the ground was a strange symbol carved in stone."

In her peripheral sight, Secret saw Old Woman go to the bench that had been recently moved near the hearth, next to the large cauldron, which had always been in that same place. "What frightened you? How did you feel?"

"I had to get away. Whatever chased me meant me harm. I knew the symbol would lead me somewhere safe."

"How would you describe it?"

"There was a square, and inside of it were shapes. A circle, a triangle, and something that resembled a flame. No, not quite a flame," Secret said as she realized the last shape was one she had drawn and colored at the lecture she'd attended with her father many months before. She chose to ignore the coincidence. "The center is like the intersection between two circles."

Secret looked up to see Old Woman staring at her clasped hands.

"Have you dreamed of it since?" Old Woman asked.

"Yes. Several times. Usually I only see the symbol. I'm not always chased."

In a flailing frenzy, Cyril sprinted across Secret's lap, spilled the seeds, crawled up Old Woman's arm, and pressed his face into her neck chattering as if he'd escaped a goshawk's pursuit. Old Woman stroked his tail in silence, her mouth a narrow line.

Secret was relieved by his interruption. She didn't know

whether her friend would continue to question her, or how much she could stand to contain. What her parents had done and what the adults had witnessed caused her shame.

"I'm glad you were willing to share your dream with me, child. When you speak of something, you change its power. How do you feel now?" Old Woman asked.

"A little better," Secret said, and she did, at least about the dream.

Weeks later, the unsettled feelings hadn't left her. Nikolas had asked before if she were ill or if someone had been teasing her at school, and she claimed all was well. One day when they were alone in the woods, he questioned her again.

"You haven't seemed like yourself for a while. Are you sure nothing is wrong?"

"Yes, I'm sure," Secret said, tossing a rock into the stream. She lied outright, to someone who caused and meant her no harm, her loyal and trustworthy friend. Her face burned with shame both for the lie and for what her father had done. Regardless, Secret couldn't imagine admitting what had taken place. There was too much to explain, so little understood.

Worse yet, Secret had begun to have new doubts about herself. What if she was mistaken and had seen the symbol somewhere, months, even years, before, not in a dream alone? What if she couldn't tell the truth because she couldn't remember?

Nikolas blinked at her, his expression patient.

She decided she could at least tell him what she told Old Woman. "It's only that I've been having dreams that frighten me. Something chases me, and I see this." She grabbed a stick and drew the symbol in the soil behind her. "Have you seen that before? Anywhere?"

"No," he said, after a long look from all sides. "And this came to you in a dream?"

"Yes."

"I would've remembered it when I woke up, too," he said.

Nikolas knelt and traced it with his finger. Secret felt the hair rise on her arms at the same time that he shivered. They looked at each other for a long moment. She sensed an understanding between them neither could articulate but both knew nonetheless.

When Nikolas stood up, she scratched through the drawing until no shapes were left.

Secret couldn't have imagined then where the symbol would one day appear, and in how many places, some far, far away.

XXII

Her Mother Receives an
Arcane Manuscript

THE MATTER OF THE SYMBOL SEEMED TO HAVE BEEN COMpletely forgotten. There were no more questions. Not a single reference was insinuated. Her father didn't apologize for his actions, show any remorse for what he'd done, or admit he had made any mistake. He never explained why what she'd drawn was so important, why he behaved as he did, or why Fewmany was involved.

Secret, however, forgot nothing. She was unable to return to the way things were before.

She avoided Bren, and when she couldn't, she kept conversations brief and excused herself from outings with the claim of schoolwork, a reason her father found unquestionably valid.

She was well into her seventh year of school, age twelve, before she could manage not to flinch if he reached a hand in her direction. Bren seemed perplexed by her avoidance. He attempted to make light of it—she was growing up, too old for him—but Secret knew he was hurt. But nothing she could do to him could possibly wound him as he had wounded her.

Of course, there was no change in Zavet. She remained meticulous in her work, dutiful as a mother, and attentive as a wife. Secret and her mother had always had a practical relationship. The distance between them only grew by an increment after the incident with the symbol drawing.

Then came the summer before Secret turned thirteen.

On the day the messenger arrived, Secret was home from the

woodcut printmaking class she attended three afternoons a week.
She had slipped off to the woods with Cyril when he appeared in
the doorway and had to carve her blocks at night in her room to
keep up with the other students. Cyril didn't arrive to escort her
every afternoon, and for whatever reason, he hadn't on this particular day.

Secret went into the kitchen to make tea.

Her mother sat at her worktables, her thick black hair tied back.

"Mother, would you like a cup?" Secret asked as she placed the
kettle to boil.

"Mint and lemon balm, please."

There was a steady *knock, knock, knock* at the front door. Zavet
rose to answer. Footsteps approached, more than her mother's, and
Secret assumed it was the parcel man delivering a new box of her
mother's grid paper. Instead, a woman followed Zavet into her
workspace. Although Secret rarely took notice of what the parcel
man or couriers brought, Secret felt curious, in fact compelled,
to see what had arrived. She removed the kettle from the fire and
walked toward her mother.

The young woman wore a well-fitted uniform of a coat and
skirt with prominent blue buttons. She introduced herself as Bea, a
messenger.

"There's a note for you to read first," Bea said. She handed
Zavet an envelope sealed with gold wax. Secret stood close to her
mother as Zavet laid the letter flat and ran her fingertips over the
typeset words.

> *You are known to be an exceptionally gifted translator of languages
> common and arcane. The search has been long for one with such
> profound knowledge. Please attempt, as others have not succeeded.*

There was no signature.

"What is it?" Zavet asked.

Bea reached into her thick leather satchel, covered with many pockets. She handed a deftly made wooden box to Zavet. "A man-uscript," she said.

Secret glanced from her mother's imperceptible smile to Bea's intelligent face. A warm sensation filled Secret, and she felt drawn to the young woman. The messenger must have noticed the atten-tion, even though Secret didn't stare.

"Good day to you, Miss," Bea said to her.

"Yes, good day," Secret replied.

Zavet rubbed her hands across the top and edges of the box. She pulled a pin from a latch, which dangled from a delicate chain. She reached for the contents.

The manuscript was unbound. Its separate sheets were stacked one upon the next, several dozen, at least one hundred, likely more. Even Secret knew immediately that this was a unique document. It was not made of parchment but of an old paper, thin to the point of translucence. The text was written with great economy in mi-nuscule characters on only one side of each page.

Spontaneously, Secret drifted her fingertips across a line of words. Her mother said nothing, no hiss, no rebuke.

Zavet turned the pages slowly. Near her, held under one of her glass grids, was a lengthy contract, and several feet away, a book out of its old binding, a few ancient threads poking from the folded signatures. "I am quite busy and haven't much time for another as-signment."

Secret cut her eyes at her mother. Years had passed since Zavet accepted a tattered book or disorganized ephemera from collec-tors of oddities and antiquities who appeared at her door. Secret remembered the tall stacks that once sat on her mother's tables. But since they'd moved into the row house when she was four, Zavet attended to stacks of documents instead. Only one book or manu-script required Zavet's attention at any given time. Secret suddenly remembered the manuscript Zavet's old professor sent her to trans-late, one she had to send back because of an agreement she had to honor. Secret wondered who among all of her mother's patrons had secured her exclusive service for all those years.

"When does the owner wish to have the completed work?" Zavet asked.

"As soon as you're able, but there is no rush," Bea said.

Zavet continued to study the pages and caress the manuscript with reverence. "This is unlike anything I've seen before. However, if I'm able to interpret the script, what does the owner want? I provide one handwritten translation, unless I'm asked to provide another handwritten copy or arrange for one to be typeset."

"One handwritten translation will do," Bea said.

"Are you authorized to discuss the fee?" Zavet asked.

Bea again reached into her satchel, into the deepest recess. She withdrew a leather bag cinched with a leather string. Zavet peered inside, then carefully poured the contents on her table.

Little gold bars, a small fortune in ingots, tumbled out.

Secret had seen her mother paid in gold, silver, and copper coins, but never in ingots, never so much.

"This may be four times what I would charge for completion. Please take most of it back," Zavet said.

"I was told to pay you this full amount now."

"What if I'm unable to translate the text?"

"Your payment is to try," Bea said. "You will see me again in one year. If you should finish before I return, please hold the manuscript until then."

Secret led Bea to the front door.

"What is your name, Miss?" Bea asked with a curious look.

"My name is Secret," she said.

"Very well then," she said. She waved as she walked into the busy street.

When Secret returned to her mother, Zavet was slowly tracing her hand along a page. The girl stared at the unusual marks unlike any alphabet or system she'd ever seen.

"In what is it written?" Secret asked.

"Blood," Zavet said.

Secret looked at the brownish-red ink, the alchemy of pigments. "That's not funny, Mother," she said, "and that isn't what I meant."

Zavet curved her lips in an impish smile. "The condition is remarkable. At first, I suspected it was a hoax. Such tricks have been played before, and I know of colleagues who were duped. What a shame. But this . . ." Zavet turned several pages with great care, touching the beginning and end and going back to the first page. Her fingers skimmed it once more, then again. "A translator's quest is the opposite of any other. We don't find these treasures. Somehow they find us."

Secret couldn't recall the last time she had seen her mother so enthralled. "Well, can you read any part of it?" Secret asked.

"Yes, one word here, unlike any of the rest. It's not in the same language," Zavet said. "A name. Aoife."

Her mother had spoken with an ancient tongue.

Secret's whole body vibrated with the sound, her being a bell struck with full force. She felt suddenly heavy and strong, as if her body were no longer her own. Zavet swept her eyes from her daughter's feet to her head. For the briefest instant, Secret felt her mother's eyes make contact with her own. Zavet bit her lip and blinked once, slowly, then looked away. The ringing within Secret settled to a hum, then faded into silence.

Hesitant to move, Secret stood there as her mother placed the arcane manuscript back in the wooden box. Zavet clasped it to her chest and walked past the dining table. She paused before she reached the stairs.

"You will not mention this to your father," Zavet said, her voice forbidding.

The night after the arcane manuscript arrived, Secret thought she heard a noise in her father's study. She wondered if he had returned late from his recent trip. She crept from her room to the third floor and spied Zavet bent over the map table surrounded by candles. So much beeswax was aflame that the hall smelled of honey. In shadow lay the wooden box in which the arcane manuscript had been stored. Secret held her breath and listened to the whisper of a turned page. As she left unnoticed, she wondered what compelled her mother's furtive study in the dark.

Secret returned to her bed, almost tempted to go back and reveal her interest. Although she was told not to tell her father, Secret was given no specific instructions herself. But the fact that Zavet was reading in the middle of the night was enough of a hint her mother wanted to be alone.

In the days that followed, Secret expected her mother to be in good spirits. Zavet had been so happily intrigued when the arcane manuscript arrived that Secret expected the mood to last for a while. Instead, Secret sensed to keep away. Zavet was uncommonly silent, far beyond the absence of muttering. Secret noticed, with apprehension, that her ever-busy mother had begun to sit in a dark room, motionless, as if numb with shock. When asked if she felt well, Zavet replied, "As well as ever."

Secret couldn't help but think Zavet's behavior was somehow connected to the manuscript.

One night, Secret could resist no more. She lit a candle and crept to her mother's tables. Ever since she was a little girl, her mother allowed her to look at but never to touch the texts being translated. Secret did as she was told, no matter how tempted she was to study what was within the hidden pages when her mother wasn't looking. But at last, curiosity had become a compulsion. Secret was perplexed that she felt so drawn to see it again, especially considering she couldn't even read it.

She searched among the materials on Zavet's tables. As usual, the area was orderly, the grid-marked paper stacked neatly, the ink bottles capped, the pens lined up in a row, the framed glass grids one on top of the other. The most recent book her mother was translating was closed with a ribbon marking her place. The translation in progress was placed on top of its tattered cover. In the center of the table, in front of her chair, was a lengthy document written in a dramatic, curly script. A note with a broken wax seal lay on top. Secret unfolded it.

Her eyes widened with surprise. It was written on stationery from Fewmany Incorporated. The letter was addressed to Zavet and read,

> *Rowland cannot tolerate the penmanship.*
> *With gratitude,*
> G

Carefully, Secret placed the letter exactly as she found it. She flipped through the papers in a rectangular bin and discovered three more documents and one brief letter from G. So, her mother worked for Fewmany, too, likely helping her father with whatever acquisitions he was expected to make. Secret felt a twinge of annoyance that her parents hadn't told her, even though there was no particular reason for her to know that fact. She stopped herself from wondering if what her mother did had any link to what happened with the scissors so many months before.

She turned to her mother's shelves. Nothing seemed unusual. The vase was high in a corner. The same books were in the same order, ones Secret had been rarely allowed to see when she was a child. She ran her hand behind the books to see if anything had been hidden there, but the space was empty. The arcane manuscript wasn't on the shelves either.

But then Secret realized she could check the records her mother kept of her work. Secret pulled the bound books down and sat on the floor next to her candle. She skimmed for mention of the mysterious text.

Zavet had always kept logs of her work and diaries of translations. The oldest ones were boxed in the storage room on the second floor. Zavet kept the most recent records near her. Among these, Secret had been granted the indulgence of a curious look now and then.

The logs noted each text Zavet received—the date, its title or description, total pages, materials used, the name and address of the owner, payment given, payment due. As a younger child, Secret wondered about where the books and manuscripts had been and from how far away many of them had come.

Yet when Secret opened the two logs she found on the shelves, she saw only dates and titles on page after page. She had taken only one year of classical languages, but she was able to discern some of the original titles. She observed groupings of certain subjects— natural science, philosophy, history. These were the works her mother had received one at a time for years from a single patron. No name or address was mentioned. Secret had assumed these were written in an old log stored away.

Then, Secret read the last, most recent, entry Zavet wrote. *Manuscript. Unbound. Handwritten. Arcane. 154 pages, one side. No signatures. No known provenance. Handwritten translation. Paid in full.*

Secret replaced the logs and looked next at the diaries. These chronicled Zavet's efforts. Scribbles, sketches, and phrases were scrawled in the margins. Written in a precise, almost elegant hand with black ink of a purple shade, Zavet made comments regarding the texts, sometimes comparing them to others she had translated. She noted questions about syntax, connotation, and other subtle forces that bore upon understanding. These she answered in green tinged with blue. Sometimes in the margins, Zavet wrote a note to herself, a mundane reminder of an errand, or scrawled a loose rendering of an image from her mind's eye. However, Secret couldn't read most of it. Zavet wrote in whatever language suited her at the time.

No indication appeared that Zavet had even begun the translation of what the messenger had delivered.

Secret wondered where Zavet had hidden the arcane manuscript.

When Bren finally returned from his latest trip, Secret was relieved. No matter what Secret did or didn't do, she was unable to soothe her mother, but Bren managed to offer comfort in some way to ease the trouble. She hoped whatever he did would help this time.

But after dinner, only hours after he arrived, Secret overheard her parents in Bren's study. There was a shrill tone in Zavet's voice. A reference to a letter. Secret dared to creep closer to the door.

"Never visit. Never write. Never invite me stay. Lovely time with you and granddaughter," Zavet said, mocking the accent of her native land. "The hag wonders why?"

There was a long pause. Then Secret's father, a shrewd negotiator in all spheres of his life, offered a solution.

"Send Secret by herself next summer. She's no longer a little girl. She's responsible and respectful and would cause no worry or trouble. I think she'd enjoy the journey. We need not be concerned about the classes she'd miss at the start of the term. She would catch up quickly. If you sent her, it may settle matters for some time."

Zavet didn't respond. An exaggerated kiss snapped the air.

"Yes, dear, would be an acceptable reply," he said.

"I'll consider the suggestion," Zavet said.

Secret went back to her room, excitement racing through her pulse. She remembered fragments of the only visit she'd made to see her grandmother. The experience had formed a warm place in her memory—the feeling of the woods and its peace, the welcome of people who shared her blood. If allowed, she would return to the faraway village of her mother's birth and the beautiful land that surrounded it.

However, Secret felt the coldness of all that was unsaid and what was. She had never heard a kind word ever spoken of her grandmother, but then her mother hardly mentioned Ahmama at all. If Secret was told anything, it was the same story in a different form—Zavet's mother had sent her daughter away. That fact alone was meant to explain everything.

Because she had eavesdropped on her parents' conversation, Secret decided she must be indirect if she was to learn more about what they had discussed. One late morning, as her mother was dusting, Secret said she dreamed of her ahmama and the village and woke up wondering how she was. Secret had no such dream, in fact.

Zavet wiped an oiled cloth along her shelves. Her glance skimmed across Secret's face. The girl kept her body and mind guarded.

"Your ahmama is alive and old and frail," Zavet said as she turned back to her dusting.

"We live so far away. Don't you miss her?" Secret asked.

"No. I am too busy to bother," Zavet said.

"Don't you miss the village? Your home?"

"No, I lived few years there. It was hardly a home at all."

"I remember our visit when I was little. I enjoyed it very much."

"I remember being stung by bees and being so swollen and sick I thought I might die."

Secret's forehead twinged. She rubbed the spot gently. She remembered that, too—and the bee in the tree that told of the wound and the wolf. "I know you have your work, and it's important to you, but perhaps, if you could take leave, we could go again?"

Zavet braced her arms against her worktable. "My last visit was the final one."

"But surely Ahmama would like to see you again." Secret hesitated. "To see me again."

"My last visit was the final one. Do you understand?"

Secret choked down the sadness that welled up for her mother, and for herself, as a gnarl of anger rose against it. "But—" Secret said.

"*Do you understand?*" Zavet asked again.

"Yes, Mother."

Secret wanted to, but didn't, couldn't. Her mother kept her reasons and meaning hidden, as always. With an aching chest, Secret went to her room to read.

Not long after she was lost in concentration, Secret heard noises on the floor below—shrieks and exclamations. She walked halfway down the stairs. Zavet's rapid babbling was unintelligible but nonetheless seemed ordered, syntactical. The girl listened. She wasn't certain but thought the language was her mother's native tongue.

The frenetic repetition of a phrase escaped Zavet's throat. There were thuds and slaps against the plaster walls and stone floors, the crash of a dish. Several years had passed since Zavet had a fit that progressed much beyond mutters. That day, something had been unleashed in her.

Secret couldn't escape unnoticed to the courtyard or through the front door. Panic quickened her heart and heated her bowels. She ran upstairs to hide. She grabbed a quilt from her bed, squeezed in the space next to her large wardrobe, and covered herself head to toe.

In that moment, Secret began to breathe with shallow sips. She closed her eyes. She felt the inside of herself become still and black. Her mother's noise was unable to reach her. Not only did Secret feel unafraid, she also felt nothing at all. She lingered in the absence of thought and feeling, a space where she felt disembodied, untouchable. She realized she had been in this dark place before, in other moments like this, but she had never descended so deeply.

When her mother entered the room—the inevitable end of these fits, minor and severe—Zavet couldn't find Secret. The girl was aware of her mother's presence beyond the cover but didn't move or speak or breathe. The woman crept only inches away from Secret's body, opened and closed the wardrobe several times, and tossed aside the coverings on her bed.

"Where are you, my little fungus?" Zavet hissed, her tongue back in place. "You naughty thing, come out." Finally, her mother left.

Secret curled into the corner, deadened. When her stomach growled, she was angry at its insistence. When the urge came to relieve herself, she was resentful of her body's demand. Hungry and uncomfortable, Secret finally went downstairs. The moon had taken its turn at light.

Her father was home. He took three plates from a shelf and placed them on the table. Her mother stirred a heavy stew, pungent with mushrooms and onions.

"Hello, Secret," Bren said. "A usual quiet day for you?"

"Yes, Father," she replied.

"She seemed to disappear into her books," Zavet said. "Didn't you, girl?"

"Yes, Mother," she said.

After dinner, in the dark, Secret went to Fig Tree. She leaned her back against her friend's trunk.

Tell me what you sense, she said without saying. Secret drew infrequent hints of air into her flattened lungs.

Breathe, child, breathe, Fig Tree said with alarm. *You are scarcely alive.*

Scarcely alive? Secret asked.

You are chilled and without light, Fig Tree said. *Please stop.*

Secret took a full breath and hugged the tree. She was sorry she frightened her friend. However, she felt good about what she had discovered. She had found a way to disappear, better than under her hair or cloak. Yes, she had done this before, but not for so long to see its effect. Her body remained where it was, a mere shell, but the rest of her vanished to another place where she couldn't be found. This discovery made her feel safe, in control, which was without a doubt better than being afraid.

XXIII

What Happened to Fig Tree

SOON AFTER SECRET'S THIRTEENTH BIRTHDAY, DURING HER eighth year of school, her parents finally agreed to renovate the row house. For so long, she overheard random conversations and arguments her mother and father had about the old place's condition. With the exception of the modern water closet and freshly painted walls, the house had been untouched by previous owners. Secret rather liked its character with its heavy old doors, cracked plaster, and tall windows. Her mother certainly paid no mind to any of the house's flaws.

The purchase of the row house had been a reluctant one. Bren had always wanted to move to one of the manors north of town—so prominent had he become at Fewmany Incorporated that he could afford the luxury and wanted to indulge it—but Zavet insisted they remain within the wards. Bren had agreed so that Zavet would be near shops and markets, but the understanding had been they would renovate the row house soon enough. Nine years later, aside from acquiring a few beautiful decorations, nothing had changed.

Bren had finally had enough. One evening, Secret heard the clash of voices downstairs and tiptoed to the second-floor landing to listen.

"I don't want the bother of strange workmen in every corner of the house, not to mention the filth and vapors they will leave behind," Zavet said.

"Then I'll arrange a nice room for you in the best inn where you can work in comfort," Bren said.

There was a long pause before Zavet replied. "You know how important a familiar environment is for me."

"The time there would be temporary," he said.

"I didn't mean the inn."

He sighed. "It will be familiar, your same house, only one that looks as if it belongs to a family of our means. It's reprehensible that I live this way—the outside as fine as any other on the block, the inside dilapidated, out of fashion, frankly, it's an embarrassment," Bren said.

Alone in the shadows, Secret raised her eyebrows in astonishment. She had no idea her father was so angry about this and was amazed he'd held it in for so long. For an instant, and no more, she wondered why he had invited Fewmany into the house at all that awful night if this was how he truly felt.

"You exaggerate," Zavet said.

"Oh, it's clean and orderly—we have a good maid—but I need not settle for that alone. Now, either I will purchase a manor as I wanted to years ago, pristine from top to bottom, inside and out, and we'll move there—no filth, no bother—or we will stay here and do what must be done."

After several moments, Zavet said, "I want to stay."

"Then we shall stay."

That autumn, they prepared to transform the old row house. Despite her earlier resistance, Zavet did attempt to find some pleasure in the effort. The three of them visited shops to choose new furniture, linens, and drapes. Zavet swept her hands along every surface. She admired sturdy joins, turned legs, and fine carvings. Fabrics cascaded over her arms and slipped through her fingers. She rallied for down pillows for the beds and horsehair cushions for seating. Secret's parents took considerable delight in the search, and she did, too. They argued, discussed, and laughed in a way they never had before. Secret had no idea what inspired the congeniality—perhaps the novelty alone—but she enjoyed it. She was especially pleased when she was allowed to choose whatever she wanted for her room and took her own pleasure in that.

The selections were made, bills of sale signed, and delivery dates decided.

Zavet was less amenable once the renovations began. She insisted that Bren's study be completely finished first. She relocated her tables under the south-facing windows there and tried to work despite the noise and activity. She was short-tempered with everyone, including the laborers, whom Secret found diligent in their work and masterful in their crafts. Regardless of what her mother thought, Bren had apparently hired the best men to patch, replace, paint, and mortar.

Several weeks later, Secret returned from school, entered the house, and saw that everything new had arrived. Excited, Secret called for her mother and received no response. Secret assumed Zavet was away for a winter's day walk. Still wearing her cloak and carrying her satchel, Secret opened the new drapes in the parlor and looked at the beautiful furniture and decorations.

Walking past her mother's workspace, the walls and windows repaired and painted but everything else the same, Secret went into the kitchen. She tested the copper spigot on the new water basin near the new, more modern wood-burning stove, then admired the hefty dining table and chairs, and walked to the stairs. She swept her hand against the restored banister rail as she went to the second floor.

She stood in the doorway as she had when her father first showed his little daughter her new room. To Secret's left, in the narrow corner between the doorway and the fireplace, was a full-length mirror. Across the room, under the first large window was a desk with many drawers and the old carved chair she'd chosen at an antiquity shop. Next to that was the little faded blue chest with the painted animals, still locked, as it always had been, with a quilt neatly folded on top. Her new bed was in the same place as the old one, under the windows tucked in the corner. There was a square table near the headboard topped with a pewter candlestick, brass lamp, and silver vesta. On the wall opposite the fireplace was a much larger wardrobe, and where the cupboard had been, there was a tall cabinet with doors at the bottom and shelves on the top. Her nesting dolls filled an uppermost corner, and the books were stacked exactly in the order they'd been before. The toy chest was gone, her playthings stored on the third floor.

She smiled, delighted by the changes, and dropped her satchel near her desk.

Finding the house rather cold, she kept her cloak on as she inspected the other rooms on the second and third floors. She returned to the kitchen, found a new plate in the new cupboard, and made a snack of jam and bread. Wishing to feel the last of the day's sunlight, she went to the heavy back door, the only part of the house she begged her father not to replace, pulled the great bobbin and latch, and stepped into the courtyard. She turned to the left with a greeting on her lips.

But before she could speak, she saw the butchered stump where Fig Tree had been.

Secret's knees toppled against her weight. Her chest ached as if she'd fallen from a great height. The plate lay broken in pieces.

"My tree," she said. "My friend—is dead."

A dove lit upon the wall where Fig Tree had cast her shade. He told without telling that a man had come with an ax. The birds and ants and other insects tried to stop him with the means they could, but their tiny strength wasn't enough to thwart his might.

Tears raced down Secret's cheeks, then she held them without a sound. She feared she would scream and never stop. She sat where the thick trunk had been. Fig Tree's friends began to gather around her, all of them sad for the sudden loss.

A sparrow—the great-great-great-granddaughter of the sparrow whose hatchlings had flown from the branches—clutched one of Secret's grasping fingers. She chirped, and Secret looked into her dark little eye. Without words or sound, but in a realm of seeing through knowing, Secret saw herself as a tiny child with a wooden pail in her arms. She put the bucket on the ground and tipped it until water trickled on the soil. A pale green leaf, wide but sick from lack of light and love, caressed her face.

You renewed Fig Tree with your love and attention, a pigeon said without saying.

Your care made it possible for her to care for us, a starling told without telling.

Fig Tree was not alone, Secret, a mouse squeaked without squeaking.

Secret's face was dry, but it felt bruised and broken. She composed herself and went inside to her room. Curled on her bed, Secret starved herself of air and vanished into the darkness that left her numb. She became hungry and thirsty, but she resisted her body's urge for her to return. She didn't move until called for dinner.

She said nothing as her parents talked. At last, she asked, "Why was the fig tree cut down?"

"It was in the way. We're going to cover the courtyard with nice slate tile and purchase new planters and shrubs. The pitiful tree is finally out of its misery. I was pained to look at that crippled thing," her father said.

She wasn't crippled, Secret thought. She swallowed her grief, consumed the fruit of the sour loss whole.

Secret attempted to eat her dinner. Parsnips, cabbage, broad beans.

"There was no point in telling you," her mother said. "This way, there would be no moping or histrionics. It was for your own good."

The girl chewed and chewed, but her throat remained closed. They knew she cared for Fig Tree—and killed her anyway.

"It was only a tree," Zavet said.

"Fig Tree was my friend," Secret shouted. She pressed her lips together. Too late. The words were out.

Her parents widened their eyes at her outburst.

"Your friend? What could it ever do for you?" her father said.

"Childish nonsense," her mother said.

Her parents glanced at each other. An understanding passed between them. Secret's cheeks reddened. She knew this look of silent judgment well.

Secret picked up her plate, left it in the kitchen basin, and went to her room with all of her new things and old feelings.

Why didn't you keep your mouth shut? she asked herself. You knew how they'd respond.

Secret wrapped a thick quilt around her from head to toe. Her mind filled with the blank space where Fig Tree had been, then the memories returned. Fig Tree's sickly leaves becoming healthy and plentiful. The welcomed shade under her branches. A first taste of the sweet fruit. A leather ball rolling between Secret's little feet and the tree's lowest branches. Birds above, singing. Fig Tree's stories about the families who had lived there, the children who had sought her company, too. Fig Tree keeping all the secrets the lonely child wished to tell.

Her lungs burned as she wept without a sound. Her grief seemed to have always been part of her, a well tapped with no end to its source. No one else knew what Fig Tree was. No one else, not even her family, could recognize her loss. When her head began to pound, she sat up and tried to force the sobs to stop.

As she struggled to calm down, a current of anger swelled within her. She had loved Fig Tree, and she wished she had not. This pain wouldn't be possible if she had seen it as a tree like anyone else. The anger grew stronger, pushing the grief away, down, back to the place from which it came.

Secret clenched her jaw. Yes, if she were like anyone else, who didn't think twice about smashing an insect or cutting down an old tree, she wouldn't feel like this. Why had she sat on the fig tree's branch and held herself open to what might come? It had been a mistake, she decided. She should have remained closed. Her temper flared.

The anger felt better than the grief, but it couldn't keep its hold for long.

Days later, she had her father take her to Old Wheel. She told the truth, that she was meeting school friends at a play, but as soon as it began, Cyril appeared at her feet and led her away. Secret intended only to go for a long walk in the freezing cold, but her feet took a turn toward Old Woman's cottage.

Once inside, Secret curled in front of Old Woman's steady fire. The large cauldron near the hearth radiated from the absorbed heat. Secret hadn't mentioned what happened to Nikolas, but after Old Woman placed a cup of tea in her hands and sat down, Secret let the words spill.

Old Woman tried to take Secret in her arms, but Secret pulled away.

"I am so very sorry for your loss," Old Woman said.

"But I shouldn't feel this way. It was old. And it was only a tree," Secret said.

"Not to you. As you know, trees hold secrets. Sometimes, they are the only things that stand still long enough to listen and remember."

Cyril chattered and jumped into Secret's arms. "Why do you say things like that to me? There's no *proof*, you know. No one believes that. It's stupid and silly and childish," Secret said with a scowl. Old Woman's comfort had piqued her. She wanted to be told she was making too much of what happened, *and* she wanted sympathy. Secret couldn't figure out why she was so torn between the two.

Old Woman paused, breathing out quietly from her parted lips. She stood and walked to the table. "Only to those who've forgotten the tender bond of all things." She wove a quick braid halfway down the length of her white hair and tied the end with a blue ribbon. She crumbled a dry flower head on a cloth and began to pick out the seeds. One by one, she dropped them in a small pouch embroidered with a rendering of its blossom, leaves, and stem.

As she stored the seeds, Old Woman told Secret that the pods and heads and dried vegetables on the table were of strong, enduring stock. They carried old stories, told in part through their physical nature. The hue of a bean, the tenderness of a leaf, the firmness of a root. Over time, yes, they changed, revealed new qualities, but what endured was their essence. Further, Old Woman knew that Secret knew they had memory, too, of matters of the world few imagined or contemplated.

Each beast as well, Old Woman continued, had the same mystery. They had the stories of their own days—and deep within, of those from whence they came. Yet those stories, like those of plants, included the stories of others—of creatures who neither looked nor felt nor smelled nor tasted nor sounded as they did.

"We speak to one another with words and gestures, but before either, there are thoughts. Before thought, there is awareness, the greatest enigma of all," Old Woman said. "You, Secret, knew Fig Tree was aware of you, and you of her. You shared more than the same plot of land or pleasant company. You shared each other's story."

The girl smoothed the squirrel's red fur. Silver strands flecked Cyril's tail.

"Fig Tree was your witness. Whatever you said or felt, she listened without judgment. She heard you. That is a powerful, loving deed to do for another. Do you remember the story of the red dragon and how she came to know All That Is? Before her lesson of the deer?" Old Woman asked.

"When she became as small as pollen and big as a whale?"

"Yes. What did you *feel* from that myth?"

Secret tensed her eyebrows. She repeated the beginning of that myth to herself. The red dragon had changed into various sizes and shapes and spent time among all things of the world, from rocks to beasts. "I feel Egnis wanted to understand things from their perspectives. To see the world as it is, which isn't only one way but many."

The girl stared at her friend. The conversation made her uncomfortable. Her skin tingled, her body ached, and her head was dizzy. She hadn't had one of those bizarre occurrences with unexplainable images since she dreamed of the symbol, and she tensed every muscle hoping it wouldn't happen now.

Old Woman peered back, serene and reassuring. "Beautiful. Simply beautiful. Very well put, child."

Secret released Cyril. She waited until she was steady and walked to the table to help with sorting. She held her hands poised when she sensed Old Woman's attention on her. The eerie sensation had not completely waned. She felt as if she'd glimpsed something behind her she dare not confront directly.

"What is it?" Secret asked.

"I wish to tell you something I've kept to myself for a long time," Old Woman said. Cyril jumped on the table and helped himself to a shelled walnut.

Secret let the air become stale in her lungs.

"When you were a little girl and sat outside my walls, I knew you were there. Many times I was tempted to show myself. For a child to hide as you did, with such uncanny, careful quiet, such an ability to listen, I knew to be patient. You wouldn't reveal yourself before it was time. That is your natural wisdom, a rich gift of discernment beyond your years." Old Woman paused. "I know you're reticent, Secret. I realize it's difficult for you to speak of ceratin things. Telling me about your connection to plants and animals when you were a little girl was a brave act and one of trust. I take that seriously."

Secret nodded. She didn't know what to say in response.

"You're thirteen now, aren't you?" Old Woman asked.

"Yes, this past autumn."

"What have you been told of your transition into womanhood?"

Secret stared at the floor. She had watched what happened to the older girls at school and heard them speak of blood, hair, and bending bones. Her own body had started to become a stranger, shape-shifting into someone else. But Old Woman had prepared her as well. There was no formal discussion but an instructive comment now and then, often when a particular plant could be used for a woman's purposes, some Secret wondered if she'd ever need herself. "We've talked of this. I know what changes are to be."

"These changes aren't only physical. Of course, you'll have the conflicting and intense feelings of anyone your age. And sometimes, your emotions will get the better of you. But you are not an ordinary girl, Secret. You may be challenged in ways others girls, and boys, never will be. Your gifts could become greater."

"What do you mean?" Secret said.

"What you receive from animals and plants could begin to come from people. A sense of their thoughts, now, or the past or future."

Secret turned her head with a dismissive shake. Secret thought of her mother, who told her daughter she once knew the thoughts of others and then wholly denied such a thing had happened, claiming she had been confused, mistaken. She wanted no unwelcome burden like that.

"And there could be dreams unlike typical dreams. The meanings could be hidden through symbols or clear and obvious. They may recur in some form. And you will have a profound sense they are meant to be heeded as messages."

The blood in Secret's face pooled at her feet.

"Has any of this happened to you, child?" Old Woman asked.

"No," Secret said, willing herself to look Old Woman in the eye.

"I meant no accusation, and I don't mean to frighten you. I hope after all the years you have known me, you've come to trust me. My intent is to prepare you, as I have by telling you what natural things will happen as you grow into a woman and what plant lore you should know for your own well-being. In this matter, I want you to feel safe if you begin to experience what most young women won't," Old Woman said.

"And I hope I don't," Secret said.

"Why not?"

"Who wants to be different like that? What I have to live with now is more than enough, and I wish that would go away in a way I didn't before," she said.

"Considering what you've endured, I understand why you'd feel as you do. Some gifts carry a burden, and some don't reveal their purpose until later. Be gentle with yourself and what you think to reject." Old Woman waited for a reply. Secret remained quiet. "Please, will you go to the stream?"

Secret found an empty pail near the hearth.

She followed Cyril's bounding lead. As she sat upon the bank and watched the flowing water, she wondered if she should have told Old Woman that the dreams she used to have of the blue men and of the symbol didn't seem like her other dreams. She thought about those times when her body ached and she felt as if she knew things there was no rational explanation for her to know. Old Woman would have believed her, without a doubt, just as she had believed Secret when she said she could speak with creatures and plants.

But Secret didn't want to be believed. Given the choice, she wished her supposed gift, as well as the unpleasant occurrences, would vanish as easily as they first came. And if they did not, she didn't want things to get worse.

Carefully, she leaned toward the water and filled the pail. As she did, she wondered what other girls were doing at that moment. Schoolwork, reading, having tea with a mother, playing a game with a brother or sister, walking to visit a friend, sharing a secret, dreaming about the future, sitting on a front step, lying on the ground in a courtyard watching the clouds.

Secret steadied the pail next to her. She looked all around and listened to the layers of sound. It was so beautiful there in the woods, no matter the season. How lucky I am to see this, she thought. She was sincere, despite what she'd said and thought only moments before, even though that still remained true. To be angry and grateful at once was confusing.

The cold began to seep through her skin, spreading to her bones. She felt invigorated and took a breath to intensify the sensation. Her mind was muddled, then clear. With no effort or intent, she slipped open. She felt her presence connected to all the elements around her. The stream flowed, the clouds floated, and the evergreen boughs swayed. A bird chirped, a fox yipped, a deer bellowed. She clutched a root's curve and pressed the frigid soil. Secret was by herself, but she did not feel alone. With peace, she sighed. She heard a low, distant groan. A jolt went through her hip, making her twitch, and she knocked over the pail. The water seeped into the ground. She watched it disappear, curious about what it carried in its descent.

A ruffling of feathers made her look up to a bare branch, stark black against a white cloud. The crow bobbed his beak and cawed. Yes, he confirmed, he was the one who revealed there had been a village in the woods, before the town. As she stared at the bird, a thought came to her—through him, the earth, the wind, she couldn't discern—and the thought was, *There are witnesses to all that's been and all that will be done. They are not all human, but they all know.*

XXIV

What The People of the Town Experience in Their Dreams

ENTER ANOTHER REALM, THE ONE OF SLEEP. JOIN THE dreaming, boundless, full of strangers and strangeness. Beauty and impossibility.

Everywhere, the sleepers visit places they have never been. Snow-peaked mountains hold up the sky. A beast with a sheep's face, long neck, and thin legs waits patiently. It is dressed in a cap and saddle bags made of a colorful woven fabric. The animal scales a narrow, rocky path on a long, long journey.

For someone, the trail crumbles away. A slow fall ends with a gentle landing in a valley. Butterflies blur among the bursts of blossoms. A wolf leaps at a grasshopper and chases it. The trail left by its body reaches a river.

A dreamer discovers the ability to walk on water. Music takes the form of air, and the dreamer dances in circles to the shore. Steps from the water, there is a high stone wall with no portal or reasonable end. A decision must be made.

Someone leaps upon the ledge. Below the wall, one side is a desert and the other side is an ocean. A magnificent bird alights in the sand. A handsome ship appears on the water. The stone wall gives way to a steep stair which leads to a narrow road.

The dreamer chooses to dive into the ocean. Within the deep, there are cities populated by fanciful creatures. Six gray beasts with fins, large tails, and intelligent eyes enter an ice cave and exit its maze. When all pierce the surface, there is a beach of jewels.

Someone fills his pockets with gems and enters a vast garden. The tended walkways lead to a gated city. A bell hangs at the entrance, but no one responds to the ring. Metal bars bend like saplings. The streets are empty. A beautiful person runs to give greeting. At the center of the city, there is a celebration. Welcome.

To awaken now could be a disappointment, or a mercy.

XXV

Nikolas's Birthday Celebration

UNDER A HEAVY ROCK AT REACH'S ROOTS THE SUMMER SHE was thirteen, Secret found an envelope addressed to her in the finest of scripts, dusted ever so lovely with gold. She was asked to be a guest at the prince's fourteenth birthday celebration. On the invitation, in Nikolas's boyish print, were the words,

> *Please come, Secret.*
> *Surprises await.*

She hadn't been to The Castle since her first visit, seven years earlier, when she met the likes of Fewmany and the light of Nikolas. Although her mother and father attended the annual ball every year after, she didn't accompany them again. She didn't ask why, and they didn't explain. Instead, she remained home with Auntie. Her parents stayed out until the next morning, when they returned with curious grins, once concealed behind elaborate feathered masks.

Nikolas had invited her to his private parties since then, but she felt out of place and worried she would do something to embarrass herself. Her regrets disappointed him, but his acceptance hinted he knew the reasons she wouldn't reveal outright. They had forged a friendship close enough that some things could remain unspoken.

But if she were truthful with herself, she had wanted to go to several of those parties. As much as she liked being alone with her courtyard companions and her books, sometimes she wished to be like everyone else her age. Most of Nikolas's friends were not hers, but some were, and they shared common interests and good conversation. Surely, their mutual friends would attend this celebration. She might not need to find refuge in the Great Hall's unlit corners after all.

If she were going, a new dress was necessary. Her wardrobe consisted of school uniforms, three frocks for the times she went to performances with her parents, and several everyday blouses, skirts, and dresses. None of that would do for this occasion.

So, she told her mother about the party.

"Prince Nikolas invited you?" Zavet said, not bothering to mask the surprise in her voice. "Are all of your schoolmates attending?"

"I don't think so. May I get a new dress and go?"

"Yes, and yes," her mother said. "Ask your father what amount you may spend."

Then Secret told her father what she needed and why. He blinked at her and asked, "Prince Nikolas invited you? How did this come about?"

"We're in the same class," she said.

"Then all your schoolfellows received invitations?"

"No."

"How well do you know our young liege?" Bren asked.

"Well enough."

"You've never spoken of him before."

Of course not, she thought, for reasons such as this. She could sense her father plotting a map of affiliation in his head. "What is there to tell?" she asked.

Her father grinned. "Very well. Seeing as this happens so rarely and we can, with fortune, afford it, I will give you plenty enough for a dress and shoes and combs to match. Have your mother take you out."

"Thank you, Father," she said.

The next morning, Secret and her mother walked through several wards, past the shop where she'd found her beloved purple cloak, and entered Fewmany's Fine Young Lady.

Once inside, the shop woman claimed all the new fashions arrived there first and began to show them what had come in recently.

Secret obliged her mother and the shop woman's insistence that she try on this one, and this one, and this one. Secret felt she looked hopelessly silly in the puffy round sleeves, waists well above her waist, and too-long skirts. Zavet declared she looked appropriate, but Secret was in despair. The patient shop clerk, nearer Secret's age than her mother's, rolled out a metal rack from behind a curtain.

"These are from our Antiquity line," the shop clerk said. "They are the latest couture in other kingdoms but for some reason have little appeal here."

Secret scowled at the garish colors and superfluous folds. Then she saw one unlike any other. Her mother and the clerk winced. One of them clucked her tongue. She whisked into a dressing space, stared long at her reflection, and exited with it on her arm.

"I want this one," she said.

"You're not attending a masquerade ball, Secret," her mother said.

"Apparently not, because I've chosen no mask to wear with it," Secret replied. "This is the one I want." She dashed off to find simple black shoes, quickly chosen, and refused any decorations for her hair.

As the shop woman tallied the bill, Zavet asked what gift Secret planned to get for Nikolas. Secret said she already took care of that matter. Zavet didn't question her, and Secret was glad. She knew no one but Nikolas would appreciate the surprise she had in mind.

On the night of Nikolas's party, Secret dressed then waited in the parlor. Her mother remarked that she looked well groomed, her father that she looked whimsical. Bren fetched the two-horse cart and met her at their doorstep. As they rode through the streets, Secret held Nikolas's gift on her lap as Bren spoke of courtesy, propriety, and deference. Secret nodded. She had no compulsion to make it clear that Nikolas was, in fact, her best friend, and just happened to be of royal lineage. Her father, she knew, was easily held in sway by wealth and power, both of which he desired.

Once beyond The Castle's wall, they traveled up the path, through the gatehouse, and turned around into the courtyard right inside the walls. Bren said he would come to get her in the same place and wished her a good night. She glanced behind her as she walked toward the Great Hall. Bren and another father reached out past their carts to shake hands.

Inside the hall, a loud quartet blared merriment from the dais. Guests clustered together in small groups. From the second-floor gallery, The King and the Queen peered down. Nikolas's sister Charming—Pretty had married first, of course—greeted her and handed her a cloth pouch.

"I'm Charming, Nikolas's sister," she said.

"My name is Secret."

"Oh, you're Secret," she said, not unkindly but curiously. "Nikolas talks about you all the time. I almost thought you were imaginary. We've never met."

"We have, but it was only an introduction at the grand ball several years ago. There's no reason why you should remember."

"I will remember you now. Enjoy yourself. Don't peek in your bag until you're told to. There's a clue inside," she said. "Oh, and you may place the gift on the table a few paces behind me."

Secret slipped the pouch's drawstring loop around her wrist. She went to the table and held the wrapped box in her hands, trying to decide what to do.

"You're in the right place," a girl said lightly as she plopped a gift next to the rest.

Secret looked at the girl, who was among Nikolas's circle of friends that didn't overlap with hers. Secret didn't like the girl because she often made cutting remarks about others, including her closest friends. "Yes, now to choose a spot."

"Oh, it's you, Secret. This is a first, isn't it? I haven't seen you at one of these festivities, have I?" The girl gave Secret a critical glance. "Odd frock, but it actually looks decent on you. But that present—were you attacked by knife-wielding bandits and fended them off with a box?"

Secret turned the gift around in her hands. "I'm afraid it met trouble on the way here."

"You can't give it to him like that."

"I think he'll understand."

"That's still no excuse to give a damaged gift," the girl said as she flounced the silk ribbon on the one she had brought. "So then—have a good evening."

"And you as well," Secret said.

Secret cut her eyes around as she considered what to do, then glanced up. Nikolas was several paces away but walking in her direction. She waved. He squinted, his return gesture cautious. Then his face relaxed with recognition. He approached her.

"You looked like someone else for a moment," he said.

"Who?"

"I don't know, but it wasn't you. The dress is befitting, though. You look nice and rather—self-assured. Yes, quite bold." He smiled.

"Thank you," she said, pleased with the compliment.

She had stood long in the mirror in her bedroom after she prepared for the party. The dress was the color of ripe plums and rare sunsets. Along the neck was a loose drape that served as both shawl and hood. Secret used it to cover her head and attached it at her temples with unadorned silver clips. The sleeves were fitted from shoulder to elbow but almost a second skin from elbow to wrist. At the cuffs were triangular cascades of matching silk, affixed to the mid-forearms in the tight seams. Down the darted bodice to the hem was a placket embroidered with a violet vine bearing flowers. A molded silver button centered each bloom. The waist was narrow above the hips' curves. Thin tucks striped the skirt, which pulled gracefully toward the floor.

Perhaps it was, as her mother suggested, a costume. But wearing it, Secret felt brave and powerful. She wished to pretend she was both, if only for a night.

"I'm glad you came," Nikolas said.

"At the end of the night, I hope I feel the same way."

"Oh, Secret. Everything will be fine."

"Yes, well, regardless." She decided then what to do with his gift. She held it out to him. "Happy birthday. I know you're supposed to open gifts later, but please take this now and open it in private."

"Ah, so mysterious. Why?" he asked as he accepted it.

"You'll see. But be careful. There's glass inside. It's fragile. And you must keep it upright."

Nikolas drew it close to his chest. "Thank you. I'm curious." He glanced at her wrist. "Good. I see Charming gave you a pouch. She's devised a great hunt. *You* might think to check places you've been before." He winked and stepped away. Secret was puzzled by what he meant.

A few minutes later, he stood on the dais to welcome everyone and directed them to tables full of food and drinks and the wide hall for dancing. Secret managed to find fruits and nuts among a feast spread of game birds and meat pies. She ate nervously as she kept close to three other girls, one whose face turned pink as a cat's nose when a boy asked her to join him for a waltz. Then, after Nikolas opened his presents, Charming gathered the large group together and sent them on the search.

They were allowed the run of the castle. However, while some doors were open, others were locked or marked with signs not to enter. Open doors yielded nothing or a coveted item from the list. Screams and laughter arose when some decided to enter where it was forbidden. Guards stood in wait and rapped them on the heads with wool-stuffed clubs.

Secret was merry with shared excitement, running around and laughing with her friends. Her cloth pouch became heavier with each found item. They compared their trinkets, speculating on who might be ahead as the winner.

She dashed toward a stairway that led to the hall's gallery but noticed movement in the shadows before she touched the railing. With a pause, she searched the floor. The tiniest mouse she had ever seen poked her whiskery nose into an arc of light.

She wanted to ignore her and continue with the game. She wanted a normal evening, just like any other guest there would have. But the mouse chased after Secret and squeaked.

With a quick glance over her shoulder, Secret reached down to scoop the creature into her palm. Secret traced the tip of her gray ear.

Would you like me to take you outside? Secret asked.

No, there is a place you must see, the mouse said. She revealed the image of a large chamber with a long table and heavy drapes.

The mouse guided Secret from her perch in Secret's hand. Secret walked into a familiar corridor that ran along one side of the Great Hall. Lamps, hung at somewhat even intervals, provided some illumination. The whispering couple who stood in the dark—the girl with her back to a column caged loosely between a boy's extended arms—didn't seem to notice her. As she passed them, she blushed. Then the mouse told her to open a door to the right.

Secret had been to the chamber before. Nikolas had taken her there to hide the night of the grand ball long ago. She placed the mouse on the floor, and it skittered toward the curtained panels. The room was the same as she remembered it. Secret walked up to the crest on the wall opposite the panels. In the dim light, she could see its gold rim and the reddish tone of the flat objects arranged in rows.

So, there are the dragon scales from every prince's quest from generations long past, she thought as she looked at the crest. Nikolas will be the next to add to the display when he returns from his.

The mouse squeaked again. Secret went to her and stood outside the panels. Secret searched for the latch, which clicked as she crept into the clandestine little room within the room. Light drifted through the woven panels like mist. Her fingertips traced the bench's edge, then its top. An object toppled. She grabbed it.

Secret exited the hidden space, closed the thin door, and went to the windows. In her palm was a carved stag. This prize, without a doubt, was meant only for her.

Unnoticed, she slipped into the corridor. Instead of turning left to go out as she had come in, she turned right. She expected to find another entrance into the Great Hall. The corridor met a perpendicular hallway. A crossroads. There were no sounds or movement, no signs or barriers. The passage ahead was in full shadow, but in the distance were two stripes of light, one vertical, one horizontal, meeting at a right angle on the floor.

Secret looked from side to side. She stood tall. Her dress shifted softly against her skin. Tonight, she was brave. Tonight, she chose adventure.

She walked into the passage. Her hands searched for a knob or a latch. Her fingers entered the bright vertical gap and wrapped around the dark edge. The wood in her palms didn't move back or forth on hinges. It did shake, so she pushed the door aside, and the gap widened.

The pocket door gave entry to a gilded corridor. She remembered the legend her father told her when she was small, the one about the gold roads that covered the land, removed and melted when the kingdom triumphed from The Mapmaker's War. Perhaps there was some truth in what he said.

Oil lamps burned from old torch hangers in the walls. She was glad at the moment that she'd chosen soft-soled shoes. Secret tiptoed along the stone floor, which sloped more and more with each step. To her left and her right were heavy wooden doors, chained and locked. She couldn't believe there was no armed man there.

The hall ended with arrow loops in the wall, sealed with a mix of stone and mortar. Yet she discovered one last door. It yawned wide open. Secret peeked inside.

No sound startled her, but she realized she wasn't the only live creature there. Slowly, her eyes searched the chamber. In a high-backed cushioned chair sat the King. He wore no crown or robe.

His hair lay disheveled. He was dressed in a simple tunic, long loose pants, and tattered slippers. The King rubbed his right thigh as if pained. A small groan rumbled in his throat. She watched him—this man was her ruler, who had power she could only imagine—this man who was a stranger to her, yet the father of her best friend. The King squinted with a wince. She felt a sudden sadness for him, as if she'd felt his own hidden pain.

Then he sneezed.

Secret jumped into the shadows. As she crept backward, silent as fog, she noticed the ornately carved cabinet against the wall opposite the door and the weapons displayed above it. Among the pole-arms, swords, axes, and maces, a particular sword caught her eye. The hilt seemed to be made of gold and embedded with jewels. Unlike the other weapons that somehow hung on the stone wall, the sword was placed on a shelf. From where she stood, she could discern no specific details, but the longer she looked, the more she wanted to study it.

Her toes cramped as her arches drew up, sore as bruises. Her

limbs loosened as if she were being slowly quartered. Secret shut her eyes against the tension. A curl of heat spiraled from her navel, and the vision ripped through her flesh. There was a beautiful dark-haired man, as graceful as a stag, who held a sword in his hands and dueled with a morning sky. A sword he found amid a vast treasure.

As soon as she could move again, Secret ran from the King's private chamber and the corridor of gold into a shadowy corner of the Great Hall.

The scavenger hunt ended, and the young people placed their finds on a table with cards bearing their names tucked in the bags. Secret stayed where she was, both to hide and to keep the bag with her because it held the carved stag.

The entire evening had been more fun than she had expected, but what had happened in the chamber had ruined it. Why didn't she just go the other way and continue with the hunt? Why did she sneak down a corridor she clearly wasn't supposed to enter? And why had she endured that rupture—yes, that's what it was, a tearing release in her body and mind, some force breaking free.

Of course, it wasn't the first one, but it was one of the worst. As she pressed into the corner, squeezing her eyes shut, she saw the sword, and then the symbol, and the rock, and the nesting dolls—

Secret gripped the top of her head. Stop, she whispered. Piercing jabs streaked into her hands and feet. She focused on the tips of her nails digging into her hair and skin. The images remained fixed and still. Within herself, she observed them at a distance. She was suddenly aware that they were even more similar than she had thought to those images she received from creatures and plants. Within each image was a feeling, a story, a message. She was petrified of what she might discover if she were to fully open herself to them and what she would be forced to put into words. She didn't want to know.

When she lifted her eyes again, the quartet was playing as the others ate, drank, danced, and talked. Secret glanced toward the upper gallery. Some of the boys had joined together to spar with wooden swords. The tall, chestnut-haired boy she found handsome lifted his blade, ready to strike his smaller opponent. She welcomed the giddy lightness and wholly different trembling that rushed into her as she watched him. The boy won, then faced Nikolas, for whom he was no match. Nikolas was focused but fluid, light but sharp. He might have begrudged the practice his father required of him, but he took the lessons, and the skill, seriously. Nikolas had a boy's body, she observed, but he moved like a man. She forced herself not to think about the other sword.

She emerged when clamoring bells called the guests to the dais to declare a winner of the scavenger hunt. Muriel, a clever friend with a competitive spirit, won a prize that made the boys and girls gasp. Envy cloaked many in green. She received her very own Tell-a-Bell, the latest incarnation. Less obtrusive than those worn on belts, the miniature ones were expensive and required a long wait on a list. Secret flinched at the memory of Fewmany, in that same hall, the same tiny contraption dangling next to the spiral of his ear.

As everyone began to leave, Secret clutched the carved stag and left the half-full bag on the table with the items she'd found during the hunt. She smoothed her dress, lifted her shoulders, and fixed a pleasant smile. Outside in the courtyard, the guests waited for their rides home. She saw Nikolas stroll among his friends, thanking them for their attendance and gifts. Secret joined a circle of friends who were discussing their plans for the rest of the summer. Some were staying in town, others planning to travel to see relatives. Nikolas, as Secret knew, was leaving the next week with his father to visit a southwest region of the kingdom. Secret planned to take a botany class and read for pleasure. Her friends laughed at her with affection, agreeing that she might as well be in school.

The group dwindled as parents arrived to take them home. Other clusters of guests grew smaller.

Secret was left next to Nikolas. She opened her hand to show what she'd found in the meeting chamber.

He smiled, delighted and mischievous. "I hoped you'd find it." He leaned closer in to whisper. "Proof of a recent encounter with Old Man. I wanted you to have it."

"Thank you. It's beautiful. Whoever carved it has great skill," she said.

"And thank you for my gift. Truly. I understand why you wanted me to open it alone. No one would be able to fathom why I received a chrysalis and didn't find that bizarre."

Secret smiled. She paused for a moment. She realized how steady his voice had been throughout the evening. She didn't want to embarrass him, so she didn't mention it seemed his voice had finally changed. The tone was clear and warm. "Yes, I remember when you said some time ago you wished to know what it was like to see a butterfly emerge. I searched long and hard for a chrysalis I could remove without harming it. They are so vulnerable, and crumpled, when they crawl out. I hope you're near it when the time comes."

"If not, I'll have the pleasure of setting it free for its first flight. What kind of butterfly is it?"

"That's part of the surprise," she said.

They were content in silence until Nikolas said, "I'm glad you came, although you seemed to disappear for a long while. I didn't see you anywhere."

"I'm glad, too, and I didn't mean to be away from everyone, however . . ." She decided she could tell part of the truth of what happened that night.

"Yes?"

"I went somewhere I shouldn't have. A corridor, near your father's private chamber." She locked her knees when she felt them quiver.

Nikolas laughed. "Someone should have been there near the door. Hugh must be in his service tonight. He has a weak bladder. Good thing you're no threat to the King."

His humor relieved her, and she smiled. The guard's name sounded familiar. She searched her thoughts. A young man with a cleft chin. "He's the one who found us in that hidden room at the ball, where we went for hide-and-seek."

"Good memory. A shame you didn't have an opportunity to get reacquainted, yet again in a place you shouldn't have been," Nikolas said.

Secret heard the approach of a cart. She looked up to watch her father rein in the two horses and halt the cart precisely in front of her.

"Good evening, Mr. Riven," Nikolas said.

"Good evening to you, my liege, and a happy birthday as well. I trust you had a jubilant celebration." He bowed from his seat.

"I did, sir, thank you." Nikolas turned to Secret. "I'll see you at the end of the summer then? We won't return until a few days before the next term."

She nodded, gave a small wave with the hand that held the

carved stag, and climbed onto the cart, sweeping her skirt with a flourish.

Nikolas raised his hand as they departed.

Once they passed out of the gatehouse, Bren nudged her with his elbow. "So—you had the prince's attention," her father said.

"We were having a conversation."

"Does my Secret have a secret?" he asked.

"No, Father."

Bren brushed his daughter's cheek with affection and chuckled. Secret blushed, appalled at the mistaken notion her father had in his head.

"He's only a friend. Besides, I'm common by comparison. The wrong blood, as you would probably say."

"My fault, is it?" Bren said with a bitter tone.

Secret's body tensed against his strange reply. She seemed to have scratched through a veneer of feelings she hadn't known was so present and so thin. "I meant no harm, Father."

He took a deep breath, cut his eyes at her, then relaxed. "Yes. Tell me about the party," he said lightly.

Anxious to appease him and keep her own worries at bay, she recounted every happy detail.

The Messenger Returns for the Arcane Manuscript

NOT LONG AFTER NIKOLAS'S PARTY, THAT SAME SUMMER BE-
fore she turned fourteen, Secret anticipated the return of the messenger who had brought her mother the arcane manuscript.

In the months that had passed, Secret wondered what became
of the text. The first weeks after it arrived, Zavet had entered one
of the darkest periods Secret had ever witnessed. When the mood
finally lifted and Zavet returned to her usual distant self, Secret
never knew for certain whether the manuscript had any bearing on
her mother's behavior.

Secret's initial fascination waned, too. She had scanned through
Zavet's logs and diaries and had also, when neither parent was
home, made a quick search under beds, on bookshelves, and in the
second- and third-floor storage rooms. The strange reaction Secret
had had to the name in the manuscript, as well as Zavet's deliberate
secrecy, stirred her. But as her mother calmed, so had she.

Out of sight, out of mind.

One year after the arcane manuscript's arrival, Secret was home
from her botany class and was studying her notes in her room. She
hoped she would be in the house on the day Bea returned so that
she could find out the manuscript's fate. She got her wish.

Sharp, efficient knocks announced a visitor at the front door. Secret leapt from her desk and waited at the second-floor landing. Two
female voices caught her ear. She feigned the need for a snack and
listened to their conversation as she filled a small bowl with cherries.

"The script bears no logical resemblance to any language family I know," Zavet said.

"How interesting," Bea said. "You haven't a clue?"

"I've not had many moments to solve the puzzle," Zavet said. "I apologize for the delay."

Secret walked over to her mother, a cherry hidden in her mouth. Bea peered directly at her. The girl turned her face to the floor. When she looked up again, Bea was staring at Zavet's eyes.

"If you haven't the availability, or no longer wish to attempt the task, I can return the manuscript. Perhaps another translator can solve the mystery," Bea said.

Zavet thrust backward as if she'd been slapped. Her face conveyed shock. Secret winced as though she'd felt a physical blow to her mother's reputation. But the girl was mistaken.

"No—please. I wish to study it and discover its meaning. Please, give me more time," Zavet said.

To Secret's ears, her mother's tone had been faintly desperate. Secret wondered if her mother had been presented with a language she couldn't understand.

"Of course. There's no intent to rush you," Bea said. "No doubt, when the time is right, all will be revealed. Your reputation engenders considerable faith."

Zavet, who always appeared to look around or through others, pierced Bea with a violet gaze, then turned her mouth as if unsatisfied. "Thank you," she said.

Bea reached into a pocket of her huge satchel. She handed a small card to Zavet. "If you should complete the translation before I return again, you may send a note to this address."

Zavet took it between her fingers without reading a word.

"Good day to you both," Bea said.

"I'll see you out," Secret said. When Bea walked ahead of her, Secret spit a pit into her bowl and left it on the dining table.

She escorted the messenger to the door. Secret was full of

questions she could not ask. They exchanged courteous good-byes as Bea stepped past the threshold.

Secret paused with her hand on the fireplace mantel in the parlor. That the arcane manuscript confounded Zavet gave Secret a certain bitter glee as well as a feeling of disappointment in her failure. She went to get her bowl from the table and bit a cherry from its stem. Zavet was sitting in her chair with her face toward the window.

Her mother had no way to know by sight or sound what Secret had been thinking, but Zavet said in a stoic tone, "I've yet to make sense of it, Secret."

The girl stopped chewing. She had received a precise answer to a question she had not spoken.

Zavet sighed, reached for a glass grid, and resumed her work.

After Bea's return visit, the fall of twilight bestirred her mother. Night brought unrest. Secret's slumber was more often disturbed by Zavet's unusual activity. Her mother had, until then, been a deep sleeper difficult to rouse.

When Secret heard noises downstairs, she crept out to listen. She shallowed her breathing until it nearly stopped. She hid behind doorways and chairs. As it had been since Secret was a baby, Zavet mumbled in languages the girl couldn't understand, yet sometimes in the one they shared.

This continued for weeks, until her actions took a turn.

"I've been robbed," Zavet said one night. She fluttered through her workspace, her arms outstretched to slip a book from its place, move a bin to another spot, stack this grid here then there.

"I've been robbed," Zavet said another night. She paced through the parlor, bumping furniture as if she'd forgotten its placement.

"I've been robbed," Zavet said again and again, until Secret was convinced that something important was gone.

Secret searched the house when her parents were away or

absorbed in their work. They had many beautiful things, collected as her parents became more and more able to acquire, but all objects were accounted for, if only out of place because Zavet had moved them.

With dread, Secret wondered if the missing item was the manuscript itself.

One afternoon, when her mother went for a walk, Secret went to her father in his study. This was one of his prized days to spend with his books, maps, and notes in his own hand. He was in pursuit of the elusive connection to a lost past again. His favorite map was on the wall.

It was a spectacular artifact of cartography, at least three hundred years old, or so Bren was told when he purchased it. He had been a young man recently finished with his high academy studies. The luxury cost him the loss of many well-balanced meals and a room of his own. Hand colored, the map depicted the topography of their continent with attention to forest types, mountain ranges, and bodies of water. Although significant towns were noted, there were no boundaries that demarcated kingdoms.

Bren had taken pains to create transparent overlays, and the one Secret remembered most was of the great battles of The Mapmaker's War combined with the ancient trade routes. As a young child, she had stood before it when her father helped her with her schoolwork.

"See, our kingdom reached through here," he had said, running his finger over the veil, along the sea to the west, under the river to the north, and through forests to the south. "But since The Mapmaker's War, it is here." Bren traced the lines on the veil that showed the kingdom had doubled its realm, well across the river. He explained how far north and east the war had been waged. It extended into the region where her mother had lived as a girl but no farther. Some scholars believed the great plain and fierce cold there thwarted the expansion.

Even as a little girl, Secret had been transfixed by that map, the fine detail and rich colors and generous legend. So that day, years later, when she stood at her father's door, a trace of affection drew through her worry.

"Father," Secret said. His back was to her, his finger on the overlays marked with symbols meaningful only to him. Books lay open and stacked across his table.

"Yes, what is it?" he asked, his attention unmoved.

"Mother is ill," she said when he finally turned away from the chart.

"How so?" he asked.

"She says she's been robbed, but nothing is missing, at least as far as I can tell. I checked the shelves and tabletops and walls and chests," she said.

"She must have misplaced something and is making too much of it. What do you think it is?" he asked.

"I don't know. I'm not sure." Secret paused. Her mother had told her not to tell her father about the arcane manuscript, but perhaps Zavet had mentioned it to him since then. If the manuscript was the source of Zavet's distress, maybe she shared her troubles with her husband. Surely he would be sympathetic. "Maybe she's upset about something, like the manuscript she's been studying."

"What manuscript?"

"The one she hasn't been able to translate."

He chuckled as if he'd heard a wry joke. "I don't know what you're talking about. No such thing as that baffles her. You must be mistaken."

Secret searched her father for a sign that he knew more than he was saying. He blinked at her, guileless.

"Then it must be something valuable," Secret said, "a ring or a bracelet. But whatever it is, she mutters and searches at night while you're asleep."

"Ah, then, she's tired and can't think clearly. She works more than is required of her. Don't worry yourself, my pet."

Bren smiled at her, but his eyes did not. Secret understood that her father knew of her mother's odd behavior, even though he didn't know the cause.

Secret walked downstairs, pushed the great bobbin that lifted the latch, and stepped out to the courtyard.

She took a seat on the wooden bench and table her father had given her for her thirteenth birthday. Birds visited the shallow bath and raised platform where she served fruit and seeds. In the corner that was always dark and damp, new mushrooms emerged. She looked to the empty place where the fig tree had been. As quickly as the grief stirred again, Secret forced it down.

Secret was sincere in her concern. She hoped her father would make an effort to talk to her mother and then wished he would talk to her to explain what was wrong. But such directness was unlikely. Secret knew Zavet would divulge nothing. Neither parent was so straightforward.

Besides, there was the inviolable bond they shared. Secret thought they surely knew of people's tolerant, yet suspicious, attitude toward her mother and general high regard for her father, but this appeared to create no dissonance between them. They were ruthlessly protective of each other, their mutual respect and admiration undaunted. Together, they were affectionate in words and gestures with a frequency and intensity Secret never experienced with either. In all the years as their child, she had never had one complain to her about the other, rally for her favor over the other or secure her in their confidence. The love between them existed before and without Secret. She was never part of it and never could be. That love eclipsed her, then and always.

Soon after Secret tried to speak to her father, Zavet's wanderings through the house after dark gave way to nightmares. She heard Zavet call out in words Secret didn't understand. The floors and walls only muted the language Secret was certain, in all the routine mumblings, she'd never heard before. The sound of it made her body vibrate, as if the smallest fibers within her trembled in unison.

Secret lay in bed with her eyes on the ceiling.

"Wake up, Zavet! It's only a dream!" her father shouted. Then a pause, the sound of crying, and her father again, "I am your husband. This is your home. You're safe. No one is taking you away. Open your eyes and look at me!"

Secret listened in terrible pain, a poison of shame and anger leaching from her blood and bones. Why did she have a mother like this? Zavet couldn't look at her daughter the same way she gazed upon her dead words. She didn't have friends for tea and their children running through the house in laughter. Where was the mother invoked in the old tales, who cooed, kissed, and cuddled, who let this one take her place?

A hot, black pressure surged into her chest and throat. Rage, pure and vicious, wanted out. It goaded her to kick, scream, pound, flail, destroy. She fought it as she feared it, a hidden force she hadn't known was so potent.

As it quieted, throbbing in her temples as punishment for its rejection, Secret put her face in her hands. Then came the sadness for a cold mother she could not comfort and a father helpless in his blind love. Secret cried for a misery beyond, and which contained, her own.

Then almost as suddenly as they began, Zavet's late wanderings and nightmares stopped. All returned to normal, day in, day out, as if that period itself had been a dream. But Secret knew, because it always did, the darkness would return.

XXVII

The Dreams of the Town's Children

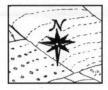

FOLLOW THE CHILDREN INTO SLEEP. YOUNG AS THEY ARE, they, too, climb mountains and cross valleys. They swim in deep oceans and stroll through gardens. Such beauty is within them from birth. In the open spaces between dreams and waking, there is peace. They are empty of everything but their own selves.

Then the void blinks and ripples, and dreams form.

Follow a frightened boy who rides a small horse through a dark wood. Stand powerless as a bandit jumps through the trees and beats him with a whip. Run behind the escaping boy.

Fall through a hole in the ground next to an anxious girl. Sit with her and the terrible knowledge that she broke her mother's dish, broke her mother's dish, broke her mother's dish.

Leave, because nothing can be done now, and discover a skeletal waif dressed in elegant clothes serving its heart to a man and woman with sunken chests.

Step backward into another room where a crowd's laughter peels the light from a boy's face. He stands next to a slate square, his chalk-written answer to a simple problem incorrect. Watch him melt like wax.

Jump out of a window and run through a tunnel that ends with a gilded cell. Do not disturb the sleeping girl who dreams she is not shackled there, naked.

Leap upon a sailboat that floats back to the light. Approach a boy who stands at the edge of a village. He cuts his eyes to the sky and behind his back. "Help me," he whispers. A winged shadow blocks the sun as angry voices come closer. "Help me!" he shouts. His scream crosses the boundary into consciousness and joins the others.

"Dragon!" the children cry as the bells in cages rouse the adults to mutter about their day.

It was only a dream, the children are told in harried, or kind, or teasing voices.

XXVIII

Secret Sickens with a Fever

SOON AFTER SECRET BEGAN HER NINTH YEAR OF SCHOOL, and the day before her fourteenth birthday, she walked to Old Wheel to see a performance after school. She checked her pockets and satchel and realized she'd forgotten her money at home. Her desire to attend the amusement was strong enough for her to risk going to The Tallest Building to ask her father for coins, which she had been compelled to do only twice before.

Anxious not to miss the start of the bard troupe's tales, Secret whisked into the lobby of Fewmany Incorporated. No one was behind the carved desk. She rang the bell. By count, she noticed two more names had been carved into stones in the wall. Again, she struck the bell. She knew she needed a visitor's pass—such were the rules—but she hadn't much time. Secret walked with purpose to the stairwell. She would take no risk with dallying in the open waiting for the slow pulley lift.

On the twelfth floor, she arrived breathless. The staircase was opposite the lift, and as she paused to think which way to turn, Fewmany emerged straight ahead.

She froze in place like a cautious rabbit.

Ever since the incident three years earlier, Secret had tried to avoid Fewmany. She knew he was most likely to attend performances at two halls in particular, and if her parents were taking her there, she did her best to excuse herself from going. When that didn't work, she engaged in the niceties with her parents' acquaintances and the classmates she saw but kept her eyes moving. If she spotted him, she dashed off to the water closet or found some other way to dodge even a polite exchange of "Good evening." She suspected he had noticed her now and then despite her furtiveness, but he did not come near.

But there, on the top floor of his building, she was trapped.

Fewmany seemed attentive to his private thoughts as he walked and nodded in acknowledgment that another person stood in front of him. Then he paused, stared, and finally smiled.

Secret braced herself. She had dreaded a moment like this, but the circumstances that day were worse than she imagined. There she was alone with him. She knew rationally there was little chance he would mention the matter for which he'd visited her house those three years back. Yet, she remembered well the uncomfortable feelings he seemed to provoke in her. She wanted no conflict.

"Oh-ho, what have we here?" Fewmany said. "Miss Secret Riven! No mere glimpse today, but a full gander. You look lost. Trying to find your father?"

"Yes, sir," she said.

"Come with me." Fewmany escorted her down the corridor to Bren's office, but her father wasn't there. The magnate led her back to the central hall.

"I spoke with him quite recently. He will no doubt return soon," Fewmany said.

"I appreciate your kindness, but please don't let me keep you from your duties," she said.

"I've a moment or two to spare, especially to ensure you aren't rounded up for trespassing," he said with a grin. "Unless the badge is hidden on your person."

Secret flinched and realized there was no chance for a quick escape. "I was in a hurry to see my father. The man wasn't at the lobby desk at the moment."

"Well, then, I'll have to see to that. 'Twouldn't do to let the riff-raff run about the place. One never knows what shall crawl in off the streets these days."

She didn't know what to say.

His comment snagged her attention not only for what he said but more so for the way he said it. Although she had heard his voice before, she hadn't noticed he spoke with an accent she couldn't identify. His choice and order of words were sometimes unusual. She knew he and her father were born and reared in the same region of the kingdom across the river, her father in the populated former seat, Fewmany outside among the pastures. That subtlety alone may have accounted for the difference, but she could think of no one she'd ever known who sounded quite as he did. Then again, neither did she know anyone else like him.

She peered into the glass case that had stood in the central hall as long as her father had worked there, no doubt for some time before. She didn't feel as alarmed now, but she did will him to leave. She was content to wait for her father without supervision.

"Beautiful, are they not?" Fewmany asked as he walked toward the display. Inside were mechanisms made of gears and bells, which ranged in size from that of a young child to one as tiny as a tailless mouse. The smallest of all Tell-a-Bells hung at his ear.

"'Twas only the simple ring of one that gave me the idea for the invention that everyone wants now. When I was but a knob-kneed lad, I heard the old ram out in the pasture with the bell a-clanking at his neck and the ewes giving chase. I thought, We're no different from sheep. You and I—everyone—we're conditioned to respond to the sound of a bell. Dinner to death, and all that's between. A bell says, Pay attention. A bell says, There's a message. A bell says, Be alert. When we're reminded, or intend to remind, we invoke it—something rings a bell.

"All those years ago, I had neither the means nor the know-how, or how I'd get either. Later, I had the former and could hire the latter. I recruited men hungry with ambition who took my idea, made it work, and scaled it down from one that ticked loudly and obtrusively on a table to one that whirs as quietly as a thought and rings as lightly as a sigh."

He tapped the little cage on the side of his head. "Now, everywhere, people get through their days with more clarity and success. The bells ring, and they talk to themselves about what must be accomplished, what they need at the market, what chore requires completion. They repeat their bell toll."

Secret looked at the tiny contraption at his ear, in the same place it had been the first time she met him and each encounter thereafter. "They are everywhere, without a doubt," Secret said.

"*Baaah, baaah, baaah,*" Fewmany said. "Of course, now, I have men at work on a device to capture sound. Imagine how *maaaad* the masses would go for that."

Secret nodded, but only to acknowledge she heard what he said. She didn't know what to think of the man at all.

"What grand ideas have you for the future?" he asked.

"I haven't thought so far," Secret said.

"Your father says you're a smart girl, a touch dreamy, uncommonly quiet, not a lick foolhardy, without a rebellious bone in your body."

Secret looked away as she tried to think of a reply. Opposite the glass case of Tell-a-Bells was another sparse with antiquities. They were everyday objects—a cup, a clasp, a necklace missing several beads, a knife, and more—but they were exquisitely crafted and remarkably beautiful. All of a sudden, a clammy coldness spread under her skin.

"I do my best to be good," Secret said at last.

"Yes, you do, don't you? An intelligent, respectful, and forthright young person you are. I think you'd make a fine apprentice, in the right department." Fewmany tucked his fingertips into the edges of his coat pockets. The chain of his timepiece curved over the lumpy swell of one of them. He gave a sharp sniff and squinted his eyes ever so incrementally. "'Twould be essential to make a match with your interests and capabilities, but all the better if that revealed any hidden talents."

There. She was certain she'd sensed the shadow of the symbol rise behind his words.

"I shall have a talk with your father about you—oh-ho, and here he is," Fewmany said.

Bren greeted them and asked what sparked Secret's unexpected visit. She said she'd forgotten her allowance to pay for a bard troupe performance and wished to borrow the sum. As Bren searched his pockets, Secret's head began to ache. Secret took the coins, said her thanks and good-byes, and put her hand on the staircase rail to leave.

"Next time, Secret," Fewmany said, "remember your pass. We have ways of dealing with those who don't cooperate."

"Yes, I will, sir," she said, her eyes on stairs below.

When Secret stepped into the street, her head hurt, her body ached, and her belly felt leaden. She searched her cloak's inner pocket for the coins her father loaned her. She stopped at an FM Apothecary for a packet of willow powder. The clerk gave her a glass of water to take with the medicine.

As she turned to leave, Cyril stood in the doorway, his ears alert. Secret watched the passersby. None of them gave the squirrel a glance, the same as it had always been. She decided a rest in Old Woman's quiet cottage might provide comfort.

She followed him to the alley and entered the tunnel. The cool air and sound of trickling water gave her some relief. Secret hoped a visit to Old Woman would soothe her enough so she'd feel better on her return home.

Her friend was away when Secret arrived. Cyril told Secret that Old Woman was foraging for mushrooms. The thought of them made her nauseated. She lay down on the soft bed and looked around at the roof. She studied the shelves built along each wall above the windows and doors. Glass vials and ceramic jars vied for space. Secret remembered when she helped to harvest, dry, and store many of the seeds and herbs. She thought of the logbook, with its few blank pages left, in which she recorded what Old Woman taught her.

Then she saw on a joist, well beyond a tall man's reach, the curl of a snakeskin, wholly shed. The translucent scales gave no hint of its body's true colors. With a groan, Secret wished she could writhe out of whatever had taken hold of her. No sooner did she close her eyes than Old Woman returned with a basket on her arm.

"You look ill, child," Old Woman said. "Let me fix you some tea. How do you feel?"

Secret described her aches and queasiness. Old Woman brought a ladder from outside and climbed to the shelves. Secret passed between sleeping and waking as her friend prepared an infusion.

"Here, swallow this spoonful of garlic and honey before you drink your tea. It sometimes makes a body inhospitable to illness."

"It's so strange. I felt completely well an hour ago, and then suddenly, I didn't."

Old Woman sat next to the bed. "I've been in a mood myself, not quite at ease. There may be something in the air. But you're also at an age of growing pains, which can come and go quickly. You could be fully well by morning."

Secret rested as Old Woman tended to a task in the cottage with Cyril at her elbow. When she felt stronger, Secret rose to leave. Old Woman took her hands and looked into her eyes the colors of night and day with a gaze that made Secret feel vulnerable and revealed. When she glanced down, Old Woman placed a tender kiss on her forehead.

Secret went straight home and right to bed.

She had no stomach for dinner. Her mother served her vegetable broth and a slice of bread in bed. Zavet placed her hand dutifully on Secret's brow.

"You are a bit feverish. Try to sleep," Zavet said.

In the night, Secret wobbled down the stairs to get a drink of water. Her skin felt as if it were a membrane about to burst into moist shreds. She pressed apart the back door's great bobbin and latch and stepped outside to the courtyard.

She could hardly look at the place where the fig tree had stood. But the courtyard was now quite beautiful with slate tiles from end to end, growing evergreen shrubs on the east wall, and enormous ceramic pots filled with herbs and flowers Secret had planted and cared for as Old Woman had taught her.

The autumn air was cool and sharp. The moon was waxing. She connected the twinkling stars with the shapes she'd been taught in lessons, but Secret suddenly realized the connections were not inherent. They were determined. Any number of patterns could be imagined among the same fixed points.

The idea thus formed in her mind made Secret dizzy. She shuffled back inside and let the latch fall. *Clunk, click.* The sound pulsed through her stomach, her viscera tight with unexplainable fear.

The next morning, her father found her first, covered only in a sleeveless shift and burning with fever. She felt him lift her into his arms—how long it had been since he carried her—and place her into the copper tub. Her parents let the water rise to her neck and draped damp cloths over her head. When she began to shiver, her father carried her back to bed, tucking the covers around her.

"I'll leave for the office," Bren said to his wife. "Fewmany will know the best physician to tend her. Do not leave her alone."

Zavet gave her a cup of water and a dropper full of bloodwort tincture. Secret could not stop shaking. The drink spilled down her chin and neck. Her mother spoke to her, then left the room, but Secret didn't understand what she said.

Alone, she watched a pigeon, a dove, and a sparrow fly to the ledge and peek into the closed window. Secret opened the sash with feeble strength. The birds tried to communicate with her, but her head was thick with mist and fog. They seemed so distant, so out of reach.

Back and forth she swayed until she collapsed against her pillow and spiraled into a realm of dreams.

A doorway. Inlaid in the lintel, she saw two joined circles of gold and silver, their union made of amethyst. Across the threshold, a spiral stair, illuminated by reflec-  tions. She walked with the sound of footsteps behind her. From the top of the stair and mountain, she could see the wideness of the world.

She returned to the cave below the spiral stair. Metals and jewels filled the space. Swords, shields, daggers, armor. Cauldrons, pots, vessels, cups. Buckles and brooches, rings and bracelets.

Treasure beyond the wildest dream.

And then: She was on the ground in the dark in a forest. Her ankle circled in a metal ring attached to a chain. A man's hand on her thigh, a gross  weight. Terrified.

A blade glimmered.

His fingers entered her body.

She screamed and struggled.

She ran for miles. A kind man took her across a river. He did not leave her. She placed her hand on a large rock and oriented herself from that center.

And then: A fire blazed against night, a dancer near the flames. A costume covered the dancer. Large head with flared nostrils, wings that fluttered, a long curv-  ing tail, broad heavy chest. Red, so much red.

She was a child dressed in white, painted blue. A man with a gold breastplate stood in shadow among warriors. She felt him let her go without a touch or a word. Her father.

Then she was the dancer, merged with the rhythm of drums, spiraling toward the child dressed in white, painted blue. Her daughter.

With a leap, she entered the dance, white sleeves waving. She and the dancer circled the flames. The drumming became faster. The crowd began to hum. The child felt weightless. She took the dancer's hands.

She touched her child, The Orphan.

She touched her mother, The Red Dragon.

In this moment, they were myth.

XXIX

She Awakens Able to Speak
an Ancient Language

SECRET AWAKENED. HER EYES WERE CLOSED. SHE SENSED SHE was in her room, on her bed. A cool draft swept across her face. The fresh air stirred faint scents of beeswax and juniper but did not carry away a feral stink. As she lay there, her body felt heavy as if she'd walked too far without rest. Her mouth puffed woolen.

"I want water," she heard herself say with her own voice in a foreign language.

Her mother poured water from a pitcher. Vivid pink scratches lined her face and hands. She had circles under her eyes and a slight tremble in her hands.

"Drink slowly. You've had only sips for many days," Zavet said in the same unexpected tongue.

Secret sat up and looked around. Yes, she was in her room, but perhaps she was dreaming again, and the language they were speaking was part of that ethereal world.

"How long have I been sick?" she asked.

"Twelve days and nights. You could barely be roused to eat. Your flesh has become thin," Zavet said.

"I'm hungry," Secret said.

Her mother exited, favoring her left leg.

Secret looked at the windows. Nearly all of the panes she could see were cracked and some were missing. The window closest to the head of her bed had a pane with three wispy black feathers stuck to the glass, glued there with a dark substance. Blood, she thought. Why did the bird fly into the window? She doubted it survived the impact and wondered what had happened to cause all of this damage.

She dropped her legs at the edge of the bed. A gust of wind swirled in her room. As it settled, she saw bits scatter across the floor. She leaned over and peered down. She saw dead insects, whole and parts, feathers, tufts of fur, and long strands of black hair. Secret found this very strange. The maid regularly cleaned her room, and even if she hadn't been allowed inside during Secret's illness, there was no way to explain the fur, feathers, or insect parts. The feral odor rose in her nostrils.

She stood on gelatinous legs and tottered to the window near the foot of her bed. She opened it weakly, slowly, careful not to upset the cracked glass. There were scratches on the sill. Secret closed her eyes. The last memory she had before she became unconscious was of a pigeon, dove, and sparrow at the ledge. Her fourteenth birthday. A visit from them, as on her seventh. But she could remember nothing since, other than wonderful, perplexing, and sometimes horrifying dreams.

She tried to imagine what could have caused the mess inside and outside her room. A knot twisted in her stomach and yanked at her navel. Not hunger, not fear, but a warning.

Then she went to study herself in the full-length mirror. She did look thin. Her skin looked unripe. Her eyes gave a faint reflection. Her hair was limp but shiny at the crown. She pushed her fingers against her scalp. Every strand was silver at the start of the root. She prodded a greenish bruise under her eye and a soreness across the bridge of her nose. Secret felt a dull ache around her navel drop to a throbbing lurch in her belly.

She left her room, leaning against the walls, noticing scratches on the steps, and went to the water closet downstairs. She used the privy, then stood, then noticed other changes had taken place during the fever.

The blood didn't surprise her, but the timing did. Why now?

she thought. Was this part of the fever's violence? She tended her woman's body and crawled back into her childhood bed.

That night, her father rushed into her room.

"I didn't lose you," he said as he stroked her hair with a tenderness she could hardly remember from him. She allowed the gesture as she pushed away the drifting memory of what he'd once done to those same black locks.

Secret shook her head against the pillow. She understood what her father said, but her tongue wouldn't let her use their shared language. He continued to speak. She acknowledged him with nods. His face looked crestfallen as his tone rose higher. The young woman sensed what he didn't ask. She knew he was afraid she'd become silent again as she'd been as a child. She moved her lips in a whisper, nothing but air, and tapped her throat.

Bren sighed. "Your voice is weak. You're tired. I'll leave you to rest."

She was glad when he departed a day later for a postponed trip so that she wouldn't have to endure his expectations about when she would speak again. Secret stopped talking to her mother entirely. She knew the wrong words would spew out. But Zavet continued to use the strange tongue as if to test, or to trick, her.

Although she felt stronger, Secret kept to her room. Tired but unable to sleep, she decided to draw the images she could remember and gathered her coloring sticks and paper from under her bed. There she found the hidden stack of drawings she'd made as a child. The woods where her grandmother lived. The plants and creatures from the courtyard. The men in their blue coats. The woods outside of town. The symbol. She put them aside without a closer look.

On a rough-edged sheet of paper, she sketched two overlapping circles above a doorway. She had no gold or silver sticks and used yellow and gray instead. She began to color the intersection in purple. As she filled in the space, she remembered the circles she'd drawn at the lecture she attended with her father . . . and the symbol she rendered that caused him to cut her hair inch by inch. And in the same dream of the linked circles, there was a cave filled with treasure, one with vessels and rings and swords . . . magnificent swords like the one she saw in the king's private chamber that night when her body ruptured and a beautiful man dueled with the sky.

Secret crossed her arms against her chest and held herself. Her breath was shallow. She slipped into the images, careful not to go too far, to feel too much.

Logic isolated them as random.

Image linked them in relationship.

The dream and ruptures, not separate, only separated.

In the shackled struggle with the man, there was an escape and then the rock—the rock that marked one place and guided a traveler to the next—

Beyond the fire, a child in white—painted blue—Azul the orphan—men in blue coats—

The man near the fire—gold chestplate—man, father, warrior—

As she began to toss everything back in the box, she named the nexus of it all—the bee in the tree, which told of the wound and the wolf.

The connection among them all eluded her.

She wondered if the ancient language provided a clue. While sick, she hadn't dreamed of the blue men, not that she could recall. When she tried to remember those comforting dreams, she knew she had comprehended their words in the realm of sleep but had awakened with the perception of nonsense. Yet the sound of their speech—the rhythm, inflection, tone—reminded her of the one she heard in some of the fever dreams, the language she now magically spoke.

Secret whispered the unusual name that her mother had read aloud from the arcane manuscript. Aoife. She lingered over the syllables—*ee-fah, ee-fah*—unable to repeat the nuanced and certainly accurate pronunciation her mother had achieved.

That word's language was not the ancient one Secret somehow

knew. Zavet had told her so when her mother received the manuscript, and she could sense it now herself.

Her head felt thick. As she settled against her pillow and under
her quilts, her thoughts scattered, drifted, conflicted. One began to
persist—what if the ancient language she now spoke was the same
as the one in the arcane manuscript? If she was correct, Secret realized she might be able to read it, too. And her mother might be
able to help solve the mystery of what was happening to her.

As much as she wanted to know, she was terrified to find out.

The next morning, Secret walked downstairs to eat.

"Good morning, Mother," she said without thinking first. She
had spoken in her native language. Secret nearly cried with relief.

Zavet didn't acknowledge the tongue's return, served Secret
breakfast without comment, and took her seat at her workspace.

Secret gripped the edge of the dining table. A scream flowed
into her palms. She stared at her mother's back. The table rattled on
thick legs.

"*SSSSsssssss!*" Zavet hissed, wet and heavy.

Secret glared until Zavet turned around.

"What happened while I was sick? All the broken windows,
the scratches in the stairway?" she asked in the language she first
learned and spoke.

"There was a violent storm with much lightning, wind, and flying debris, thus the damaged windows. As for the scratches, I tried
to move some boxes out of storage alone. I damaged the stairs dragging them down," Zavet said.

"Is that when you got the scrapes on your skin and the limp in
your leg?" Secret asked.

"Yes," Zavet said.

A chill rippled under Secret's flesh. These were somewhat plau-
sible answers, but Secret didn't believe them.

"And what happened to me?" Secret asked.

Zavet shrugged. "An illness can change someone. Your fever was
very high."

"I can speak a language I never used before. One I've never heard spoken in my life. Is that why you are like you are—because of a sickness?"

When Zavet opened her mouth, the language from her daughter's fever dreams told the tale.

"They thought so." Zavet spun her chair toward Secret and lowered her face. "When I was near your age, I was sent to another foster home as far from my village as I'd ever been. The woman and the man who took me in told me I was possessed. No pure creature could have a tongue such as mine. They tied me naked to a bed and put a bag of salt in my mouth and left me alone through the night. When they let me loose the next morning, I drank and drank until I vomited. The woman watched me for proof that the evil was out. I've wondered what might have happened had the sputum not taken the form that pleased her. After that, I spoke only when spoken to, until I left that place to return to my fatherland, where I was allowed to use only my mother tongue."

The story shocked her. Secret felt pity for her mother, but her anger was undaunted. "It didn't begin for you when you were my age. You were far younger," Secret replied in her native words.

Zavet sighed and brushed her fingertips against her wedding ring. "I was born that way. You were not. You will not be like me." She lifted her eyes to her daughter.

Briefly, Secret stared into an open gaze that seemed to hold her and the entire world in bright violet innocence, the treasure of a beautiful child.

When Secret blinked and looked again, her mother's focus was diffuse as ever. The moment of wonder had vanished.

Secret watched her mother's features shift to their typical states, creased brow, narrowed lids, and firm, straight mouth. Zavet had returned to herself.

"Oh, no," Zavet said, as if in warning, almost teasing. "You will not be like me at all. This I know. This I've always known."

Secret's skin flushed cold. She felt small then, the way she had when she reached for the nesting dolls seven years before, witnessed by the specters of dead brothers.

"But I am different. Strange," Secret forced herself to say, as if this were her only chance to speak the truth. "Since I was little, I've had dreams, not like ordinary dreams."

Zavet bit into the grooves of her lips.

"And I have odd moments when I'm awake. Sometimes they come when I see or touch something, and the images are similar to dreams. My body aches when it happens, and they seem to rupture out of me."

"You've always had such a vivid imagination, haven't you? It was to be expected in a little girl, but now—"

"This is not my imagination. You don't know what I feel, what I see and hear. I think these dreams and ruptures are connected. I think they mean something."

Zavet turned her lips into a dismissive grin. "You know, I fault your father. He insisted on telling you those silly stories when you were small and impressionable."

"I'm fourteen now, Mother. I know the difference between what is fantasy and what is real."

"Then you're old enough to know that dreams, while asleep or awake, are meant to be forgotten."

Secret crossed her arms against her chest to contain the fury that threatened to crack her bones.

"Simply ignore the bothersome thing and, in time, it will leave you alone," Zavet said.

"Yes, you gave me such helpful advice before. You remember, don't you? Some things don't go away. It's not true."

"Then perhaps you need to try harder."

"Well, the language I awoke speaking isn't my imagination. You spoke it back to me."

Zavet remained silent.

"I want to see the manuscript," Secret said.

"Why?"

"I want to know if the language in which it's written is the same as the one we speak."

"There is a phenomenon called coincidence," Zavet said.

"And sometimes a coincidence isn't merely that."

"Simply because one can speak a language doesn't mean one can read it."

"You can."

"That is my gift. True. But the general rule applies to everyone else."

"I think something uncanny is happening to me, and—" Secret grasped for courage, for meaning. "I think I am—perhaps we are—part of something? I don't—I'm not sure."

"You are your father's daughter, aren't you? His lost past, your hidden future?"

Secret pressed her tongue against the back of her teeth. "Bring me the manuscript."

Zavet shifted her feet flat on the floor. She appeared to stare at and look through her daughter. Her face was expressionless. Then she smirked. "Wait there."

Secret watched her mother step past, favoring her left leg, then disappear up the stairs. She was away for several minutes, making noise somewhere on another floor, and returned with the familiar wooden box.

Gently, Zavet placed the arcane manuscript at the corner of the table near Secret's elbow. A soft ringing filled Secret's ears. She stared at the text. The minute handwriting was straight despite the absence of lines. She touched the paper and curled the top edge of the first page to turn to the second. She waited for the recognition to come. Both shocked and relieved, Secret shook her head.

"I can't read it," she said.

Zavet whisked the manuscript away and stored it in the box.

"Can you?" Secret asked.

"Oh yes."

"What kind of text is it, then?"

"A history."

"So what language is it?"

"The language of truth," she replied in the ancient tongue.

"That's no answer," Secret said.

"But it is the only one you shall get. Now, go rest. I have work to do." Zavet took the box and went up the stairs.

Secret gripped her head in her hands. She exhaled with a hiss of her own, long, slow, poisonous. She took the plate of jam and bread and a cup of cold tea to her room. There she remained the entire day, resentful that she went to her mother for an explanation, understanding, perhaps even comfort, and received nothing more than she ever had.

An ache wholly different from the ruptures wrenched her palms and soles, the source at her desolate heart. She tried to settle herself by imagining how Old Woman would console her, what her friend might have said if she were her mother. But the comparison somehow made the pain even worse. If Secret could choose not to have her mother and not to endure her own peculiarities—the communication with creatures and plants, the dreams and ruptures, her watchfulness, the eyes the colors of night and day—she would choose to forsake both. And if she had to pick one, she didn't know which it would be. Secret buried herself in her quilts, sipped the air, and released herself to the numb darkness.

That evening, her father returned home from his brief trip. Secret went downstairs as Zavet set dinner on the table. Bren kissed his daughter's kerchief-covered head once she sat down.

Then, for no reason Secret could comprehend, her mother revealed what the fever had wrought.

"Your daughter awoke from the fever able to speak a language she did not know before," Zavet said.

Bren's mouth curved into a dark smile and his eyes flickered with wicked humor as he studied his child.

"Once upon a time, we burned women like you at the stake," he said.

Secret glanced at her mother. She had been eating her pork and stewed apples and was then dabbing a bead of blood from her bottom lip. Her teeth were red at the edges.

"Bit your tongue again, dear?" Bren asked his wife.

Zavet nodded.

A little too late, Secret thought.

When her parents glanced toward her, then each other, Secret suppressed the urge to break every dish within reach. She ground her teeth as she remembered another dinner, another revelation, one that made her parents look at her this same way.

"Don't you have anything to say, Secret?" her father asked.

She shook her head and loosened the rage that filled her throat. Zavet had exposed her to her father. He didn't need to know what happened. It wasn't obvious like the silver in her hair. There was no need to shame her.

Secret forced a bite of food into her mouth and slit her eyes toward her mother. Better they should have burned you, she thought.

Without a word, Zavet swept her hand across the table, pushed the saltcellar toward her daughter, and tipped it suddenly at the edge of Secret's plate.

"Mind what is spilled, girl, and watch it doesn't spread."

XXX

Nikolas's Visit and the Festival

A WEEK AFTER THE FEVER BROKE, SECRET FELT WEAKENED but not unwell and wanted to return to school. The physician had no inkling what had caused Secret's mysterious illness. To his knowledge, no one else in town had become sick with this ailment. He advised her parents to keep her home to rest for another month. They all agreed she could resume her studies in the comfort of her room. Arrangements were made to get her books and assignments. A classmate would be asked to volunteer to deliver her belongings and serve as a tutor.

One afternoon, Secret heard a strong knock at the front door. Her mother answered, then arrived in Secret's room moments later with Nikolas. Zavet seemed astonished by his presence. He had book satchels on each shoulder, one his, one hers. With a shrug, the straps slipped down his arms to the floor.

As her mother closed the door, Secret heard her ask someone if they would like a cup of tea. She realized Nikolas's guard was in the hall.

Nikolas stood in the middle of her room without a word. The sight of him made her sigh with relief.

"Say something," Secret said.

"There were rumors you were dying," he said.

"Maybe I was, but now I'm not."

Nikolas pulled the carved chair next to her bed. His demeanor was timid. He looked at her with worry. His hands found no rest at his knees.

"Be still," Secret said. Then she noticed the tender pink stripe at the meat under his right thumb, a scab at the thickest end. "What happened to your hand?"

"It was cut," he said, covering the wound with the other palm.

"Yes, I can see that. What did you do?"

"It happened one night. I wasn't quite awake, I think. I'm not sure what happened. A dream about a hunt. It's a long story. I'm fine. It's healing," he said.

She sensed she shouldn't goad him, but the mention that he'd had a dream made the hair rise on her arms and neck.

"You look as if you haven't slept in weeks," he said, then paused. "Sorry. That was rude."

Secret shook her head. "You meant no harm. I was asleep while I was sick, but I didn't rest. I had strange and terrible dreams." He glanced away for an instant then didn't quite meet her eyes.

"Your fever must have been very high, then." Nikolas stared at the top of her head. "Why are you wearing such a heavy kerchief?"

She paused to think of an excuse, but the effort was pointless. Everyone would know eventually. She removed the cover and bent her head to him. The root of every single hair had gone silver.

"When the fever broke, the silver appeared," she said. "I expect it to be permanent."

"Much like our friendship," he said. "Even though you'll look far older than I from now on, you crone." He raised an eyebrow at her, a good-natured smirk on his mouth.

She laughed until a cry coiled itself around the sound. She couldn't recall the last time she laughed, but she was almost certain it had been with Nikolas.

Secret grabbed her pillow tight as the impulse to hug him surged into her arms.

He smiled then dug into his satchel. Between his fingertips, he twirled a blue feather. She took it by the quill instead of the web, and he slipped his hand around her wrist gently. Tears were in his eyes when he let go.

"I found it the week of your birthday. I've been waiting to give it to you."

She held the feather. "Thank you. It's beautiful. Where did you find it?"

"At the top of a tower. Strange to find it there of all places."

"A good place to hide and play. I never thought of how much fun that would be," she said.

"Play? I go there to practice being lord of all I survey." He swept his arm in a dramatic arc, and she laughed again.

He reached into his satchel once more and handed her a little bundle held with twine. She untied the knot. There was a broadside that announced a traveling festival and a stack of folded notes. She read one, then another. Her school friends had written to wish her a quick recovery and to tell her about what she had missed while she'd been away. Her lashes moistened with tears, which she quickly brushed away. The thoughtfulness surprised her.

"Charlotte, your acerbic but good-hearted seatmate, was the one who organized the note writing. We've missed you, you know. And the festival is next week. Some of the others wanted to know if you can go," Nikolas said.

"I doubt I'll be allowed to leave the house, especially if I'm not even being allowed to attend school."

"Let me speak to your mother about that," he said as he pulled a book from Secret's satchel.

Then a week later, a long covered cart arrived at Secret's house to take her, Nikolas, and several friends to the festival. She let her cloak's hood fall away and, when someone asked about her hair, she explained plainly that the fever had made her hair start to turn silver. Some of them flinched and pushed back into their seats.

"I hope I don't get that fever," one of the boys said.

"You must have been very sick," one of the girls said.

"I'm better now," Secret said. "I don't believe it's catching."

The festival was set up in the grassy gap between the west edge of town and the distant woods. A long corridor of booths and stages stretched from north to south. Colorful banners, open laughter, fragrant smoke, and bright tunes were everywhere. Jugglers and acrobats defied the weight of the air. Costumed men invited revelers to test their muscles and wits in games. Ribbon-haired women served mugs of ale, plates of roasted meat, and trays of sweets. Storytellers whispered fantastic tales to those who stopped to listen. At the end of the corridor, a tent's flaps opened and closed at intervals, men waiting to go in as other men trailed out.

Secret noticed that people from wards all over town mingled together, all caught in the spirit of celebration. Secret couldn't recall ever seeing such friendliness among so many different people, from the patch-worn residents of the southeast to the finely fashioned ones of the northwest, and all in between. The day itself mirrored the joyfulness—clear, cool, sunny. What a relief from our mundane routines, Secret thought.

After hours of running to and fro with her friends, she sat for a while in a shady spot near a pony that nuzzled her neck. Secret rubbed his front leg and shiny little hoof. She was in a pleasant mood, warm and open, and because she felt like it then, she listened when the pony asked to tell of his adventures. He told her of his travels from kingdom to kingdom, exhausting but interesting. He was given enough to eat and drink and his owners did their best to let him rest. He always had other horses or his handlers for company.

Then she saw Nikolas with an older boy from their school. He showed the boy an object he held in his hands. Curious, Secret said good-bye to the pony and walked up to Nikolas when the boy left, still studying whatever he held.

"Meet my new friend," Nikolas said as he lifted a small, long-jawed skull up to her. The jagged teeth were menacing.

"Is it real?" she asked as he handed it to her.

"That depends on what you think it is. I won it, and the man in the game booth swore it's a baby dragon skull, to the wonder and amazement of all who stood by."

Secret glanced up at the glint in his eyes. A tremor whipped lightly through her knees, hips, and shoulders. She pressed her fingers into the bleached bones. "Very convincing."

He took the skull and held it to his ear. "What's that? She's heard tell of your kind, has she? Of all people, she should be prostrate with awe to meet proof of a living, oh yes, sorry, dead legend. Say again? You want to whisper to her?"

The blind head floated toward her left ear. For an instant, Secret closed her eyes and remembered one of the fever dreams, the ritual fire, the dancing red dragon. When her lashes fluttered open, the skull had vanished. Nikolas grinned in its place.

Then she pointed to the sky behind him. It had become a flow of warm, muted colors around the sinking sun. He turned as a murmuration covered the horizon, hundreds of starlings in a looping, spiraling, twisting dance. The birds twirled inward, circled round. Each individual bird giving its motion to the whole wave. Secret tore her eyes away only to notice the astonishment of the people around her. Little children leapt as they pointed. Young people stared with parted lips. Adults reached for their beloveds' hands. Several brushed tears from their cheeks. All was silent except for the flutter of the wind.

"What was the skull going to tell me?" she whispered as they peered into the patterns.

"To see is a trick of the mind, but to believe is a trick of the heart," Nikolas said.

Secret stood next to him with nothing to say. The moment was perfectly beautiful as it was.

XXXI

Her Mother Dies

AFTER THE FESTIVAL, SECRET PERSUADED HER PARENTS TO allow her to return to school. She missed her classes and seeing her friends, especially Nikolas. She felt caged between the house and the courtyard all the time. Her father protested most, wishing not to go against physician's orders, but her mother was more reasonable.

"She needs to be away from here, Bren, to go on with what she must do," Zavet said, her hand stroking the back of his neck.

A night or two later, in the wee hours after she and her parents went their beds, Secret awoke to a musical noise. She glanced out of her windows for a passerby, but the street was empty. A distant newsbox was hardly audible. She listened for a neighbor at an open sash, but none was near. Secret entered the second-floor hall and went downstairs. She could hear a distinct melody. She followed the song to the kitchen and looked into her mother's office. Zavet stood with her hand on the great bobbin. The door was open. Night traced her in silhouette.

In shadow, Secret listened—for the first time in all her fourteen years—to her mother sing. There were no words, only tones, fluid and clear. The song had a simple melody.

Secret wanted to touch the sounds or swallow them whole or breathe them into her blood. She felt light and pure, bathed in music that sounded primordial yet newborn. That voice must have always been within her, Secret thought. Why had that beauty emerged now?

She tiptoed back to bed. Secret was filled with an urge for

kindness in spite of how angry she still was at her mother for what happened after the fever. A part of Secret didn't want to be so bitter. That part wanted Zavet to share more of her songs.

But the next morning, when Secret told Zavet what she had seen and heard, her mother shook her head and said, "I don't sing. You must have been dreaming."

Secret knew better than to question why Zavet denied it. She worried that her mother would stop if given such attention again. She said nothing to her father and lay in bed in anticipation. For several more nights, somewhere on the first floor, Zavet hummed, toned, and warbled until she exhausted herself and returned to bed. The mornings and days that followed were calmer, quieter.

Then silence took the place of the singing.

This awoke Secret next. She crept downstairs and saw her mother's dark back against a glow of light. Zavet sat at her worktables bent over a task. She didn't move as if she were reading but did as if she were writing. Secret stood in the shadows with the shallowest of breaths. Zavet paused, straightened, and turned in her chair. Secret held her breath until the scratching sounds resumed. Puzzled, Secret went back to her room. She wondered what her mother could be doing that required the secrecy of night. She couldn't be certain, but Secret suspected her mother's work involved the arcane manuscript.

She mistook the silence for peace. In retrospect, it was a warning.

Years later, during the Plague of Silences, when its great hush would sicken one and all, Secret would remember this eerie quiet. Zavet didn't mutter or babble during the day or sing or stir in the night. Zavet nodded and pointed and avoided words. In the absence of sound, her mother seemed to disappear, her body an echo of what gave it form.

Neither would Secret forget Cyril's final escort one afternoon and the events that followed.

She met Nikolas in Old Wheel at a lecture they didn't plan to attend. They had both had the same idea earlier in the day. There was nothing unusual about their meeting—they'd done this dozens of times before—but the mutual invitation had an urgent spontaneity about it. Somehow, Cyril knew, too, because he arrived at the hall to take them to the alley.

Secret was anxious to return to the woods for the first time since she was ill. She missed the space to roam in peace.

Cyril perched next to the grate with his paws in a gentlemanly clutch. *This is the last time I will lead you through this thin place. From now on, you must trust you know the way,* he said. He darted into the hole.

Thin place? she asked.

Where things are closer than they appear.

Is this a trick? Secret asked. She and Nikolas entered the tunnel.

Never was, and not now.

Secret tugged Nikolas's sleeve and told him Cyril would no longer be their escort.

"Why not?" Nikolas asked.

Only children see magic squirrels, Cyril said.

Secret shared the reply.

Nikolas stomped in the dark until he caught Cyril's tail. Their red- and gray-furred friend squealed. "Real enough to touch," Nikolas said with a subdued laugh.

But Cyril, why? she asked.

You are not the girl you once were, he said, then closed himself to her, a sensation as heavy as if he'd shut a door in her face.

Secret puzzled at his abruptness and what he meant. However, she didn't argue with his statement because he was right. She was no longer silent. She was more ambivalent about her ability to speak to creatures and plants than she was as a little girl. She was well aware something had changed in her during the fever, although she wasn't certain what that was.

After she and Nikolas crawled through the hole in the hollow, they greeted Reach then wandered into the trees. Cyril climbed into the branches and followed above their heads. They walked toward the setting sun.

Nikolas was as likely to speak as he was to be quiet on days like this, and on that one, he wasn't talkative. She attempted conversation, but he was terse.

"I need quiet, but I didn't want to be alone. Can you honor that for me?" he asked.

"I will," she replied. "All is well?"

He shrugged.

She nodded and followed at his side. He stopped when two owls began to call to each other among the bare treetops. She noticed he rubbed the scar under his thumb as if it hurt. Although she wondered how he got the wound and why it pained him now, she remained silent. Secret tried to enter the owls' conversation, but they refused her.

Nikolas resumed their walk. The sky changed from a faded blue to a rich violet. She saw him extend his right hand toward her. At first she thought he was about to speak and this was only a gesture before his remark. She glanced at him. She couldn't read his expression, but there was a brotherly softness in her best friend's eyes. Then he turned his palm up, and she understood what he intended. Nikolas had never done such a thing before. She didn't know whether to be touched or concerned.

She hesitated, then placed her hand in his. His grip was light as they strode ahead. She found it reassuring.

"Is there something you want to tell me?" she asked.

"No," he said. "And you?"

"No," she said, then felt a sudden urge to tell him about the fever and about the dreams and ruptures she'd had since she was a child. The words pushed into her chest and throat. Nikolas looked at her with expectation although she made no sound. She forced the words down, right through her toes and heels. Not now, she thought. Do not spoil this contentment with your strangeness. He asked for silence anyway.

Once the fallen leaves lost their red, orange, and yellow colors to the evening shadows, they turned back toward town under a sprawl of darkness. They realized Cyril had not alerted them to go on their way home. They released their hands to run back to the hole in the tree.

When they left the alley and entered the nearest lamplit street, a man's voice shouted to Nikolas. The guard raced toward them.

"Where have you been?" the guard asked. He was stocky with dark curly hair and pockmarks on his face. He gave Secret a glare but not nearly as harsh as the one with which he pierced Nikolas. "Your father will have my head if he learns I let you out of my sight, not to mention how late we are."

"He's always late for dinner. He won't notice," Nikolas said.

"But your mother isn't, and she will, if she hasn't already."

"I'm sorry. I didn't realize how late it was. We can go now, but—" Nikolas looked at Secret. "We have to take you home first. It's dark, and you're too far away to walk alone."

She didn't argue. The guard gave a high whistle, and a carriage approached. He held the door for her as she climbed inside and sat opposite Nikolas.

"I've never been caught like that before," Nikolas said.

"Neither have I," Secret said. She was always home when she was supposed to be. She expected to be in serious trouble.

She huddled in her cloak and watched the glow of the streetlamps. As they rode without another word, a noise within her gathered to meet the noise on the streets—clattering, ringing, muttering—a din of alarm.

When the carriage stopped, Secret hardly heard herself wish Nikolas a good night or his reply. Her ears filled with a rush as she unlocked the front door, crossed the threshold, and saw her father as a shadow rise from his chair in the dark.

"Your mother is dead," he told her.

Her inner balance shifted but she was still on her feet.

"An accident. I believe she choked," Bren said to his daughter.

He had found his wife slumped on the floor near her work-tables. There was an empty bowl and a half-eaten slice of bread at the corner of one. The furniture was out of place as if suddenly, violently, bumped.

Secret collapsed and shuddered. Her father rushed to comfort her. He had no idea that the first noises were laughter, not cries.

Choked. Choked! Secret thought. My muttering mother choked!

The cruel joke tore itself into tragedy while Secret herself could make no sense of the split. She cried against her father's shoulder.

Secret was the outward and the inward, the revealed and the hidden, two sides of the same coin, two places at once. She knew how she was supposed to feel—the old tales told her so—but that orphaned grief did not strike her.

Through the immediacy that followed, she remained steady and dry-eyed.

Her father's unprecedented embraces and requisite tears.

Her mother's body cool and yellowed like a forgotten tome, prepared for a colder tomb. The burial of her mother's flesh and all the memories it contained.

The shuffle of those bereaved on their behalf, friends and associates of her father, her friends and their horrified parents. Nikolas's stare of sadness, which almost broke her; Fewmany's glimpse of pity, which mended the crack.

The newsboxes repeating announcements of the death of a prominent man's wife.

The flow of sympathy carried by letters, from her mother's admiring patrons and colleagues far and wide, which wouldn't ebb for months.

Auntie filling in, feeding them.

One of those nights, as Zavet lay in the ground, Secret stood at her bedroom window. All of the panes broken while she was sick with the fever had been replaced. The feral scent had faded. The floors were nearly clean of fur, feathers, and insect wings. The house was so quiet. So quiet. She grasped her hair until the roots pulled at her scalp. She shuddered.

Her mother was dead, and she felt an irreconcilable sense of abandonment and release.

XXXII

The Months After

IN THE HOUSE SHE SHARED WITH HER FATHER, SECRET SAW her mother's absence. There was the empty place where her mother once sat, once slept, the space she once took as her own, the one in her daughter's life. Zavet's place was there, then gone.

In those first days, Secret felt the shock that her mother was dead, a physical rending of her body. Her organs seemed wrenched out of place, her heart dangling on its strings, her arms and legs weak as if pulled from their sockets. She assumed the jolt of the sudden loss is what shook her locks loose. One morning, she awoke on a nest of sliver-tipped black hair. She clutched her head, fearing she was bald, then combed her fingers through thick metallic strands that curved over her small breasts. She pushed away the memory of another time when her hair had been mysteriously restored. When she studied herself in the full-length mirror, she was intrigued by the silver's radiance and equally repelled. In the weak light, she appeared both numinous and gruesome.

Her father was transformed as well. The good-natured man he was went missing. He had tended to the necessary details in those first days. The funeral arrangements. The choosing of Zavet's burial dress. The notifications to the families they knew socially, to the high academy she attended, and to Zavet's mother for whom he had only a village name and no certainty she was still alive.

For a week, he didn't go to work, and Secret didn't go to school. She kept to her room as he silently roamed the house. When she couldn't avoid him, she listened as he talked and talked, babbling his disbelief, and allowed him to hold her as if he feared she would leave him, too. At night, she heard him above her, alone in his room, but she couldn't join him in his grieving. After her initial tears on the night Zavet died, Secret had none left. She knew, but would not name, the deep hidden truth of why that was so. Her feelings about her mother were unspeakable.

In the following weeks, sometimes, she went to the woods because she didn't know what else to do. For hours, she sat under Reach wanting no more than his stable trunk at her back. If gentle creatures approached her, she acknowledged their presence with a direct look but didn't open herself to them. With respect, it seemed, they didn't intrude their thoughts upon her. There was a formality between her and them that hadn't existed before. An effect of the fever, the culmination of a wish, an inevitability of growing older—whatever the reason, Secret didn't lament the distance.

Occasionally, she went to visit Old Woman. The first time Secret went after Zavet's death, her hair was fully silver and she told her friend what had recently happened. She tolerated Old Woman's embrace and sympathetic tears. She nodded when Old Woman remarked on the waves of grief she would endure, the times she would forget then remember her mother was gone, and the gentleness it would behoove her to have for herself as she moved through her feelings. During other visits, Secret helped with chores or followed along to forage as Old Woman reminded her of details she already knew.

Now and then, Old Woman asked whether she wanted to speak of her mother, but of these things Secret said little. Old Woman encouraged her to share her grief, but Secret could find no words to describe how she felt. That Secret didn't cry in her presence concerned the elderly woman, so Secret claimed she did at home. Secret knew if she said she didn't at all, Old Woman would worry and urge her to talk.

Nikolas, however, let her be.

He had attended the funeral and expressed his condolences then, and she allowed her father to let him in the house once a few days later. In her parlor, Nikolas sat across from her and said he didn't know how she felt but could imagine her pain. He gave her no platitudes, no idle chatter, no pressing questions, neither about her feelings nor about why she didn't weep. Once she went back to school, he didn't avoid her. Somehow, he managed to stay close even as he gave her space.

"Leave me, Nikolas. I must be alone," she sometimes said.

And he would go.

"Stay with me," she said.

And he would stay, his company quiet.

"I don't know what I want," she said.

And he would guess, sometimes rightly, sometimes wrongly, but he tried. She appreciated his patient effort more than she knew how to express.

At school that ninth year, Secret wished to be treated as if nothing had happened. But of course, it had. Her friends, although awkward, didn't ignore her, but everyone else seemed to make an effort to keep away from the most casual encounter, as if she had an affliction that would spread to them as well. She saw how schoolmates pointed and stared. Their fingertips raked across their heads, perplexed at how her hair had become so completely silver so quickly.

This roused an unwelcome, familiar shame. She hadn't forgotten her first school and the taunts she endured because of what made her different. Her appearance with that black hair, those eyes the colors of night and day, and that tawny skin. Her silence, which no one understood. Her attention to the creatures and plants. Neither had she forgotten how she was teased at this school, among these same children, for sharing tales of the plants and animals and insects. She remembered how they had invoked her mother and madness then.

Now, her dead mother was a blemish on her, replacing the stain of a peculiar one.

Secret did what she could to keep herself occupied. She was diligent with her schoolwork, excelling at history and classical languages, which shouldn't have surprised her but did nonetheless and perturbed her even more if she thought about it for too long. She didn't intend to follow in either parent's footsteps, but their influence couldn't be denied.

Her father attempted to busy himself as well.

For a while, he limited his travels and hired Auntie to stay with Secret the nights he had to be away. When he and Secret were home together, many evenings they went to their respective rooms for private study. Bren stood at his maps, flipped through books and documents, and scratched notes in large bound journals.

But Bren's nature wouldn't allow him to withdraw for long. Three months after Zavet's death, despite his grief or because of it, he began to attend performances and dine out again. When he could, he talked Secret into joining him. She did so sometimes because she wanted to hear music, see the play, or eat a good meal. Other times, she went to make the forlorn look in his eyes go away.

She watched her father with a greater curiosity than she had before. Bren had always spoken easily with anyone nearby. It wasn't unusual for him to have full conversations with complete strangers. He seemed to know the right question to ask, compliment to give, or, if he had met the person before, remark referring to a previous interaction. Bren remembered names and faces as well as familial, social, and collegial connections. People swept toward him with wide smiles and extended hands.

The amiable boy that he told Secret he'd been was mirrored in the man she saw. Secret, in some moments, thought him golden, bright, and warm in a world that welcomed him. Quietly, she envied her father, whom she little resembled in body and disposition.

Without warning, on occasion, Secret thought of her mother and what she had seen in the man who became her father. Other women ascertained his charm. Some, married or not, batted their eyes, twittered at his clever observations, and whisked their hands across his sleeve. Visiting female friends and relations of those in his circle glanced at Secret to determine her age and at her father's left hand to find a ring, which he still wore.

Although Bren had regular contact with people, Secret knew he called them associates but possibly none was a true friend. This made Secret sad for her father, who she felt was lonelier than he would admit.

Perhaps in his wife's absence, Bren noticed what he perceived as loneliness in his daughter. He remarked that she rarely told him of schoolmates she planned to join for afternoon performances or at a party.

"I know you miss your mother, but she would want you to enjoy yourself. I want that, too," Bren told her more than once.

Secret only nodded.

When that encouragement held no sway, he tried a bit of humor.

"Youth is meant to be lived," her father said. "It's a time of passion and exuberance. Confusion as well, yes, but that adds to the fun. Get out, get out! Trouble me with antics. Test my nerves with the chatter of spirited girls. Worry me with an objectionable swain."

"I'm sorry to disappoint you, Father," Secret said.

He dropped his jaw to speak but swallowed what he intended to say. "You're a good girl," he said. "No matter that you're an odd little duck."

Yes, she thought, as much as ever, if not more.

Soon enough, spring returned. Zavet had been dead six months. Secret became used to arriving home from school to find a warm dinner in an iron pot, prepared by the cleaning woman. Elinor was paid now to go to the market, cook a meal, and tidy the house five days a week. Secret and her father did their best to remember when Hildith the laundry woman made her stop and to pay on time those who gave service.

What hadn't been attended to in all this time was Zavet's workspace. Bren sometimes lingered among the belongings that hadn't been moved. Secret noticed he had taken care to return the documents that belonged to Fewmany Incorporated and the lone text Zavet was translating for her only patron. Everything else was

exactly as Zavet left it. Elinor was allowed to dust, but Bren refused
Secret's offer to store away what remained. Secret knew he hadn't
even cleared her mother's wardrobe, jewelry, or perfumes.

Secret tolerated this until she could stand it no more. The next
time her father was away on a trip, she decided to risk his anger
and take care of the duty herself.

On a day when Elinor wasn't there, Secret opened the back
door and most of the windows on each floor. She felt the breezes
swirl through the rooms. For a moment, she stood near Zavet's empty chair. How much quieter the house has been, Secret
thought. No muttering, babbling, or hissing. No hidden thread of
tension waiting to be plucked, the consequence unleashed.

She wove her hair into a tight braid and set to work. She went
into the third-floor storage room, created some order among the
boxes strewn near the door, and searched for empty crates. She
found four of various sizes. With the smallest one, she went downstairs and packed away the pens, inks, straightedges, and blank grid
paper. Next, she found clean rags in the water closet that she used
to wrap the glass grids, still murky from Zavet's fingerprints. With
that carefully placed in the storage room, Secret returned for what
was on Zavet's shelves.

All the while, as she attended her task, Secret tried to keep the
arcane manuscript out of her mind. She was embarrassed that she
claimed she'd be able to read it. But that day she'd been so angry
and desperate for answers.

What she'd said to her mother after the fever seemed like an
addled raving now. In the months since Zavet's death, Secret settled
on an explanation for what happened. She was understandably
frightened by the illness and not thinking clearly. She was wrong
about her ability to read the manuscript, and she had tried to force
meaning on the dreams and ruptures.

She needed a story—one that would explain what came to her.
The story would contain it all, instead of leaving the images un-
connected and random. She wanted the pieces to make sense, even

if the whole remained mysterious, the way the tales and lore she loved made sense. At least there was a beginning, middle, and end, and a message to it all.

But as she climbed the stairs with an armful of books, reminding herself of what she'd decided, the core of her body became tight as if it protected something hidden.

The last items on the shelves were the vase that had replaced the nesting dolls, three grammar texts, and Zavet's log and diary. Secret's hand hovered over the log. Perhaps Zavet had recorded the address Bea had given her on the little card. Secret hoped, desperately, that her mother had completed the translation and returned the manuscript to the anonymous owner.

Secret flipped to the last page she'd seen when she looked almost two years before. After the entry for the arcane manuscript, there were only titles and descriptions listed. The final entry was for an incunable with gilded edges and woodcut illustrations. No additional mention of the arcane manuscript.

She placed the log aside and skimmed the diary. The writing was a jumble of languages, one Secret's native tongue, one she could read with difficulty, three she couldn't identify. On the last page, scrawled under a lengthy paragraph, was one sentence.

A map is to space as an alphabet is to sound.

For a long moment, Secret stared at the words. She wondered what the incunable contained that prompted her mother to jot that quote or personal observation.

It was her mother's final comment.

A little cry rattled in Secret's throat. She coughed it free.

After she carried the remaining five books to the storage room, she took the vase and placed it with ceremony in the middle of her father's map table. He couldn't miss seeing it there.

Downstairs again, Secret closed the back door to block the flooding sunlight. She made a quick lunch and sat at the dining table. While she ate, she allowed herself to wonder about the arcane manuscript. Surely, since Zavet said she could read it, she had completed the work and sent it on its way. There had been time for her to finish between their awful conversation after Secret's fever and before her own sudden death.

Eight nights later, when Bren returned from his travels, Secret went downstairs to greet him. She found him with a lamp in one hand and a piece of bread in the other standing in the dark of her mother's workspace.

"What happened here? I gave Elinor the strictest instructions," Bren said.

"I cleared it. Nothing is lost. I stored it all away," she said.

"Why?"

"She's not coming back. It was time."

"It's as if I found her dead again," he said with a crack in his voice.

"Father—"

He strode passed her with his palm raised.

She stared at the back door. The moon's glow through the windows illuminated the great bobbin and latch. The door appeared to open a gap, a trick of the light or the tears in her eyes.

Bren remained cold to her for weeks.

Then as summer approached and the school term was near its end, Secret worried whether Bea would return. Secret had been told not to tell her father, but now with Zavet dead, she didn't think it mattered to keep quiet for her mother's sake. But she was concerned for her own. If she told Bren, she would have much to explain. She also didn't want to upset him again.

Once her classes were finished and Secret had long hours alone, she made an escape to the woods. She couldn't be asked what became of the manuscript if she wasn't home to be questioned. Besides that, she did feel guilty for not visiting Old Woman in several months. Secret didn't understand why Old Woman's kindness after Zavet's death stung her more than it comforted. She was sure anyone else would have welcomed the sympathy.

One bright morning, Secret walked to Old Woman's cottage.

Secret didn't see her, and there was no response when she called out her name. Although she hadn't in some time, Secret stood among the trees and asked the animals for help. A robin leapt from under a shrub.

Follow me, she said.

The bird led her to a wide glade where berry vines curled at the margins. Old Woman's back was turned, but Cyril noticed Secret. He bounded toward her and jumped into her arms. She hugged him tightly.

Old Woman spun around. Secret pressed her lips into a line, waiting to see her friend's reaction. The woman's eyes revealed an old hurt, but her smile was sincere.

"So good to see you, Secret," she said, trapping Cyril between them in an embrace. "Come, I've found a lovely new plant that is growing from a very old root."

When Old Woman released her and Cyril jumped down, Secret looked at her friend. "I want to say I'm sorry. These months have been difficult. That's why I didn't come."

"We all grieve in our own ways. I've missed you, but I under-stand," Old Woman said.

They strolled and talked. At some point, Secret felt it would do no harm to ask her friend's advice. Old Woman knew what kind of work Zavet had done.

"Before my mother died, she received an old manuscript to translate. I don't know whether she completed what she was asked to do. Someone will come to ask about its progress soon, and I don't know what I'll say," Secret said.

"Tell the truth. You can return the text, and surely someone else will be given the chance to translate it."

"But there's a problem. If she didn't complete it—and didn't return it—I don't know where the manuscript is. It may be hidden somewhere."

"What makes you think so?"

"I cleared her shelves and tables myself, and I once searched the house," she said.

Old Woman looked at her calmly for a long moment. She seemed to be considering her words with great care.

"Isn't it possible she returned it without your knowing?" Old Woman asked.

"Yes, that's possible. But it's also possible she didn't."

"Do your best when the time comes. You can't be expected to do more than that. If it was given to your mother, it was her responsibility. Her death was sudden. She didn't have the chance to make arrangements. Be as helpful as you can, but know that if it's missing, that is not your fault," Old Woman said.

Secret exhaled a deep breath. "I feel somewhat better now."

"Very good," Old Woman said. She looked past Secret into the glade and clapped her hands with mirth.

"Look, a swallow!" Old Woman said. She clapped again and laughed like a child.

Secret scanned the air and grass, then saw a blue swallow twirl with grace and speed. She followed its dramatic dance and felt glad at the sight.

"So it is told, there's not been one of its kind here in many, many years," Old Woman said.

"Why not?" Secret asked.

"A disruption in their course. Its visit is a hopeful sign," Old Woman said. She looked at Secret with such tenderness that the young woman felt tears in her eyes.

And it was a hopeful sign, she thought, because the summer came and went without a visit from Bea or any letter of inquiry about the manuscript.

Then came autumn.

XXXIII

The Messenger Comes Once More

ZAVET HAD BEEN DEAD ALMOST ONE YEAR WHEN SECRET EN-tered her tenth year of school. By then, the shock was long gone and her father was more like himself, but not quite as he had been before.

At the start of the term, she received her class assignments and saw she wasn't enrolled in the ones she had requested. There were courses for students who planned to attend the most prestigious high academies, and because Secret intended to do just that, she knew she must have those placements.

When she met with the headmaster to ask if there had been a mistake, he thumbed through the file on his desk.

"Neither your marks nor your capabilities are at issue. Our policy is to assign the seats to those who will make use of them," he said.

"I don't understand. I'm going to attend high academy."

He leaned back in his chair and folded his hands across his pro-digious belly. "For a girl from a good family, that isn't necessary, is it?"

Secret swallowed hard as she tried to keep all emotion from her face. She understood the implication. A girl like her was expected to marry well, not further her education, certainly not to the extent Secret intended. Then Secret realized she couldn't think of a single girl who'd been placed in those courses in all the years she had at-tended her school. None of her female friends, not even Charlotte or Muriel, had mentioned they'd asked for the placements. She as-sumed this was because they had more modest expectations.

"I see," Secret said with forced calm. "Thank you for your time, sir."

That night, Secret asked her father for his help, although she didn't tell him why she believed she'd been denied. He would figure it out on his own or be told directly, if that were the case.

"They can't pull an extra chair for my clever daughter among those highborn dolts? Leave it to me. This will not stand," Bren said.

Within the week, Secret was granted the courses she wanted. Soon enough, Secret heard rumors of a generous gift her father supposedly made to restore one of the school's older wings. She understood quite well the insinuation that her place had been bought. This angered her, knowing she rightly deserved to be in those classes based on her own merit.

What she didn't anticipate was the attention she drew. Although she had been taught by some of the teachers before, they seemed almost appalled that she was there, her presence a violation of established order. They were not outwardly cruel, but she could sense she was not wanted.

Then she had to contend with the taunts and snide comments from boys in her new classes as well as other schoolmates who weren't. The remarks annoyed and hurt her. Bookworm. Good morning, *Mr.* Riven. Does that skirt hide a secret?

But what frightened her were the few boys who stood in her way, blocked her path as she walked down a hall, or pressed her against a wall. The last was the worst. Most of the time, they didn't touch her, the intimidation of their presence enough, but on occasion, one boy in particular would ease his shoulder against her chest, his eyes savage, his breathing hard. She hated the fear and rage that welled up in her, useless because she couldn't act.

She remembered her father's advice when she was a child—don't cry, or others will be on her like a pack of wolves. She knew he was right. When keeping her head down and attempting to ignore them wasn't effective, she learned the power of a silent stare, all the more disconcerting because of her mismatched eyes. She felt hard and defiant in those moments, surprised she had the strength of will to face them so directly. She learned what routes certain boys took and how to avoid them at certain times.

However, she'd hold the tension until the end of the day and sometimes collapse in tears on her bed. She knew she was intelligent and worthy of the seat she took, but on the worst days, she wondered why she bothered. She worried she would confront the same derision later at high academy or that it would be worse.

She told none of this to her father, who would have intervened had she asked, but she didn't want the humiliation. She was grateful her friends remained true and steadfast, coming to her defense at times. Charlotte was quick with retorts, Muriel had a skill for interruption, and Nikolas merely had to stand next to her without a word.

In the end, had she not enjoyed the challenge of her studies, she would have returned to her former classes. As much as she hated how she was treated, ultimately, she didn't want to fail herself. She knew attending a high academy was her means to leave the town and her past behind, a way to begin again and never come back.

Beyond that struggle, there were other changes Secret couldn't wholly avoid.

She and her classmates found themselves between childhood and adulthood. Through considerable primping and posturing, there were attractions answered and unrequited. There was all manner of jealousy, betrayal, alliance, and ambition. These feelings she felt too but kept them all to herself. Better to remain quiet and avoid trouble.

She and Nikolas were no different toward each other, but Secret observed a change in how others were around him, especially the boys—louder laughter at his jokes, more enthusiastic agreement with his opinions, more effort to gain his attention. They were the sons of men with land, titles, and enterprises, some of whom where advisers to the King. The jostle for favor had begun in earnest, all of them aware what boons he could offer in the coming years. In general, Nikolas seemed happy in the company of many friends, as well as with the blatant adoration of several lovely girls.

Secret watched her schoolmates from a distance prone to sudden bursts of affection—a hand clapped on a shoulder, arm-in-arm, a girl's fingertips glanced across a boy's arm. They practiced at the limits they all knew—flirting words and gestures, in the right circumstances stolen kisses and caresses, attempts at courting before any formal intent was expected. Soon enough, there would be engagements and marriages and what intimately followed, finally granted by custom.

Aside from feeling awkward, Secret felt inadequate. She didn't think herself to be wholly unpleasant, but she was no match for other girls who seemed to sparkle. She knew she was capable of engaging conversation, but she was unable to fawn, coquet, or charm. Although she had some interesting qualities, these hardly seemed to matter, she thought, considering her appearance. She didn't believe any boy could see beyond her tawny skin, silver hair, and eyes the colors of night and day.

Once, in the girls' water closet, a schoolmate one year ahead watched her adjust the combs in her metallic hair. The girl had petal-pale skin, frond-like lashes, and crystal-bright eyes.

"I wonder where you might ever be considered pretty," the girl remarked with cruel inquisitiveness.

Secret had scowled into the mirror then cast her eyes away from her own face, angry because of the comment and envious of the girl's beauty.

Then a few weeks after Secret's fifteenth birthday, at the end of an unusually grueling day of school, she returned home looking forward to some quiet. Elinor was already gone. Secret checked the mail on the parlor table where it was always left. As a matter of habit, Secret flipped through the stack even though she rarely received anything except a periodical.

Her palms went cold when she saw a letter addressed to her mother. Bren handled the maudlin correspondence with patrons and colleagues who hadn't learned she was dead, but Secret knew this wasn't one of those letters. The front bore an embossed stamp from a courier service, and the back was sealed with a round of blue wax.

Secret rushed to her room with it in hand. She dropped her satchel, tore off her cloak, and cracked the seal. It was a typeset form letter. It requested a reply to indicate a day and time when one of their messengers might make a call. There were instructions where to post the letter and to note the attention of the Antiquities, Relics, and Curios Division. At the bottom of the page was a handwritten asterisk with the words *per your prior request.*

"Why this, why now?" Secret muttered.

For a moment, she considering having her father tend to the matter. As Old Woman had said, the manuscript was her mother's responsibility, not hers. But Secret didn't want to explain to him how the manuscript came into her mother's possession and what had happened afterward. Whether she liked it or not, she had been present when the manuscript first arrived, then when Bea returned the next year to ask about it, and then saw it herself before Zavet's death. This was Secret's problem now.

Secret pulled stationery from her desk drawer and jotted a terse response with agitated strokes of the pen. She listed several afternoons when she expected to be home—alone. She struck a match on her silver vesta, melted wax on the envelope, and dropped the letter on her satchel so she would remember to send it the next morning.

She stretched across her bed with a frustrated sigh. A prick of anger stabbed at her stomach, the needling bother of what her mother left behind. She glanced at the nesting dolls on her shelves, then closed her eyes. What she would say to the messenger, she had no idea.

On the first day Secret noted she would be home, she answered a knock at the door. She wasn't certain Bea would be the one to return, but she was. They sat across from each other in the parlor. Bea placed her heavy satchel on the floor.

After cursory greetings, Bea asked, "Where is your mother?"

"She's dead."

Bea raised her hand to her chest. "I didn't know. I'm so sorry for your loss. Please accept my condolences for you and your family."

"Thank you. You're very kind. She died nearly a year ago."

Bea folded her hands in her lap. Her brow creased and her mouth drew taut. "I'm told only what is appropriate for me to know, and perhaps the owner was aware of her death, but it is my understanding this visit was meant to be scheduled."

"I don't understand," Secret said.

"Your mother must have asked for more time to complete her task. She knew how to contact the service."

"Yes, you gave her a card when last you came."

"Well," Bea said. She paused. Her shoulders rose ever so slightly. She exhaled with an audible whisper. She reached into one of her satchel's pockets and referred to a small bound book. "My instructions for today were to obtain the manuscript and the translation."

Secret couldn't breathe. "I have neither."

Bea remained still.

"My mother must have anticipated she'd finish but couldn't fulfill the obligation," Secret said.

"I don't wish to be indelicate, but do you know where the manuscript might be?"

"I sorted the effects related to her work. I didn't find it then, and I don't know where she might have put it."

Bea nodded.

"She would have ensured its safety. My mother recognized it was a unique, valuable work. She would have done nothing to compromise it."

"Not destroyed, then."

Secret reared back in her father's chair. "Of course not. She thought it was magnificent. What cause would she have for an action like that?"

"I once had a call to make in which the person entrusted with a text decided it was incendiary. So he ensured no one would ever know again what it contained. That isn't the only instance I know of, and it won't be the last."

"How terrible."

"I agree."

"My mother wouldn't do such a thing."

"And I presume you don't think her the type to have sold it."

"No, of course not. But that's happened, too?"

"Yes, although it's rare. And you don't believe it was stolen?"

"Stolen?" A memory surfaced of Zavet's voice repeating, *I've been robbed, I've been robbed.* Zavet hadn't meant the manuscript, but Secret never learned what, if anything, had been taken. "No. She kept it hidden. I never saw it left in the open."

"I had to ask." Bea paused. "There have been unfortunate incidents throughout the years involving one treasure or another."

Secret detected an ominous tone in her voice and didn't ask her to explain. "I think it's missing. That's all."

Bea remained quiet as if she were thinking.

"What do you know about the manuscript?" Secret asked.

"I wasn't told this directly, but sometimes one learns a bit of information in other ways. I've heard it's a precious thing, the only one of its kind and unbelievably valuable. I've heard some people think it's not written in a legitimate language all, but if it is, no one has been able to decipher what's written. Some think it's worthless and the owner is a fool. Regardless of the truth, it's a mystery."

"Do you know to whom it belongs?"

"No. My connection is indirect. I'm only the messenger."

"I imagine the owner will be angry to learn it's missing. I'd expect a return of the fee might be in order."

Bea shook her head. "I believe in this instance the payment was for the trouble. For whoever owns it, the value of the manuscript is well beyond the fee."

"Do you think the owner will try to contact me directly?" Secret asked with a hesitant tone. She didn't want to endure that confrontation.

"I can't say for certain, but I will convey what you've told me," Bea said. "As for the manuscript, you have the address for the courier service. Please, write to the division if you find the manuscript or discover any information about what became of it."

Secret felt her muscles tense. She didn't want this burden. Unless she planned to divulge the matter to her father, she was now responsible for whatever followed.

"I understand," Secret said.

With an efficient flurry, Bea tucked her little bound book away, raised the satchel to her shoulder, and smoothed her skirt as she stood. "I hope you do find it."

Secret opened the front door. A cat scurried from the steps.

"I'm sorry you must deliver this disappointing news," Secret said.

"That is part of my job. Again, I am so sorry to learn of your mother's death."

Secret nodded.

Bea huffed with effort as she shifted the many-pocketed satchel against her hip. "The last time I saw you, you more resembled a girl, and your hair was black as a crow. Look at you now. You are striking draped in silver. You are beautiful. A good day to you."

Secret couldn't utter a reply through her bewilderment. No one had ever said anything like that to her. She most certainly was not, and she couldn't imagine why Bea would say such a thing. She felt a sudden urge to cloak herself but had no cover.

After Bea departed, Secret sat at the dining table and stared at the empty space where her mother once worked. Resentment pulsed thick and noxious in her veins. As far as Secret was concerned, the arcane manuscript could remain lost forever.

XXXIV

What the People of the Town Endure in Their Nightmares

IN DREAM AFTER DREAM, DOORS APPEAR IN THE WALLS where there were no portals before. One looks ancient, with elaborate carvings and an iron latch. Another is flat and narrow; another is wide and stout; this one is locked, missing its key; that one is cast in shadow, its bottom edged with light. The last looks foreboding. It leads where one does not wish to go but must anyway.

Open the door. A child cowers in a corner. The small one uncovers its eyes. The child is asked, "Do you not recognize me?" Notice the threadbare garments, the thin limbs, the gaunt face, the shivering. The child runs away. Pursue it.

Hands grab the child and beat it. "Run again! Dare to run again!" a voice says.

The chase goes on and on until the child collapses. "Don't be that way. Give a cuddle," a voice says.

The pace slows, then stops. The child returns of its own accord. A shunning silence makes it disappear in full view.

A voice shouts, "One . . . two . . ." The child stands still before the count of three. Eye contact is forced. "Answer the question—now!" a voice says.

Someone feels a grip on the shoulder. Someone hears a terrible noise. Someone has a bad feeling. Turn around. See the monster with a haunting face. Run. Where does not matter. Run! Turn a corner, jump through a window, dart around a door. Get away.

The dreamers find themselves in places they don't want to be with no idea how they arrived. Notice the chamber has no exit. Take a forgotten key from a pocket and feel it break in the lock. Pull against the shackles. Watch the hourglass trickle seconds of sand. Realize there is someone else in the room.

Wake up.

Trapped hearts pound in gasping chests. Eyes and hands scramble for familiar holds. Babies cry. Bodies need relief. Bells in cages ring.

The people stumble dazed from their doors, to their carts, to their work. All the while, newsboxes herald the day's tidings. Everything seems the same, except for the numbers and names. A scarcity here, the threat of war there. The prince from an allied land injured on his quest to acquire a dragon scale will survive as they all do. As it should be.

XXXV

A Ride to the Edge of Town

IN THE MONTHS AFTER BEA'S VISIT, SECRET DIDN'T SEARCH the house for the manuscript or mention a word about it to her father.

Instead, she focused on her studies. Her resentful teachers gave her rare encouraging remarks. Most of the teasing had given way to a perplexed tolerance. By then, it was clear the covert intimidation wasn't going to deter her.

As for the other trouble, the encounters in the halls rarely happened anymore. The most threatening of it stopped after the boy who physically pushed her came to school one day with a black eye and gashed cheek. Nikolas claimed his swollen bruised knuckles were from a bad strike while sparring with his sword and that the pale red streaks and blotches on his face were harmless rashes. She spared him a demand for the truth, and he spared her questions she was too proud to answer.

Along with the respite at school, Secret continued to have a welcomed reprieve from certain dreams and disturbing ruptures. Nothing like that had happened since the fever, and she hoped it wouldn't again. In all that time, her communication with creatures and plants had lessened as well. There were far fewer opportunities because she rarely went to the woods anymore and she'd asked her father to hire a gardener to tend the courtyard. She simply didn't have the time.

When her tenth school year ended, Secret spent the first of her summer mornings sleeping and the rest of her day as she wished, sometimes reading, sometimes attending an afternoon performance with a friend.

One evening, as she walked home after a lecture, she took a detour through a ward she had seen a few times before. The closest newsbox could be heard faintly. Children played on quiet streets. She stopped to admire a vendor's cut flowers. She leaned the blossoms to her nose. Not even the faintest scent tickled her.

"The latest hybrids," the florist said. "All the vibrant colors we expect with none of the cloying smells."

"Where are they grown?" Secret asked.

"I haven't a clue. I only sell them," the woman said.

In the pause between the florist's words and Secret's good-bye, an odd chirp pierced the air. As Secret went on her way, the noise reached her ears again. She searched windowsills and lampposts for an uncommon bird but saw none. Secret looked toward the ground as passersby hurried along, expecting to see a creature there.

Suddenly, a man ran into a small child with the full force of his walking legs. Secret gasped as the child tumbled to the sidewalk. The man glanced back but kept moving. The child sat up, pushed yellow-tinted spectacles against its nose, and looked around. Adults scurried by, muttering their Tell-a-Bell tolls into the air or scowling at the thoughts in their heads. No other person appeared to take notice.

As Secret began to cross the street, the little one stood up, chimed "No scents, nonsense," and walked off as if it had poor balance. Around a corner the child went, peeping in the distance with a flower in its hand.

Secret followed. She rushed to the child's side. "Are you hurt? I saw you fall down."

The child stopped and raised its head but didn't look at her directly. "That happens all the time."

"Where is your mother?" Secret asked.

"I don't know,"

"Are you lost?"

The child tapped its nose with a flower. "No, I'm *found*," the little one said emphatically.

"Is that your name? Found?" she asked with a grin.

"No! My name is Harmyn, and I'm found, too."

Secret knelt on the sidewalk. She looked at the child's long, loose, yellow tunic, brown leggings, and old tan shoes. Dark blond hair stuck out in tufts. Sudden affection stirred her heart. As the warm feeling made her smile, she was surprised. She had felt this way countless times for creatures of all kinds, but never for a child.

"My name is Secret, Harmyn. What do you mean that you're found?"

"Aunt and Uncle call me 'found' sometimes."

Secret suppressed a laugh. A foundling, she thought. "Where are your aunt and uncle now?"

"Not here, not there, but somewhere," Harmyn said.

"Someone is nearby to look after you, then?" Secret asked.

Harmyn faced upward. "I look after myself."

"Does anyone know where you are at the moment?" Secret asked.

"You do, and now you won't. But first," Harmyn said, and held out the flower to her, "this is for you."

Secret accepted the gift, and before she could say thank you, Harmyn was toddling away, chirping with each step.

On an early morning not too long after, Secret awoke to a tapping noise at her bedroom window. She expected to see a bird pecking for insects in the corners, but none was there. It was still dark, not quite dawn. She opened the window sash nearest her a little wider. Close to a glowing streetlamp, she saw a young man on a horse holding the reins of another. He almost hit her with a rock as she peered out.

"Come down," he said. "It's Nikolas."

"What are you doing here?" she asked in a loud whisper.

"Come down, and I'll tell you."

She was wide-awake then. She had crept off without anyone's knowledge many times before, but this was different somehow.

She hurried into a skirt and blouse and her most comfortable shoes. Without bothering with a brush or comb, she twisted her hair back and held it with a ribbon she found in a box in her wardrobe.

Her feet pattered down the stairs. She unlocked the front door and locked it again with her own key. When she walked away from the doorstep, she noticed Nikolas was dressed in drab clothing, which she had never seen him wear before. She hardly recognized him.

"Either you have a new tailor with suspect tastes, or you're in disguise," she said.

"A bonus mark for you."

"Where is your guard?"

"Standing at my chamber door, sworn to claim I'm dead asleep, because if he doesn't I will reveal to my father he was—how shall I put this?—otherwise distracted in the middle of the night," Nikolas said.

Secret's face burned. "Would you tell?"

"Of course not. The threat is enough, and who knows when we might need to trade favors again. Now then, here," he said, holding the reins out for the smaller horse.

"But—I've never ridden before."

"I considered that. She's the gentlest in the stables. She was trained for my sisters. You'll have no trouble riding sidesaddle."

Secret glanced down at her long skirt. "Where are we going?"

"On an adventure," he said.

"Why can't we walk?"

"We have too far to go. You aren't frightened, are you?" Nikolas asked with a hint of sarcasm.

Secret glanced at him then looked into the horse's eyes. Although she hadn't done so with an animal in a long while, Secret attempted to speak with the mare. The horse was receptive and promised Secret she would be safe. When Secret asked if she knew where they were going, the mare whiffled and tossed her head. No answer.

Secret stared at the horse, trying to figure out how to get herself up. She decided she didn't want to sit angled off to the side. She grabbed the highest point of the saddle, rooted her foot on the stirrup, and felt a surge in her legs. She threw one leg over the horse's back and sat down. Instantly, she felt anchored. She adjusted her skirt, aware that her calves showed and no proper young woman should ride this way.

Nikolas raised his eyebrows.

"I'm less likely to fall," she said, her face flushed, spirited more than embarrassed.

"And with that I can't argue—or won't with you."

They traveled from her northwest ward to the southeast, crossing where wealth bordered want and back again. He waved at people along the way. A few of them waved with casual recognition.

"Some of them greet you as if they saw you recently," Secret said.

"Some have. A few weeks ago, I had an encounter, so to speak, with Old Man. He encouraged me to begin seeing the kingdom with my own eyes, without the influence of another's view. So, I thought to ride through town alone to discover what I hadn't noticed."

"Which is?"

"There's much to learn about people and places I know so shockingly little about." He slowed his stallion to allow a little boy with patched pants to rub the beast's thick shoulder.

Secret remembered a cart ride through town many years before with her father. He had been angry at the child who approached at his side, shouting that he had no coins. Then she thought of Harmyn, the shabby clothes, no one there to watch.

"As my mother says, fate has its favorites," Nikolas said.

"What do you think?" Secret asked.

"Even if that's true, that doesn't mean things can't be done differently. Circumstances can change, can't they? What do you think?"

"I suppose it depends. My parents came from humble origins. My father says he lived in a ward much like the one we're in now. If he hadn't been so amiable, or smart, or ambitious, he might never have left. But that he was able to make a different life, why is that? Fate? Luck? Chance? Why were you born to your station, and that boy we passed to his?"

"I have no answer," Nikolas said.

Secret looked to her open side and noticed stairways and thresholds that needed repair. "On my way home several nights ago, I saw a child about four or five years old wandering alone. An orphan, I think, with blond hair and yellow spectacles that chirped like a bird and walked with an unsteady gait. I worried if it's all right. On your rides, have you seen a little one like that?"

Nikolas was silent for a moment. "No. With a description like that, I would recall if I had, I think. Did the child seem in danger or need?"

"Danger? No, not right then. In need, probably."

"Yes, well, sadly, your friend isn't alone. If you can, find out where the family lives, one of my mother's charities can surely help."

"Thank you. Now, as for this adventure for which you woke me before dawn," she said.

"Not much longer," he said.

Touched by hints of morning light, The Tallest Building rose, then fell, at their right shoulders. Nikolas led them around Old Wheel, past the edge of town, and along a dirt road where the land was flat and covered with thick grass. Farther south they went, the sun beginning to glow, and then he stopped.

They slipped off their horses and stood at a field.

Secret had been born in this town and lived her entire life there, but never once had seen the arable lands outside the borders.

"It's so lovely and peaceful. Look at how the sun rises," she said. She lifted her face to a light breeze and felt a rush of contentment.

"That isn't why I brought you." He pointed in the distance.

"Look into the field, softly, as if it were about to vanish," he said.

Across the entire field, among the rise and fall of the dense gold stalks, spiderwebs gleamed like jeweled necklaces. Their threads draped heavy with dew, which reflected the misty dawn and cast a hazy pool of light that floated above the rye. Under the drone of hidden insects, a rustle stirred the field and set the webs to swaying. She stepped among the stalks, which reached above her waist, and peered closely at a web. There was a tear in one corner where a moth lost his struggle. The symmetrical strands drooped low with round beads of water strung like diamonds against each other. Clinging to the tip of a rye blade, a spider watched for movement below. Secret opened herself to the sun and stalks, the flailing death and the spinning life. She sighed as her heart beat its part in the matrix of rhythms.

Oh, she had forgotten how she missed this feeling until it came again.

"Amazing, don't you think?" Nikolas said. "Imagine how many spiders are here. All in this one place. I didn't notice the webs until a few days ago. I suppose the rye will be gathered up soon enough, and this will disappear until next year."

"Why did you take me here?" she asked as she returned to the field's edge.

"This was too beautiful to experience alone. No one else would appreciate it as you would. After all, you are the one who taught me to see this way."

"What do you mean?" she asked.

"To wait and see what will be revealed. There is wonder in what appears to be ordinary. A field of rye is magical, in the right slant of light," he said.

"Perhaps every child discovers that somehow," she said.

"And if that's true, most forget as they get older. I didn't, and that's why I could bring you here." Nikolas paused. "Perhaps you, too, needed a reminder."

He was right, but she didn't say so. She tried to remember the last time they'd walked through the woods together simply for the quiet and the company. Months ago. Secret looked into his eyes and smiled with affection. "Thank you, Nikolas."

"You're welcome."

They looked toward the eastern horizon as the horses grazed nearby.

"You're leaving for your summer trip soon," she said.

"Day after next. No more traveling with my mother—at last. My father insists I must learn my duties as his father taught him. So, this summer, we're going to a seaport region. We might get to go on a ship."

"Careful not to fall over the edge of the world."

"We'll be eaten by some dragon-like monster before then, right?"

"You should hope. A quicker end that way than tumbling into an abyss."

"Bloody though," he said.

"Only for the ones waiting their turn at the maw," she said.

"Perhaps I'll remain onshore, then." He grinned and called to the horses, which ignored him, three times.

Secret bade their attention without a sound. They looked at her, bobbed their heads, and stepped toward their riders.

Nikolas gave her a knowing glance. He didn't say a word. He remembered her hidden gift. "Back to civilization," he said as he handed her the reins.

XXXVI

The Apprenticeship

ON THE EVENING OF SECRET'S SIXTEENTH BIRTHDAY, HER FA-
ther treated her to a fine dinner at an exclusive eatery near The
Tallest Building. Bren kept his attention, for the most part, on his
daughter, except for an occasional wave or handshake with an as-
sociate and his lovely family. Secret had a rich mushroom soup, a
warm chicory salad, and a plate of delicate cheeses and fine-milled
bread. Her father attempted to consume an entire roasted peacock,
served with the iridescent plumes from his tail as decoration. When
she could, Secret averted her eyes from the sight, which would have
disturbed her only slightly more if it were being eaten raw.

As they enjoyed a spiced pudding for dessert, Bren looked
across the table at his silver-haired daughter.

"Secret, I've been thinking that you may have an unexplored
gift," he said.

"What might that be?" she asked.

"You've had superior marks in your language courses. That is
no doubt due in part to your diligence, but you may have, as it
were, a latent ability."

Secret put her spoon across the top of her bowl.

"Perhaps not as comprehensive as your mother's, I imagine. But
she remarked on this possibility not long before . . ."

She nodded. She saw no reason to refute what he said. It was
possible he was correct, and his veiled phrasing pointed at his rea-
soning. He wouldn't be so crass as to name what had happened
after she awoke from the fever. She hadn't forgotten the remark
he made about women being burned at the stake. However, Secret

wished not to ponder the ancient language, remembered and un-spoken. For her, what had gone dormant was a thing of the past. "You may be right," she said.

Bren looked back at her quietly. He blinked. The new Tell-a-Bell at his ear glinted from the lamplight above. He leaned his wrists against the table and twisted his ring. "She so enjoyed the pudding here, didn't she?" he said.

A few days later, Secret found her father opening a parcel at the dining table. A collector Zavet had helped years earlier didn't know she was dead and had sent a slim volume to translate. Bren hated these reminders and the duty of sending a letter to accompany the text's return.

"I'll inform the patron and send it back," she said. The task wouldn't pain her as it always did her father, who was often melancholy for days afterward.

His lashes were damp. "Thank you."

She sensed him looking at her as she skimmed the note the patron had included with the book.

"Your mother was proud of you, you know. A good daughter, polite and gentle. Of course, she appreciated how quickly you learn and how curious you are," he said.

Secret faced him. What did he mean by curious? she thought. As for the whole of what he said, Secret had never been told any of that in those words. So much of what her mother felt about her had been implied.

"Oh," she said.

Bren cocked his head imperceptibly. A glint flitted through his eyes.

"I'll bring this to the courier's tomorrow," she said as she gathered the book and turned to walk up the stairs.

One early evening soon after, Bren found her at the bench and table in the courtyard focused on her studies.

"Secret, I received this in my bin today," her father said.

She quickly skimmed what he handed her. The booklet and

application were for young people who wished to learn about the work at Fewmany Incorporated. They would be taught about a discipline under the direction of adept professionals.

"I would be most glad if you applied to my department," Bren said.

"I'm sorry, but I haven't your passion for what maps reveal or land acquisitions. And it seems you must talk a lot, to many people, often," she said. "Which is not exactly my forte."

"I realize you haven't an interest in the former or the disposition for the latter, but you are well suited for careful, thoughtful study. Two offices within my department will accept apprentices in research and translation," he said.

A quiver jolted through her stomach.

He sat down next to her. "Consider this. You have to find a direction for your future. You aren't meant to tend a litter and a house alone or with help. You aren't meant to toil as a maid or a shop clerk. We—I—haven't sent you to the finest school for such a fate, and I wouldn't have demanded you have a place in those courses if I didn't believe you capable. Soon, sooner than you expect, you will have to think about the high academies you'd like to attend. I expect you'll have your eye on the most prestigious institutions. A recommendation from Fewmany Incorporated would be a boon."

She looked at him.

"And let's not forget this: You have always been a fond reader of ancient stories. We retain language experts to assist with our ventures—"

"Mother was one, wasn't she?" Secret said.

"Yes." He paused as if surprised that she knew. "I suppose she told you at some point."

Secret nodded. She wouldn't reveal she'd learned this from looking on her mother's tables when she was forbidden to.

"Well, then, as I was saying, some of the translators serve as tutors for the right pupils. In time, you would be able to read many favorite tales in their original languages."

She knew her father sometimes had a web of hidden priorities behind his words as well as his actions. She never learned why she had once stood vulnerable at his shearing hands, unsure of his motives. This time, unlike the last, however, he truly seemed to have her best interest at heart.

But if she was wrong and he had a reason he wouldn't reveal, she glimpsed her father's genius then. Aware of the seduction, she was seduced nonetheless. This was how he swept land from under people's feet. He understood desire. For some, it was money, and he arranged fair settlement. For others, it was dignity, and he made no spectacle. For the rest, it was honor, and he organized an act of naming and homage.

Her head and heart argued all sides at once as she drummed her fingers against the booklet.

"If I were accepted, where would I do my work? Would I be on your floor?" she asked.

"The researchers and translators are on the third floor, and many of the apprentices share a room on the sixth," he said.

"I'll think about it," she told him.

That night, she did. She wondered what it would be like to learn from someone with skills she assumed were greater than her teachers'. She thought about renowned high academies she might attend, her admittance made easier if she were to apprentice. Perhaps that would help negate the fact she was a girl, vying for a place traditionally meant for a boy. She imagined how many tales she could enjoy and study in a new way if only she understood the languages.

Her mother briefly came to mind. Secret would always be in the shadow of Zavet's gifts, but that didn't mean Secret couldn't claim her own. Then she thought of her father, who wished to force the world open for her, proud of his ability to do so as much as of her intelligence and her promise.

Then, unexpectedly, she thought of Fewmany. Without him, the opportunity wouldn't even be possible. She hadn't forgotten what had happened when she was eleven or the uneasiness she felt near him although he had done nothing to harm or threaten her. She didn't understand why she was so conflicted about him. A part of her wanted to keep away, sensing danger, while another wanted to approach with curious interest. The gap between the two impulses intrigued her. In that space, she wasn't afraid. She was shocked at the realization.

If she received an apprenticeship, Secret knew she would rarely see Fewmany in the building. And regardless of that, she wished to know for herself what she could achieve, given the chance. So, Secret completed the application and left it at her father's place at the dining table where he was sure to find it.

Two weeks later, she received a letter addressed to Miss Secret Riven on the parlor table. The wax seal was embossed with Fewmany Incorporated's mark. When she read she had been accepted as an apprentice, she wasn't entirely surprised. She was a worthy candidate, but her father's position likely guaranteed hers within the new group. Bren wasn't surprised either when she told him at dinner, but that didn't dampen his elation at the news. She was excited as well, more than she thought she would be.

Nikolas congratulated her when she told him she'd been selected. He understood quite well what opportunities she might have because of it. Although he was glad for her, even proud, he did suggest caution.

"My opinion of Fewmany hasn't improved with time. I overhear things from my father and the Council now and then. He's a man of complex motives. Be careful if you're around him," he said.

"I'm sure I'll rarely, if ever, see him. Besides, I'll only be an apprentice," she said.

The day of the apprentices' orientation, two mahogany carriages with gilded trim arrived after school to take them to The Tallest Building. She was one of ten students and the only girl, even though she knew other girls had applied.

On the ride to Fewmany Incorporated, she listened as the boys discussed the departments to which they hoped to be assigned and made remarks about friends who were not sharing their good fortune. She looked out the window at the people on the sidewalks as she pondered her luck.

When they arrived at the building, a tall, tonsured man in a gravy-brown suit approached them with a board in his hand. His greeting was friendly enough, but his tone was no-nonsense as he read off the names on a list. Once everyone was accounted for—he seemed relieved that the count matched—he led them to the stairwell to the right of the lobby's carved desk.

They climbed to the sixth floor and were led to a room near the end of the hall. Secret counted ten double-sided desks with twenty chairs, three coatracks, and two built-in cabinets with brass labels on the doors. Lamps brightened the space to compensate for the dim light coming through the huge windows at the end of the room.

There was a table with refreshments and another table where an aging man sat with a quill pen. One by one, the students sat before him to have their portraits quickly drawn on tiny squares of paper. Secret realized they would all get badges to wear, similar to the one her father wore each day. She remembered a moment twelve years earlier, when Bren brought her to the building's lobby to pick up his first badge, days before starting his position as a Geo-Archeo Historian.

"Smile, Miss," the old man said, brushing the feather's plume against the tip of her nose, then she did, if only because of nerves.

The man with the board returned again. He placed a stack of booklets on a desk for them to review and invited them to sit with their tea and cakes. Secret chose a seat toward the front of the room. She studied the booklet's cover. There was a detailed illustration of the building on the front with the words FEWMANY INCORPORATED: MANUAL OF RULES AND RESPONSIBILITIES.

She skimmed the booklet's introduction and learned Fewmany Incorporated was involved in all manner of ownership and commerce—acquiring land, materials, goods, and ideas. Anything that could be bought or sold, it seemed.

She saw the old man gather his belongings and leave with a nod. The apprentices continued to eat, and their talk became a little louder. She and the boy closest to her stumbled through nervous small talk.

All eyes lifted when a jaunty *rap-rap, rap-rap* tapped on the door. Fewmany entered alone.

Some of Secret's fellow apprentices murmured to their desk mates.

"Welcome, sir," the man said cheerfully. "How good of you to accommodate this event on your schedule."

Everyone joined in a round of modest applause. The magnate smiled appropriately and raised a splayed hand to invite silence.

Secret thought she'd never seen anyone dress as Fewmany did, formal, proper, and somehow too stylish. His ascot bulged white and wide like a singing frog's throat. He wore a coat with black lapels and cuffs, the fabric dark gray with lavender stripes, thin-legged black trousers, and black boots with decorative buckles. Light from the nearby lamps reflected off the ring on his right hand and his Tell-a-Bell.

"Welcome to Fewmany Incorporated, inspired by innovation, anchored in tradition. I am Fewmany, in the flesh, and 'tis an honor and a pleasure to see each one of you here today. This is a favorite time of year for me, when we bring our finest young heads together after an arduous culling. I imagine you're eager to meet your adepts and begin to learn what we can teach you, so I will be brief. First, be willing to try because that is how you learn. Second, be willing to fail because that is how you learn in what ways you are strong. And third, be willing to succeed because that is how you learn the span of your worth. I became the man I am today because I followed my own sage advice." He grinned with a hint of self-deprecation.

A few of the apprentices chuckled softly.

"I hope to meet with each of you for an informal visit at some point during your time here. In the meantime, if you have questions, please ask your adepts. They are here to guide you. So then, be well, do well, and enjoy being a member of our exceptional fold. They're all yours, my good man."

Fewmany nodded toward the corner of the room, surveying the young people seated at the desks. He didn't smile or draw any undue attention, but he briefly met Secret's eye. She kept her head up and didn't glance away. He turned toward the door.

Male voices conferred outside the open door when the magnate stepped out. Moments later, six men in almost identical gray coats and trousers entered.

"You will find your names on the tags on the cabinets, and there you may leave your belongings and assignments. Some of you will use this room, six twenty-one, to do your work, but the fellows here could possibly find you a seat closer to their offices." He said the name of one of the men, and the man stepped forward. "Would the following please line up to join him?"

As one fellow's group was complete, he departed with his students and the next waited in turn.

Secret was the last in her seat. For an instant, she wondered if there had been a mistake, but one gray-suited man remained. The tonsured man lowered his board.

"Congratulations. It's a girl," he said as he left.

Secret rose from her chair. She looked at the stranger ahead of her. Although he was likely old enough to be her father, he was some years younger than her own. He was tall with narrow shoulders. His hair was light brown, trimmed but unruly, and his eyes were a warm hazel.

"So, you're Bren Riven's daughter," the man said as she approached. He studied her with curiosity as though she wasn't quite what he expected yet he wasn't disappointed.

"Yes, that is correct, sir," she said.

"You may call me Mr. Gray, Miss Riven."

She paused. Mr. Gray. Translator. The letter among the documents on her mother's table signed only with G.

"I am called Secret," she said.

"Is that what you prefer?"

"Yes, s—Mr. Gray."

"I'm supposed to refer to you as Miss Riven. Such familiarity is against the rules—but we translators follow far too many as it is. Between us, you may call me Leo."

Secret tempered her grin, afraid too much of a smile would make her appear nervous, which she was, or ingratiating, which she wasn't. She was, however, much relieved. She had worried she would be assigned to someone unpleasant and humorless. Leo seemed kind and not at all irritated that she wasn't a boy.

"Your father is an affable man, tenacious as well, and roundly admired," he said.

"That is a pleasure to hear."

"I didn't know your mother well. We met on very few occasions. I confess, I envied her reputation and talents. She was highly renowned in our circle. A legend, really."

"I can imagine."

"I was so sorry to learn of her loss. Quite tragic."

"Yes, thank you for your kindness."

"Well then, with parents such as that, you realize we expect great things from you."

"I will do my best."

"That's all we demand," he said with a light tone. Leo stepped to the side and gestured to the door. "Now, follow me to where we unravel tongues and twist them again."

XXXVII

The Estrangement

So it was that during the autumn of her eleventh year of school, she became an apprentice at Fewmany Incorporated.

On the third floor of The Tallest Building was the translations office. There were four desks in the center of the room that faced the corners. Along the walls to the left and right of the door were shelves and cabinets filled with labeled bins, reference books, paper and parchment, bottles of ink, boxes of nibs, and sticks of wax.

Nearest the door, to the right, sat a young man named Wesley, a copyist with a harelip and round brown eyes who, Secret was told, was paid to translate the scrawl of one of the translators. On the left sat Leo, who kept among the essentials of his work a clay figurine made by his little son, a vesta decorated with a moon and stars, and a miniature portrait of his pretty wife. Behind the copyist and Leo, the other two translators hunched over their spaces. Cuthbert was excruciatingly tidy and smelled of bay rum. Rowland was dreadfully messy and reeked of garlic. After her introduction to them, neither bothered to acknowledge her presence. Leo instructed her not to take their foul manners to heart. They were relics from a time when few could read and the fewest of those were women.

Every time she went into the office, the men were bent over their desks, lamps aglow on cloudy days, scratching word after word. The bins were always full of correspondence, orders, documents, and contracts to translate in one of any number of languages. Almost every negotiation and transaction of the conglomerate passed through that room.

This is why Secret had had to sign a confidentiality agreement.

What she knew, she promised not to divulge. However, she was given the most routine assignments, which she determined was a wise precaution on Leo's part. There was no need to involve her in sensitive matters.

Still, she was kept quite busy. Her fellow apprentices complained that they were given nothing to do but tedious errands and menial tasks and sometimes had to sit through endless meetings. They spent more time watching rather than doing.

She thought herself fortunate then, with possibly the best adept in the building. Leo gave her assignments every day. At first, the documents and correspondence she translated had already been done by others, and she was instructed to compare her attempts with the final versions. She sat with dictionaries and grammar texts to check her efforts. Leo Gray realized she learned best on her own and through her particular mistakes. Then at the end of almost every day, he sat with her at her desk in the apprentice's office closest to the west-facing window, answering questions and helping her correct her work.

As expected, Secret proved to be an excellent apprentice. She was a natural scholar, more so than a linguist, and the former was what compelled her to succeed as she did. Her enthusiasm sustained her through many hours of study and practice on grammar, conjugation, and syntax. She had pride in her work, and she liked feeling competent and useful.

She also found pleasure in the routine.

After school, she attended to her apprentice duties until she heard the rumble of people leaving the floors at the end of the day. She sat at her desk on the sixth floor and did her schoolwork until her father came down from the twelfth to fetch her. Together, they rode the two-horse cart home, entered a clean house to have the warm meal Elinor made, and settled into their quiet evening. If her father was away on a trip, she left with everyone else, herding down the halls, out the doors, and into the streets. She walked one of the same three routes home, ate the dinner left on the stove, and completed her school assignments for the day. By then, she was old enough not to need Auntie's supervision, which left her feeling responsible and trusted.

On the nights she wasn't too tired, she studied folklore and tales written in languages she could now read fluently. She welcomed the return of an old, almost forgotten, enchantment. She discovered again the promise of wonder no matter what good and evil was involved. She began to keep charts of images and themes she observed, the variations often subtle. The fates of good girls and boys, the rewards of beauty and virtue, the wrath of the powerful, the help of magical objects and mysterious beings. Through tale, legend, and myth, there were cycles and patterns to order and chaos.

And then, at the end of each day, she slept, content in knowing what the next one would bring.

This continued through the autumn and winter, and then, at the first of spring, Secret had a disturbing dream.

She dreamed of a forest thick with evergreens. A white-haired hag with a clouded eye danced on a rag doll. She cackled as she tore the doll apart. A fox and a rooster ran toward her shouting in the ancient language of the fever and chased her up a tree. The animals locked the doll's fragments in a box. An infant fell from the tree. It crushed the fox and rooster, swallowed the key to the box, and turned toward a rustle in the forest. An ogress with teeth of stone snatched the baby and swallowed it whole.

Secret awoke in a panic that made her breathe as if she'd been chased for miles.

The next day, she had no rational explanation for why she had an urge to go to the woods. Her body simply craved a nourishment only that place could sate. She didn't have school or her apprenticeship, so she left a note for her father saying that she was going to Old Wheel to see a troupe.

She walked the shortest route through the wards to reach the alley. She no longer anticipated Cyril's escort. She entered the tunnel in his absence and crawled out of the hole in the tree.

Despite the afternoon chill, she removed her light cloak, stockings, and shoes and left them in a pile near the hollowing tree. She ran fast to force a burn in her lungs. Her long hair splashed against her back. Frightened animals scurried. Birds lifted in flight. When she came to Reach, she walked across his roots. His low drone hummed through the marrow of her bones, persistent and urgent, but as it had always been, she couldn't comprehend his message. She left him to go to a favorite place along the stream where a boulder forced a split in the current.

She gathered her skirt high. The water's cold shocked her head to toe. The rush cut at her knees. Carefully, she climbed on the boulder and balanced at its center. She closed her eyes.

"All is well, and there is no worry," she whispered.

She lost herself in birdsong, breaking water, blowing wind. She pressed her hands against the boulder. It seemed to rise to greet her. Her palms rooted beyond its surface, into its fixed and fluid place in time, there for eons, slowly worn away.

She envied the tranquility of its fate.

"What is mine?" she asked, expecting no answer.

When Secret opened her eyes, a fox peered at her from the bank. Secret shivered but not from the crisp evening. The vixen barked once as she scampered out of sight. A deer's bell seemed to reply. A succession of animal calls carried through the trees.

She sat in silence until her thighs became numb and her feet hurt from the cold.

When she stepped back on land, she heard a human voice somewhere near. She stood still to locate the direction. Then Cyril ran a circle around her legs.

"What has gotten into you? Cyril! This isn't like—Oh!" Old Woman cried. "Secret! I didn't expect to see anyone here."

Secret gave the squirrel a leveling glance. "I'm sorry you were startled," she said. "What's wrong with Cyril?"

"I have no idea. He started to run around as if he were having a fit. I thought he might have been bitten by something. But I understand now. He wanted to find you." She saw Secret's bare feet. She wrapped her blue shawl tighter around her shoulders. "Come with me before you catch your death of cold."

In front of the cottage's fire, the two of them sat on the floor. Secret drank tea and listened to Old Woman tell of her recent visit to her native village. Her eldest granddaughter and her family had moved there the year before and served as doting hosts.

"You traveled at the end of winter? My father hates when he must travel at that time of year. Dismal, wet, and cold," she said.

"Fine weather and shortcuts made for an easy journey, fortunately. I enjoyed my time with them, but I'm glad to be home now," Old Woman said. "Months have passed since I last saw you. Before the start of your school term, I believe. Are your courses as challenging now as the year before?"

"Yes, but I don't mind. I prefer it this way, being busy," she said.

"I've not asked in some time, but have you found what was missing?"

Old Woman's tone was conversational, not prying. The question agitated Secret even though it shouldn't have. She was the one who had told Old Woman about the arcane manuscript in the first place. After Bea's return more than a year before, the day Secret had to tell Bea her mother was dead and the manuscript was missing, Secret had a random visit with Old Woman. Her friend had asked if Secret had learned any more of what became of the manuscript. Secret told Old Woman that her mother, in fact, had not returned it and she'd been unable to find it. The subject hadn't been raised since then by either of them, until that spring day.

"No," Secret said, not admitting she hadn't searched at all. "I'm afraid not."

"She must have hidden it like a treasure. I suppose she was a cautious steward," Old Woman said.

"Yes, she was that."

"And what has your attention now?"

Secret told her of the apprenticeship at Fewmany Incorporated that she'd started months before.

"What do you enjoy about the work?" Old Woman asked.

"I've done well in my language courses in school, so I know I have an aptitude. The work there makes me think differently, it's more practical, and I like that. I find my comprehension is much better, and that makes reading old tales in their native languages even better. I can only do that with four languages now, including our own. I'm learning more all the time."

"And how do you feel about this? Are you doing what you truly want to do?"

Secret thought the question was odd. "Well, of course. What I learn will benefit my future. I want to attend a good high academy, you know. This will help no matter what area I choose to study. And I know my father is proud. I'm glad about that."

"As he should be. As I am." Old Woman looked into Secret's eyes. A slow, soft exhale drifted from her nostrils. "A person never knows precisely where a choice will lead, does she, and that is hers to decide. I hope you're doing your best to be led by what is true to yourself, without obligation to the desires of others."

Secret bristled even though she saw concern in her friend's expression. "And that's what you've done?"

"In time, when I discovered what my own desires were. I was fortunate in that I could choose from the whole realm of possibility. Very few things were proscribed where I lived my earliest years. I had a full life there, rich in love, rich in knowing I was loved. When I left to come to this kingdom, I did so because I wanted to. Then many years later, I felt a call to live in these woods, and my answer was to do that. It was my deepest heart's desire. Somehow, I knew what I was meant to do. I believe most of us have a sense of our purpose but are too often confused or discouraged or wounded to heed it."

Secret curled her knees to her chest. How was it that Old Woman could be so comforting and disconcerting at once?

Old Woman studied Secret's features. "The little girl who hid among the leaves and shadows now hides in your face. And for a long while, I've felt you've hidden from me."

Secret remained quiet.

"I know there are things you haven't wished to tell me. Things you keep inside because you fear what will happen if you allow them out. What was between you and your mother, for example."

Secret pulled her knees closer and held her breath.

"You bear a complicated grief, I know, but that's only one matter among many," Old Woman said.

Cyril startled them both when he jumped through the curtains and sprinted to leap on the table.

Secret looked at Old Woman. "I'm sixteen. Everything is troublesome now, isn't it? You talk as if I carry the weight of the world," she said, dismissive.

"That's because I think you do."

The squirrel toppled a small bowl. Apples rolled across the floor. Old Woman picked up one that touched her knee. "I worry about you, Secret. I'm sure you mask very well the burdens you carry, but that doesn't make them disappear, and they aren't invisible to me. I can't force you to speak, but I wish you would. There are matters I want to discuss with you. It's time. But I require your trust and honesty to do so."

The impulse to flee quickened in her blood. Secret stared at the base of the large cauldron near the hearth. She hadn't meant to see Old Woman that day. She only wanted some peace, not to be provoked. Her pulse raced when she realized the animals had called to one another, announcing where she was, as if they wanted her found. Her anxiety turned to anger.

"I don't want to talk. And why do you care so much anyway?"

"Because I love you, child."

Tears welled into Secret's eyes. Her heart seemed to bloom, full of space and light, then, just as quickly, it collapsed in one beat. She realized no one had ever said those words to her. Ever.

"What's wrong, Secret?" Old Woman asked, her voice soft.

A sob pressed against Secret's throat, and she fought its release. She shook her head and began to rise to her feet.

"Something I said has upset you deeply—"

"I have to go. I'll be late for dinner," Secret said, making her way to the door.

"Please, don't leave. Tell me what's troubling you."

"Leave me alone. I don't want to talk. Not to you, not to anyone," Secret said.

"I think you need to. Desperately. And I need to talk to you. There are things you must understand—"

Into the twilight and through the woods, Secret pounded her bare feet over stones and sticks scattered on the dark ground. She ran from Old Woman's tender words, afraid of the hollow place they'd touched within her. She fled from what Old Woman had not spoken, fearful of what Old Woman wanted to reveal. Although no creature followed her, Secret felt chased, as if something she had always sensed had stepped up its pursuit.

XXXVIII

The Cipher

NOT LONG AFTER HER ENCOUNTER WITH OLD WOMAN, SE-
cret received a multivolume set of botany texts from her father. He
said he'd seen them in an antiquarian shop while on a trip months
before, but the owner hemmed and hawed at parting with them.
Bren left his card and told the man to send a letter if he changed
his mind. To Bren's surprise, the man did. Bren said he thought to
hold them for her next birthday, but he wanted to give her a surprise for all her hard work the past few months.

As she looked at them, she noticed they were printed in a language in which she was fluent. The drawings were so detailed that
a magnifier must have been used to aid the illustrator. Many were
hand-colored by someone with delicate skill. A pang of longing
moved through her finger as she traced an exceptionally rendered
curl of a fern.

"Thank you, Father. They are beautiful. I'll enjoy studying
them," she said, her hand placed gently on the stack.

Bren gave the top of her head a little pat as he passed her to go
up the stairs.

Secret carried her new books to her room and placed them on
her bed. She lit the lamp on her bedside table, turning it bright, and
stood at her shelves. There, she would have to make room and possibly store some books away.

As she tried to determine where to place them, she thought of
her father. Time and again, he had returned home with marvelous
things from his travels, from exotic foods to lovely objects to precious stories. He spared no expense, she realized even as a child.

The books he had given her when she was a girl were often bound in leather, set in crisp type, with the woodcut or etched illustrations fully colored. She loved some more than others, but she couldn't bear to part with any from her own little library.

She stared at a row of books she received during her first years of school. Those she hadn't read in a long time, but the thought of boxing them away to make room for more made her somewhat sad.

A fly spiraled at her ear. Her hand waved it away.

Then the fly whipped in front of her in zigzags. It landed at one end of a middle shelf and crawled over the uneven hills of the spines. It stopped on the top edge of the largest, least worn book and twitched its front legs against each other. Secret watched it, the tiny eyes glinting back at her.

She stretched out her finger toward it as it danced across the top of the spine. As the fly lifted into the air, her fingertip fell into the valley between the front and back covers of the book. Secret pulled the volume toward her.

That one she had received when she was seven, written in her mother's native language and one Zavet resisted reading from the page. Silly folktales, her mother had called them, full of the allure of nonsense. Secret had thrilled at the drawings, created with such detail and emotion, and imagined the stories she wasn't told.

Secret turned through the tales again. She lingered on one page and remembered how long she once looked with pleasure at the animals crammed among and on top of one another under one roof. When she flipped to the next tale, she found a dry brown, pressed leaf from the old fig tree. She left it where it was, ignoring the threat of bittersweet tears.

Then the center yawned open to a ragged edge. Secret couldn't remember what illustration was missing, but she was certain she hadn't torn it away. In the page's place was an object she had never seen before. It was not drawn or crafted in haste. It was beautiful, brilliantly colored.

Two concentric circles, one within the other, were mounted in the center of a thick square of paper. Both circles moved round and round. The outer circumference of the larger circle had the letters of her language's alphabet. Beyond this circle, drawn around it on the square, were small images. Secret could identify most of them— a tree, a bird, a flower. There were fewer drawings than there were letters. The smaller circle had a tiny triangular window cut near its edge, which pointed outward to the larger circle.

As Secret turned the circle, the window revealed figures, no— symbols, but precisely, yes—an alphabet. One she didn't know, but as she studied the shapes, she realized she had seen it before.

The alphabet of the arcane manuscript.

Secret held a cipher in her hands.

Before any other thoughts entered her head, she grabbed her lamp, went to her desk, and pulled out a sheet of paper. She studied the little drawings and turned the circle to reveal each letter of the strange alphabet again. Secret wondered if the letters were in order, if there was one, and whether the order mattered.

She clutched a pen and began to write each letter in black ink, first in a row, then in a column, then randomly scattered on the sheet.

Then she wrote the letters of her native language's alphabet in the same way next to the others in brown ink. She had to scratch out three because when she checked the cipher again, three letters were missing.

For a long while, she stared at what she'd written. She touched the letters when the ink was dry and traced her fingertip against the small drawings on the cipher itself.

Secret decided then that the strange alphabet wasn't from another language at all. To simply substitute the letters from one language for another would result in unintelligible gibberish.

This had to be a code, one Zavet had broken.

Why her mother hadn't provided a simpler means to decipher the manuscript—other than this puzzle of circles—Secret had no idea.

Calmly, she slipped the cipher into the old book and returned it to its place on the shelves. The nesting dolls stared down through the shadows. She placed the botany volumes on the edge of her desk. The fly buzzed once around her head as she extinguished the lamp.

Secret curled into a ball under her quilt.

This she knew: First, her mother had broken the arcane manuscript's code, which meant she could read it, as she had claimed she could.

Second, Zavet did not transcribe the manuscript and return it to the owner.

Third, deliberately, Zavet had made a cipher and put it in a place where her daughter would likely be the only person to ever find it.

Secret pulled the covers over her face. She inhaled the stale air into her shallow lungs.

The cipher was useless without the arcane manuscript, but Secret didn't know where the text was. When she cleared Zavet's tables and shelves, she hadn't found it. Wherever Zavet kept it hidden, surely it was there still, but Secret was left with no clue.

No clue either about why her mother would leave the task to her. How peculiar.

Peculiar as her death. Sudden. Unexplained.

The darkness pulled Secret into the empty place where all was quiet, all was calm.

In the days that followed, she was late to her apprenticeship almost every afternoon. She apologized to Leo, who seemed more surprised than perturbed. When she went to the sixth-floor room to do her work, she found herself slow and inefficient, prone to errors she otherwise never made. Leo sat with her privately to review her mistakes, which humiliated her although he wasn't harsh in his correction.

"This isn't like you, Secret," he said. "I trust all is well, at school . . ."

"I'm sorry. I'm a bit overwrought these days. I'll be better soon," she said.

One of those afternoons, she infuriated Cuthbert when she dropped a bottle of ink that splattered the side of his desk, then enraged Rowland when she tried to move the pile of papers near his feet when she went to clean the spill. *Little scourge*, she heard in her head. Leo sent her home early that day with paternal insistence that she get some rest.

At school, Secret's teachers barked for her attention in class and shook their heads in puzzlement when they returned her marked assignments.

One particular gray morning, her geometry teacher asked, "Miss Riven, does Mr. Lyle hold you in thrall above today's lesson?"

She blinked as she heard the male laughter fill the room. Her eyes focused again. She realized she had been looking straight at the chestnut-haired boy, who turned his face to his desk as his seatmate smacked him against the chest.

"No, sir. I'm sorry. I was thinking of something else."

"Lyle's honeyed lips," a boy shouted.

The teacher gave her a sharp glance as he attempted to bring the roar under control.

It was that same day when Nikolas rushed after her as she was leaving school to go home instead of to her apprenticeship. She was already off the grounds when he called to her. She stopped to face him as other children slipped by, alone or in groups.

"I'm having a party at the start of our summer break. Muriel already said she'd attend, and Charlotte might, along with a couple of other friends." He slipped a folded note from his pocket and gave it to her.

She read the invitation in his handwriting, which indicated the date and time.

"I'm sorry I can't attend."

Nikolas creased his brow. "Why not?"

Her breath caught. She expected him to repeat what had so often been rote between them. He would say *Very well then*, and she would say *Thank you*, and that would be that. Nikolas had never asked why before.

"My father has reservations for a musical performance."

"What performance?"

She tried to think of a recent announcement from a newsbox or listing from a longsheet.

"A quintet with a solo soprano," she said.

He looked at her blankly then shook his head. "Honestly, I rarely ever ask even though I have parties all the time. I know you keep your circle small, and I know who you avoid and for the most part why."

She remained quiet. There was more to why she didn't want to attend than what he assumed.

"You can't tell me you haven't had fun at some of the bigger events. My birthday, when we had the scavenger hunt? Or the fall festival, that same year, too? I don't think I'd ever seen you smile so often, or so easily."

"I did enjoy that day."

"Yet?"

Secret looked away from him and gnawed the edge of her lip. She had no simple answer. There was much she kept to herself, of which she was too embarrassed to speak. She never felt she fit in and secretly wished she were a girl with matching eyes, plain dark hair, a pleasant disposition, and a degree of charm. If she hadn't been a silent child who could speak to creatures and plants, she wouldn't have grown up so strange.

But those worries weren't the reason why she didn't want to go to the party. She couldn't stop thinking about the cipher, the lost manuscript, and her dead mother.

"Secret? Well? Do you have an answer?"

"Circumstances were different then."

The frustration in Nikolas's eyes lifted. His shoulders softened and he leaned toward her. "You've honored a proper time of mourning, haven't you? What more do you owe to her memory?" he said softly.

The remark flayed off a skin she hadn't known was so thin until he brushed against it. She held herself against the rage that made her quake but couldn't keep its violence from her voice. "Owe her memory? My mother's? I owe her nothing. What would you know? What would anyone know?"

He tried to touch her but she backed away.

The gesture raked the rawness again.

There was the wound of her need, the knit of his friendship across one weeping edge. She suddenly hated him for his loyalty, for the protection he gave her, because through its presence, she couldn't deny the dark vulnerable hole within that could not be filled.

Afraid she was going to cry, she began to walk off, glancing at the schoolmates whose eyes flicked toward them, curious about what transpired yet trained to look away.

Nikolas grabbed the strap of her satchel. "Come with me," he said, turning her around.

She was furious but didn't want to draw more attention, so she followed him to the carriage that was always waiting for him at the end of every school day. His guard opened the door, Nikolas told the coachman her address, and she clambered up. The wood inside was polished, the seats were brown leather, and the windows had deep-red curtains pushed aside to let in light.

Nikolas closed them inside and sat next to her. "You've been distant for weeks. Clearly, something is bothering you."

"I've had much to do lately. I'm tired and irritated."

"You always have much to do. That's not the trouble."

"That's my answer."

"I don't believe you," he said softly. "What's wrong?"

Secret stared at her hands and held her breath.

"You're not prone to outbursts. You were angry a few moments ago."

She eyed the door. If she slipped across the seat quickly enough and lunged for the latch, she'd be gone in seconds.

"Is this about your mother, Secret?"

Her chest heaved.

"Are you missing her?"

She shook her head. Tears streaked from her closed eyes. She raised a hand to her throat. The pressure swelled until she thought she'd choke. Stop it, she said to herself.

"Will you tell me?" he asked, his voice as gentle as his grip on her arm.

The tenderness split her open.

Unintelligible fragments spewed from her mouth, the whole of what she held back for so long forcing itself from within, out of order, between sobs. "A messenger came . . . manuscript . . . she left a cipher . . . she choked . . . the symbol . . . my fig tree . . . blue men . . . and there was a sword . . . ruptures, *tearing* out of me . . . don't understand . . . and the fever . . . a language . . . never heard it before . . . hate her . . . it's lost . . ."

He didn't try to quiet her. He let her babble out every word without interruption. His hand never moved.

Once the words ceased, the sobs consumed her. Nikolas wrapped his arm around her back. He took a punch in the chest when he pulled her close and pressed her head against his shoulder.

"Stop. I'm not going to let you go," he said quietly as she struggled.

When she realized he meant it, she slumped against him as she cried.

"Shhhh," he whispered. "Easy now."

The carriage stopped and the door opened. Nikolas waved off whoever was outside, and they were closed in again. Wiping her face on her sleeve, she eased away from his arms. Her breathing hitched as she tried to calm down. She felt empty and tired and ashamed. She'd never cried in front of him before.

Nikolas gave her a handkerchief.

"What you told me, I'm afraid I understood little of it. Why don't you try again, now that you've settled?"

Embarrassed as she was, she was glad she'd been incoherent. Much of what she said, she hadn't meant to share at all. She didn't know why it had spilled out then. She glanced at him. "What do you remember I said?"

"Something about a manuscript, but the rest, well, you were distraught." He blinked at her while she sat in silence. "If you can't trust me with whatever you're keeping to yourself, who can you trust?"

She rubbed her eyes. "You can't speak of this."

"Understood."

"Almost four years ago, my mother received a manuscript to translate," Secret said, taking a moment to summarize the basic facts of what happened for him. "Then a few weeks ago, I found a cipher for it." She briefly described the unfamiliar alphabet and the drawings.

Nikolas scowled in confusion. "If she could read it, why take the time to make a cipher instead of transcribing it?"

"I don't know. Regardless, it's useless without the manuscript."

"You said she kept it hidden. Surely it's in the same place she last left it."

Secret shrugged.

"You haven't searched to find it."

His bluntness piqued her. "I didn't ask for this."

"Perhaps not, but it seems to me she not only trusted that you could finish what she didn't, but also that you would."

"Quite a gamble."

"I doubt she thought so. She obviously meant for you to know what it contains."

Secret met his eyes. A sudden shiver passed through his body, a twitch as quick as the fly that had crawled along the edge of her book, and she felt the wordless portent raise the hair on her arms. She dismissed the connection to other times they'd shared an uncanny feeling, the first night they met, the afternoon she drew the symbol.

Nikolas crossed his arms as if he were cold. "But it is strange, leaving the cipher like that, not finishing the work, as if . . ." His expression was flat. Then, he pressed his lips in a tight line and his eyes narrowed.

Secret couldn't bring herself to ponder, let alone say, the thought he didn't finish. As if her mother knew—

She pulled her satchel on her shoulder. "What happened earlier, I'm sorry."

"You feel how you feel, and sometimes, it's too much to hold by yourself. It's all right."

Secret reached for the latch on the carriage door and turned to face him. She took a deep breath. "I'm—what you—I appreciate—"

"I know," he said, his hand over his heart.

XXXIX

The Future Quest

EARLIER IN THE SPRING, SECRET AND HER FATHER HAD RE-
ceived an invitation to Charming's summer wedding. They hadn't
been invited for Pretty's nuptials several years before, but her father's status had grown. Bren told her he'd know a position with
Fewmany would lead to great things. Secret understood her father
felt a place at the King's right hand move within reach. The favor
he thought had once cast his ancestors aside could reverse to once
again bring fortune, prestige, and power. Bren was delighted by the
inclusion, but Secret dreaded the search for a gown.

Bren told her to spare no expense. So yet again, for another
celebration at The Castle, Secret went in search of an appropriate
frock. She was determined to choose something typical and taste-
ful, as the occasion dictated. She visited clothiers from one ward to
the next, where they all seemed to have nearly the same thing, and
nothing seemed appropriate.

Finally, at a shop only a block from Old Wheel, she settled on a
gown she was assured was the latest fashion. The two shop women
said it was flattering on her figure and a lovely color against her
skin. Although Secret didn't think she looked quite right in it, the
dress would have to do. She had the seams taken in and said she
would pick it up when the alterations were done.

Two weeks later, after she left The Tallest Building for the day,
Secret returned to get the dress. It was carefully folded within delicate sheets of paper and tied with a wide silk ribbon, and her shoes
were placed in a soft velvet drawstring bag.

On her way home, she shifted the dress in her arms. The bag

she'd slipped on her elbow banged against her hip. The sidewalks were crowded. The streets were filling with carts and horses. A shouting woman bumped Secret as she rushed by. The jolt surprised Secret, and she almost dropped the dress on a sewer drain, still damp from a recent street cleaning.

A chirp reached her ears, then a little voice said, "Hello, Secret."

Leaning against the nearby lamppost was Harmyn. There was no mistaking the yellow spectacles, messy light hair now almost shoulder-length, or strange clothing. This time the waif wore a green tunic with a ragged hem, breeches that were too long, and low boots with one missing buckle. For a moment, Secret wondered where the child got such peculiar things to wear.

"Hello, Harmyn. I'm surprised you remember me."

"I know who you are," Harmyn said. "You looked at the flowers and then you spoke to me." The child seemed to look at her peripherally, not directly.

When she stood next to the little one, Secret sensed, more than saw, that the child was ill. She felt a weariness, long endured, and almost asked what was the matter, but then did not.

"Shouldn't you be home now? Where is your aunt or uncle? I think you know better than to walk around alone, especially as it gets so close to dark. It's dangerous," she said.

"Only if someone notices you," Harmyn said.

Secret blinked in response to the strange comment. A man walked past them dragging a little girl by the arm behind him. Harmyn recoiled as if struck in the face.

The waif reached into a pocket. "I want to give this to you."

Secret shifted the dress under one arm, reached out her hand, and accepted in her palm a warped bronze cogwheel missing a tooth. She thought it was curiously beautiful.

"Do you know what it is?" Harmyn asked.

"A cogwheel. It's from some kind of machine," she said.

Harmyn glimpsed at her, then quickly looked away. "Yes. You should keep it."

"Where did you find it?"

"Behind the big building where the ground isn't covered anymore. You've been there." The child pointed south.

Secret looked over her shoulder. "Behind the building, yes, I have." When she turned back, Harmyn was gone.

Then Secret heard a caw. She peered up at the lamppost. A crow stood on top. His black feathers shone lightly in the setting sun. His chest had a narrow bald stripe where feathers no longer grew.

Few times since the fever had Secret communicated with creatures and plants, and since then, none had compelled her to listen. She had been the one to address them. But the crow cawed aloud as he stared down, forcing an image. Curious but wary, she opened herself to see the village in the woods—yes, this was the same crow who visited her before—but closer then, a view of huts and little gardens and trees and a well—

She shut herself from him. She didn't want to see more. He cried out then flew away.

The cogwheel lay heavy in her hand. She almost tossed it in the sewer, but she didn't and could give no reason to herself why she kept it.

Unbidden, her memory released a whisper, *You have a mystery in your blood.*

When she returned home, Secret hung the dress in her wardrobe, put the cogwheel away in her desk, and gave not another thought to it, Harmyn, or the crow.

On the day of Charming's wedding, Secret and her father waited downstairs for their hired carriage. Bren's reaction to her dress was less than effusive.

"Where did you find that?" he asked.

"In one of the shops among the many," she said.

Bren twisted his mouth and squinted.

"I was assured any young lady wearing this gown would be well received." Secret paused, annoyed by her father's disapproval. She knew she'd done precisely what she was expected to do for a day like this. "And the cost was exorbitant."

"Was it?" His eyes darted from one detail to the next. "Well, you're sure to get noticed, which may, in some unforeseen way, help me to see you married off, after high academy of course."

"As I understand, such a decision is my choice in this day and age," she said.

"You'll be spared it altogether if you show no effort in the first place," he said.

Secret pressed her lips together. She kept them that way until she had to greet people as they found their seats for the marriage ceremony.

After trumpeting, petal flurries, and inaudible vows, the guests exited the Great Hall for feasting and revelry. Much like the grand ball she had attended when she was almost seven, the decorations were splendid. Arrangements and garlands of fresh flowers perfumed the air. Dignitaries draped in silks and jewels greeted one another. The royal families were most conspicuous in their tiaras and crowns.

As she walked across the courtyard, she recognized a few schoolmates and fellow apprentices. Their families, too, had been invited to the wedding. She did her duty to be gracious and friendly, engaging in the smallest of talk. When she was done, she went on her way to find a tent where she could sit in the shade.

She spotted her father and Fewmany talking with one of the King's advisers. Her father quickly waved at her, and Fewmany turned to follow Bren's shift of attention. The magnate nudged the top of his hat to acknowledge her. Secret nodded once then looked away.

In a corner, Secret found a seat. She wriggled in the gown and scratched at one of the seams. She saw Nikolas some distance away. His features had changed during the past year. His jaw lost its rounder lines, his eyes became deeper, somehow brighter. He'd grown a head taller, pushing him slightly above average. She tried not to think about the coming final year of school, their twelfth and the last together. By this time next year, she would be preparing to leave for high academy and he would be traveling to allied kingdoms.

She watched him stand with two princes, both older than he. The men laughed, nudging him with their elbows and winking. Nikolas regarded them with the neutral expression Secret knew well. He had some thinking to do about what he heard.

Nikolas then eased through the crowd and craned his neck left and right. Secret waved. He unbuttoned the length of his coat and flopped down on the bench next to her. He gave her a perplexed glance.

"Stand up," he said.

"Why?"

"Your gown," he said. Secret stood near her seat. He looked at her with the same impassivity as he had the two princes. "Lift your arms, please," he said. "And turn."

She complied. Secret had noticed several other young women in attendance were wearing a fashion very similar to hers. They all had dresses with a fitted bodice, billowing sleeves, and full, long skirt. Secret's was a deep rose hue, which suggested the color of petals, dead ones she thought. The silk fabric had a garish shine and strange texture.

"It has all the makings of a fine garment, but . . . you don't seem comfortable in the least."

"Formal wear is rarely comfortable," she said, flicking the collar of his coat as she sat down again.

He grinned slightly. Then in the pause of their silence, he frowned.

"Nikolas, for goodness' sake. Stand up, my prince!" the Queen, regal as legend, said, sweeping toward her son.

He cut his eyes at Secret, who fixed a polite smile. They stood at the same time, Secret to curtsy, Nikolas to obey. His mother began to button his coat. He leaned back, which strained her reach. He fastened the buttons himself as she questioned him.

Had he greeted specific guests and dignitaries, whose titles were as long as their arms?

"Yes, Mother, of course," Nikolas said.

And had he paid compliments to and promised to dance with certain princesses and young ladies, whose faces, virtues, and dowries were equally fine?

"Yes, Mother," he said.

And did he remember that he would see many of these important people again on his goodwill visits soon after he finished his last school term?

"Yes, Mother. Father reminded me, too."

The Queen squared his crown and fussed about his hair. Nikolas tensed his jaw, his color high.

"Remember who you are, Nikolas. Remember what suitable royal match must be made. Remember your duty. The fate of this kingdom will be in your hands one day," the Queen said.

"How frequently I'm reminded," he said.

The Queen turned toward Secret. "Miss Riven, isn't it?"

"Yes, Your Majesty."

"Don't you look lovely? That is a fashionable gown to be certain," the Queen said.

"Thank you, Your Majesty," she said.

"You're sure to catch the eye of many young gentlemen today." She swept a critical gaze over Secret's hair and face. "I trust your father has made introductions."

"As any good, devoted father should, Your Majesty."

The Queen gave her son one last reminder in a whisper, then whisked back into the crowd.

A vein snaked across his temple as he shut his eyes and exhaled with slow restraint. Secret had seen him angry before, but he was seething then.

"Let's go," he said.

Secret followed him toward the front walls of the castle. Nikolas darted into an arched doorway. The stairwell was dark and confined.

As she followed him up the curving stairs, she tensed against an anxious pulse at the center of her body. She dismissed it.

Nikolas shouted a call before he stepped into the light. A sentinel in full uniform greeted him formally. Nikolas asked him to leave and wait at the base of the tower. As if taken by surprise, the sentinel widened his eyes, then winked at him, and disappeared down the stairs.

He removed his crown and coat. He leaned against the battlement, his palms toward the sun. Opposite The Castle, across town, The Tallest Building was fully visible. Below, the streets and buildings filled the gap between the two structures. To the left were the meadows bisected by the tree lines. To the right, in the distance, were the woods. Secret looked behind her and saw the structure of the rest of the castle. The purple and red flags above them fluttered in the breeze. She would remember this moment when she stood with him there once again, as the Plague of Silences took its toll on every person in town.

"Crossing the green space between town and the woods seems to take far longer than using the tunnel. Perhaps it seems that way because it's aboveground, not in the dark."

"I never tried that way. I'd be afraid to get lost entering from an unfamiliar place," she said, her tone neutral.

"You could ask for help. You had it the first time and many times thereafter," he said.

"I suppose," she said. "That was so long ago."

Nikolas leaned his weight against the wall. "We haven't spent a day together there in years, have we? Funny, isn't it, considering how much time we spent in the woods when we were little. It's almost impossible to get away by myself now. The last time I went into town alone, my father somehow found out I didn't take my guard. I had to beg him to keep the man on. He was so angry." Nikolas became quiet as if he decided not to say what was on his mind. "How long has it been since you've gone?"

"A while," Secret said.

She turned away from him to look over her shoulder beyond the northwest wards. The last time she went to the woods was the last time she spoke to Old Woman. Secret's cheeks burned as she remembered what Old Woman said and how she had run away. The pain of that memory was like a bruise that didn't hurt unless it was touched. To return to the woods would mean facing the shame for her behavior and the fear of what else Old Woman had wanted to say.

She had told none of this to Nikolas.

"It was difficult enough when all I had to do was schoolwork. Then came the apprenticeship," she said as she faced him again.

"Yes, I know." Nikolas sighed. "My suspicions about Fewmany remain neither confirmed nor refuted. He and several cohorts visit here regularly. Your father among them. I've seen him leaving after certain Council meetings. Some agreement is under negotiation."

"There are whispers in the halls about a Very Important Project," she said with emphasis, "that has Fewmany's full attention. I think I've heard allusions to it as The King's Ransom. I'm not sure if that's a joke."

He nodded. "Appropriate then. I've heard my father grumble about the coffers more often."

"Do you know what's proposed?" she asked.

"I think it's a wall. There was one here a long time ago, but it was torn down to make way for more wards. Now there's far more to surround. I've heard references to potential threats and preparation, but nothing that suggests there's immediate danger from another kingdom, or even the so-called dragon menace. A wall takes longer to build than an army anyway. That's why I think it's the former. But why Fewmany is involved, I have no idea."

"I have a guess. Materials, rather than strategy. Fewmany Incorporated holds quarries and mines and several enterprises in construction."

Nikolas scowled. "Convenient, isn't it, if a wall that protects his interests is one he is compensated to build."

"How unusually cynical of you," Secret said.

"As I said, I have my suspicions."

They stood together looking out across the town and what lay beyond it. How small, how vulnerable it all seems, Secret thought. How exposed. She imagined a wall around it, but the image made her feel sad, not safe. For a moment, she wondered where Harmyn was wandering far below, then why the crow had revealed the village, its huts, the well . . . Secret tossed her head to shake the thoughts free. She glanced at Nikolas. He peered ahead but, Secret observed, without outer focus.

"I want to ask you something with absolute sincerity and in confidence," he said after a long silence.

Cautious, she looked at him.

"Do you think the dragon exists?"

She took a deep breath and stared at the sky past him. Her memory drifted to the old tales her father had first read to her, stories of a beast that was sometimes mercurial, sometimes cunning, very strong, occasionally wise, and almost always greedy. It loved and protected its treasure, its hoard, and woe to those who robbed the stores. The myths she learned from Old Woman told of a creature as old as time, capable of violence and mercy, regret and joy, who impossibly gave rise to each day and the descent of night. And every so often, news-boxes repeated reports of the dragon menace that ravaged a distant land or wreaked some sort of havoc as a means of warning. Even Secret had seen evidence of it, the red scales on the mounted display in the meeting chamber with the paneled, hidden room.

"Before I answer, tell me why you asked," she said.

"Several months ago, I was preoccupied with thoughts of the quest. More than I'd been before, for whatever reason. As always, a conversation about it with my father resulted in the same talk of duty and tradition and assurance that I, his son, would understand the purpose upon my return but not before."

Nikolas pressed the scar under his thumb as if it hurt, and continued.

"Then sometime in the spring, the trees were in full leaf, I remember, I took a walk with Old Man. That might have been a dream. Or not. I can never quite determine. He leaves me with such a strange feeling. Regardless, I told him I was troubled. All I could think about was my ambivalence about the journey, that, and the risk involved. Old Man said he'd heard many tales of quests. Many versions of the same tales. Rare was any mention of doubt, but that didn't mean a man felt none. We spoke about discernment and courage and choice and fate. Not as platitudes but as ideals, genuine and true. When our walk was done, he said in a way that made my hair stand on end, 'You must find what you seek.'"

"I once had moments like that," she said, then added, "with Old Woman."

When Nikolas realized she would say no more, he continued.

"Then today, I spoke with two princes who completed their quests several years ago. I asked what guidance they could give me for when my turn came. I was prepared for them to be trite or even secretive, but they began to laugh and traded stories of food, drink, and certain company they had along the way. They told me I'd be given a map when it was my time, and they said the confrontation wasn't as harrowing as I probably imagined. They said no more, and I left confused."

"But why did you ask whether I think the dragon exists?"

"Think about it. Isn't it strange that no one kills this dragon, or seems to try, and it doesn't kill us, the ones who confront it, even though it's supposed to have destructive powers greater than an army of men? I'm expected to believe it can destroy a whole village alone, but not a single man bearing a sword? Still, the quests continue and the world remains intact."

Secret considered his words. "What if the threat is real, but fortunately, nothing has provoked it to commit anything more than its random acts?"

"Look, I understand I serve as a symbol for the kingdom, the one who stares evil in the eye. But what if—" his gaze the color of myth met hers of night and day—"what if the meaning of the quest is obsolete? What does that say about us, every one of us, with a prince as its proxy, that we cannot move beyond it? If there is nothing to face, Secret, then why am I going?"

"Those are subversive questions," she said, a tone of warning in her voice despite her agreement.

"I know. And that confounds all I've been taught and what's expected of me." He paused. "So, do you think it exists?"

"The dragon is a matter of fact and figment. There's a kernel of proof, it seems, because it has endured for so many ages. I suppose you'll learn for yourself soon enough," she said.

He leaned against the battlement's ledge with crossed arms. His chin dropped and his shoulders tightened.

"Are you afraid?" she asked.

"Yes, I am. But of what, I don't know."

Secret had never seen him so vulnerable. How deeply he thinks, she thought, how deeply he feels. An impulse to reach out to him surged into her hands. She hovered her left palm near his back, then withdrew it. He might not like that. He might not want to be touched, she said to herself. Nikolas clutched the edge of the wall and stared into the distance. She watched him, her blood rushing in her veins, afraid of a rebuke for the comfort she wanted to give. Her heart thudded faster as she forced her hand toward him and placed it gently on his shoulder.

Nikolas sighed at the contact. She could feel him relax, as if whatever he'd held tight had vanished. She exhaled with relief that he hadn't pulled away. She dropped her hand and slipped it around his elbow. He stood straight, linking his arm with hers. With affection, he leaned toward her, and she tilted to his side. He felt solid and strong. She welcomed the sun and the wind. Right then, in that moment, everything was perfect.

A bird darted so close by she could see the dot of its eye.

Then her feet began to throb as if she'd walked too many miles. When the ache rushed into her hips and shoulders, she froze. Not now, not again, she thought.

Secret felt her body echo—yes, the feeling was like a sound striking her heart, the palms of her hands. The ground became sky, then ground again, and she swayed against a man with green eyes who was once a boy—

Secret looked up to see who stood next to her.

For a moment, she didn't recognize him.

His name was—his name was—

"Secret, what's wrong?" Nikolas clutched the sides of her arms.

She closed her eyes. Panic flared through her muscles and bones. Her body felt heavy, but her blood felt light. She thought of her glimpse into the king's private chamber and the gold-hilted sword and the rupture that had come then.

"Can you answer me? What's the matter?" Nikolas asked.

"I became dizzy from the height," she said. She turned from his grasp and stepped back from the wall. "I guess I must keep my eyes afar, not down."

"Are you sure? You seemed—lost—for a moment. I called your name but you didn't reply. You just stood there," Nikolas said. "Has this happened before?"

She looked into his eyes. Not green.

"No, it hasn't," she said, the lie far easier than the truth. "I must be sensitive to heights."

Nikolas stepped close and put his arm around her shoulders. She flinched, which made him draw her tighter to his side.

"You won't fall on my watch," Nikolas said.

– XL –

What Is Within the Town

THE DAY IS DONE. NIGHT BRINGS ITS OWN ILLUMINATION.

Slip into the private spaces. Notice how they are all the same. Chairs, tables, beds, an area in which to cook, an area in which to wash. There are objects for warmth and comfort; others kept for beauty or function. Observe how they are different. Some people live with sparse possessions by aesthetic choice or destitute necessity. Those with the room to fill do so in the manner of shrines, each object imbued with power. Others, regardless of space, scurry through pace-worn paths edged with belongings, so many that a map is needed to find what is forgotten. Between the lack and plenty, there is enough. That is often difficult to see.

Walk out into the streets. The moon is new, and thus its glow can be no guide. Lamplights keep a safe path. There may be danger along the way—more so than ever—so be alert. Pay attention to goose bumps and shivers, the impulse to strike or run away.

Continue on. Pass the closed doors. Be quiet. Strangeness accompanies this walk. The foreboding seems to widen. All at once, it is sourceless, distant, and immediate.

Pause at a doorway. Move to the next. Linger at this threshold, then another. Go round and through town, where there are rich and poor, young and old. Everywhere, it is the same.

In the light of day, they hide the children they beat, the wives they batter, the husbands they belittle. There is no tangible brutality in silence, no obvious scars through neglect. They keep the mute company of liquor, pills, and food. Unspeakable things remain unspoken. They contain the workaday frustrations until they release over spilled milk, at the drop of a hat, for no reason at all, with no warning. The resulting questions are unanswerable. *Why can't you behave? Why do you provoke me? Why won't you listen?*

Remember, there are children present. Target or bystander, they are witness.

The children see what was seen before by the eyes of the ones who came before them. They are made in those images. Over and over again, they will be told it is for their own good, how it is done, what little boys and girls do to make their elders happy, not for them to question. Do as they say, not as they do. This is nothing to cry over, they're told. They'll be given something to cry about.

Make no mistake. They know moments of joy, laughter, contentment, and love. Some know more than others. For none is there ever too much.

XLI

A Private Meeting with the Magnate

THROUGHOUT THE SUMMER BEFORE SECRET TURNED SEV-
enteen, before her twelfth year of school, she spent most of her
days at Fewmany Incorporated. Although she had assignments to
occupy her three afternoons a week, she spent almost every full day
between the translations office and the sixth floor.

Leo indulged her, perhaps more than he might have another
apprentice. The teacher in him—he had told her of that former
aspiration—delighted in her voracity and quick learning. His instruction, challenge, and praise, more so than her lessons in school,
had encouraged Secret to test her own capabilities. Leo allowed her
to bring in books from her own collection, and he devised creative
assignments for him to evaluate.

In the different languages in which she was becoming more
fluent, she wrote truces between eons-long enemies, villains' con-
fessions, and detailed tallies of kings' coffers. The inventive tales
amused them both.

Her earnestness delighted her father. This reflected well on him,
of course, and he was greatly pleased to hear reports of her mas-
tery. Because of his traveling, Bren could converse in three other
languages, but could read and write only in his native tongue with
proficiency. Secret was accomplished in these, improving in three
others, and curious about several more, which were quite unlike
her own.

When Bren invoked her mother, Secret nodded but kept her
mouth shut. She didn't want the comparison. What had come with
ease for her mother required hard work from her. She knew Zavet

had been motivated by what she could not pursue. She desired the rare and remarkable, like the tablet she'd seen as a student at the high academy, artifacts which were one day found in a mixed stack of old books, a buried chamber, or a discovered cave. But Secret found the most commonplace texts to have their own fascination. With them, Secret sought understanding, which could be achieved or lost with a single word.

Too soon, too abruptly, it seemed to Secret, the summer ended. She would miss the morning light at her desk in room 621, lunches outside in a shady spot in Old Wheel, and Leo's additional tutelage. She was surprised by the melancholy mood that came over her the last full day she worked.

But then her days and evenings returned to a familiar rhythm. Her twelfth school year began, which meant the return to lectures and schoolwork. Her apprenticeship resumed its former three-day-a-week schedule. The only new matter she had to attend was reviewing materials from high academies.

Not long after her seventeenth birthday that autumn, there was a disruption to her ordinary days.

She had been an apprentice for almost a year but had not been asked to a meeting with Fewmany. At the apprentices' orientation, he had mentioned he hoped to sit with each one of them to talk. Through the months that had passed, she heard some of the boys speak of their meetings while they stored their schoolbooks in the cabinets in room 621. She had asked a few directly if they'd spoken with him. By then, most of them had.

All of them in some way revealed they admired or respected Fewmany, but not a single one had the same experience.

"My father said he had a certain . . . vitality . . . about him. I think that was an understatement," one boy said.

"He asked what I wanted to study at high academy, and I asked him some questions. It was nothing," another said.

"We discussed how he developed the Tell-a-Bell, and I told him I had ideas for a long-distance message device that would eliminate the need for posted letters. He didn't even give his toll when his bell rang. I say, impress him if you can," replied a third.

"I'm not sure whether he or his office was more intimidating. I have no memory of what I said while I sat there," stated the next.

"He's going to eat you alive, Riven," the last one she asked told her with vicious glee.

Then she finally received her summons, a brief note written by his secretary and sealed with the Fewmany Incorporated mark.

On the appointed day and time, Secret climbed the stairs to the twelfth floor. The physical effort kept her mind off what was to come. In the central hall on the top floor, beyond the displays of antiquities and Tell-a-Bells, was a reception lobby. Toward the back of the room was a desk. There sat a dour secretary with a fierce bun in her hair and the longest fingernails Secret had ever seen.

Behind the secretary was a detailed portrait of the magnate. Perhaps it only seemed to be larger than life-size, but it was imposing indeed. Dressed in a black coat and trousers, a dark-plum double-breasted vest, and a crimson cravat, he stood with his right hand on his hip, the other relaxed at his side. His eyes seemed to peer into the distance, focused on a faraway point. Secret wondered how the woman worked as he loomed over her.

After Secret gave her name, the woman led her to a closed chamber to the left of the desk. Shut inside, Secret saw a long, rectangular table surrounded by twenty-one high-backed leather chairs. A globe marked with silver pins on a marble stand claimed one of the heads. A freezing draft slipped between the heavy drapes at the hidden windows. She looked at the paintings on the walls—each aggressive in color or contrast—and approached one that had embossed text, which read: FABER EST QUISQUE FORTUNAE SUAE

That is, *Every man is architect of his own fortune.*

She heard the muffled sound of a large bell. Moments later, two carved doors, which bore no congruence to the building's architecture, rattled at the knobs and opened out into the chamber.

"Join me in my inner sanctum," Fewmany said. "This is where I hold my most important meetings."

She noticed his deft flick behind his right ear. He had disengaged his Tell-a-Bell. He stepped aside, raised his arm to direct her, and closed the door behind him.

On the wall ahead, there was a fireplace filled with burning logs. To her left, animals watched her enter the chamber from their places on the wall. She held a gasp in her chest and the cry that chased it. Their glass eyes reflected light from the windows and the brass lamps that flanked the desk. Only one of the beasts was prized for its meat. The rest were trophies, killed for sport, creatures she had seen only as illustrations in books.

She sensed the display was meant to be acknowledged. To ignore it might have been considered rude.

"A comprehensive menagerie," she said, looking straight at him.

"Thank you. A mere portion of my collection. There are yet a few rare and exotic heads I intend to acquire. One day perhaps I shall wrestle a white tiger with a dagger in my teeth, or slay a dragon and mount its head where I can hang my top hat."

Secret forced a smile in response to what was surely a joke. She continued to look at him, telling herself to act as she had to in her classes, refusing to be intimidated.

"Please, sit down," Fewmany said, gesturing to the two elaborately carved chairs that faced the window. He stepped behind his leather-topped desk and flung himself into a brown tufted chair with a high back. He heaved his shiny boots onto the desk's corner.

"Oh-ho, 'tis a mercy to lighten my load," he said. Fewmany crossed his arms and blinked at her with interest. "A change has come about you since we last spoke at length. Mature—and rather dramatic, I think."

Secret pressed her elbows into her sides and hid a fist behind the other hand in her lap. She refused to flinch. "I have grayed young, sir."

She saw the covert grin ripple through the small muscles under his flesh, so subtle she knew he hadn't meant it to be seen. He looked at her with the same scrutiny—and amusement—as he had the night her hair grew before his eyes. Neither of them had forgotten, nor would they speak of it. What had happened then was not resolved, but Secret hoped the matter had been put to rest. She couldn't provide him with knowledge she didn't have. No blood comes from a stone, she thought.

Fewmany shifted in his seat for comfort. "Yes, I had noticed that before today. To be clear, I intended to remark that you now look me in the eye. Confidence suits you."

"Thank you, sir," she said.

"So—your mother, peace be to the dead, and your father, clever cunning fellow he is, raised a good girl, didn't they?" Fewmany said.

"So it's been said," she said.

"Smart and quick learning as well, I know. Mr. Gray reports you're a superior apprentice. Work hard and continue to do well here. You're granted time to learn and to see how this world works. I keep the brightest nearby. You'll not want for better. Tell me, what are your plans after your graduation next year?"

"I expect to attend high academy. There are four or five that interest me in particular, any of which I would be honored to attend."

"'Twouldn't be a surprise if you were forced to take your pick," he said.

"I should be so fortunate," she said.

"Have you decided upon an area of study?"

"No. I have many interests and haven't chosen one."

"So, Miss Riven, do you have questions for me?"

The silent beasts behind her and the man in front watched without hurry. As she paused to think, she studied the objects nearby. The pen and inkstand guarded by its bronze-cast griffin. The blotter lightly stained. Three bins within his arm's reach stacked with documents of all sizes. On a stand in the corner, a dismembered arm and shoulder carved from alabaster. A rack near the door held a long coat with a shiny black fur collar and black hat with a high lid and gold band above the brim.

She knew she couldn't ask the questions she wanted answered. Why had her father shown the drawing of the symbol to him? Why was it so important? Why had she been allowed to apprentice, the only girl among them? So, instead, she thought to ask what might reveal more about him.

"I appreciate Mr. Gray's generosity with his time and instruction, and I've been glad to have practical assignments throughout my apprenticeship. I've done my best with the work I've been given. What do you expect in return for this investment in my training?"

"That's one question I don't believe I've been posed, and now that it has been, my answer isn't what I'd anticipate I would give. What do I expect?" He regarded her with full attention. "Enthusiasm . . . gratitude . . . fealty."

"When I read the manual we were given, I was interested to learn that you started with one small dry-goods shop. The manual listed many enterprises, and I noticed their names are chiseled behind the lobby's reception desk."

"Quite a number, yes," Fewmany said.

"Why are there so many along with the one you first founded?"

He tugged a handkerchief from a breast pocket and set about dusting the toes of his boots, keeping an eye on her.

"I found one key to profitability is uniformity. I understood quite young that we creatures of habit exhibit a mechanism, if you will, for more than a favorite tea or route home. One clings to the promise of consistency—yes?—for better or worse. With venture after venture, I ensured that whatever was made was reliably the same and where it was obtained recognizable as well. This is why, no matter where you go in town or in this kingdom—or several lands beyond it—you will precisely know where to go, what to expect, what you will find, see, smell, taste, and hear. This creates a form of loyalty which is almost inviolable as long as the familiarity holds.

"There are so many," he continued, "because I have an instinct to discover a bright idea or clever good, then make it accessible, especially appealing, and provide it to those who find benefit. In this, I have no equal. No one does this better. No one trumps me."

Secret detected frankness with a hint of conceit in his tone. As far as she knew, Fewmany had no equal, but then she had never met anyone else like him. "You surely have other matters on your schedule, and you've been generous with your time. I have one last question."

"And what is that?"

"What compels you to strive as you do?"

Fewmany gave a slight grin. "I shall turn the query to you first."

"What do you mean?" she asked.

"As it appears, 'tis not enough for you to be an acceptable student because you are an exceptional one. Your father boasts of you on occasion, and I know what information your application contained. That achievement alone would have ensured your choice among many fine high academies, yet you chose to apprentice here. In this case, too, I'm well aware of the value of a recommendation from my enterprise. While other young women your age have more modest intellectual aspirations, perhaps entertain the occasional nuptial daydream and visions of what follows, you seem in pursuit of something, even if you cannot identify what it is. So—to the question, what compels you?"

She returned his direct gaze. In the space of a pause, the words came complete. "I'm curious to discover what I don't know and wish to seek the boundaries of what I do."

"Quite well said," Fewmany replied, evidently impressed.

Secret allowed the brief reveal of a gratified smile. She was pleased with her clever yet honest response. "The question returns to you."

"What compels me to strive? The truth is, Miss Riven, the memory of hunger. 'Tis a common tale, isn't it, men who've made themselves out of nothing who later acquire everything they want," he said.

"And what of the things such men need?" she asked.

"Easily sated. Let me tell you a funny story. When I was but a wet-nosed laddie, I went on my way to the village to fetch some such for my father. I chanced upon a little pouch of copper coins. Filthy, it was, trampled, I'd say, and no one was near. 'Twasn't much, but a fortune to me, who'd never so much as rubbed two together. Off to the village I went with the copper in hand. I bought as much bread as the coins would buy and hid myself behind a tree and ate and ate. I stuffed the crumbs into my mouth and pocketed the crusts I could not swallow. Sparrows and whatnot pestered me for the crusts. 'Greedy little birds, mine!' I shouted. I ran from them, belly near to bursting, and heaved the meal from my gut. A mongrel chanced upon me and ate what I heaved. Angry, I chased him until he heaved, and it was taken up by a crow. Then the dog and I chased the crow and pelted it with sticks until it heaved in the river, feeding the fish. And that was the end of that."

Fewmany chortled and wiped a tear from his eye. "The sight we must have been!"

"Two lessons from that day," he said. "First, never run on a full stomach because it will leave you empty. Second, squirrel away for survival. My supper that night was but a cup of milk and the crusts I'd kept. The coins were spent except for two and those I rub together to this day." His coat's left sleeve moved as a patting sound rose from behind the desk.

She knew he meant to amuse her, perhaps impress her with his rise above adversity. She heard what he said, but more so what he didn't intend to expose. Under it all was a wounding despair. A tender tremor rippled through her heart.

"Poor Fewmany," Secret said before she could stop herself.

He whipped his feet to the ground, lurched forward across his desk, and swept his arms out with an easy flourish. "Not anymore," he said with quiet restraint.

Secret dared not move or speak until the shadow in his eyes returned to whence it came. Her stillness let the sadness she'd felt for him pass by and allowed the alarm to set in.

Fewmany—for all of his innate brilliance, blatant ambition, and apparent generosity—was a volatile man. She would forget, and remember, again and again.

XLII

The Search for the Manuscript

LATE IN THE AUTUMN OF HER TWELFTH YEAR OF SCHOOL, SE-
cret began to sort through booklets from and correspondence
with high academies within three kingdoms. By winter, she had
narrowed her choices to five, all renowned, and started to compile
what each required.

She vacillated between anticipation and dread.

Some days, she imagined kissing her father's cheek before she
stepped into a hired carriage, her trunks strapped to the roof, and
fidgeting in her seat as the horses pulled her away toward a new
life. She wondered what it would be like to start again in a place
where she had no history, where no one knew she'd once been
black-haired and silent. She saw herself entering a room of fellow
scholars and sitting next to someone, perhaps a young man with
spectacles whose eyes repeatedly passed over the same line of a
book because he, too, was nervous about his first day. There were
possibilities ahead, knowledge to gain, friends to make, and she felt
hope as if it were a living thing with a beating heart.

But then she would catch a glimpse of herself, her eyes the colors of night and day, her solitary ways, the secrets she held within,
and she wondered if there was no escape she could make, no matter
where she went.

She considered, too, what would be left behind. There was her
father, who would surely miss her and she believed she would miss
him. He had been the one to give her the gift of stories, take her
on outings she enjoyed, and concern himself with her studies and

interests. Bren had provided well for her, and she knew he would continue to do so until she could make her own way.

And there were her friends. Although some of them weren't certain yet what they would do after graduation, Secret knew Charlotte was going to travel to see distant relatives and Muriel, who played the piano, wished to attend a small, female-only conservatory.

As for Nikolas, by the coming summer's end, he would leave for goodwill visits to allied kingdoms, an act of diplomacy that had been a family tradition for generations. He had told her he would be away for at least two years, and soon after his return would depart again, that time for his quest to obtain a dragon's scale. Although no one required it of him, he hoped to attend high academy after that. Regardless of whether he went on to further study, soon enough Nikolas would be given responsibilities to tend to in the kingdom, awaiting the day he would become king. During those years, he would marry and have children, as expected. His life was destined in a way Secret's was not. She wondered what she would make of hers, aware her bond with him would fray until it broke. It was inevitable.

Although formal applications weren't due until the first of spring, Secret decided to prepare hers early. She asked her father to obtain the proper documentation from school, and she asked Leo for recommendations to send as well.

One bitter winter afternoon, Secret went to the translations office to get her letters from Leo. The room wasn't quite warm enough, despite the stove Wesley kept stoking. Each of the men huddled within his coat, his fingertips poking through his gloves. A sharp draft came through a crack in a window and stirred the smells of bay rum, garlic, smoke, and discomfort.

"I had Wesley make a copy of your letters so you may keep a record." Leo handed her envelopes sealed with Fewmany Incorporated's mark and a folded stack of paper. "Of course, you understand I gave a most tepid recommendation considering you are so lazy and slow-witted."

Secret smiled. "How generous of you to say."

"You didn't ask for a letter for the academy that I thought would well suit you. The one your mother attended," Leo said.

She shook her head as she felt herself shrink from the mention.

"Didn't want the comparison?" a rheumy voice called out.

She wasn't sure whether Cuthbert had addressed her or had merely made a remark.

"Well?" Cuthbert asked, lifting his head from his work but not facing her.

"I may not choose that discipline, and there are other fine schools that teach the same if I do," Secret said.

A waft of garlic rose when Rowland twisted in his seat. "That woman was a witch."

"Quiet, Rowland," Leo said.

"She was, Gray. Oh, it wasn't only the way she looked. Those eyes—turned a man's blood one way or the other—"

Cuthbert and Wesley laughed as Leo said, "That will do."

"What she knew was unfathomable. Fewmany had his whims, and the strangest scraps and half-missing pieces would pass through us—remember, men?—and what we couldn't interpret, he'd have sent to that woman. Nothing was a mystery to her. How was that possible?" Rowland said.

"The reek of envy masks your other, Rowland," Leo said.

"I'm asking the girl," Rowland said.

Secret clutched the letters to her chest and felt the men's eyes on her. "I only know what I was told, sir, and that was she was born with the ability."

"A witch born then, not spell-made," Rowland said. "Which are you, her silver-haired daughter?"

"Wesley, why don't you help Rowland find his tonic? I believe he's in need of a sip," Leo said as he stood, gestured to Secret, and led her into the hall.

He shut the office door. "I apologize. Rowland has these moments at times. He's an old man. You mustn't take him seriously."

"You said he envied her," Secret said.

"We all did. I once asked your mother what it was like to have her gift. To be honest, I was surprised because she spoke with pain, not joy. She said, 'I hear screams that never cease.'"

Secret bit her lip as she remembered her mother's muttering and burbling and dark moods. No, there was no joy.

"Rowland was also Fewmany's favorite, until your mother took that place," Leo said, then whispered under his breath a phrase in another language. He cast his eyes upward and gave a quick nod.

"Mr. Gray, Miss Riven," Fewmany said as he strode toward them with two men following behind.

"Sir," they said in unison as he passed.

Alone again, she asked Leo, "What did you say a moment ago?"

"It translates to, Speak of the wolf and he appears at the door."

Soon after that day, the nightmares began.

The first was merely disturbing, a harbinger of what would be worse.

In the dream, Secret walked in a forest of fir trees. She was tired—she had journeyed far—but she was content, even happy. She chanced upon the square that contained the circle, triangle, and flame—the symbol carved into a stone, left along her path. She looked ahead. It was night then, and the moon lit a narrow trail. There stood a man who was not a man but a grotesque menagerie. He had a wolf's head and a sheep's trunk with two legs, boar and stag, and two arms, pheasant and bear. *Follow me*, he said in Fewmany's voice. Too afraid to flee, knowing she'd be chased, she did. He led her to the door of a cottage, its threshold edged in bones, and said, *You've been expected here.*

Secret awoke before she stepped through the door. She rationalized the dream easily enough. Nothing more than a terrible combination of the past and the symbol and the present and Fewmany's wall of dead beasts.

In the weeks that followed, Secret dreaded going to sleep, knowing she would find herself where she wished not to be.

The nightmares came with minor variations. In each one, a beast's back appeared in shadow, human in form. It moved with a brute's gait and heavy gestures, but it was not male. The creature was an ogress. Within its reach was a container—a barrel, or cage, or cauldron—and it stretched its arm to whisk something from the depths again and again. The beast grew fatter, sloughing off a skin to grow. It made horrible noises—smacking, chewing, crunching. There was a glimpse of infant arms and legs.

Once, those infant limbs were a shade of blue, and Secret awakened after that horror thinking of her brothers who never were.

Secret knew these were not like the uncanny dreams of the blue men, the symbol, and the ones from the fever. Neither were the ogress dreams like ordinary nightmares, which drifted from her thoughts upon waking if they lingered long at all.

For a month, she endured this until the last one revealed its message.

Secret dreamed she was trapped in a cage too small for her to stand. Her nose ached as if she'd been struck hard. An animal reek, oily and feral, tainted the air. Close by, a porcine beast pulled a screaming baby from a huge stone pestle. The cries stopped as the ogress gobbled it up. The beast reached for another child, limp at the end of a cord attached to its belly, and then another, tethered around the neck with a rope. As the beast fed, Secret realized she was being saved for last. Then the ogress defecated with a grunt, an odious rupture of fingernails, hair, and bones—and one small key.

Secret thrashed in the gap between sleeping and waking. As her eyes opened in the dark, she thought, The key is in the body.

She awoke in a fright. The key is in the body the key is in the body, her mind repeated in a maddening loop. The mental effort it would take to ignore the thought would be more difficult than the attempt to find what was hidden. She could no longer avoid the search.

Her shaking hands pushed open the curtains to allow in the streetlamp's light. There was no moon. She stumbled to her bookcase and grabbed the nesting dolls from their high place on an ignored shelf. She sat on the floor, twisted their bodies apart, and paused at the evident emptiness of the twelfth one. Where the solid, last little one should have been was a folded sheet of paper. Within the folds was a key, and on the torn-edged paper was an illustration. Secret grabbed the book of folktales from her mother's native land, put the cipher to the side, and flattened the page back in place.

A hag stood in front of a cottage made of bones. The woods surrounded her in the dead of winter. Secret studied the picture—how it had once frightened her—and then she noticed a detail she didn't recall. She went to the window and squinted. A blue rectangle, with sides and a top, was drawn on top of the roof.

Secret held the images in her mind. The nesting dolls. The cipher. Fragments of the illustration. Blue box. She believed she knew where the manuscript was.

Key in hand, she knelt at the foot of her bed in front of the faded blue chest her mother had kept since she was a child. The lock released with a click. Her hands claimed the contents.

A bag of gold ingots.

The thirteenth doll.

A letter sealed with wax.

Secret opened it and read, *A map is to space as an alphabet is to sound.* A scream of confusion boiled in her chest. That was the sentence her mother had written on the last page of her diary. Why was it repeated in the letter and left here for her to find?

She swept her hands along the inside of the chest, searching for a package or a catch for a false bottom. Nothing. The arcane manuscript wasn't there. Secret didn't understand why her mother would separate clues for the manuscript from the source itself. Dazed, she returned the items to the chest, locked it, and slipped into the breathless blackness where there was nothing but silence.

The next morning, Secret awoke and went downstairs for a bite to eat. Her father was away again, and Elinor wasn't scheduled to come on that day. She would be alone to search undisturbed.

Secret pulled the great bobbin and latch on the back door and went outside. She needed the sun and air and the space to think. Where would her mother have hidden the manuscript?

Secret wandered around the courtyard, her feet directing the way. She focused on the splay of each toe within her slippers, which calmed the roil of what was within her. Her steps led her to the place where the fig tree had stood. Her body lowered to the ground, where she sat with crossed legs, the slate tiles cold under her thighs.

With closed eyes, she lifted her face to the morning sun. She surrendered to the heat as it became a vibration. The silent hum moved through the center of the queen bee's sting and was transformed into a white light in her head. For several breaths, she knew bliss. The escape didn't last long because as soon as she rubbed her lashes, she remembered what she had to do.

She went to her father's study on the third floor. His favorite map, hundreds of years old and covered with transparent layers, fluttered when Secret rushed into the room. She opened the curtains of the south-facing windows and lit a lamp. She checked every drawer, below every surface, under every map, book, and document Bren had left out. She looked behind the maps on his wall where there might be a hidden panel. With a lamp, she peered as best she could behind his shelves. One by one, his books came down, her hands lightly powdered with dust, and one by one, they were replaced in the order he'd chosen. All that was in there seemed to belong to him.

Then she went to the second-floor storage room.

Box after box was crammed within the space. She opened some of the boxes to check the contents, finding some of her mother's old logs and diaries, but the longer she looked, the more she questioned whether her search there made sense. Her mother would have been more likely to secret the arcane manuscript away in an accessible place rather than bury it like this. How else would Secret find it?

She remembered the illustration torn from the book. The blue

rectangle was drawn on the roof, not on the ground. The placement of the box had to be a clue.

The garret, Secret thought.

She stood in the hall on the third floor, staring up at the wood
panel that closed the space. If her mother had kept the manuscript
there, Zavet must have had a ladder nearby.

The door to her father's bedroom was closed. Secret turned
the knob and entered. Everything in the room was the same as it
had been since the row house's renovation four years earlier. The
curtains were open on the four-poster bed. Zavet's slippers were on
the floor near the bed where she'd always kept them. Secret looked
into her father's wardrobe, then her mother's. All of her clothes and
accessories were still there. The table near the fireplace appeared
untouched. There was her mother's silver brush, comb, and mirror set, the inlaid box where she kept her jewelry, and the row of
perfumes in beautiful bottles. Her wedding ring lay in the center
of it all.

Secret's breath caught in her chest. Oh, Father, she thought.

She went to the wardrobes again, Zavet's on the right, Bren's
on the left. She peeked under the stubby claw-foot legs. There was
something against the wall. Behind Zavet's wardrobe Secret found
a ladder.

Secret dragged it into the hall and balanced it so she could
climb. She pushed the garret's wooden panel out of the way. Her
tiptoes pressed against a rung as she pushed herself up.

It was dark but for the angles of light coming through the ven-
tilation slats. Not wanting to be startled, she asked any rats, mice, or
bats to announce themselves. She received no answer.

Then she saw a metallic skitter, tiny and alive, crawling on the
side of a box. Silverfish darted in all directions. Their presence was
no surprise if there were books stored in the garret on which they
could feast.

On top of a box was a smaller one.

Secret took it in her hands. She brushed her thumbs against the dovetailed joints. She touched the pin in the latch. This was the wooden box that had held the arcane manuscript.

Her blood pounded under her flesh. The relief, excitement, fear, rage as she lifted the lid and found—

Nothing.

The arcane manuscript was gone.

Within the box, a silverfish crawled over a strand of hair, across her hand, and disappeared into the darkness.

She threw the box into a corner.

"Where is it? What am I supposed to do now? How could you do this to me?" she screamed into the rooftop.

As she climbed down the ladder and sealed the garret's access again, she stored away what tried to break free, what she could not yet face. She went to her room, grabbed the carved stag from her side table, dropped on her bed, and rounded her knees to her chest.

Her mother was dead.

She had not choked.

The manuscript was the key to why.

XLIII

A Change of Plans

DURING THE LAST WEEKS OF SCHOOL, SECRET SEARCHED THE parlor table the moment she walked in the door. High academies were sending their acceptance letters, and Secret was anxious to learn where she would be going in autumn. The evenings she and her father returned home together, Bren stood in the distance, his eyes wide, waiting as she sorted through what had been delivered. The afternoons she didn't have her apprenticeship, she went straight home from school and riffled through what Elinor had placed on the table already.

When the first rejection arrived, she was disappointed but not terribly. That school had been her last choice. With the next two rejections, she became more disappointed, then worried. Her father decried the academies' lack of judgment and remained confident all would be well.

Secret was alone the day the last two letters arrived. The academy of her third choice lauded her outstanding record, regretted they couldn't offer admittance at that time, and stated she was on their waiting list in the event a place opened. The academy of her first choice sent a rejection so perfunctory she wondered if her application had been declined without review.

Devastated, she went to her room and lay on her bed in tears until the lamplighter passed on her street. She ignored her growling stomach as night fell. When she heard her father downstairs, she wanted to vanish. She could have waited to tell him, but that wouldn't change the news.

Bren knocked on her door softly and opened it a crack.

"Are you asleep?" he whispered. The lamp in his hand illuminated his face and the gap where he stood.

"I'm awake."

"Did you eat dinner?"

"I'm not hungry," she said, her belly empty except for the dread and anger.

Bren entered with caution, as if he sensed something was wrong. He stood in the middle of the room holding the light.

"Father."

"What is it?"

"I've heard from the last two. My first rejected me, and my third has placed me on a waiting list." Secret thought she heard him choke back a cry.

He raised his free hand to his face and exhaled long and low. "Secret, I'm sorry."

She curled into the corner of her bed.

Bren sat down near her, placing the lamp on her table. His Tell-a-Bell began to chime. The delicate *tinktinktinktinktink* startled him, even though it went off at that same time every day. He fumbled behind his ear to find the quieting catch. "There is the waiting list. That is a very fine academy," he said.

"I didn't want to be on a list. I wanted an acceptance. I wanted to pack my trunk and leave here and go somewhere—somewhere—else," Secret said, her throat hard from fighting tears.

Bren tried to touch her, but she drew farther back.

"You could wait, as you've been offered, but there are other academies you decided against. You could reconsider those," Bren said, unconvincing.

Secret shook her head. "I worked for this. You have no idea what I endured these past three years so I could apply to the best academies, not ones that would *just do*."

"Perhaps your ambition was too high."

"You're the one who encouraged me and the one who went to the headmaster when he wouldn't listen to me. Didn't you want me to attend the best? Didn't you buy that chance—only for it not to pay off now?"

Bren dropped his head. "It was inconceivable you wouldn't get in. You went to the finest school, received the highest marks."

Secret suddenly realized what he missed and she didn't want to admit. "I completed my forms with my given name and noted what I'm called. The same reason you had to fight for me is likely the same reason I won't be attending high academy this autumn."

"But you're exceptional, like your mother—"

The mention sent a streak of fury straight to her head. "Why does everyone keep mentioning her? I am not like my mother! I don't know how she managed to achieve what she did or what luck was on her side, but whatever it is, I don't have it. I don't know what I'm going to do."

Bren leaned over slowly with an outstretched hand toward the side of her face. "Don't touch me," she said, threatening.

"We will find a solution. It may not happen in time for the coming term, but we will find one," he said.

Secret put her face in her hands. Suddenly, she thought of her blue brothers. Had either lived, her father might not have been sitting there disappointed and sad. He might not have encouraged her, his pet, at all, having had someone else to carry his name and fulfill his hopes.

Bren sighed. "I *am* proud of you, Secret. You know that."

"You'd be prouder if I'd received an acceptance."

He didn't reply. He took the lamp from the table, walked to the door, and stood at the threshold. "I'll bring up a plate."

At school, there was no way to hide what happened. The high academies also sent letters to the schools announcing who had been admitted. Although she told only her friends of the replies she received, the headmaster's announcements celebrated who had been accepted and conspicuously left out her name. When asked directly, she lied and said she was still waiting to receive word, even though she was almost certain every academy had sent their notifications by then. She did at least muster the manners to congratulate her classmates on their good news.

She forced herself through the final weeks. She deflected her friends' concerns, assuring them she was hopeful a notice would come and she'd be on her way to her third choice at the end of the summer. They weren't convinced, she didn't think, but they didn't needle her with questions about what she would do if that didn't happen. If they had, she had no answer.

On the evening of her graduation, Secret felt none of the hope that had filled her daydreams weeks and months before. She summoned a practiced smile through the ceremony and managed a sincere thank-you when she received a certificate as the third-ranking student in her class. The irony did not escape her.

She promised Nikolas to attend his party afterward only because he begged her and because it was being held at The Castle. If she needed to sneak away, she knew exactly what chamber she would choose. That evening, her father took her on the two-horse cart, their ride silent, and grabbed her sleeve before she stepped down.

"Please, try to enjoy yourself. This is a grand night, no matter what tomorrow brings," he said.

She nodded, pushing the scroll of her certificate against his leg. "I won't be too late. Remember, carriages have been arranged to take us home."

A guard pointed her to a servant who led her to a courtyard deeper within the castle's walls. Pretty lanterns strung across the space gave a soft glow. It was a fine evening, unusually warm for so early in the summer but pleasant. All of the boys were in their vests, coats set aside, and some of the girls had pinned or tied their hair away from their necks. There were small tables and chairs and blankets and cushions where the guests could sit. In one corner a quintet played lively music, and in another was a table spread with plenty to eat and drink.

Nikolas noticed her at the entrance. He looked relaxed and

happy. The neck of his shirt was open, and the cuffs of his sleeves were rolled above his wrists. She smiled as he gestured for her to walk forward. He led her to Charlotte and Muriel, who in an uncharacteristic burst of affection kissed her lightly on the cheeks. Secret laughed and attempted an awkward return of the gesture.

They sat on the ground with their full plates and cups. They spoke of good memories, and Secret was truly glad for her friends as they shared their forthcoming plans. Kindly, neither girl prodded her to tell what she expected to do in the coming months.

Across from the three of them, Secret observed Nikolas and a girl talking together in what seemed to be a halting but attentive discussion. They shifted their cushions closer until their arms were forced to touch. The girl wore a pretty green dress with flattering darts in the bodice. Her hair was set in loose curls that framed her heart-shaped face. In the dim light, Secret could see the flush in his cheeks, not due to the evening's heat. She looked down and smiled at how flustered he was.

Throughout the evening, friends and acquaintances stopped to chat, then moved along, everyone in a good mood. Secret tensed against her fluttering stomach when the conversations lulled for a moment and she was aware the chestnut-haired boy was right behind her. After a while, twitching with nervous energy, Charlotte and Muriel decided to dance, leaving Secret alone on the blanket.

At that moment, she saw a mouser peer around the courtyard entrance. Secret made no sound but called him to her. The cat padded across the ground. She heard someone mutter, "Ugh. A cat. Disgusting creatures." With a purring meow, he crawled into her lap.

"Resting from your work, are you?" she said as she scratched under his white chin and stroked his gray fur.

"Do you like cats?" a voice behind her asked.

She turned to see the chestnut-haired boy facing her. His eyes were the color of moss after a soft rain.

Her stomach flipped, and she couldn't seem to breathe in. "I do," she said after an awkward pause she would ruminate about long after this happened. "Do you?"

"Yes. We have one, but she's a prancing little thing who's afraid of mice. Not like this fellow."

Before she could reply, Nikolas crouched down next to her. The boy's and Secret's eyes met for a moment, then looked away. Secret gave Nikolas a piercing stare, which he didn't notice at all. The dazed expression on his face explained why. Secret cut her glance to the girl in the green dress whispering to a friend, making furtive glances toward Nikolas.

The mouser walked toward him, but he pushed it away.

"I need to talk to you," he said. She knew then the look in his eyes wasn't because of the girl. "Come with me."

Secret followed him away from the group and into a vestibule not too far away.

"I'm leaving tomorrow morning," he said.

"You told me you weren't leaving until the end of the summer," she said.

"My father decided he wants me to accompany him to see how a feud is settled before it spreads."

"So you'll be back afterward."

"No. I'm off to the first kingdom on my itinerary after that."

"But—you haven't had time to pack."

"Someone does that for me."

Secret pressed her back against the wall and pounded her head once on the stones.

"I'm sorry. I wasn't told until a few moments ago. My father has a tendency to make decisions and announce them when there's no time left to argue," he said.

"And apparently with no regard for what might be happening when he does so."

They stood in silence, both shocked. Secret had not imagined how their parting would happen, but it wouldn't have been like this.

"We won't see each other for years," he said, stunned. "The goodwill visits will take two, at least. I'd return in summer, or autumn. And then soon after that, I'll leave again for the quest. So I might not see you again for three years. Three years assuming nothing happens on the quest and"—his voice caught—"and you're here when I come back. But you won't be. You'll be at high academy."

"I have to be admitted to one first," she said.

"You will."

The vestibule was dark, but the nearby lamplight reflected the tears in his eyes. A falling sensation rushed through her torso and legs, as if she'd been thrown from a ledge.

He lunged and wrapped his arms around her shoulders. She pressed her forehead against the top of his chest and gripped the back of his vest. She gasped as a sob tore free, violent but soundless. He pulled her tighter. She felt his staggered breathing. Once she calmed herself enough to face him, she stepped back. A tangible rip seared across her sternum. She realized he hadn't been ready to let go, and neither had she.

Secret looked at him, remembering what she thought on the first night they met. His eyes were still the color of myth. She wiped her thumb against his cheek. He caught her wrist. "I'll see myself back to the gatehouse," she said.

"You're leaving now?"

"I can't do this again later."

"I'll walk with you."

"Go back to your guests. Please."

Still sniffling, he nodded.

She slipped her hand through his and stepped toward the entryway.

"Secret, I—"

"Yes?"

"I'll miss you," he said.

"I'll miss you, too," she said.

He watched her walk away. When she turned to look back, he was leaning with his hands against the wall where she had stood. She heard the release of a sharp cry. She forced herself to move on, to the gatehouse, where she climbed into one of the waiting carriages to go home.

Hidden near the steps of the row house, she found the key and went inside. All was quiet. Her father had left a lamp burning low on the mantel. She stumbled toward the dining table, threw herself in a chair, and braced the sides of her head in her hands. She couldn't believe her best friend had been ripped away from her, no warning, no good reason.

Tears blurred her focus on the back door's great bobbin and latch. As she took a thin breath, the arches of her feet pulled up as the wells of her hips and shoulders drew down.

"I've had enough pain tonight," she said as this rupture opened wider than one had ever done before.

A dark-haired man stood at the threshold of the door.

He was a king. He had been her lover.

She had drawn maps in his service, and this one would be her last—and a lie.

His name was—his name was—

Secret's vision returned to the shape of her hands on the table, but her focus remained within, her sense of time and place fluid. This dark-haired man had cut the sky with a sword and swayed far above the ground at her side. There he was again, at the threshold, waiting. For her. But who was *she*?

Her breathing quickened until she became cold and then shallowed until she slipped into the blackness. Before she surrendered, she heard the distant hum of bees.

XLIV

Fewmany's Library

To avoid being idle and the despair that it would bring, Secret arranged to continue as an apprentice through the summer. Between the disappointment of not getting an acceptance and the shock of Nikolas's sudden departure, Secret was numb. Leo suggested that she contact the academies to learn why she had been declined, but Secret wasn't sure she wanted to know the truth. She couldn't change what she was, if being a girl was the reason, and she couldn't have been any better as a student, if her record was the issue. Regardless of the answer, she would have the same problems applying elsewhere.

One morning, she went to her desk on the sixth floor with a file in hand and saw a letter centered on her desk. It bore Fewmany's personal seal. The letter, written in his hand, requested a brief meeting. She couldn't imagine what he wanted.

When she approached the magnate's reception desk, his secretary, efficient and sour as ever, asked her to wait and disappeared through the door behind her. Moments later, the woman held the entrance open, instructed her to go to the inner sanctum, and told her to knock.

Secret did as she was told. Fewmany's voice bade her entry.

He offered her a seat. The dead beasts on the walls glared blindly at her back.

Fewmany clasped his hands and dropped them on his desk. He appeared to be in a good mood, as if he'd recently had a long-needed rest. "Mr. Gray informed me you requested to remain in our service for several more weeks."

"Yes, sir," she said. Her face blazed when she realized he certainly knew why that was so.

"I'm aware you've had an unexpected impediment to your plans."

She nodded once, sharply.

"I am sorry to learn of that, Miss Riven," he said.

She searched him to see if his eyes betrayed his words, but she detected no incongruence. She believed he was sincere. "Thank you."

"I heard on good authority that you have a fondness for old books," Fewmany said.

"Old books, yes, but the tales within more so," Secret said.

"Well, for some time, I've not been able to remove a task from my bell toll. Then . . . Eureka! Why not ask one of our brightest and most loyal apprentices?" Fewmany said.

Secret kept her back straight and her attention on him. That instant, she thought, possibly, he would ask her to remain in the translations office. But Secret had never once seen a book among the piles of work left in the office's bins, and aside from that, it would contradict what she knew from Leo. He had told her he'd heard of no plans to offer positions to any of the apprentices. They were expected to attend high academies or venture out in the world for a time. Some future alignment of circumstances might lead them back to the conglomerate.

"Yes, sir?"

"To the point—I have a grand library filled with great works, many of them rarities and oddities, an enviable collection, especially for those who appreciate such things. A number of these texts your mother—peace be to the dead—deciphered for my delight."

Her pulse began to race. "Did she? How many?" Secret asked.

"Throughout the years, a hundred, perhaps more."

She remembered the books and manuscripts that had appeared on her mother's tables, one by one, year after year. There had never been one mention of the sole patron's name or where he lived. Zavet was bound by an agreement to translate for that person alone, but she had violated this arrangement when she accepted the arcane manuscript. Of course, Zavet didn't tell her husband and forbade Secret to breathe a word of it. Zavet, like Bren, worked only for Fewmany.

"I found she was especially gifted with esoteric works, the best I ever retained," Fewmany said.

"Was she?" Secret said, forcing a tone of interest. Secret thought then about the lost manuscript. It could not be his, she knew. There would have been no reason for the messenger, bag of ingots, or return visits if it were.

"She was," Fewmany said.

"Why have you asked me to meet with you? I haven't the breadth of knowledge she did," Secret said.

"I require a thorough, respectful archivist to catalog and organize the collection."

Secret paused, expected to think of a few words of polite rejection, but instead she replied, "How intriguing, but as you know, I do want to attend high academy. I might hear from the one for which I am waiting. And there are options with less rigorous requirements."

"I suspect the latter is not your preference. My offer stands," he said.

"I'm honored but surely a person more knowledgeable and skilled than I would be better suited," she said, even as she resisted an unwelcome curiosity.

"You doubt your powers?" Fewmany asked. He leaned forward, his eyes set on hers.

"I'm young and realize I have much to learn."

"Modesty has its charms, but ambition has its rewards. My risk on your skill has calculable returns for both of us," Fewmany said. "I know you are a diligent worker—concerned with precision. I require such an ethic in this duty. I also know you can be trusted with valuable materials. Mr. Gray claims never to have had a worrisome lapse with you."

Secret felt baited, allured. She knew she couldn't decline right then. This game she had to play and, to her astonishment, believed she wanted to play. A sharp whispering memory cut into her thoughts as a warning, but she ignored it. Something had taken a turn. "Must I give you an answer now?"

"'Twould be foolish for you to do so without seeing the library itself. Tomorrow, come to my estate at six o' the clock. My secretary will provide the directions. Is that agreeable to you?" Fewmany asked.

"Yes," Secret said.

He smiled as he stood up and flicked his finger behind his ear, engaging the Tell-a-Bell once again. He escorted her across his office, barking *Splendid*! and *Huzzah*!, and opened the door for her. He smelled faintly of sausage and cloves as she stepped past his fine-suited bulk.

The secretary handed her a slip of paper with the information. Secret decided to see whether her father was in his office and to tell him what Fewmany had proposed. She suspected Bren was already aware.

She whisked past the shelves of Tell-a-Bells and antiquities, knocked on her father's office door, and waited for an answer. She entered without an invitation. He wasn't there. She glanced at the clutter on his desk—piles of loose papers, several bound ledgers, an open bottle of ink, the handbill for a lecture.

On his walls and stacked on a square table were maps of distant places. The ones that were hanging had the transparent sheets her father liked to use to annotate without marring them. She thought of the treasured map at home in his study and the veil for The Mapmaker's War. As Secret perused the charts, she saw her father's familiar marks used in the service of the present. Some of the lands had yet to be acquired—his role was to see that they were—where timber, mines, and fertile ground awaited new fates. Her father ensured that Fewmany's grasp extended as far as his reach.

Secret walked to the windows, cooler because they faced north, and looked out at the town and distant castle. Her imagination replaced the streets and buildings with a forest of trees, as it was in a primordial time when boundaries were marked by scent and sound, not by the decisions of men and the symbols of mapmakers.

A hard, rhythmic knock startled her. She turned to see a young man in a messenger's uniform carrying a long leather tube.

"Apprentice, make sure he gets this," he said, handing her the object.

She accepted the delivery and signed the receipt book he pulled from a pocket. He wished her a good day then rushed out. She leaned the tube on her father's chair—another map, she knew.

The longer she waited, the more agitated she became. She had an assignment to complete, but she wished to be outside, away from the building. Down to the third floor she went to see Leo.

Wesley opened the door when she knocked. Cuthbert and Rowland glanced over their shoulders but didn't speak to her. Leo leaned back in his high chair, ruffling his hair like a mane.

"Finished already?" he asked.

"No, soon. I'd like to ask permission to leave early this afternoon. There's a lecture I'd like to attend."

"Permission granted, Miss Riven, especially considering you've never asked to leave early before. Your sense of duty could do with a little corruption." He drummed his stained fingertips on his desk.

She nodded with a narrow smile, thanked him, and left the room.

At the moment she reached the stairwell, she heard Leo call her name.

"I do believe I caused you offense just now, and I want to apologize. Your dedication is mature for your age, but it was not right of me to suggest you should be otherwise," he said quietly.

"Thank you, but no offense was taken," she said.

"Yes, well, you seemed out of sorts." He paused, his hazel eyes focused with concern. "Is there something the matter?"

Secret almost brushed him aside but sensed no harm in the

facts. "I'm not quite over a moment of surprise. I met with Few-many earlier, and he has offered a position to me as the archivist of his private library. He didn't tell me not to speak of it, so I trust I may with whom I wish."

"How did you answer?"

"I had none. I'm to visit the library tomorrow, then decide."

Leo curled his fingers at his mouth and blinked at her.

"What is it?" she asked.

"Aren't you waiting to see whether you're admitted?"

"Yes, of course, and that's what I'll do if and when I hear word. But for this, to decline outright didn't feel appropriate. You understand."

"Hmph, well, I do. This is altogether different somehow," Leo said, his tone perplexed. "Apprentices come and go. Only the most talented are granted positions within the enterprises, not only here, but also elsewhere in the kingdom, even abroad. You would be an obvious candidate because of your skills." He looked at her squarely. "You've been placed in special favor. Have no doubt in that."

"But I did nothing to do so."

"Oh, but you did. As others have as well, who might have had a glimpse of why they rose but rarely of why they fell. Fewmany can be capricious."

"Then I should view this as an honor?"

The corners of his eyes tensed. He crossed his arms and shrugged. "One must be careful of the bargain, so I'll be careful with my counsel: Be mindful for the path you've laid for yourself. Watch for temptations to stray."

She nodded. She felt gratitude for his candor and for not speaking to her as a child.

"Get your things and go. Make your wizened adept happy and be idle through the rest of the day. Think of me while I'm chained to my desk." He moved his arms in a mime of bondage.

She laughed with him, retrieved her satchel from room 621, and left the building.

As she crossed the long, gold-toned tile plaza, she denied the impulse to walk barefoot in the shade of trees. Instead, she went to a teahouse where she and her father had shared several afternoons. It had been under different proprietorship when she was a young girl. Since then, its interior decor, tea and cakes, and name had changed—the latter chiseled in the marble wall in the lobby she passed almost daily. Nevertheless, she ordered a cup and sat at a table alone.

She held the warm rim of the cup against her lips. She tried to conjure a reassuring daydream of a teahouse she would one day frequent, where she would sit to think through a difficult assignment or rest from a long day. No details came, only a haze as thin as the one rising from her tea. She shut her eyes as the disappointment that she wasn't going away crushed her chest. How can this be? she asked herself.

Then she set down her cup, looked out, and watched passersby. In a pause of the flow, she saw across the street an antiquarian shop with furniture and objects displayed in the window. She thought of the alabaster statue in Fewmany's office and wondered what he might have displayed at his manor. She was certainly curious about the library. That moment, her despondency eased. If the worst happened and she didn't get into high academy this autumn, perhaps she would like working in the library. Perhaps that would give her something purposeful to do until circumstances changed.

The following day, she walked to Fewmany's residence with a map of the route. The walk was much farther than she had expected, and most of it was outside of the main boundary of town. When she arrived at the main gate, a man with a plumed hat and ruffed collar required her name in order for her to enter. He gave her a minted token as her pass, which she was instructed to return to him when she left.

The pleasant stroll led past several enormous houses set back on tidy lawns. She appreciated the openness and the presence of shrubs and trees, regardless that some were pruned in such a way that it was impossible to know their true shapes. She heard stray human mumbles, which at first disturbed her because she couldn't locate the source. Then she noticed a manor here and there had its very own newsbox near the front entrance. What an extravagance, she thought.

At the gate of Fewmany's manor, a man dressed similarly to the first she saw stepped from his covered post. He asked to see her token, then allowed her access.

Fewmany's manor was at the apex of a wide, paved, curved lane. The great house resembled The Tallest Building with its thick columns at the entrance and symmetrical windows, of which there were twenty-four windows on the left and twenty-four on the right, grouped in twos. There was a second story, not as long as the first, and with the same windows. There seemed to be a basement story as well, with small windows above the grade of the foundation. Chimney stacks jutted from the rooftops. This view only hinted at its sprawl and grandeur.

Secret climbed the marble stairs and stood at the heavy, wood-paneled double doors with two keyholes, one above the other, covered with gold escutcheons. There was no brass knocker, but to the left of the threshold she saw a braided cord—silky to the touch—and pulled it.

A hidden bell rang out, its deep timbre hinting at its size.

Metal fumbled in the locks, and the mechanisms turned with ease. The door opened.

The man was of ordinary height and features, his thinning brown hair swept back over his crown, his cheeks and jowls slightly drooped. His eyes were very bright and dark brown, his pupils nearly lost in the color. He wore a tidy, formal long coat and breeches of a handsome gray- and blue-flecked tweed. His sedate smile put her at ease.

"Miss Riven, I presume. Do come in," he said.

He led her through the marble hall, the ceiling at least thirty feet high. A round table with a thick, talon-footed pedestal, large enough for a conference of men, directed their gait to one side.

Along the length of the hall were twelve identical doors, six on each side. Between the doors were smooth plaster recesses. Within these were marble statues of angular human forms. A rug spanned the length from entry to end. Its tight weave held fast a wordless bestiary. At the end of the hall was a grand staircase, in green marble with dark, wooden railings, which split to the left and right on either side of the landing. There, in that waiting place, was a bay of beautiful leaded windows and a long, cushioned bench underneath.

The man invited her to sit. When he disappeared up one of the stairwells, Secret turned to look outside. Past a gold-toned tile courtyard, a row of trees gave way to one obvious gap, framed by a metal arch. There hung a fanciful gate. Between the vertical lines of the trees she could discern iron bars, a high fence.

He lives like a king, Secret thought.

Fewmany bounded down the stairs to her right.

"Welcome," he said. "Follow me."

The staircase curved to a second level and yawned open to a hall with identical proportions to the first floor. Paintings instead of statues covered the walls between the doors. An elaborate, repetitive design appeared in the tile floor. The doors were the style as those on the first floor, except for the one to which he led her. That one was made of wood, ornately carved with figures, many of them scorched black. Secret stared at the burned relief.

"A survivor," Fewmany said. "Fire destroyed the library to which it gave passage. Behold its scar."

"It's lovely," Secret said. As Fewmany opened the door, she glanced around the second floor. Treasures such as this were not strange to her. She had lingered before a few at The Castle. Had she accepted more of Nikolas's invitations, she guessed she might have spent more time admiring such pieces. However, Secret felt compelled to gaze now, to be moved by a wholly human beauty.

"After you," Fewmany said.

Secret drew a spellbound breath. Words fail what splendor it was for her.

From one end of the library to the other was a central corridor, flanked by perpendicular cabinets filled with bookshelves. It appeared to extend the entire length of that floor, six enormous rooms long. The gallery was accessible by spiral staircases with brass sconces on both sides of each landing. On the west wall, windows let in shafts of light between the stacks, and these were decorated with sumptuous drapes.

She walked toward a table large enough for a banquet, which held book stands, a stack of blank paper, and three pen and inkstands. At the other end of the table was a stone fireplace, built in the middle of the corridor, the chimney reaching solidly to the roof. Her hands brushed over the table's waxed surface as she approached the hearth. She felt radiant and warm although there was no fire. The afternoon's heat swept through the library's open windows. She touched the mantel, admiring the woodwork, and then stepped around the fireplace as Fewmany followed.

"Oh-ho, speechless, are you?" Fewmany asked.

"There is much to take in," Secret said.

He stepped to the cabinet closest to him, opened a glass door, and brushed a row of books with his fingertips. With a pinch, he withdrew two volumes.

Secret accepted the books from his hands. She placed them on the table. The older text was in an archaic form of one of the languages she had learned. She could read it with minimal difficulty. The newer volume was handsomely bound, set in type. Slipped before the title page was a sheet of paper with some kind of description.

"I insist that my dealer provide an annotation of each work," he said. "It's a bother, for which he's well compensated, but sometimes he forgets.

"See here," he said. "I read, write, and speak what I first learned but can read one language dead to us all in which others are rooted, which I taught myself. Some of the volumes I hold I've had translated for my enjoyment. There are many that await such a fate.

What good is a book that can't be read, I say, and I'm certain you'd agree. These are among my dear treasures—the only ones of their kind or a surviving few of a former many."

"Do you read often?" Secret asked.

"When I'm so inclined," he said. "Let's walk among them, shall we?"

He gestured for her to step ahead. She scanned the cases left and right, with only a few shelves vacant. She paused to look at a series of volumes as tall as a young child. Illustrated and rare, she assumed. "What's in your collection?"

"Geographies, histories, philosophies, chronicles, treatises on nature, diaries, annals, codices, esoterica, apocrypha, compendia, texts of the spagyric arts, and a wee bit of poetry," he said.

"Diverse material," Secret said.

"Oh-ho, yes, as well as mythologies, legends, fables, and folktales." Secret's face bloomed with a smile.

Fewmany grinned with a hint of teeth and twitched his brow. One of the six staircases was nearby, so she began to climb, her fingers welcoming the smooth curve of the rail.

"So," he said, "your responsibility, if you choose to accept the position, would be to provide me with a catalog to tally what I have and find my way through it all. I wish to have the volumes grouped by subject matter and coded thusly. I expect any translation to remain with its original at all times. The annotations should provide you with enough information to categorize each work. If not, you may take the time you need to read it and write one on your own, or request assistance for a translation if the language is unfamiliar."

Secret noticed the room had darkened. Through the shadows, the library beguiled her.

She opened a glass cabinet door. She breathed in a faint, musty perfume as she traced her fingertips across the ridged spines. Fewmany stood aside with his hands behind his back as she removed one book, then another, studying the binding and the pages within. He didn't interrupt her exploration.

Her mother came to mind. She remembered all of the books and manuscripts Zavet had never let her touch, this simple pleasure forbidden.

"Did she come here?" Secret asked.

"Who? Oh. Yes. Once. She said she'd never seen a collection to rival this one. I took that on good authority," he said.

Secret closed that door and moved to another. She noticed how quiet it was, like the slow descent into a deep sleep.

"Consider you could lead your own study here, like great scholars and philosophers of times past. You are capable of such discipline, I presume," he said.

She glanced at him with a tweak of suspicion. Surely there had been no interference on his part, or on his behalf, to see she wasn't admitted to an academy. Her memory flashed to the illustration in the book he held open the night her hair grew. He would have no reason to have a book meant for children, but she wondered if it was there, among the thousands in safekeeping.

"Sir?"

"Yes."

"Why would you offer this position to me when you know I intend to leave to pursue my studies as soon as I'm able?"

"A man for whom I once worked told me one can hire the best who will serve exceptionally for a short time or hire those who will do to serve adequately for the long term. I sense you are exceptional, Miss Riven, and I would be glad to see you begin the work someone else may need to carry on," he said.

Secret looked down to hide the pleased smile that bowed her lips. "So, I would be free to go once circumstances change?"

"Of course," he said. "Aside from that, I recall you once said, and I paraphrase, that you wish to find what you don't know and to discover the limits of what you do. That includes both knowledge and experience, does it not? and here—" he swept his arm wide, "you will have that opportunity."

Secret heard the door open. She and Fewmany peered over the gallery's edge. The manservant entered with a candle.

"I've come to light the lamps, sir," he said.

"Carry on, Naughton. There's a good man. Chase away the eerie," Fewmany said.

She slipped a small text from the shelves, held the book open in her palm, and traced her fingers across the print. She could feel the subtle impression of the type in the thick paper. There was a force of greed in her blood, strong and unanticipated.

"You would be here alone to work. Does that concern you?" Fewmany asked.

"Not in the least."

He stood at a window with his fingertips against the muntins. "You do like music, do you not?"

"Yes."

"A quartet numbers among my staff. They would be at your call."

"I prefer to work in silence."

"Very well. The cook here concocts delicacies."

"I prefer simple fare."

"As you wish. If you desired to rest from your duties, you'd have the run of the gardens and can view the galleries where my beauties are held. You may walk through any door you find open but must not force one you find locked."

"I appreciate the gesture."

"Did I mention I will pay you amply in silver?" He named a sum that made her eyebrows lift. With that salary, she could have her own little place, if she weren't going away soon.

"That seems fair," she said.

Secret replaced the little book and selected a nibbled codex. The words were unintelligible, a language she didn't know, but the writing was done with meticulous care, calligraphy straight on faint, hand-drawn lines, initials painted with rich colors. Her mind twirled with wonder at how he obtained such things, that such things even existed. Its weight, texture, and promise felt as good as any caress of a gentle animal's back, roundness of every apple, tilth of the rich earth.

"What do you think of the terms?" he asked.

"Quite generous," she said.

"I should divulge I took the liberty to speak to your father. He had no objection, if that in any way bears upon your decision."

She eased the ancient text closed. "How reassuring."

"Did I fail to mention, Miss Riven, that you may borrow any volume? Any one at all, regardless of its condition or rarity. Consider it a boon, as well as an act of trust."

A bark echoed in the hall, a high persistent summons. The noise startled her, but no more than what burst out of her mouth.

"I accept, sir."

"You may take time to consider," he said. He seemed taken aback by her quick response.

"I have no need of it."

"Let us shake hands to seal our *nudum pactum* then," Fewmany said.

Secret's body tremored with polarity. Fewmany's warm, smooth, firm hand struck the freezing cord that spiraled from her head to her feet. A part of her did not agree with this decision.

Fewmany released her palm.

"When shall I start?" she asked.

"What do you say to the first of the coming week?" Fewmany asked.

"I will inform Mr. Gray," she said.

"All preparations will be made for your arrival. My good man" he said, "hail the carriage for my bonny new archivist, my keeper of tales. 'Twouldn't do to let the quickening darkness wreak its havoc on her."

XLV

Harmyn and a Revelation

THAT EVENING WHEN SHE RETURNED HOME FROM FEWMA-
ny's manor, Bren was seated in the parlor reading a book. He had
been waiting for her. When she told him she had accepted, her father looked relieved and delighted.

"Congratulations," he said. "What a boon this is for you."

Leo's response was tempered but genuine. He said he hoped
the academy would admit her in time for the new term, but in the
meanwhile, this was surely an opportunity she could not decline.

On her last day as an apprentice, Secret reported to the translations office to see what final assignment she had to do. To her
surprise, when Wesley opened the door, Leo's desk was laid out
with a small banquet. Even the two old translators joined the festive
mood, at least enough to mumble congratulations and farewell and
to take heaped plates to their desks, turned halfway to listen to the
room's conversations.

Secret thanked them for their kindness and answered Wesley's
questions about Fewmany's manor and Leo's about the library. She
regaled them with all the details she could recall. For the remainder
of the day, she helped with several brief letters and restored some
order to the drawers of ink and paper.

As the afternoon brought its shadows, Secret's chest grew
heavier, her palms tender. She hadn't realized how sad she would be
to leave. Cuthbert and Rowland muttered their good-byes, and Wesley shook her hand with formality. Leo walked her to the stairwell.

"One day, you will do something great. I'm honored you were
my apprentice," he said.

"I'm grateful you were my adept. You've been an excellent teacher."

"Here." Leo handed her a small wrapped package.

Secret opened it. Inside the case was a green pen with a fine gold nib. She looked up, blinking back tears. "Thank you, Leo."

"A little token to remember us by," he said.

"Of course I'll remember you, and the others. Always."

As she descended the stairs, she held her breath so she wouldn't cry.

She turned in her badge at the lobby's front desk, exited the building, and crossed the plaza. She had a vague awareness of the people who walked past, the carts and horses that swept by, the peals of Tell-a-Bells and the chatter of newsboxes. There was no reason to rush home. She felt suddenly vacant, absent from her body, which moved like a lonesome shadow, unnoticed, along the sidewalk.

As she turned a corner, she glanced ahead and almost doubled back her steps to take another route. There, yards away, Harmyn spun around a tree wearing a clean but faded red coat with the sleeves cut off and low boots. The yellow spectacles appeared to be the same as before. Sharp, hushed peeps escaped the child's lips.

"Hello, Secret," the child said without looking at her as she approached.

"Hello, Harmyn." Neither spoke as Harmyn continued to twirl. A hollow grumbling reached Secret's ears. "Would you like something to eat? I was planning to get a bite for myself," Secret said.

The child nodded.

The two stepped into a bakery about to close for the day. Harmyn sat at a round table and asked Secret for a pie and bun. A man with a tall, blue hat stepped up to the counter to assist her.

"A gooseberry pie, a cinnamon bun, and the last tart, please," Secret said.

"Ravenous after a long day?" he asked.

"Not terribly," she said. He put the treats on one plate, which Secret found odd but didn't complain. She paid the man and served the child, who thanked her and then said nothing else until every crumb was gone.

A tiny, green face peered around Harmyn's neck. Secret blinked, certain she'd imagined the sight, then looked again. The triangular visage with mysterious eyes stared back.

Secret could feel it urging her to open. "There's an insect on you," she said.

"That's my manic mantic mantis," Harmyn said.

The creature crept to perch on the child's shoulder. Its stalk legs appeared too thin for its long body. Secret had seen drawings of the insect but had never found one.

"Where did it come from?"

"The sky. It flew on me one day and has been my friend ever since. I think it likes you," Harmyn said, licking the plate clean.

"How do you know?" Secret asked. She wondered if the child had her ability, too.

"Because I do."

Take me on your finger, the praying mantis said without saying.

Secret reached across the table with more instinct than volition. The mantis crawled with otherworldly grace upon her fingertip and stood still.

"She dances. Move your other hand near her head but not too close," Harmyn said.

Secret drew ribbons in the air. The insect swayed as if entranced. In spite of herself, Secret smiled with a glimmer of contentment she had not felt for some time. When the dance ended, the mantis tilted her head and twitched her antenna.

The child is real, but no one else can see it, the mantis said.

I don't understand, Secret said.

Watch.

Without provocation, Harmyn began to chirp a sweet melody. The baker with the blue hat cocked his head then shrugged, and an assistant at the shelves counted loaves without glancing up. Moments later, one after the other, a woman and a man came in. The woman asked for a sourdough loaf to take home. As she waited, she looked at Secret, stared at her finger, and twisted her face into a grimace. Harmyn continued to twitter. Once the woman left, the other customer ordered a cherry pie and turned to find a place to sit. At the only other table in the bakery, there was no chair.

Watch, the mantis said.

"May I take this extra chair near you?" the man asked.

Secret stared in disbelief. Harmyn was small, but the child was clearly seated there, its dark-blond head resting on the back.

"Yes, you may," Secret said, thinking of no other way to learn whether the man would notice the waif.

He thanked her and reached for the chair's flat slat edge. Harmyn fell to the floor with a loud squawk.

A spontaneous rage rushed to Secret's head, blinding her for an instant. Harmyn looked toward the man with a blank expression. Secret wanted to point the man's attention to the child but knew it was fruitless. She wanted to comfort Harmyn but couldn't imagine how to explain the adult's behavior.

The town is sick, the mantis said. *Heed what will be revealed.*

I wish not to heed, Mantis.

Such is your choice, Secret, but that which is already open is harder to close.

The mantis spread its hidden wings and flew through the transom above the door. Harmyn ran to call it down from a lamppost.

"Mantis! Mantis! Manic monster, come down!" the child shouted.

Secret stood patiently on the street as the mantis crawled to meet Harmyn's waiting hand. A wing twirled away from the insect's mandibles. The mantis took her seat on the child's shoulder.

"May I walk you home, at least to your ward?" Secret asked. She felt protective although she didn't want to.

"Close, but not too far."

"Why is that?"

"Aunt and Uncle don't like strangers."

Secret took Harmyn's lead and headed south. The sun had almost set. The streets were crowded with more and more carts. Where the hoof clatter quieted, the newsbox din seemed louder than usual. Even with the noise, she could distinguish the tingle of nearby Tell-a-Bells and the muttering tolls that followed the chimes.

"The middle of town is in the wrong place. Did you know that?" Harmyn asked.

"Where should it be?" Her skin puckered into goose bumps.

"Do you really want to know?"

Secret swallowed the inevitability. "Yes," she said.

Harmyn skipped ahead, a red blur among the people who dotted the sidewalk, moving with ease among them. Secret stepped into a brisk pace to keep up. The child stopped short at the plaza in front of The Tallest Building. The gold-toned tiles were still warm from the day's light. Harmyn moved forward with the gait of a fearful animal.

Then they entered Old Wheel.

Her body battled with its torn will—to flee or to follow. Harmyn led her along the streets and through alley passages she didn't know existed.

Secret's heart throbbed into her throat as they approached the square in which she'd heard many fantastic tales. She thought of kind, drowsy Auntie and of Nikolas, who had followed her lead so many years before. Her knees were rendered almost useless, as the child pulled her into the alley where the grate led to the tunnel to the woods.

"The middle is here," Harmyn said. The child stood upon the entrance.

"Have you been here before?" Secret asked.

"Yes. I like the story times in Old Wheel," Harmyn said.

"As I do, too, Harmyn, but I mean this very spot. Have you visited this grate before?" Secret asked.

"I like to sit on it sometimes. If you stay very still, you can feel it was once a good place. Calm and happy," Harmyn said.

Secret knelt in front of the child. The shadows were about to claim the light's narrow territory. No lamplighter had reason to enter the vacant alley. She had difficulty seeing Harmyn's features.

"Have you ever seen an animal here? A squirrel? A red one?" Secret asked.

"Yes. With a bushy tail. I don't like it because it came after me with chattering teeth. I chased it away again and again until it didn't come anymore."

"Have you ever lifted the top and gone into the hole?" Secret asked. She thought of herself at the age of five, standing in that place and the gentle rupture that revealed the stone-walled well.

"Into the closed dark? No. *No*."

"Who told you this place is the center?" Secret asked, her tone serious, her pitch high. She reached to grab the child's arms, but Harmyn leapt back as if the clutch were anticipated. The child wouldn't look at her.

"No one."

"Then how can you say that?"

Harmyn quivered from head to toe. "I know."

"How do you know?" Secret demanded.

"I don't know, but I do, and I know you do, too, but I don't know why."

Secret's blood went cold. Her hips and shoulders ached as if they'd been wrung at the sockets. She touched her palms to the ground as she lost the equilibrium of her body and thoughts. For an instant, she stood at a well, then at a rock; she looked into a man's green eyes and felt the grasp of another's rough hand. Secret pulled away from what seized her. She pressed her hands and knees into the old cobblestones. "No more rhymes, Harmyn. Tell me plainly."

When she looked up, Harmyn had disappeared.

The mantis crept toward her fingers.

You can doubt but you cannot deny, the mantis said. Her wings flared, and then she was gone.

XLVI

Old Woman Tells of What Is to Come

THE MORNING AFTER SECRET'S LAST DAY AS AN APPRENTICE, she awoke to a dissonant noise at her window. A pigeon, a dove, and a sparrow tapped their beaks against the glass as they chirped and cooed like incessant mechanical toys.

When she sat up in bed, groggy from sleep, she stared at them and tried to remember what day it was. The birds had appeared on the evening she was born and on her seventh and fourteenth birthdays. Her eighteenth was weeks away.

What happened with Harmyn and the mantis the previous afternoon rushed to her mind. Secret shut her eyes and released an agitated huff. She had enough to contend with—her failure to get into an academy, Nikolas's unexpected departure, and her new job beginning in two days. She didn't want creatures compelling her to listen or to think of that strange child who said stranger things or to rouse the dreams and ruptures in her memory. She realized then how much she wanted the seclusion of Fewmany's library with no one and nothing to bother her, only quiet and books and the promise of beautiful things to see.

She heard the crack of glass and looked up. The pigeon had broken a pane. Infuriated, Secret opened the window all the way. The three birds stepped to the middle of the sill.

We are here to deliver a message, the pigeon said.

It is simple, the dove said.

You must go to Old Woman now, the sparrow said.

Why? Secret asked.

A change wishes to know its course, the pigeon said.

I don't understand, Secret said.

Go to her, so that you might, the dove said.

Why didn't she come to me then? Secret asked.

This choice is yours, not hers, the sparrow said.

The birds circled to face the sky and lifted into the air.

Secret hadn't seen Old Woman in almost two years. A confrontation was to have its due. As she dressed, she dreaded her return to the woods, a feeling that as a small child she could never have fathomed.

She walked to Old Wheel, slipped into the alley, entered the grate, and emerged through the hole in the tree into the woods. Before she approached Reach, she felt his low drone rise through her feet, incomprehensible as ever but stronger, resonant, urgent.

She gave his trunk a dismissive pat as she went on her way to the stream to sate her thirst. Not far from the water's edge, Secret noticed a cluster of mushrooms. She peered closely to see if they were edible or poisonous. She remembered Old Woman teaching her how to identify them, the subtleties that meant the difference between life and death.

Secret continued slowly toward Old Woman's cottage. As she observed what was taking its turn to bloom and to fade, she recalled herself as a little girl who thought she would have been content forever to live among the green, alone. But she was no longer that girl, and the quiet that filled her suddenly began to feel like a hunger that would consume her whole. Secret drew back and focused on the fall of her soles.

When she saw the cottage's open door and blue shutters from a distance, Secret halted her steps. A hidden owl's hoot startled her, an unexpected sound for morning. A moment later, Cyril scrambled down a tree, ran up to her, and placed his paws on the toe of her shoe. She nudged him away gently and crossed the glade.

Old Woman's head peeked up from the herbs growing near the cottage's shadiest wall. She looked toward Secret then rose to her feet. As Secret came closer, she expected Old Woman to approach her, even to smile, but her friend remained rooted in place.

Old Woman's expression wasn't hurt or angry but somewhat bemused. "Why did you come today, of all days, when you've so long been away?"

"I was told to."

"By whom?"

"Three birds," Secret said reluctantly.

Old Woman's eyes squinted as if she didn't understand. "What were you told?"

"A change wishes to know its course. That's how I understood what I received."

For a moment, Old Woman appeared to be confused. Then a glint of clear reckoning flickered in her eyes. "Yes, of course, that's the kind of summons you would receive. The time has finally come to speak to you. Let's sit inside."

Secret stepped into the cottage. The room seemed so much smaller now. A cobweb stretched from a rafter to the top of the cupboard. There were old stains on the table, and one chair had a mended leg. On the bed were the same lumpy pillows and summer quilt.

A cold dread weighed Secret in her chair as Old Woman lowered slowly to the seat across from her. The white hair at Old Woman's temples was wispy, and her cheeks drooped. But there was no hint of frailty in her eyes.

"There's no point to small talk," Old Woman said. "What I will tell you requires a faith that is open rather than blind. You'll want a rational explanation that fits your understanding of things now, but that I can't give you.

"I'm not merely an eccentric old woman who lives in the woods. When you were a little girl, I told you I was from a village not of this kingdom, and I shared stories of my people, how we live and our tales. Our myths.

"Whatever you believe to be the truth in such myths, the people who have repeated them for generations are real. We consider ourselves descendants of Azul. To this day, we keep our vow to guard the dragon," Old Woman said.

Secret's tension cracked with laughter. "You can't be serious. That's charming, but you can't expect me to believe it. I'm a bit old for that now."

Old Woman removed the sash from her waist and stretched it across the table between them. She rested her wrinkled hand in the center of the blue band. "We wear this color as a reminder of who we are. There are some who wear it more prominently as they have for ages. The dream you had as a child, of the men in blue coats? It may have been coincidence, or something deep within you knows."

Secret pressed her lips together. She had expected no such evocation.

"I chose to live on the margins not only because I enjoy the solitude," Old Woman said. "I believe in the haven we old men and women provide. Those who find their way to our doors, or our domains, are searching, seeking, even if they don't realize that they are.

"I also believe in what may come, although I knew the ones who have been waited for might not appear in my lifetime or to me, individually, at all. I knew to look for you, Secret, even though I didn't know who you might be.

"That you found your way to my door didn't reveal you, and neither did your ability to speak to plants and creatures, although both gave me pause. Once you got older, I knew I must be patient and cautious. That was the time you had told me about your other dream," Old Woman said.

Old Woman walked to the fireplace. With surprising strength, she pushed the large cauldron away from the hearth. There it was, carved in stone—the square with the circle, triangle, and flame within. The symbol.

Secret's mouth dropped open. "You let me believe I dreamed it, but one was here all along. You—lied to me."

"Because to force a matter into consciousness can be

destructive. You weren't ready for the truth beyond the fact. Now, you must know," Old Woman said.

"The fact is that one was hidden in your house. Why didn't you tell me?"

"I intended to, but Cyril interrupted me that day. He must have known you weren't ready to hear yet. He was right to distract me and make me pause. Something was emerging within you, unfolding in its own time, and you were frightened."

Secret's memory hissed with the sound of cutting shears and flashed with the image of her drawing, the bowl of pears, and Fewmany's resting hand.

"So what does it mean?" Secret asked, although a part of her didn't want to know.

"This symbol is not the only one. There are others throughout the known world. They connect one to the next, serving as guides for those who know how to follow them. Some are in abandoned places, and some are like mine, in the cottages of those who wait. There are places beyond our havens, too, where the symbols lead— villages of my people and farther still, other realms our people guard," Old Woman said.

Emotion rather than image surfaced in Secret's thoughts. She remembered feeling safe in the dreams of the blue men and knowing, somehow, if she could go with them, all would be well. Even some of the symbol dreams evoked that longing and trust to follow. Then Secret wondered what Fewmany knew, or believed he knew, about the symbol. Whatever it was, it had compelled him to question her when she was only a child.

"That isn't frightening. You could have told me," Secret said.

"It wasn't time." Old Woman paused for a long, deep breath. "Then came your fever. Your hair changed, which for anyone else would have indicated how severe the illness had been. But for you, I believe it was an outward sign of an inward shift. Tell me, what happened while you were sick?"

Secret closed her eyes. The feral stink that had filled her room burned in her nostrils. Her lids flew open again, and she stared at the tabletop. She remembered some of the fever dreams, beautiful and terrible, an endless stretch of land, a great treasure, the fire where a child danced with a dragon. Within her still, silent now, was the ancient language that had come forth as she slept.

"My fever was very high. I had strange dreams."

"Similar to the ones of the men and the symbol?" Old Woman asked.

"In a way."

"And still you don't wish to speak of them? Your reluctance only makes this more difficult, Secret."

"Continue with what you have to say."

"Very well." Old Woman paused and lowered her gaze. She seemed to be thinking. "Not long after your illness, your mother died."

Secret's body went rigid.

"There were others who knew to watch for a child with a gift like hers. This gift especially suited that person for a specific task," Old Woman said. "Along with our myths, our people tell an ancient legend. The legend is of a woman who came from a land far away. She was an exile who escaped a terrible war. This woman was able to harness the power of image and symbol and, with it, encoded our stories and deeds. As you and I would say, she could write.

"Our collective history is spoken to this day, but whatever knowledge she gathered died soon after her body. She had taught her daughter and her granddaughter what she created, but there was no need or desire for the skill among our people. But an ancient Voice told the daughter to protect what her mother had made. She foretold that a time would come for these works to appear again, and, with it, the birth of children who must continue with the legacy the

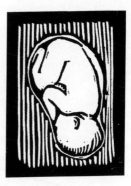

tomes contained. Among these children would be one who could decipher what the woman left behind."

Secret's eyes squeezed shut as her joints began to ache and her body seemed to pull apart. Fragments of the dreams and ruptures whirled in her mind without order.

"Elders, far older than I, believed your mother was the child who would read the text. Her death and the loss of the manuscript were terrible shocks. Neither was foreseen, but even portents are prone to the unexpected."

"And what does this preposterous story have to do with me?" Secret asked, her body seizing in pain with the words.

"Secret, you're one of these children. You are here to shift a balance, one with the potential to deepen our darkness or bear forth a hidden light. The elders don't know what form the events will take, but they believe nothing and no one will be spared its wake. Whatever gifts you possess will be necessary when the time comes.

"You won't be alone—there will be allies—and one of them is Nikolas. Just as I believe you sense a purpose that isn't yet clear, Nikolas has one, too, far beyond his duty as a future king. When you were sick with your fever, he endured a trial of his own. An old man confirmed this to me."

"Nikolas would have told me so," Secret said defiantly. As soon as the words spewed from her mouth, she thought of the scar under his thumb that he had never explained.

"Did you tell him what happened during your illness?" Old Woman asked.

"Not clearly, no," Secret said.

Old Woman folded her hands and looked into Secret's eyes. "Have you looked for the manuscript since I last saw you?"

"Do you mean when you asked about it as if it were only a matter of polite conversation?"

"I was told to guide you to the degree that I could. I wasn't and haven't been told everything. There remains much I don't know. Not until I returned to my village for that winter visit was I informed how important that manuscript is believed to be. I tried to speak with you then, as you'll recall, and I've regretted my failure ever since. I withheld too much, I was too indirect out of fear you would close yourself even more, and I had no idea stating my love for you would make you run away," Old Woman said.

Secret pressed her hands against her eyes, hiding the shame she still felt for fleeing. Even as she decided she wouldn't mention the cipher or the unexplained reason Zavet left it for her, Secret wondered what her mother had read in the arcane manuscript. If any part of what Old Woman said was true, what had it revealed? Finally, Secret answered, "I looked for the manuscript. I found no trace of it."

Old Woman rubbed her forehead softly. "She must have been concerned with its protection if she hid it so well. How sad she was lost so suddenly. So strange a death."

"The end of life is prone to the unexpected, too," Secret said with mocking bitterness. "Do you have anything else to say to me?"

Old Woman's eyes simmered with frustration. "You don't believe what I'm telling you. I have no reason to convince you of an elaborate story, Secret. You create far greater dangers for yourself with your denial. What is to come depends on your choices as much as on those of others."

"What is to come is I will enter a high academy. The choices of others have thwarted me for now. Unless I'm taken from a waiting list, I won't go this autumn—you didn't know that—but I will go somehow, somewhere. In the meantime, I've chosen to take a position offered to me. It was an honor to be asked and an honor to accept," Secret said.

Old Woman tilted her head and furrowed her brow. "A position? Where?"

"I'll be the archivist in a private library. The man who founded Fewmany Incorporated asked me," Secret said.

"*That* is the meaning behind the message," Old Woman said to herself, seizing an elusive thought. "I understand now. I wasn't only supposed to reveal what your future will bring. There's a warning to give as well."

"For what?" Secret asked.

"We know of the man Fewmany who seeks to own the land where the symbols lie. We know he has acquired some of these places and removed the stones that were found. He clearly understands they have meaning, otherwise he wouldn't make the effort to take them. What's unknown is what he seeks, beyond what the lands provide," Old Woman said.

"Then why hasn't he taken yours? It's right under his nose," Secret said. She wondered if she had unwittingly protected Old Woman before, being able to truthfully claim she'd seen the symbol in a dream.

"I can't answer that. Perhaps it's only a matter of time now," Old Woman said, her tone worried. She stared at Secret until each held the other's eyes. Secret felt herself close against the scrutiny.

"I've done nothing wrong," Secret said in protest.

"I believe you, just as I believe you don't intend to do so. But something is different now. I think you're in danger."

"I'll be working in his library. How dangerous can that be?" Secret asked.

"He's been watched, too, as you, your mother, and Nikolas, and no doubt others have been."

"And if that's true?"

"No man attains the power he has without having a ruthless sense of perception, either within himself or through those he surrounds himself with. There may be a reason he can't explain why he asked you to take a job that seems so innocent."

"I proved myself as an apprentice. He hired me on my merit. That's all," Secret said.

"For your sake, I hope you're right. But something is amiss. That message—a change wishes to know its course—worries me."

Secret placed her palms against the table and rose from her seat, leaning forward with a scowl. "Well, it doesn't worry me. If anything you've told me is valid, I want no part of it. I want to work in the library and go to high academy and leave this place, begin anew, and never come back." She meant every word as it left her mouth.

Old Woman wrapped the blue belt around her waist. "This is your destiny. You have a choice in how to meet it. Deny, resist, or accept. You can leave now, but I will never abandon you. I love you, Secret, and I'm here as a guide when you're ready."

"Then expect a wait to outlast you," Secret said, even though in that moment, beyond all reason, she knew in her blood and bones what she'd been told was true.

When Secret stepped to the threshold and glanced back, she saw tears coursing down the soft wrinkles of Old Woman's face. "Take good care of Cyril."

Her stride quickened as she crossed the glade. As she ran toward the trees, the ground rumbled under her feet, a sensation more than a noise. She clutched her head as the quiet of the woods ascended to a din—*whir chirp hum yip grunt bell screech howl*—and she screamed for it to stop.

Secret hitched her skirt as she approached the hollowing tree. She looked up before she crawled down the hole. Surrounded by a haze of light, a bee hovered between her eyes. Her forehead pulsed once, and then the bee was gone.

She rushed through the tunnel and into the town's streets, her thoughts frenzied. The dreams and ruptures, her connection to creatures and plants, the arcane manuscript, the ancient language— each was part of a whole she could not and did not want to see.

As she hurried, she brushed past others, knocking into some without apology. She muttered curses under her breath when cart traffic blocked an intersection for longer than seemed reasonable. A crying child and its exhausted mother received a harsh bark when they stepped into her path. A flower vendor's bucket was out of place, and she kicked it, sending blossoms through the air and spilling water across the sidewalk. Through ward after ward, she walked and ran, but she couldn't flee her building rage.

With a violent clamor, Secret entered her house and pounded up the stairs to her room. Her stomach empty and needy, full of questions and wanting, Secret crawled onto her bed, pressed her forehead to her knees, and drew shallow breaths. Silent, she told herself. Be silent. The wild thoughts that had chased her across the woods, through the streets, and to her room slipped away. She disappeared into the familiar, dark still place somewhere within where no one could find, touch, or speak to her. There she escaped from all that plagued her, every feeling, thought, memory, and dream.

When she roused, the street below was quiet and the moon out of sight. She had slept through the remainder of the day. She crept to the water closet, then to her room again, and changed into her nightclothes.

Secret sat on her bed with a sheet wrapped over her head. She drew in the stale air, welcoming the darkness again, and as she waited, there was a flame, a flicker, Nikolas, a blond boy with a gold cup, so long ago.

Enough, she thought. She held her breath until the vision was extinguished, then held another, and another, each one shut behind a door and sealed against what she never wanted to think, feel, or believe again.

XLVII

What the Town Cannot See or Hear

AT NIGHT UNDER A NEW MOON, A CHILD WANDERS ALONE through the wards. This child has a home where it does not wish to be, yet it has no choice in the matter. No choice, except for some nights, some days, when the child escapes to find a solitary freedom.

No one sees the child who swings around the lampposts, climbs over benches, and peers into windows with sticky fingers and moist breath. No one catches the child as it snatches dry buns from clean shelves, plucks bruised apples from dark corners, and gnaws tough meat from old bones.

Well into the night, as most of the newsboxes are silent, the child peeps and chirps. The cheerful sound falls on deaf ears as the people who cannot see the child are lost in sleep. Neither do they hear the child sing with a voice so pure, so true, that it seems born from the essence of light.

The child sits on the curb of a street. Far below the cobblestones and drains, beyond the old vein where water once flowed, the earth shifts. The child no one sees or hears can feel the disturbance.

This is a warning no one can heed, except for one.

For now, she is asleep, wrapped in silver and linen, not ready to awaken to the groan in the ground that calls her name.

APPENDIX I

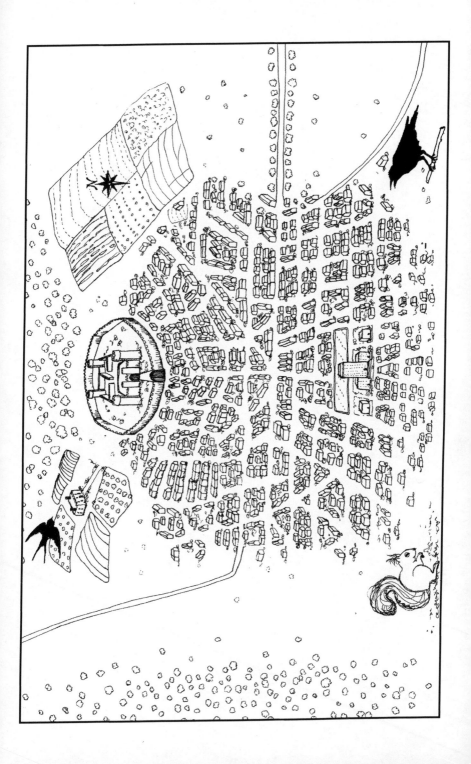

APPENDIX II

Myths of the Four

The Great Sleep

THE GREAT SLEEP DREAMED A wish to awaken. All was quiet and still, no color or sound, shape or feel. The Great Sleep wondered within what it could be without. Its eyes moved under the veil to watch the question become a thought and then its lids lifted and there was a pucker and a pop in the deep dark, the echo turned inside out, a hum then a rumble.

In the distance, an orb of fire pulsed inside a blue cloud. The Great Sleep peered ever closer. Slowly, the orb formed a strange gray skin that shifted and turned. For an instant, the thrashing stopped and the skin ripped red and wet. There came a howl so loud and powerful that The Great Sleep moved back into the darkness. A spiral of flame curled skyward through plumes of vapor and rains of metal. Around the spiral blew a fierce wind, which cooled the molten skin and made a mountain. The orb heaved mightily as the fire spiral found its tail and coiled at last to enter the world.

There at the mountain's navel stood the creature that had come forth, a red dragon. Its first call was a sputter, its second a bellow, its third a roar. And with that roar, the dragon found it had lifted into the air upon magnificent wings and began to fly with turns and twists of joy. It was she who first saw the world.

Now and then, The Great Sleep returned to watch the dragon's delight, and when its gaze fell again on the orb, there were always new things to see. The skin became blue and rippled, brown and buckled, green and wide. Then on this skin there crawled tiny creatures, so small that The Great Sleep had to come close and squint. There was all manner of bustle and buzz above and below, things moving in, among, and through water, air, and earth, leafed and flowered, furred and feathered, shelled and scaled.

One visit, The Great Sleep saw that the dragon was not on the wing. The creature sat upon the top of the mountain, looking this way and that. Then it flew to the ground, searching here and there. Noises rattled the mountain, and the dragon lay in wait for what would erupt.

All at once, a cave tumbled open to the right and a geyser rushed up to the left. After the last boulder rolled away, a giant among dwarfs appeared, golden from the point of his cap to the round of his shoes. Under the final drops of spray landed a womanly wisp, white from the shine of her hair to the tips of her toes. The dwarf and the wisp shook their heads as if shaken from long naps. They looked at the dragon, the dragon looked at them, and The Great Sleep laughed and laughed until the Gold Dwarf and the White Wisp asked the other, "What in the world is that sound?" And The Great Sleep laughed all the more.

What Powers They Possessed

IN A VALLEY NEAR AN ocean, a desert, and a forest was a mountain, and near this mountain lived the Red Dragon, the Gold Dwarf, and the White Wisp. They came to call one another by names that suited them. The dragon was named Egnis, the dwarf was Ingot, and the wisp was Incant.

They had never been before, yet the Three came into being with great abilities.

Egnis had the power of air and fire. She who first saw All stirred the winds with her tremendous wings. When she was angry, the wind tore across the lands. When she was happy, gentle breezes swayed. It was Egnis who crept under the earth and burst through the molten ruptures. It was she who scorched the meadows and forests to dust. It was she who ate the sun every night and breathed it anew every morning.

Ingot knew the veins of the earth, hard with metals and bright with jewels. He smelled the sharp scents through cracks in the rocks. With strong hands, he tore away the stone to reveal the glint and glow. He crawled into small spaces to mine dense rock with brute strength. It was he who brought the metals and jewels to light.

Incant moved with the earth and the water. She delighted in the rush to seed and spore, the blossom into being, and the call of every creature. She spoke with the roar, whisper, and trickles of the seas and rivers, lakes and ponds. She drifted with the silent springs and fell with the rain. She spoke with rumbles and grumbles but most often with silence.

The Three—Egnis, Ingot, and Incant—delighted in their gifts but realized they were ever more powerful when working together.

With stick and stone, Incant carved seedlings from the earth and planted them hither and yon. She filled her hands with seed, sent Egnis on the wing to stir the wind, and threw the seeds into the breeze. Egnis partnered with the seas to dance, and rain fell upon the lands. She watched the creatures discover the beauty and food in what they found. They carried on the spread and rebirth where the land welcomed it.

Ingot asked Egnis to breathe upon the wall of the cave inside the mountain. The iron inside flowed like blood. The iron filled a crevice in the shape of an ax, then spilled through the cave's mouth. Ingot seared his hands on the hot shape, toughening them like leather. He took the ax and beat it against the mountain's walls and faces. Pieces of metal and jewels fell at his feet.

Ingot danced with joy, Incant wept for his happiness, and Egnis laughed in fiery gusts.

The mountain bled where it was touched by Egnis's breath. Incant's tears pooled near the molten flow. The two combined in a cloud of steam. Ingot rapped his knuckles against the hardened flood. They looked with wonder at proof of their combined strength, but the invisible and most powerful force was their love for each other.

It was Incant who noticed that Egnis's claws sparked against certain rocks. It was Ingot who struck these rocks together over dried grasses that Incant had gathered. It was Egnis who gently blew on the sparks to create fire. Again, they danced and laughed.

How Fire Came to the Humans

INCANT HEARD THE SHIVERING OF the human creatures and their sighs when Egnis returned the sun. She had long moved among them, quietly, guiding them to food and shelter. As a silent whisper, she shared with them the gifts of the earth and the use of simple tools.

So she asked Ingot to appear with her to give them the power of fire. They went to a boy and a girl, young enough to be curious yet not too fearful, old enough to speak and be understood. Incant approached them as a thin woman clothed in a gown of mist. Her hair waved like boughs in the winds and weeds in the sea. She told them they were chosen to share a power with their kind. At their feet she laid a bundle of sticks and dried grass. Ingot stepped beside the White Wisp. He wore a triangular cap, a tunic, a vest, heavy pants, high boots, and a wide pouch. His eyes shone like jet through his whiskered face. Head to toe, he was the color of gold. He knelt before the children and took rocks from his pouch.

The boy, the girl, and Ingot struck their rocks all at once. Sparks flew into the kindling. Ingot told them to take deep breaths and slowly blow upon the light. Flames took to their eyes, then to the grasses. The children pressed their palms near the heat. They reached for larger sticks to feed the fire. The flames grew. Ingot taught them to tend the embers, and Incant taught them to extinguish the glow.

From high upon the mountain, as the sun slept in Egnis's belly, the Three could see a glow in the distance, one that would multiply across the land like stars.

What Tools Were Given

INGOT BUILT A FORGE INTO the mountainside. He fueled it with wood gathered from the forest. He dug pits and buried heaps of metals and jewels.

With zeal, he shaped the metal into form. He had watched the humans with curiosity, noting their clever thumbs and tongues. They made use of good tools, which Incant gave them, but the materials became worn and quickly broken. So it was that Ingot made long tools that could cut, slice, and chop, and wide ones meant to dig and scoop, and hollow ones ready to fill and store.

Ingot and Incant noticed the humans liked adornment. They carved rocks with rocks. They made clay beads to string with gut or grass. With colors taken from plants and the earth, they painted vessels of all sizes, human and animal shapes made of clay, and walls made of stone.

So Ingot took a lump of gold, melted it within his forge, and formed a rope. He called Incant to give aid. His thick-skinned fingertips took the cooling rope and bent it round her wet wisp of a wrist. Around the loop, Ingot placed beautiful jewels. The object shone like the sun.

They found a boy and a girl who were as young as the children who'd been given the gift of fire. Together they slept in a bed of ferns. Incant whispered for them to awaken. So gentle was she that when they opened their eyes, the boy and the girl thought they were dreaming. The Gold Dwarf and the White Wisp led the children to the cave where Ingot stored his wares. Within were scythes, shovels, and cauldrons as well as cups, bracelets, and medallions— that, and much more. The children gasped.

Ingot led them to the mines from which he dug and the forge at which he worked. He showed them how to extract the veins of the earth and to transform what they found with the sweat of their brows. The children clapped and smiled with mirth.

With a gentle hand, Incant led the boy and the girl back to their hidden nest. She sang them to sleep again. Certain that they slumbered, Incant left gifts at their feet. They would awaken from the ghost of a shared dream and to the mystery of a golden knife and silver cup, both adorned with jewels.

The Lessons of the Deer

SHE WHO SAW ALL COME into being was witness to that which came to be. She flew with the grace of birds and swam with the ease of fish. If she willed it so, she could become small as a grain of golden pollen or as large as a great gray beast of the sea. She could turn solid as stone or permeable as a spiderweb. Egnis could be that and all things in between, and because she was, she was everything.

Before the Gold Dwarf and the White Wisp emerged in the realm, Egnis experienced all that could be. Her presence was known and welcomed among all the creatures and plants of the world.

Yet Egnis had a favorite creature, and that was the deer. She found it one of beauty, grace, and gentleness. She liked to look into its clear, dark eyes and see her reflection.

There was a herd of deer she watched as the cycles turned. Egnis was present at the birth of one doe's fawns, a male and a female. She who saw All felt joy when the small ones rose upon thin legs and joined their mother by her side. When the fawns were given a place to rest, Egnis was content to drowse with them in the sun.

When a sudden snowstorm separated the brother and sister from their mother, Egnis worried. Hungry animals and freezing cold could prey upon the unprotected little ones. Although she did not interfere with the cycles and their turns, Egnis chose to lead them to a hollow tree. She blocked the opening with her body and saw them through the night.

As the fawns grew, Egnis felt envy for their lithe, graceful legs. She could swim and fly, but she could not run and leap. She did her best to move on the land so that the fawns could play chase with her. Egnis startled with surprise when they disappeared into the grasses and trees only to leap across her back.

In time, the sister and brother became a doe and a stag. The doe grew to have fine fawns of her own, and the stag sired strong young as well. Egnis was proud of their vigor.

Their mother lived long and became ill. Egnis saw that all things must die to allow renewal, but she was sad to see the old deer's decline. When Egnis found her lifeless body, she shed a lake of tears because of her grief.

Her children, the doe and the stag, emerged as great elders among their kind. Egnis visited them still.

The aged doe told Egnis that a strange matter concerned the deer and their fellow creatures. The animals accepted that the humans wanted them for food, but they were not killed only for their meat and skins. Egnis was confused by her story.

She followed the doe's brother, a mighty ancient stag. He moved with slow dignity and tough muscles. Suddenly, several young men chased the stag until he was exhausted. They pierced him with spears and arrows. When he fell, they stabbed him with daggers. Egnis shook with rage. The young men severed the stag's head, the antlers branched like a tree, and left the body on the ground. Egnis recoiled with disgust at the brutal sight.

She followed the humans to their village. A young man carried the stag's head above his own. Men, women, and children cheered. Egnis wished to know why they had killed the stag. She knew of no other creature that acted as they did. So Egnis revealed herself, red, scaled, and winged.

The humans screamed. Some ran away, and others attacked with spears, arrows, rocks, and torches. Egnis froze for a moment. She had never known fear, but she feared these creatures. She did not approach or withdraw because she wished to understand. They continued to attack. Egnis felt frustrated that they did not see she meant no harm. She began to back away, but they continued to pelt her. Egnis rose up on her legs and leaned back against her curved tail. She felt a force within her, the pure power to destroy. She breathed a plume of fire that set all before her aflame. The screams were hideous. As she fled, Egnis dropped her head with shame, for her reaction had no restraint, and many innocent humans had died.

Why the Sun Didn't Rise and How the Moon Came to Be

AFTER THE ANCIENT STAG'S DEATH, the sun did not rise for three days. The creatures and plants in every land were terrified. Upon the top of the mountain, Egnis lay curled in darkness. Ingot and Incant could not reach her by climbing the mountain, so they worked together to reach her from within. Ingot wielded his sturdy ax and cut into the mountain's belly. Incant called upon the waters to wash the pieces away. Step by step, the Gold Dwarf hewed a spiral passage into the rock. The boulders tumbled down the rough-hewn stairs and to a rushing flow that the White Wisp directed to faraway lands.

Ingot broke through the mountaintop. Egnis lifted her head.

Incant joined them in the dark, bearing a small torch. Egnis told them of the stag and the humans and how she had destroyed the village. She was asked if she had slept, and if she had, what had she dreamed.

The Red Dragon said The Great Sleep had come to her and said, "Within All That Is, there is a choice. The choice is the ultimate power, within and without." Ingot and Incant looked at each other. They told Egnis that they had shown young humans how to make fire and tools. Neither the Gold Dwarf nor the White Wisp had told them how to use what they were given. The humans made their own choices with the knowledge they had obtained.

Egnis wept with sadness for killing the people and for her friend, the stag. None of it need have happened, but it did. The dragon's tears pooled at their feet. The torchlight gave Egnis a mirror for her face. Then she wept with gladness. The moment of reflection made everything clear.

She asked Ingot to create a silver orb. He did and rolled it into the valley. Egnis asked Incant to kiss the orb. She pressed her lips to its cool surface. Egnis invited them all to look upon its face. They saw themselves.

Egnis coiled her tail around the orb and flew into the sky. She breathed the sun into morning light. Opposite its glow, halfway past her circle of the world, Egnis dropped the orb. There it turned to pull the fluidity of feeling into union with the rays of thought. The moon reminded Egnis that in darkness there was always light.

The Orphan Was Found

ON A FINE DAY, EGNIS followed the vein of a river as it flowed through a thick forest. Sunlight splashed between the branches into the water. A shape caught Egnis's eye. She circled back to what she'd seen.

There, under the current against a rock, was a human infant. Egnis pulled the limp creature from the depths. It did not move or breathe. A ragged cord hung from its belly. Its skin was blue, unlike the skin of any human Egnis had ever seen. She held it tight and returned to the mountaintop. Ingot and Incant stood near as they considered what to do.

Egnis lay the child within her nest. She breathed a gentle, red flame toward its body, and the infant wiggled its toes. Encouraged, Egnis blew a rainbow into the child, chasing the red with orange, yellow, and green. With blue, the child cried. With indigo, the eyelids opened, and with violet, light from the darkness entered its eyes.

The Three gasped, for they all believed the child was dead beyond return. The infant cried piteously. Egnis cradled it against her scaled chest with deep tenderness. It turned its head as it pursed its lips, desperate to suckle. Incant clutched her breasts. Her palms were wet with milk. She reached for the human child and took it to her body. There, the infant found nourishment.

When the infant had its fill, Ingot fetched a large basket filled with moss. Incant placed the child within. They stared at the sleeping babe.

In most ways, the child was ordinary. It had a head, two arms, two legs, and the usual number of fingers and toes. It had two ears, two eyes, one nose, one mouth. Yet its skin remained as blue as it had been when Egnis pulled it from the water. Below its waist, it was an oddity.

"The infant is male and female," Ingot said.

"The child is he and she," Incant said.

"The being is both and they," Egnis said.

The Three agreed that the child needed a name. Egnis had saved the infant, and she was given the honor of bestowing the name. So the foundling was called Azul.

Azul Grew

EGNIS, INGOT, AND INCANT RELIED on the beasts to help with Azul's care.

Incant observed that the infant beasts were fed when they were hungry, and this she did for the child. If Azul's thirst became greater than her store, the wolf, the bear, and the deer gave of their teats and milk.

Ingot saw that the small ones were given closeness, and this the Three shared. Incant was filled with love, but her touch by nature was cool. Ingot covered the child with his gold beard and held them to his chest. When Azul began to sleep through the night, Egnis took the child to her nest, circled them with her body, and blanketed them with a feathered wing.

Egnis saw that all beasts took pleasure in play. The Three called upon the animals and insects to frolic with Azul. Incant taught the child to swim, climb, and stroll. Ingot delighted in making toys, some that rolled on wheels and others that turned on clever gears. Egnis asked Ingot and Incant to craft a pouch, in which the dragon placed the child and took them round and round the world.

The Three understood the raw nature of the foundling and agreed to guide them with gentleness. The Three noticed when they responded to Azul with anger or impatience, the child cried more or took fright. Egnis had observed that some beasts cuffed their young when they misbehaved. When Egnis tried this, Azul looked at her as if they had been betrayed and wept without consolation.

The dragon reminded the Gold Dwarf and the White Wisp of the lesson of the stag and the village. To pause before action gave space for choice. The Three chose love, for it was the flame of love that brought Azul back to life and the practice of love that taught the child to trust and share.

As Azul grew, the Three gave the orphan the freedom to learn skills. All that Ingot could do, he taught to the child. All that Incant could do, she taught to the child. In these lessons, Azul learned all the skills and trades that had taken root and flourished among the humans. Azul enjoyed the many gifts their foster parents gave them. Azul could do anything.

Egnis was the one to lead Azul away from the comfort of the mountain and into the wider world. Saddled upon Egnis's strong, red neck, Azul traveled far and wide. From the sky, Egnis imparted her knowledge of the cycles within All That Is. Azul learned of cycles within cycles, of those that ended never to begin again, of those just beginning with the ends yet unknown.

Azul felt boundless and brave.

Yet a time of great doubt was ahead for the foundling.

Azul's Rage

FROM THE CHILD'S EARLIEST DAYS, Azul knew that they had been found by the dragon. There was wonder in the tale, and Azul often asked to hear how Egnis discovered them under the water and fired them to breathe for the first time.

Underneath the joy was a murky feeling that Azul ignored. The Three had bestowed a rich life on them, and Azul felt deep within that they were loved. Yet deep within, Azul, too, felt they were not.

When Azul grew into the shape of adults, they began to explore the world away from the mountain. The Three encouraged the brief journeys, trusting that Azul knew well how to take care and be cautious.

Azul was intimately familiar with all types of creatures and plants but had not been among their own kind. The foundling crept to a village's edge to watch. During one observation, Azul realized how different was the color of their skin. Azul's travels with Egnis showed them the peoples of the world and none of them was blue. When Azul returned to the mountain, Ingot assured them that they were no different from any other human. Azul's color was unique.

Then, Azul observed the bodies and clothing of the humans. Azul knew the difference between males and females from the beasts. The humans had the same distinctions, although often covered with clothing. Azul remained hidden until they saw male and female humans frolic and mate in the forest. With horror, Azul realized that they were one body with two forms. When Azul returned home, Incant tried to comfort them. Azul's body was different from most humans, but they were still human. Nature did not always follow the same plan.

Again, Azul watched the village. As among the animals, there were small groups of adults and young. Some of the groups had more adults than young or more young than adults. Azul could see that those in the village knew one another—as a herd knew its members—but the small groups clustered together with obvious attachment. A woman carried and fed one infant and no other. A man returned to one small group and no other. Children played among one another, but some resembled certain children more than others. When Azul arrived at the mountain, Egnis saw them hide in the cave.

Egnis went to Azul, who refused to speak. In the night, a horrible scream stirred the forest. Egnis rushed to find the creature that was in pain. There upon the ground was Azul. They threw the objects near their hands and pounded the earth with their fists. Wails of rage flooded from Azul's throat. Azul refused to see or speak to Egnis, Ingot, or Incant. Ceaseless, for days and nights, Azul cried and screamed. Each day and night, one of the Three approached to give comfort and was rebuked.

Then the raging stopped.

Egnis went into the forest. Azul looked wild and exhausted. At last, Azul told what caused them such agony. Azul had realized that they had been abandoned before their first breath. Their body was an aberration, and they were thrown unwanted into the water. Azul knew not the basic love a warm beast gives to its young. Azul knew not the company of their own kind or the way they belonged in the world.

Egnis could think of many things to say but said only one. "You are loved, Azul," she said. She breathed fire in her chest and urged its warmth to her child.

Azul received the love of the dragon and pressed their face into her belly.

"I must go," Azul said.

The Three knew this time would come. None tried to discourage Azul, and all understood the journey ahead was part of Azul's cycle, which began in water and whose end was a mystery.

Azul Left the Realm

AZUL RECEIVED GIFTS ON THE day they departed for the wider world. The Gold Dwarf gave the beloved child, now grown, an amulet marked with a symbol that contained a circle, triangle, and square. The White Wisp shared an incantation that promised to lead Azul home, if spoken with mindful intent. Egnis simply kissed Azul on the crown of their head and watched the journey begin.

The foundling traveled without weapons and with a sense of ease that shelter and food could be found. Although Azul missed the Three, loneliness did not too often fill them because of the quiet animal companions along the way. Azul hoped to be welcomed among their humankind but knew their difference might cause alarm.

Azul entered several villages. Each time, Azul was forced to leave. Some people ran away in fear. Some people chased Azul with violence. Some stared with such coldness that it served no purpose to linger. Azul considered that their clothing, as well as their skin, provoked scrutiny. Azul dressed comfortably, and their garments did not resemble the clothing worn by most of the people they'd seen. Although Azul was neither man nor woman but both, Azul began to dress more like a man and move with the gestures of men.

After traveling many days and nights, Azul rested in the hollow of a tree. They awakened to the sound of children whispering. Azul smiled at the boy and girl, and they smiled in return. The little ones led Azul to their home. The adults, a man and a woman, regarded

Azul with caution but also with kindness. Although Azul had never heard the language with which the people spoke, they found the words tumbling from their tongue with ease. Azul received food, shelter, and friendship.

The family who gave haven to Azul introduced them to others in the village. Not all were welcoming, but Azul was determined to dispel doubt and fear. In time, because of Azul's gentleness with human and beast and their cooperation to aid in tasks, the villagers accepted Azul among them. Azul felt immense joy and contentment.

When others asked from where Azul had come, Azul told the truth. They said that they hailed from a mountain near a valley, an ocean, a desert, and a forest. Loving foster parents found them as an infant and raised them with the world as their home and all beings as their companions. When asked why their skin was blue, Azul said that was the way they came into the world.

Because Azul could do any task, use any skill, the villagers thought them unusually bright. Azul noticed that men and women often served in different tasks. Yet Azul's presence encouraged the people to try their hands at what felt right.

Azul Returned Home

IN TIME, AZUL WISHED TO share their home and the Three with friends. The foundling gathered their closest companions and invited them on an adventure. The group set out on a fine day. Although Azul had no concern about traveling without weapons, their companions were wary. They insisted upon bringing spears and daggers. If the group needed these items only to hunt, all the better. Azul's friends thought them too trusting in a dangerous world.

To mark a trail back to the village, Azul carved an image into tree trunks along the way. The image was the symbol on the amulet Azul wore, the gift from Ingot. In time, the group became weary. Azul had not realized how far the journey was to the realm and decided to try Incant's words, which were supposed to lead the beloved child home. To Azul's surprise, the words called forth the cooperation of Nature so that the elements, the creatures, and the plants led the travelers in the correct direction.

Soon enough, Azul and their friends reached the realm.

When Azul saw the mountain in the distance, Azul began to dance. A flock of swallows over Azul's head recognized the foundling and darted over a meadow, above the trees, and to the mountain. Beautiful twinkling music welcomed the group as they gathered at the entrance to the cave. Ingot and Incant embraced Azul and greeted the guests.

Incant led them to a banquet table filled with food and drink. Ingot turned a key at the side of a metal device made of wheels, disks, and gears, from which the music sang again. The Gold Dwarf said that he'd waited many seasons to share this new invention with his beloved Azul. As the travelers ate, drank, and rested, Azul waited to see Egnis, who was away but would, as always, return in the evening.

The sky softened with fading light. Clouds floated on higher winds. One great billow turned pink, then red, and formed into a familiar shape. Azul leapt upon anxious feet and ran toward the valley. Alarmed, Azul's friends grabbed their weapons and followed with haste.

Egnis spread her magnificent wings and glided toward the ground, gentle as a bee. She fluttered with joy, sending a warm breeze to all the lands. Azul rushed toward her with open arms. Before Azul reached her, Egnis lurched backward with a claw at her chest. The handle of a spear jutted from her body. Suddenly, Azul's friends surrounded them. The people attacked Egnis with ferocity. Scales dropped from her body as sharp objects grazed her. She who saw All That Is huffed until smoke hid the people from one another. She flew backward and waited.

Azul shouted at the group. "The dragon means no harm! She is my mother!" they said.

When all became quiet, Azul asked why their friends had attacked.

"We were afraid. We thought it was a threat," their friends replied.

"There was no pause to find whether you faced friend or foe. Not a moment was given to learn or understand," Azul said.

"We could have been dead by then," one friend replied.

"And each one of you is a stranger to her. She could have killed you with one breath. Even with her awesome might, Egnis chose restraint," Azul said.

Azul's friends gasped as the Red Dragon stood behind Azul with a broken spear in one claw and a perfect white flower held in the center of the other. She dropped the spear and gripped the crown of Azul's head. She bowed to welcome the guests. Egnis extended the flower toward them. Blood dripped to the ground.

"Leave us, please," Azul said to the friends.

The foundling touched Engis's wound. Azul's love for the dragon flooded forth. A sweet song surged through Azul's throat. The orphan's hands warmed, then glowed along every contour, edged with light. The wound sealed to bleed no more, with a scar as a reminder of the hurt and the healing.

Egnis told her child that they were the same as any other human. Within, each human experienced the same feelings, and without, all needed food, shelter, and companionship. However, Egnis said, Azul had grown in love, in the absence of fear, and that made them different. Egnis urged them to forgive their friends.

Azul asked Egnis if she could die. She could, she said, in form and function. She was immortal, but she was not immutable. Then Azul asked what would happen if she no longer breathed the sun.

"All would dry in endless light or all would rot in endless dark," Egnis said.

The Dream that Urged Azul's New Way

THE NIGHT AFTER AZUL'S FRIENDS attacked Egnis, the foundling fell into a deep slumber. They walked a wide spiral to the center where there was a well. A voice called from the darkness and wetness below. "Azul," the voice said, "you are to teach what is not remembered. You are to remind others of what has been forgotten." A boulder rolled past Azul and became wrapped in a knotted net. Then the voice said, "Without the connections, it would fall apart."

Azul awoke as if shocked to be in their body. But their body was suddenly no longer one of both sexes. The flesh was female. The maleness between Azul's legs had been transformed. Azul's slight breast was now full. The orphan saw the physical change without, and felt an unexplainable difference within, and declared they was now she.

She told the Three of the remarkable shift and her dream. The Three agreed that the power of The Great Sleep had touched her. Azul must do what the transcendent guidance called her to do.

Azul and her friends departed after a breakfast feast and embraces among them all. The symbols she carved into the trees led the group home to the village. They returned amid much joy and were promised a celebration to honor them.

As the village prepared for the feast, Azul overheard friends tell of their journey. Some stories matched her memory, and others did not. She felt shocked when one friend bragged of the attack on Egnis and another told of the hoard the dragon kept within its lair. Others said they always thought Azul odd and now had an inkling as to why.

Azul wondered if she should speak to the villagers as she planned, afraid she would be ridiculed, even cast out, for what she would say.

After much eating and merriment, Azul called for silence. She thanked her friends for their companionship and good humor on such a long journey. Her return home had filled her with an impulse to build her life anew with those who felt a similar urge. She told of a place where everyone was welcomed in love, where trust and cooperation reigned and all were honored for their skills and gifts. Dark feelings would find release without violence of any kind to oneself or others.

"Where would this be?" a voice asked.

"Here, if that is where it can begin," Azul said.

"Does that make you the leader and liege over all?" another asked.

"I wish to guide. A council may lead, with guidance from all."

"What makes you think you can do this?"

"Because I believe in the possibility of a different way."

A few people mumbled and giggled. Then many others joined the laughter. Azul expected to burn with shame but stood with patience until the noise died.

"Anyone who shares the dream is welcome to join me," Azul said.

Azul chose to sleep under the full moon. She felt close to Egnis, calmed by the darkness. A noise awakened her. She sat up quickly to see a friend from the journey. He was her favorite among them and had been from her earliest days in the village.

He said he knew that some of their friends spoke falsely of what they'd seen and that some boasted of what they'd done. He did not know whether Azul knew he alone had not joined the assault on Egnis. She did not, and she asked him why he stayed behind. He said that the night before they arrived at the mountain he had had a strange dream. Azul appeared as a strong woman thatching the roof of a cottage. A dwarf poured gold upon the ground, which flowed to create a road that led to the cottage. Rain poured down, and the land became rich with plant food, green life, and animals. He walked into the cottage and saw children dancing. Through a window, he saw a red, winged serpent fly around the sun. He turned to kiss Azul, who became quick with child, and then he awoke from his dream.

For a long moment, Azul was silent. She said she must unburden a deep secret and asked for his trust. She told of her beginning, abandoned in the water, and of the mystery of her body, which was both male and female. Yet during the respite in the realm where she was first loved, she dreamed of another home to come and awoke with the body of a woman.

"I have long loved you for who you are, Azul," he said. "Let me join with you and bring the dreams into being."

They, as a man and a woman, met as two and one. In the morning, Azul and her mate left the village with a small gathering of friends. They walked toward another way.

The Death of Azul

ALTHOUGH AZUL WAS HUMAN, THEY proved to be unlike most humans.

During Azul's life, they were neither man nor woman but could be either in turn or both at once. Azul bore a girl and a boy when not a man, and sired a boy and a girl when not a woman. The children were born generations apart to two different mothers and two different fathers. Azul did not know they would outlive beloved mates and the children who brought the couples and their families such joy.

Again and again, four times with a mate and several times without, Azul built the peaceful, loving places they had dreamed of. Each settlement spiraled from a center, marked by a sweet, deep well. Ingot arrived with a team of oxen and cartloads of gold. He built beautiful roads and singing wheels for the children. Incant called upon the creatures and plants to protect their long journeys. When the shelters were complete, the crops were set to root, and the smithy was hot with fire, a group of the people traveled, bearing gifts, to see Egnis, Ingot, and Incant. The people filled the cave with swords, daggers, cauldrons, cups, bracelets, and buckles, crafted by their own hands.

Along the way to visit the Three, the travelers took comfort and shelter in cottages built within the forests. Great elders chose to live in solitude, awaiting those in need. The elders lived away from the margins of the settlements, but their cottages were connected to one another by design.

During Azul's long life, the settlements grew with prudent balance. The people lived in peace and treated one another with respect and love, from the newest newborn to the most aged elder. They were no different from their distant neighbors in the other lands, regardless of their customs and languages and ways, yet they were not the same. The tranquility and cooperation in their lives were choices they made every moment, every day. This mighty but tenuous web of understanding held them gently.

Azul was confident, although never certain, about what their long-ago dream had meant. As an ancient, Azul sat in the sun surrounded by birdsong and flowers gathered by happy children. They felt the darkness of their abandoned beginning, the end that had not been. That fact, that truth, could not be denied. Yet, too, Azul could not deny the Three's profound love, their despair to be among their kind, and the struggles and joy to build the world they dreamed of. At that moment, a young couple placed an infant in Azul's arms.

"Beloved Azul," the mother said, "what is this light in my child's eyes?"

Azul gazed at the newborn, at the darkness in the light, the pupil in the iris, and saw what the mother had seen.

Azul smiled. They touched the cheeks of the babe's mother and father.

"Dear ones," Azul said, "that light is love."

The ancient Orphan's head dropped as if in sleep. Gentle as a dream, Azul died.

The Families Venerated Azul

ACROSS THE LANDS, IN EVERY settlement, the people mourned Azul. Grief filled many hearts with heaviness. In the place where

Azul died, the people gathered to decide how to honor them. The people agreed that Azul should be taken home and for the settlements to join in an act of veneration.

Azul's closest friends wrapped the body in linen and sealed the shroud with beeswax. Ten young people were chosen to make the journey to the mountain with Azul's remains.

The young people used the ancient incantation to lead them. All of Nature was saddened by the foundling's death and took great care to ease the humans' effort.

When the ten young people arrived, Egnis, Ingot, and Incant greeted them with love and tears. They could not have known that the Three had not aged a moment in all these eras or that Egnis alone bore several scars. The Red Dragon removed a copper breastplate from her body. Her chest puckered where she had been stabbed many times.

"Majestic mother of Azul, what happened to your breast?" a young woman with violet eyes asked.

Egnis told her that time and again, bands of humans had come to raid the treasures and to try to kill her.

"But you mean and cause no harm," a young man said.

"Their perception makes it seem so," Egnis replied.

Egnis, Ingot, and Incant surrounded the cart on which Azul's body lay. The Red Dragon lifted her child, carried them to the valley, and placed them on the sweet grass next to a pyre. The others watched as Egnis melted the wax with a soft flame, removed the wraps, and cradled Azul at her breast.

When the Red Dragon lay Azul on the pyre, nine of the young people reached into their hip pouches for bells. Ingot placed bracelets of silver and gold upon the dead orphan's wrists. Incant covered Azul's skin with flowers. Egnis kissed their fragile crown. The Three who loved Azul first and always joined hands upon their child.

The Red Dragon moved to the foot of the pyre. With a heaving cry, she who first saw All drew a pained breath and blew a raging flame into the waiting wood.

As the fire rose to Azul's body, the young woman with the violet eyes began to sing. Her voice carried over the valley, beyond the ocean, across the desert, and through the forest. The young people clapped the bells in sharp, clear unison. Along the lines that marked the lands, invisible to the eye but known to the pure of heart, the bell tolls rang true. At points along the lines, solitary elders stood at their thresholds wearing blue garments and swinging bells. Between the lines, thousands of people dressed in blue as deep as the sky bowed their heads.

Tongues of fire reduced Azul to ash. The bells were silent, but the young woman continued to sing. She stared at Egnis through the flames with tears on her cheeks. The Red Dragon met her eyes and told her beyond words what The Great Sleep had said in a dream. Within All That Is, there is a choice. With that, two embers flew into the girl's eyes and blinded her, but her mind was so open she did not notice.

With the last note of her song, a flock of swallows whisked over the dying fire and scattered Azul's ashes into the wind. Incant keened until the skies clouded and rained. As she calmed, clouds drifted apart. Suddenly, a rainbow arched over the mountain.

The young woman stood in front of the line of her fellow travelers. "Great Ones," she said, "we vow to be guardians of the way of love. As you guarded and loved Azul, we will do the same for you."

"As you must for one another," the Three said with one voice.

The Three bowed to them, and they bowed to the Three. Each one stood strong and earnest, beautiful and brave in matching boots and fine blue coats.